COST OF HONOR

Acclaim for Radclyffe's Fiction

"*Dangerous Waters* is a bumpy ride through a devastating time with powerful events and resolute characters. Radclyffe gives us the strong, dedicated women we love to read in a story that keeps us turning pages until the end."—*Lambda Literary Review*

"Radclyffe's *Dangerous Waters* has the feel of a tense television drama, as the narrative interchanges between hurricane trackers and first responders. Sawyer and Dara butt heads in the beginning as each moves for some level of control during the storm's approach, and the interference of a lovely television reporter adds an engaging love triangle threat to the sexual tension brewing between them."—*RT Book Reviews*

"*Love After Hours*, the fourth in Radclyffe's Rivers Community series, evokes the sense of a continuing drama as Gina and Carrie's slow-burning romance intertwines with details of other Rivers residents. They become part of a greater picture where friends and family support each other in personal and recreational endeavors. Vivid settings and characters draw in the reader…"—*RT Book Reviews*

Secret Hearts "delivers exactly what it says on the tin: poignant story, sweet romance, great characters, chemistry and hot sex scenes. Radclyffe knows how to pen a good lesbian romance."—*LezReviewBooks Blog*

Wild Shores "will hook you early. Radclyffe weaves a chance encounter into all-out steamy romance. These strong, dynamic women have great conversations, and fantastic chemistry."—*The Romantic Reader Blog*

In **2016 RWA/OCC Book Buyers Best award winner for suspense and mystery with romantic elements** *Price of Honor* "Radclyffe is master of the action-thriller series…The old familiar characters are there, but enough new blood is introduced to give it a fresh feel and open new avenues for intrigue."—*Curve Magazine*

In *Prescription for Love* "Radclyffe populates her small town with colorful characters, among the most memorable being Flann's little sister, Margie, and Abby's 15-year-old trans son, Blake…This romantic drama has plenty of heart and soul."—*Publishers Weekly*

2013 RWA/New England Bean Pot award winner for contemporary romance *Crossroads* "will draw the reader in and make her heart ache, willing the two main characters to find love and a life together. It's a story that lingers long after coming to 'the end.'"—*Lambda Literary*

In 2012 RWA/FTHRW Lories and RWA HODRW Aspen Gold award winner *Firestorm* "Radclyffe brings another hot lesbian romance for her readers."—*The Lesbrary*

Foreword Review Book of the Year finalist and IPPY silver medalist *Trauma Alert* "is hard to put down and it will sizzle in the reader's hands. The characters are hot, the sex scenes explicit and explosive, and the book is moved along by an interesting plot with well drawn secondary characters. The real star of this show is the attraction between the two characters, both of whom resist and then fall head over heels."—*Lambda Literary Reviews*

Lambda Literary Award Finalist *Best Lesbian Romance 2010* features "stories [that] are diverse in tone, style, and subject, making for more variety than in many, similar anthologies…well written, each containing a satisfying, surprising twist. Best Lesbian Romance series editor Radclyffe has assembled a respectable crop of 17 authors for this year's offering."—*Curve Magazine*

2010 Prism award winner and ForeWord Review Book of the Year Award finalist *Secrets in the Stone* is "so powerfully [written] that the worlds of these three women shimmer between reality and dreams…A strong, must read novel that will linger in the minds of readers long after the last page is turned."—*Just About Write*

In **Benjamin Franklin Award finalist** *Desire by Starlight* "Radclyffe writes romance with such heart and her down-to-earth characters not only come to life but leap off the page until you feel like you know them. What Jenna and Gard feel for each other is not only a spark but an inferno and, as a reader, you will be washed away in this tumultuous romance until you can do nothing but succumb to it."—*Queer Magazine Online*

Lambda Literary Award winner *Stolen Moments* "is a collection of steamy stories about women who just couldn't wait. It's sex when desire overrides reason, and it's incredibly hot!"—*On Our Backs*

Lambda Literary Award winner *Distant Shores, Silent Thunder* "weaves an intricate tapestry about passion and commitment between lovers. The story explores the fragile nature of trust and the sanctuary provided by loving relationships."—*Sapphic Reader*

Lambda Literary Award Finalist *Justice Served* delivers a "crisply written, fast-paced story with twists and turns and keeps us guessing until the final explosive ending."—*Independent Gay Writer*

Lambda Literary Award finalist *Turn Back Time* "is filled with wonderful love scenes, which are both tender and hot."—*MegaScene*

Applause for L.L. Raand's Midnight Hunters Series

The Midnight Hunt
RWA 2012 VCRW Laurel Wreath winner *Blood Hunt*
Night Hunt
The Lone Hunt

"Raand has built a complex world inhabited by werewolves, vampires, and other paranormal beings...Raand has given her readers a complex plot filled with wonderful characters as well as insight into the hierarchy of Sylvan's pack and vampire clans. There are many plot twists and turns, as well as erotic sex scenes in this riveting novel that keep the pages flying until its satisfying conclusion."—*Just About Write*

"Once again, I am amazed at the storytelling ability of L.L. Raand aka Radclyffe. In *Blood Hunt*, she mixes high levels of sheer eroticism that will leave you squirming in your seat with an impeccable multi-character storyline all streaming together to form one great read."
—*Queer Magazine Online*

"*The Midnight Hunt* has a gripping story to tell, and while there are also some truly erotic sex scenes, the story always takes precedence. This is a great read which is not easily put down nor easily forgotten."—*Just About Write*

"Are you sick of the same old hetero vampire/werewolf story plastered in every bookstore and at every movie theater? Well, I've got the cure to your werewolf fever. *The Midnight Hunt* is first in, what I hope is, a long-running series of fantasy erotica for L.L. Raand (aka Radclyffe)."—*Queer Magazine Online*

"Any reader familiar with Radclyffe's writing will recognize the author's style within *The Midnight Hunt*, yet at the same time it is most definitely a new direction. The author delivers an excellent story here, one that is engrossing from the very beginning. Raand has pieced together an intricate world, and provided just enough details for the reader to become enmeshed in the new world. The action moves quickly throughout the book and it's hard to put down."—*Three Dollar Bill Reviews*

By Radclyffe

The Provincetown Tales

Safe Harbor

Beyond the Breakwater

Distant Shores, Silent Thunder

Storms of Change

Winds of Fortune

Returning Tides

Sheltering Dunes

PMC Hospitals Romances

Passion's Bright Fury (prequel)

Fated Love

Night Call

Crossroads

Passionate Rivals

Rivers Community Romances

Against Doctor's Orders

Prescription for Love

Love on Call

Love After Hours

Love to the Rescue

Honor Series

Above All, Honor

Honor Bound

Love & Honor

Honor Guards

Honor Reclaimed

Honor Under Siege

Word of Honor

Oath of Honor
(First Responders)

Code of Honor

Price of Honor

Cost of Honor

Justice Series

A Matter of Trust (prequel)

Shield of Justice

In Pursuit of Justice

Justice in the Shadows

Justice Served

Justice for All

First Responders Novels

Trauma Alert

Firestorm

Taking Fire

Wild Shores

Heart Stop

Dangerous Waters

Romances

Innocent Hearts

Promising Hearts

Love's Melody Lost

Love's Tender Warriors

Tomorrow's Promise

Love's Masquerade

shadowland

Turn Back Time

When Dreams Tremble

The Lonely Hearts Club

Secrets in the Stone

Desire by Starlight

Homestead

The Color of Love

Secret Hearts

Short Fiction

Collected Stories by Radclyffe

Erotic Interludes: *Change Of Pace*

Radical Encounters

Stacia Seaman and Radclyffe, eds.:

Erotic Interludes Vol. 2–5

Romantic Interludes Vol. 1–2

Breathless: *Tales of Celebration*

Women of the Dark Streets

Amor and More: Love Everafter

Myth & Magic: Queer Fairy Tales

Writing As L.L. Raand

Midnight Hunters

The Midnight Hunt

Blood Hunt

Night Hunt

The Lone Hunt

The Magic Hunt

Shadow Hunt

Visit us at www.boldstrokesbooks.com

COST OF HONOR

by

RADCLY*f*FE

2019

COST OF HONOR

ISBN 13: 978-1-63555-582-0

This Trade Paperback Original Is Published By
Bold Strokes Books, Inc.
P.O. Box 249
Valley Falls, NY 12185

First Edition: November 2019

Credits
Editors: Ruth Sternglantz and Stacia Seaman
Production Design: Stacia Seaman
Cover Design by Sheri (hindsightgraphics@gmail.com)

Acknowledgments

The Honor series began as a traditional work of romantic intrigue—*Above All, Honor*—intended to be a standalone novel. At the time, I firmly adhered to the axiom that you couldn't serialize a romance. I still generally find that to be true—a romance is the story of a developing love relationship between two characters that culminates in a commitment and a promise of a future together. When that is achieved, the romance *novel* is over. Sometimes, however, it takes more than one book to achieve the happily ever after, and the result is a number of books connected by the series romance arc. In the case of the Honor series, the books are connected by a central couple who appear in each book as well as by the long-running series arc of a family and friends in a changing sociopolitical world. And for the pure romance readers among us, each book also introduces a complete standalone romance with new characters. Hopefully the balance provides something for all the readers who have followed along and the new readers just giving it a try. Thank you all!

Many thanks go to: senior editor Sandy Lowe for her advice, insights, and supreme publishing skills, editor Ruth Sternglantz for understanding what I mean to say on every page, editor Stacia Seaman for treating every book like the only project she has going on her busy schedule, and my first readers Paula and Eva for feedback, suggestions, and critiques.

And as always, thanks to Lee for the continuing story. *Amo te.*

Radclyffe, 2019

To Lee

CHAPTER ONE

Washington, DC
Game Day minus 42 days
5:10 a.m.

Blair Powell woke to the teasing scent of cherry blossoms and, remembering today was going to be a special day, turned onto her side with a smile. Eyes still closed, not quite ready to relinquish the seductive cocoon of almost-sleep, she reached out for Cam, patted the still warm sheets beside her, and murmured, "Where are you and why are you awake?"

"I thought I'd go for a run before we left for the airport," Cam called from the bathroom.

Blair turned onto her back and squinted at the tiny ray of sunshine sneaking through the half-open blinds. Yes, cherry blossom season in DC was an international event, drawing hundreds of thousands to the city for those precious few weeks in April when the famed trees burst into color. Yes, their condo was perfectly situated to provide an exquisite sampling of the sight and smell of the glorious sprays of white and red blossoms. Hence the open window.

And nope, not ready to embrace even the most gorgeous of spring mornings just yet. She closed her eyes again. She was married to the sexiest, smartest, most amazing woman she'd ever met—but, hey, nothing was perfect, right? *Her* idea of a perfect morning was sleeping in until a decent hour, like, at least eight, reading the newspapers—something probably no one on the entire East Coast other than her and her father actually did any longer—and having lazy, long, multiorgasmic sex. Of course, that almost never happened, considering her wife's annoying early-morning habits. Like running at the butt crack of dawn, heading out for the office before fifty percent of the world was even awake, and just being so damn…cheery. Yes, yes, she knew Cam had a lot on her mind being Advisor to the President on Counterterrorism and Homeland Security. There were dozens of others in as many agencies charged with counterterrorism, but Cam was the only one her father relied on when it really mattered. Cam was the only one *she* trusted to protect her father, no matter how much she respected the Secret Service agents on his detail. Cam was Cam. And that was, well, everything.

"Why couldn't you have been a plumber? I like women who work with tools. Women wearing tool belts are hot."

"I work with tools," Cam said to the sound of dresser drawers opening and closing.

"That's a gun, not a tool," Blair muttered.

"Weapon. We call it a weapon. And it comes with a harness."

Blair had a quick flash of an altogether different type of harness, and heat pooled between her thighs. "Are you naked?"

"Not anymore."

"If you couldn't be a plumber, why couldn't you at least be a wolf? Why did you have to be a lion?"

"Sorry?"

"Wolves—they like to sleep in and have sex in the morning. Lions have to start running around as soon as the sun comes up."

"Okay. You're really sexy in the morning."

Blair snorted, pleased and a lot more awake. Cherry blossoms and Cam. Impossible to ignore.

"Besides"—Cam brushed a kiss over her forehead—"you can't be cranky this morning. We're going on vacation."

Blair shot out a hand, gripped Cam's T-shirt in her fist, and yanked her down for a proper kiss. When she was convinced she had Cam's attention, she loosened her grip. "If today's the first day of our vacation, why aren't you in bed doing your duty?"

Cam grinned. "That's on my agenda."

Blair would've rolled her eyes, but it was hard to do that when Cam looked so good in her running clothes. Sleeveless tee over a stretchy hardly-there jog bra, black running shorts that stopped midway down her very excellent thighs, and broad bare shoulders with just the right amount of sculpted muscles to dig her fingers into. Best of all, that gleam in her storm-gray eyes said she'd be taking very good care of her agenda in the not-too-distant future.

"You know, you could come back to bed now and run on the beach in Maui tonight."

"Maybe I've got other things on my agenda for this evening." Cam absently pushed a shock of midnight black hair off her forehead and edged her hip onto the side of the bed.

Blair propped herself up on an elbow and stroked Cam's bare thigh. "I thought you said that agenda item was scheduled for this morning."

"I was planning on a repeat performance."

"Oh. Well, then." Blair glanced at her watch on the charger next to the bed. "It's five thirty. In the a.m. We don't have to be at the airport until eleven. Which means if you're back here in an hour, you'll have plenty of time to attend to everything on my list."

"How about if I return with coffee, croissant, and purpose."

Blair laughed. "I'll take a double dose of purpose, please."

Cam kissed her again. "As you wish."

Blair cupped the back of Cam's head and drew her down. She kissed her slowly, taking her time, reminding them both of everything that mattered. "Go on, then."

"I won't be long. I love you."

"I love you too." Blair settled down into the pillows, turned her back to the glorious late-April morning, and smiled. Seven days with nothing but blue waters, warm white sand, and Cam. She wouldn't think about what waited for them when they got back. Six weeks until the convention. Six weeks, pushing 24/7 on the reelection campaign, speeches and dinners and reporters in a campaign that was going to get nasty.

Seven days before she had to think of that.

Old Executive Office Building (OEOB)
Washington, DC
5:25 a.m.

Oakes Weaver lunged for the ball, flicked her racket as her shoulder hit the floor, and watched the shot carom off the near side wall and rocket past Evyn Daniels to the front wall before she ducked, rolled, and came back up onto her feet. Evyn just managed to get her racket on it and sent it skidding onto the floor.

"Nice shot," Evyn gasped as she dragged an arm across her forehead. "Game to you."

"That makes us even," Oakes said, lifting the hem of her shirt to wipe the sweat from her face.

Evyn Daniels trotted over to her. "On the day, maybe, but I think you're still a game ahead of me on balance."

Oakes grinned. "Two."

Evyn snorted. "The first game didn't count. I was going easy on you because you were a newbie."

"And I was going easy on you because, well…you're not."

"Yeah, right. Forgot for a second you're practically a preschooler." Evyn grinned.

Oakes was used to being the youngest in just about every group and wasn't bothered by the kidding. Less than a dozen years separated her and Evyn, and Oakes wasn't the newbie on PPD any longer. Jonas Clark, the new guy, was twenty-four, a year younger than her. Funny how ten months on the president's protection detail could make such a difference. Of course, a hell of a lot had happened during those ten months, including a terrorist attack on the president's life.

"Yeah, yeah." Oakes gathered up her gear. "Barney's for breakfast?"

"Too right."

As they left the racquetball court and headed for the locker room, Evyn asked, "So, leading the advance team is pretty big-time. Nervous?"

"What? Nah," Oakes said. "It's not like I haven't done an advance before."

One of the first things Oakes had learned at FLETC was never to admit fear. Or that she wasn't totally ready for whatever was coming. She trusted her training and believed in herself. Okay, maybe she was a *little* nervous about heading up the advance team for the president's trip to his party's national convention. But she knew what needed to be done. She'd been running the list in her head ever since Tom had told her she'd be heading up the preparations for POTUS's arrival in Philadelphia. Secure and clear the airspace, map evac routes, identify safe houses, assess medical preparedness, review intelligence from the local FBI and police antiterrorist divisions, coordinate crowd control with local law enforcement, arrange surveillance of Class 3 threat individuals, establish the dog check zones, schedule highway closures for the motorcade…

"Running the list?" Evyn murmured, pushing open the door to the locker room.

Oakes laughed. "Yeah. How'd you know?"

Evyn smiled. "The first time I led the advance team, I'd wake up a couple times a night running everything through my head. Don't worry—it's not like you're out there on your own."

"Yeah," Oakes said. "I know that. The first get-to-know-everybody trip last month went fine."

"No griping over the feds moving in and bossing everyone around when a presidential visit's involved," Evyn said.

Oakes's chest tightened. "After what happened on the train trip—"

"Which somehow the White House managed to keep off the air," Evyn reminded her.

"True. But, man—I think about it. She's still out there somewhere."

"Her and probably a few thousand other loonies," Evyn said. "So we all think about it every day. That's the job, right?"

"Right." The ball of nerves in Oakes's middle unraveled. She wasn't alone anymore. She had the team. She didn't need much more than that. A couple of good friends, her parents, even though she hardly ever saw them anymore, and the team. Life was good. She didn't have time for anything else. At least that's what she told herself.

Across the Delaware River from Philadelphia
Camden, New Jersey
6:05 a.m.

"New members are arriving soon," the familiar voice said without preamble when Matthew Ford answered the phone. "We'll need you to be ready."

His contact—controller was a more honest term for the man who had determined his every move for the last fifteen months—didn't bother to apologize for waking him up. Not that he had. Matthew had been awake most of the night. The bedroom, barely large enough for the double bed, had one narrow window through which a limp breeze barely managed to stir the stale air. The girl in his bed smelled of some too-sweet perfume and sex, and for some reason, her nearness made him want to pace. When he should have been thinking about fucking her, he was trying to shake off the antsy sensation of something being not quite right.

Maybe this call would finally change all that.

"We've been ready for more than two years. Ever since the rigged election threatened to bury our identity under an ocean of color," Matthew answered, standing at the open window of the third-floor squat on Canal Street. Trash—plastic soda bottles, soggy bits of cardboard food containers, Styrofoam cups, and mountains of other unidentifiable garbage—floated up against the banks of the Delaware River below him. Philadelphia on the other side of the water rose out of a shroud of rain clouds. Rain again. He hated fucking spring and the constant drizzle. He was fucking sick of waiting too. Training and preparing so he could wait some more. He peered at the cloudy city skyline and tried to make out the Convention Center.

"Are you ready to stand up for our heritage?" his contact asked.

"We would have already if you'd given us the green light."

"Your dedication to the cause is admirable, but we needed the right stage from which to be heard. Now we have it, and the plan is in motion."

"And we are ready," Matthew swore.

"You understand there will be obstacles. Sacrifice may be required."

"We know."

"Remember, trust only those who have proven themselves."

"We'll need intelligence, and with Gary—"

"No names."

Matthew gritted his teeth. They knew *his* name, but he didn't know his controller. Oh, he knew the supreme leader's name—the whole world knew that. He even knew the names of some of central command. After all, their organization represented the real Americans, and the leaders, at least, spoke up for all the oppressed members of the white race. When he was recruited and sent to join the northeastern cell, however, they'd made it clear that his cell leader, as well as members of other cells, would remain anonymous. Security reasons. Made sense, but it also made him feel invisible. He didn't want to be invisible any longer. He'd been invisible his entire life, growing up without, watching others make it because they were special. Special. Right. Some of them weren't even Americans. When he'd discovered Identity America, with its platform of anti-immigration, anti-integration, and anti-welfare for the parasites who drained the country of resources and power, he knew he'd found his place. Now he'd have a chance to be seen.

"Timetables," he snarled, "motorcade routes, personnel lists. How are we going to get them?"

"Let us worry about that," responded the smooth baritone with just a hint of an unidentifiable accent. Matthew imagined the man to be from somewhere in the Midwest, where so many of the true believers originated.

"And what about the weapons?"

"Will be delivered in due time." A pause. "Destroy your phone as usual."

"Wait—"

The line went dead, and Matthew threw the phone across the room. It crashed against the wall and splintered.

"I could have used that," the girl in the bed said. She sat up against the pillows, her small bare breasts jutting out above the rumpled sheet draped across her waist.

"You know you can't use it."

"I could have sold it."

"No, you couldn't. Someone might trace it back to us. What do you need money for?"

She smiled. "A little blow would be nice."

"No drugs, I told you that."

She sighed and pushed the sheets aside, parting her legs. "Then maybe you can take my mind off my needs."

With a sigh, he stripped off his boxers and climbed onto the bed. At least he could pass the time while he waited for the world to learn his name.

CHAPTER TWO

Newport, Rhode Island
6:00 a.m.

Ari Rostof climbed down the boardwalk stairs from the rear of the house to the stretch of private beach on Newport Harbor. Across the way on the peninsula, the public marina bustled with boat launches as seasonal people returned. Her Jeanneau floated gently under the covered dock adjacent to the boathouse. The weather report called for highs near sixty. The water would be rough, and the sail probably cold, but she needed some time alone to recharge. Time on the water away from the phone calls, the maneuvering, the careful placement of players on the giant chessboard that was her life. Most of the time she enjoyed the game of politics, an ever-shifting battle of allegiances, of promises made and promises broken—or, more often, bent—and somewhere beneath it all, the fragility of purpose.

Staying true to purpose was always a challenge in any game where the primary goal was to win. Standing on the far end of the dock, watching the whitecaps slap against the pilings, she considered the cost of winning. Relationships were fleeting, principles more gray than black and white, and trust as transitory as the latest contract. An empty bed and contacts instead of friends were the result. So far, she'd been willing to pay the price.

"Are you thinking of going out today?" Paul called from behind her. She looked over her shoulder, smiled at their boat master. She'd known the short, square man with the weathered face and all-seeing eyes since she was a child. Sturdy, solid, unchanging, and unchangeable. Him she trusted. "Thought I would."

He shook his head. "Going to be a rough ride. Another week or two, it really will be spring."

"Another week or two, I'll be in DC."

"They got nice water down there, I hear."

"They do." *And I'll have no time to enjoy it once the race is on.*

"Imagine you won't have a lot of time," Paul said, reading her thoughts. "Senator Martinez this time, isn't it? Who you're working for?"

"That's the one," Ari said.

"So you going to get her reelected?"

Ari smiled. "You bet I am."

He nodded. "Well, I'll get the boat ready for you, then."

Ari glanced up at the house, saw her father watching her from the upper deck. She waved, and he nodded before turning back to the house. He'd expect her for breakfast.

"I'll be down in an hour or so."

"Good enough."

Her solitude postponed, Ari climbed back up to the house. Her father was in the dining room, seated at his usual place at the far end of the table, wearing his at home clothes—a casual polo and dark pants. His back was to the french doors that led out onto the wraparound deck. Ignoring the view. She sat on his left and angled her chair so she could catch a glimpse of the water.

"Bill Bailey wants to interview Martinez," he said as he added cream to his coffee. His game was golf, and his deep tan and faint crow's feet spoke of his frequent trips to the Florida courses over the winter. Trips, Ari knew, that served a dual purpose. Florida was a favorite location for foreign travelers to mix business with pleasure.

"About the immigration bill?" Ari lifted the silver dome off the platter in the center of the table, speared a slice of french toast and several pieces of bacon.

"I imagine that will be part of it."

"It's a touchy issue right now. I'll need to talk to him first, get a sense of where he's going with it before I take it to the senator."

"Give him a call, then. But if Martinez comes out strong—"

"Dad, I'll need to talk to the senator first. You know I don't discuss her policy platform with anyone outside the team."

His mouth tightened. "And you think I can't be trusted?"

She poured coffee into the china cup next to her plate. "I think you are a very astute businessman and that you have a great many interests, not all of which might be in line with those of my client."

"I'm family."

Ari met his gaze. Cool ice blue, like the ones she saw in the mirror every day. "I know that. Family is everything."

USSS Command Central, OEOB
Washington, DC
6:10 a.m.

After a shower, a change of clothes, and a quick breakfast at Barney's two blocks from the Old Executive Office Building, Oakes made it to the command center forty minutes before push. Half a dozen agents from the PPD plus surveillance and communications sat at workstations around the large room crowded with monitors, computers, and desks.

"Hey, did you bring me breakfast?" Fran Sanchez, part of the night working shift covering the president, called from across the room. Fran, straight dark hair swept back and trimmed at collar level, deep brown eyes perennially laughing, and a fast almost-always-amused smile, had been on the presidential detail a year longer than Oakes. If she minded Oakes being appointed lead on the advance to the convention, she didn't show it.

"Course." Oakes always checked who on the team had the overnight shift and brought in their breakfast orders. A little thing, but a surefire way to keep the unit tight. Food and drink were major currency in the USSS. She passed Fran the bag with a take-out egg-and-cheese burrito wrapped in aluminum foil. "The other one is for Kennedy."

"Kennedy's not here though, is he," Fran said, taking them both out of the bag.

A deep voice announced from behind them, "Kennedy is right here. Kennedy knows all."

Theodore Kennedy, tall, slim, with smooth light brown skin and starting to go gray early, close-cropped hair, glided between the forest of chairs with the graceful gait of the dancer he'd been before taking a right-hand turn into law enforcement.

Fran sniffed. "More like Kennedy has a nose like a bloodhound where food is concerned."

Kennedy snagged the unopened burrito and carried it to a nearby desk. "Kennedy knows Oakes is a champion."

Oakes grinned and slid into a chair at another station. Kennedy and Fran had been secretly dating for six months, a secret that everyone knew but didn't mention. It wasn't prohibited to date a colleague, but there was always the worry that personal relationships would become a distraction or a point of contention. No one doubted that either one would do their duty if called upon, but a team of a dozen or so people working together, sometimes 24/7 for weeks at a time, was pretty much the same as living in an extended family. Rivalries, bickering, and petty jealousies could make everyone's day a chore. Oakes had to admit, though, as she fired up her computer, Fran and Kennedy seemed to make it work. She didn't know a lot of people who could manage that. Her parents had been together forever, since right out of high school, and they seemed to have developed a kind of fond indifference, each living their own life in spheres that overlapped to some extent while going their own ways in many others. She wasn't sure she actually saw the point. If friendship was the goal, she had plenty of that right here.

"Anything doing?" Oakes asked. She'd get the formal report at the push, but she liked to check in early in case something unexpected, like an OTR presidential trip for a burger or a jog around the National Mall, had been slipped into the schedule.

"Eagle is already in the castle," Fran said.

Oakes scanned the rest of the morning schedule. POTUS wasn't due to leave the White House until late morning for a meeting at the Justice Department. Tom Turner, the Special Agent in Charge of the Presidential Protection Division, had already detailed the agents for that trip. Oakes had an advance team meeting with transport midmorning. The rest of the day she'd be busy coordinating with the supervisors of the fifteen or so departments involved in the trip.

She pulled up the intelligence report summaries that funneled through in reams every day from various agencies, flagged items prioritized at the top. The vast majority of those would be updates on worldwide or domestic events that indicated any element of terrorist activity, from movements of suspected rebel camps half a world away to social media posts from homegrown right-wing neo-Nazis. One item halfway down the list caught her attention. Location: Philadelphia.

She clicked it open and scanned just as Evyn Daniels walked in looking like a recruiting poster in a sharply tailored blue suit, white shirt, and low-heeled ankle-high boots. She fit the image of her role as Assistant Special Agent in Charge without even trying. Oakes had to remember to pick up her own dry cleaning on a regular basis, although she'd finally caved and ordered bespoke suits. All the same, button-downs, a blazer, and dark pants were her usual working uniform.

"Morning, all," Evyn said, carrying her coffee to a corner desk.

Fran and Kennedy mumbled hellos. The other agents who weren't listening to audio feeds via headsets waved.

Oakes nodded absently. Someone at Homeland was working early. The timestamp on the forwarded message from Homeland read 4:48 a.m. The report would likely come in from other sources also. The tag *Domestic Insurrectionist Org* automatically routed such items to dozens of counterterrorism agencies as well as to analysts who'd enter keywords into the intelligence databases for cross-referencing the information.

A local law enforcement counterterrorism unit—at least that's what she supposed High Profile Crimes Unit referred to—had reported a suspicious grouping of movements for individuals deemed low-level threats in the watch list database. The location changes seemed insignificant taken one by one, individuals relocating from a smattering of states all over the eastern seaboard over the last six months, and could easily be overlooked. The pattern was so subtle, even the analytic algorithms used to flag suspicious occurrences hadn't picked it up yet. A map had been included with the report.

"Look at that," Oakes murmured.

"What?" Evyn said.

Oakes motioned her over. "Take a look at this field report from the locals in Philadelphia."

Coffee in hand, Evyn leaned over Oakes's right shoulder and peered at the screen.

A series of red dots—eight of them—surrounded one central point in an arc. Lines had been drawn, all converging on the same city. Philadelphia.

"Huh," she said. "Looks like an umbrella, doesn't it."

"Yeah, and according to the geoanalysis, each of those locations is within a sixty to seventy-five-minute drive of the city."

"All identified threat targets?"

"Not all of them are in the database, but whoever did this"—she scanned down to the bottom of the report—"somebody by the name of Sloan, had access and clearance to run known associates, families, and backgrounds. There are enough connections to make a convincing pattern. She ought to be working for us somewhere. She's sharp."

"Let me check something." Evyn returned to her computer, and a few minutes later announced, "Well, that explains it."

"What?" Oakes looked up from running the searches on the names she'd set to alert for common previous addresses, work histories, family connections, criminal records, civil cases, known associates, memberships in activist organizations—anything and everything that might pinpoint connections to terrorist or seditious groups.

"This Sloan—it's a JT Sloan, right?"

"Yeah," Oakes said.

"From what I can get from the Philadelphia Police Department records, she used to be one of ours."

"Secret Service?"

"No, Justice, cyber division."

Oakes frowned. "And now she's local law in Philadelphia? That's some change. Retirement gig?"

"Not according to what I can find—she's only midthirties and most of her Justice records are redacted. Why she left is a mystery, but this HPCU she's part of now—High Profile Crimes Unit—isn't your normal bunch of LEOs. This group, as near as I can tell, has broken some major cases—internet porn, human trafficking, weapons—and Sloan was a big part of it."

"Fran is the lead advance with the Philadelphia PD, and she didn't mention this division in her first contact report," Oakes said. "I would have remembered if she had, and Fran's obsessive about details. You think they're keeping this group under wraps for some reason?"

Evyn shrugged. "Could be."

"I'll inform Turner," Oakes said, "but it looks like we're going to need some up close and personal time with them."

"Road trip," Evyn said. "You'll need company."

"I'll see if I can think of someone to drag along." Oakes glanced around. Sometime in the last few minutes, Fran, Kennedy, and the agents on the day shift had disappeared. "Crap. We need to get going or we'll be late for the push."

Tom Turner was a stickler for punctuality. If you weren't actively engaged standing post protecting POTUS at shift change, you were expected to attend the debriefing.

"We're good," Evyn said as they hurried down the hall.

Oakes slid into a seat at the long conference table a minute before seven, and thirty seconds later Tom Turner walked in. The Special Agent in Charge of the PPD was in his early forties, trim as a twenty-year-old, with dark skin and eyes and a perpetually serious expression. He'd been SAIC for all of Powell's term and part of the previous president's and had the confidence of every agent working shift.

He sat at his customary place at the head of the table, flipped open his iPad, and said, "Morning, everyone. Let's start with today's itinerary."

"You mean we actually have one?" someone muttered, and everyone laughed.

Powell's staffers were notorious for late delivery of the president's itinerary or off-the-record jaunts that put the working shift at a disadvantage when it came to providing his protection. Even a trip to the reflecting pool so he could jog required a motorcade, clearance of the route by the local motorcycle police, and organizing the press and medical staff. Oakes tried hard not to think about what a nightmare Philadelphia was going be if the itinerary she still did not have took much longer in coming.

But then, that's what she got paid for. To make it work—no matter the cost.

Rock Creek Park
Washington, DC
6:15 a.m.

Cam tapped the Bluetooth receiver to accept the incoming call and dodged a brunette in tights and a cropped pale pink tank jogging with a baby stroller. A black Lab loped beside the woman with the characteristic fumble-pawed gait of an exuberant puppy. The pup veered left and bounded after Cam, intent on making friends.

"Roberts," Cam answered as the brunette yelled, "Hamlet! Get back here."

The Lab galloped along beside Cam for a few more steps, teeth bared in a joyous grin, before dropping back to rejoin his family.

"Good morning, Commander." Light laughter infused the familiar lilting soprano.

"Good morning, Isabel." Cam turned down a path toward the duck pond. Cam's assistant deputy was a morning person, like her, which was just one of the many reasons she valued Isabel Cortez. In addition to her unceasing energy, she was astute, a good manager, and a magician when it came to handling the bureaucratic quagmire of lobbyists, politicians, and competing agencies on the Hill. Her trust in Isabel to stand in for her as Advisor to the President on Counterterrorism and Homeland Security was the main reason Cam even considered a vacation six weeks before the national convention. That and knowing Blair needed it. Blair would never admit it, but the trauma of the attack during the campaign tour and the daily grind of being the de facto First Lady, with all the accompanying public appearances, interviews, and fund-raisers, was wearing her down. Andrew knew it, too, and had gently insisted. Cam probably needed the break just as much as Blair—she just had more trouble recognizing what she needed. All except for Blair—her need for Blair was a constant hunger.

"Anything of note this morning?" Cam asked as a mating pair of ducks flew up from the water's edge as she passed.

"No red flags in the overnight reports," Isabel said briskly. Isabel must have gotten in extra early to have reviewed the dailies from the FBI, CIA, and Homeland agencies already. Usually Cam covered that as soon as she reached her office. "Are you running?" Isabel asked.

"Why, do I sound short of breath?" Cam checked her heart rate as she sprinted up an incline. Top cardio range. Perfect.

Isabel laughed. "No, you sound suspiciously relaxed."

"Just an easy jog this morning."

"I'm sending over a report for you to take a look at that came out of Philadelphia last night," Isabel said. "Not enough to tip a flag, but I thought considering the location, you'd want to see it."

Cam's antennae shot up at the mention of the city. "You're right, as usual. Something to worry about?"

"On the surface," Isabel said, "no. An interesting be aware report from the locals about increased movement from low-level targets on the watch list."

"Who's the local source? PPD antiterrorism?"

"Different division, it looks like—a High Profile Crimes Unit."

"All right, thanks. Make sure the advance team leader gets it too."

"Done."

"Are you sure I shouldn't just stay in Hawaii?" Cam cut left around a dog walker with half a dozen miniatures of various high-priced breeds spread out around him like a furry, yapping fan.

"Go enjoy your vacation, Commander."

Cam smiled, thinking about exactly how she planned to start. She could scan the report from Isabel after she delivered the coffee and her promise to her wife. "Thanks, I will."

"And turn off your damn phone."

"Done." Cam disconnected and headed back.

The bakery tucked into a side street around the corner from their building already had a short line when she arrived. The baristas knew her, and when she stepped up to the counter, her coffees were ready. She added a couple of croissants and, ten minutes later, let herself into the apartment. She carried her offerings through to the bedroom, planning exactly how she'd wake Blair. Quick sex, coffee, more sex, then croissants.

The bed was empty and the shower running in the adjoining bath. Okay, change of plans. She was nothing if not flexible—at least in some areas. She stripped off her clothes, tossed them in the laundry basket on the way past the walk-in closet, and grabbed the bakery bag off the dresser.

"Coffee out here," she said as she set the tray on the bathroom counter.

Blair opened the shower door. "Something better in here."

Cam climbed in, snaked her arms around Blair's waist, and kissed her. "I thought you were sleeping in."

"I was timing you," Blair said. "You know how much I like to share the shower."

"I seem to recall that." Cam turned Blair until Blair's back was against the shower wall. Leaning in to her, she traced the curves and slopes of her warm, water-slicked body. She never tired of touching her, never got over the wonder of her. She cupped a breast and lifted it to her mouth. Blair's fingers speared through her hair, holding her there, her deep-throated murmur signaling her pleasure. Cam's lower belly clenched at the feel of Blair's nipple hardening against her lips.

"This will be quick if you keep that up," Blair whispered through the rainfall of warm water. Blair slipped a thigh between Cam's legs and dug her fingers into Cam's hips, dragging her closer, pressing into her center.

Cam groaned softly, her senses in chaos. She wanted to hurry, wanted to take forever. Wanted all of Blair at once and longed to savor every tiny intake of breath, every faint gasp of pleasure, every tremor through the sleek taut muscles. When she knelt, her arms around Blair's hips to support her, she had a fleeting thought of just how perfect the position. Blair was a miracle in every way—more than she'd ever dared dream.

"I love you," Cam murmured as she took her.

Blair arched at the first touch of Cam's mouth, held her breath for an instant, caught on the tight wire between unbearable pleasure and the almost painful need for release. Her skin pebbled as if chilled, but she was hot, so hot, so close. She'd quickened with anticipation waiting for Cam to come home, imagining her touch, but the reality was so much more. So sharp, a knife slash of pleasure cutting to the heart of her.

"Oh God," Blair gasped.

One hand on Cam's shoulder, the other on the back of her head, she pressed close as the pressure built, the breath in her chest stilling, her heart thundering, until the pleasure peaked and she burst.

Shuddering, she finally managed a breath. Her head was still swimming, blood thundering through her pounding heart. "Did you say coffee?"

Laughing, Cam rose and pulled her close. "I did. And croissants."

Blair kissed her and rested her cheek on Cam's shoulder. "Chocolate?"

"Spinach."

Blair pushed her away. "I hate you."

Cam kissed her throat, drawing a lazy line down Blair's middle. "No, you don't. And it's chocolate."

Blair traced the curve of Cam's hip with her thumb, followed the tight line of her thigh to the delta at the base of her lean belly. Cam shook when Blair slipped her fingers between her legs. Oh yes—that's what she wanted. The fragile moments Cam gave only to her. "Thanks for the coffee, baby."

Cam pressed an arm against the wall and, head thrown back, closed her eyes and swallowed hard. "You're welcome."

Blair stroked her, her breath catching at the tremble in Cam's thighs where they touched hers. So strong, so sure, so vulnerable in this moment. Hers, all hers.

"I love you."

"Blair," Cam whispered, a warning and a benediction. "You're going to make me come."

"Oh no, really?" Blair picked up her pace and Cam came, sharp and hard against her palm. Blair held her until Cam groaned in satisfaction and drew away.

"Better than a run, even," Cam said, her voice a languid slur.

"Mm, better be." Blair patted her butt and stepped dripping into the bathroom. "I want my coffee. Then I want to do that all over again."

Cam braced both arms on the wall while water sluiced over her. "Sure thing."

Blair snagged the coffee and took a long, luxurious sip. Just the right temperature. She dug her croissant out of the bag, and an instant later, Cam joined her. Blair handed the pastry bag to Cam and leaned against the counter, Cam beside her, their shoulders touching.

Blair licked a bit of chocolate off one finger. "You know, maybe this whole morning run thing isn't such a bad idea."

"You're just deciding that now?"

"I forget how good the cooldown stage is."

Laughing, Cam kissed her. "I'll be sure to remind you every day we're away."

A burst of static, then a monotonal voice requested, "Commander Roberts, come in, over."

Blair stilled. "Cam."

Cam looked over at her radio. She'd left it on the counter before her run, and even though she wasn't on duty—technically—she'd kept the Secret Service command channel open. She always did, until she was in the air—the only place she couldn't be immediately reached.

"Sorry," Cam muttered. In the other room, her phone rang.

"Answer it," Blair said quietly.

CHAPTER THREE

Washington, DC
7:13 a.m.

"Roberts," Cam said at the same time as a forceful knock sounded at the apartment door.

Blair grabbed a robe off the hook behind the bathroom door and hurried through the apartment to answer it. Paula Stark, the SAIC of Blair's detail, stood outside with her game face on, accompanied by Secret Service Agent Will Sato, one of the recent additions to her detail who'd been standing post overnight. Blair's stomach flipped. If Paula was delivering the message, the news was bad.

A steely chill spread through her, an old and welcome shield that pushed the panic down and prepared her to do whatever she must do. She'd been here before, countless times it seemed, with countless closed faces delivering crippling news. Or news that would have crippled her if she hadn't learned survival at an early age and had the lesson repeated until she would not break. When her mother died, when Cam had been shot—the first time, when her father had come under attack in the White House, when Cam had gone missing, when Paula and other agents had been injured. Or killed.

A part of her was always waiting. Always preparing for the ultimate loss. Cam. Her father. Lucinda. Diane or Paula or any number of people she cared about, many of whom were in danger because they moved within her circle. That she had been drawn into the line of fire through no willful decision of her own no longer mattered. Her father was the president. And she was his daughter.

"What is it?" Blair said, hearing her own voice flat and empty.

"Ms. Powell," Paula said, her practiced neutral tone betraying nothing, "we need to go to the White House immediately."

Only Stark's dark brown eyes, wide and troubled, gave away her turmoil.

From behind them, Cam said, "Give us a minute."

"Of course, Commander," Stark said. "Transport will be waiting."

"Thank you, Chief. We'll be right down." Cam gently closed the door and said immediately, "It's all right. It's not your father."

Even as a stunning wave of relief made her a little weak, Blair spun around and gripped the T-shirt Cam had donned on her way to the door. She'd even managed to find sweats in record time too. Always proper, her wife. "Then what?"

"That was Bennie Caruso," Cam said, referring to the Deputy Chief of Staff. She cupped Blair's jaw. "I don't have any of the details yet. It's Adam Eisley."

"Adam?" Blair frowned. "Is he calling an emergency meeting?"

With the nominating convention bearing down on them, Adam Eisley, her father's campaign manager, was one of the most important players on the national scene. Adam assured that everything from political strategy—which often shifted with the day's events—to her father's public persona, the messages coming out of the communication division, the information provided to the press corps, and the directives to regional and state campaign offices all adhered to the all-holy campaign plan. So close to the election, his role had amplified to the point where every event and decision that came in or out of the White House was reviewed and discussed with him. Every statement her father made had the potential to ignite a media frenzy that could swing voter opinion and, if not the party's nomination, potentially the ultimate presidential election one way or the other. Adam's job was to anticipate how the public would react and to shape the president's message before a crisis ensued, all while ensuring the finance director and volunteer organizers were gathering the money and people they needed to bring in the votes.

Blair didn't envy him the job, even when he was irritating her no end with his anal obsession over every word spoken by or about anyone from the president to the most naïve campaign volunteer. She had enough to handle with the constant presence of the press, the escalating threat of terrorism—abroad and at home—and the risks to the people she loved without having her every word subject to his approval.

She sighed. Another media snafu of some kind, most likely.

"He does know we're about to leave for vacation, doesn't he?" Blair's heart rate settled down, but something still wasn't making sense. Why send Stark and an escort? And for some reason, Cam looked worried. "What?"

"Adam's dead."

Ready room, OEOB
7:15 a.m.

"Let's run down where we are with the Philadelphia advance now," Tom Turner said after they'd reviewed the president's itinerary and the accompanying working shift assignments. He focused on Oakes. "Weaver?"

"The division leads have completed preliminary assessments with main and backup airports, local police, and the Philadelphia field office," Oakes said. "We still don't have an itinerary beyond departure time, and the hotel vetting is still ongoing—so no motorcade routes."

Turner's brows flickered. He wasn't happy and Oakes didn't blame him. The greatest areas of risk for the president were along the motorcade route, where potential attack could come from buildings or intersections along the way, and the rope line, when he'd be exposed to crowds of people only a few feet away.

"Shift assignments?" Turner asked.

"Waiting to get a list of available agents from New York, Philadelphia, Pittsburgh, and DC."

"We'll want everyone in place two weeks before game time," Turner said.

"Yes, sir." Oakes knew this as well, as did every other agent in the room.

"What about the hotel?" Turner asked.

Oakes nodded to Luther Wisnicki, the agent taking the lead on securing accommodations for the president, his daughter, and the White House staffers and press. Wherever the president stayed would need to have two avenues of egress to major thoroughfares in case of immediate evacuation, and be large enough for the retinue to take over three floors, the elevators, and a major portion of the kitchen. Because of the gross disruption to business as usual, many hotels weren't all that eager for the president to stay with them.

"We're vetting five," Luther Wisnicki said when Oakes gave him the go-ahead. "Two Marriotts, a Hilton, a Sheraton, and an Omni," he said, referring to his iPad. "Security checks are completed on the Marriott and should be finished at the rest in a week. All five utilize day hires, and that's slowing down the clearances."

"The hotels that can't do without short hires for the length of POTUS's stay should move down the list," Oakes said. "It's too easy for someone to impersonate staff and go unnoticed among a lot of unfamiliar faces."

"Agreed. Unfortunately, it's pretty common in all of the hotels now."

"Everyone will be wearing security-approved IDs," another agent said, "and those won't be released until twelve hours before game time."

"Still plenty of time to have them duplicated," Turner said. "Even with embedded code cards, everyone will need a facial ID before entering for work. Let's nail down the hotel so we can get started on the database."

"We've got a list of hotel guests checking in within two weeks prior to game day," Oakes said. "So far, nothing rings a bell at any of the hotels."

Evyn added, "We're running advance reservations from airlines, train stations, and Ubers through the Terrorist Alert Database on a daily basis. Same for hotel reservations, although most don't require ID to reserve."

"Airbnb?" Turner asked.

Oakes shook her head. "There's no central database. Anyone could be staying in an apartment across the street from the Convention Center, and we wouldn't know it."

"Let's step up photo surveillance of pedestrian activity in the area and CCTV feeds of vehicles moving within midperimeter borders," Turner said.

Oakes made a note. "Roger that."

"All right," Turner said. "Where are we with hospitals? We—" Frowning, he glanced down at his phone. "Hold on."

"Turner," he said sharply and listened for a second, his eyes hardening. "Copy that. Close the grounds to tours and evacuate any unauthorized, move CAT teams to the guard posts, put Andrews on ready alert. Bring the Beast to the south circle and alert Metro motor patrol we may need a route cleared for POTUS."

Turner stood. "Weaver, Daniels, you're with me. The rest of you stand by to evacuate."

Oakes and Evyn hurried to join him as the other agents abruptly filed out to take their posts. Oakes's pulse jumped and adrenaline sharpened her sight until every object jumped into gleaming relief. Game on.

Philadelphia
7:20 a.m.

Hands dropped onto Sloan's shoulders and a soft voice murmured in her ear, "You didn't come to bed last night."

Sloan looked up from her monitors. Blue skies filled the tall windows at the far end of the loft. Huh. Morning already. A familiar scent of orange blossom shampoo and vanilla teased her. She tilted her head back and kissed her wife on the cheek. "Sorry. I just—"

"Got caught up," Michael said, her full, sensual lips lifting as she smiled. She'd caught her long blond hair back in a careless ponytail and wore one of Sloan's T-shirts with a pair of loose cotton drawstring pants. "I know."

"Sorry." Sloan spun around and pulled Michael down onto her lap. "How come you look so sexy in that shirt?"

"Eye of the beholder, lucky for me." Michael threaded her arms around Sloan's neck and twisted until she faced Sloan. The press of her breasts caught all of Sloan's attention.

"What time are you due in this morning?" Sloan asked, nuzzling her neck.

Michael chuckled. "One of the perks of being the boss is I can make my own hours. Aren't you tired?"

From behind them, the huge industrial elevator doors whooshed open, and a cacophony of voices quickly spread throughout the loft.

"Damn it," Sloan muttered.

Michael sighed. "Whatever you were about to suggest is going to have to wait, I take it."

"Let me just catch them up, and I'll meet you upstairs."

"I'll take you up on that. Don't be too long."

Sloan grabbed Michael's hand before she could get up and kissed her for a long, satisfying moment. Almost but not quite enough.

A whistle sounded from across the room.

Sloan opened an eye as Michael stepped away. The team had arrived, led by Sandy, followed close behind by Jason, Dell, Watts, and the lieutenant. Sandy Sullivan, the youngest on their team and Michael's close friend, rolled her eyes good-naturedly in their direction.

Watts, slimmed down after his recent heart attack and looking a decade younger for it, still managed to look derelict in baggy pants and a rumpled white shirt. His grizzled unshaved jawline added to his jaded, burned-out cop look, a look that had fooled many a perp just before Watts turned the key on them and locked them away. "Some of us are planning to work today."

"Good morning, Detective," Michael said, and Watts blushed.

"Morning, Michael," he said.

Michael had that effect on everyone, an involuntary rush of heat in the presence of someone so ethereally beautiful.

"I won't be long," Sloan said, rising as Michael stood.

"Do what you have to do," Michael said. "I'll be there."

Sloan squeezed Michael's hand. "Promise?"

Michael smiled again, but her eyes were dark, fathomless, endless. "Always."

More energized by the exchange than eight hours of sleep and any sort of nourishment could provide, Sloan rose to join the others as they all trooped to the far end of the huge warehouse work area, wending their way between the myriad monitors, communication arrays, surveillance equipment, and other tools of the cybersecurity trade to the conference area in the back. Lieutenant Rebecca Frye walked out of the only private area in the loft, a ten by ten room with a row of waist-high windows facing into the loft that served as her office, with a cup of coffee in her hand.

Sloan frowned. "How long have you been here?"

"An hour or so," Frye said, refilling her coffee mug from a big pot on a counter beside the table. Tall narrow windows afforded a view of the Delaware River and New Jersey on the far shore. Oil tankers and container ships floated at berth in the port or moved slowly past, heading south to the sea.

"Why didn't I know that?" Sloan said.

"Because when I came in you were in the zone, and fortunately, I'm not a cat burglar."

Sloan grinned. "I would have noticed if you'd started lifting my stuff."

Frye, as glacially cool as ever, grinned for a millisecond. "We'll have to test that out sometime. Got something?"

"Could be—still tugging threads," Sloan said.

"Hey," Jason said, dropping into a chair at the end of the table. "How come you didn't call me if you were on to something?"

"Because you're chronically sleep deprived. The baby business is killing you. Can't believe you'll have another one soon."

Jason grinned. "Hey, they're like puppies—two are no more trouble than one." He smirked, and for just an instant, Jasmine peeked out from behind Jason's preppy façade. "I could have been helpful last night, you know."

Sloan lifted a brow. Her partner in the cybersecurity wing of the team, whom she worked with day and night, could move from his preppy male identity to a sultry, sexy female named Jasmine in a heartbeat. Sloan was never sure when Jasmine would appear to tease her in a way that always stirred something beyond Sloan's control. Some primal response that intrigued and mystified. They both understood, with no words being spoken, that their bond would never extend beyond that silently acknowledged connection.

"And you shall be helpful," Sloan said. "I want to run geographic demographics."

"Mm," Jasmine purred. "One of my favorite things."

Sandy snorted. "You're both sick."

Sloan laughed. "Your point?"

In a tight pale green T-shirt with some kind of flower design and skinny jeans with holes in the knees, Sandy still didn't look more than eighteen, which had been about the time Frye had pulled her out of the mire of the streets and turned her into a confidential informant. Reluctant at first, Sandy had eventually abandoned the streets and now was a cop. Falling in love with Dell Mitchell might have been partly responsible for her transformation, but her street smarts and toughness were what made her a key contact with any number of street people. Frye had made that argument when getting her transferred back to the team from Narco.

Frye said, "All right, people, let's hear what we've got."

Sloan filled them in on the patterns she'd pulled on threat subject movements. "It's preliminary, but I've got a feeling."

Frye grimaced. "Your feelings usually mean something. You and Jason chase it."

Sloan felt the familiar rush of the hunt and nodded sharply. "We're on it."

Frye turned to Dell, who'd arrived in her usual black tee, black jeans, and biker boots. Her slicked-back jet hair and smoldering good looks completed her bad-boy look. "Dell?"

Dell had been assigned to the gang division as liaison ever since the uptick in street activity in the past six months. Dell's gender-fluid undercover persona, Mitch, managed to move among the shifting ethos of sex clubs and drug rings where regular undercover cops could not.

"Territorial disputes per usual," Dell said. "The Raptors are talking about getting into the gun trade."

"Sources for that?" Frye said.

"There's a pretty steady weapons train coming up from the south," Dell said. "Mostly small batches in private cars. They're looking for contacts."

"What are they planning to use for cash?"

"Drugs."

"Since we've cramped Colombian channels through the port, that might be difficult."

"Which means more street-level competition for what's getting through," Dell said.

"All right, let's follow the money," Rebecca said. "If they want guns, they'll need backing. Flag anything that smells like an alliance with right-wing groups. They'd make natural bedmates."

"Got it," Dell said.

Frye glanced at Sandy. "Anything heating up in that area?"

"About what we've been seeing. The white supremacist recruiters are hitting the college campuses pretty hard, and they seem to be getting some traction, especially with all the talk of cutting back on educational funding. The immigration and diversity funding proposals at the federal level are adding more fuel to that fire. A lot more heat being generated than a year or two ago."

Rebecca rubbed her eyes. "We haven't seen political unrest at the campus level like this since Vietnam."

"Which you, of course, remember personally," Sloan said.

Another flicker of a smile from Frye. Her cool elegant features and ice blue eyes, to someone who might not know her, suggested she was humorless and stiff-necked. Nothing could be further from the truth. What she *was* was absolutely solid and the bedrock of their entire team. She was also Sloan's best friend.

"My mother," Rebecca said dryly. "Big-time campus agitator. Got arrested a few times. Actually met my dad that way, who…" Frye looked away. "Well, he was a little more conventional."

"Right, he was a cop," Sloan said, giving Frye a second to regroup.

"Yeah," Frye said briskly. "In the blood and all."

"Any rate," Sandy said smoothly, "we can expect substantial street protests in June."

"Keep your files updated," Frye said. "The feds will be around at some point. Watts—you can field their requests."

Watts made a sour face. "Dandy. Probably another bunch of wet-behind-the-ears college kids with big"—he side-eyed Sandy—"guns."

She grinned.

"Probably hear sooner," Sloan cut in. "I sent my report to the Global Terrorist Database per protocol. Homeland will have it by now. So will the Secret Service."

"All right everyone, let's get to work," Frye said.

As they filed out, Watts muttered, "Anyone want to put money down on how long it takes the suits to arrive?"

"I'm in," a chorus of voices proclaimed.

Sloan looked over her shoulder and caught Frye's smile. Then she slipped away to join Michael upstairs.

CHAPTER FOUR

As Blair and Cam exited the elevator with Stark, Will Sato, who'd gone down ahead of them, opened the lobby door and spoke into his radio, alerting the driver of Blair's approach. As he spoke, he continually scanned the area east of Cam and Blair's condo building. The armored limo was visible through the glass double doors, idling at the curb. The back door was open, and a female agent Blair didn't recognize— someone probably pulled from the Washington office to cover this emergency trip—stood beside it, facing the opposite direction from Sato, covering the rest of the street.

Blair crossed the lobby, her hand just touching the back of Cam's charcoal suit jacket. No matter the crisis, she'd never seen Cam look less than magazine-cover perfect. Maybe her arresting appearance had nothing to do with her immaculately cut suit and more to do with her chiseled features and classic profile. Even now, with the edge of dread slicing through her middle, her heart sped up to look at her. And she knew too that beneath the attraction, beyond the compelling magnetism, lay the true source of Cam's charisma—her utter and unassailable strength. Cam radiated confidence and competence, and everyone around her sensed it.

Blair was glad for that unbendable strength right now as she struggled to absorb yet another unfathomable blow.

Adam, dead. How could that be? He was what? Early thirties? Not that much older than her. She'd known him longer than she'd known Cam, since the early days of her father's first campaign, when Adam had emerged as another of the wonder kids who had been instrumental in her father's sweeping and somewhat unexpected surge to the White House. She'd seen articles written about her father's White House in those critical first ninety days, about how the stern, older, business executive types who'd populated the West Wing during the last administration, slaves to decorum and protocol, had been usurped by preppies in khakis and button-down shirts and more enthusiasm than savvy. Sometimes, in the early days, her father's young staffers had exhibited more enthusiasm than skill, but that had changed, and quickly. Lucinda Washburn had guided the transformation, Blair thought, as she automatically followed the route toward the waiting vehicle she had taken hundreds of times before, striding quickly between the subtle cordon of protective agents directly into the back seat of the limo, settling against the plush leather seats with her thigh against Cam's as the agent closed the door and the limo glided away.

Lucinda, her father's Chief of Staff. Lucinda was not unskilled, unsavvy, or undisciplined. Lucinda was the woman, Blair was pretty certain, her father loved, and the one who provided a sounding board for him when critical decisions needed to be made. Lucinda saw that what needed to be done was indeed done, while simultaneously shielding the president from many of the outside forces that could distract and overburden him.

"Did Lucinda call?" Blair asked. "I didn't ask."

Cam took her hand as the limo pulled away from the curb and intertwined their fingers. "Her assistant. Lucinda was probably deciding the order of the response."

"Of course." Someone would need to tell Adam's family. The staff would need to be informed. The press. God, the press. This would spawn all kinds of conjecture and rumor if not handled properly. For the millionth time, Blair was grateful for Lucinda and just a little guilty about grumbling about all the times she'd had to stand in for her mother—and even her father, on occasion—at political functions. Sure, she hated being the object of media attention and speculation, especially when her personal life was the subject. But being annoyed and inconvenienced was nothing compared to this. "This is so horrible."

"It is," Cam murmured.

Blair leaned against Cam's shoulder, no other words necessary. They'd been here before, facing other crises, and what she loved about being with Cam was she knew she would not be alone. No matter what, Cam would be there. Maybe that was love. Surely, part of it.

She turned the ring on Cam's left ring finger. She liked seeing the gold band there, that outward symbol of not only what they shared but a little bit of possessiveness too. She liked the world knowing that Cam was hers. She couldn't imagine—

No. She *would* not imagine any life without Cam.

The motorcade moved quickly despite the morning rush, but without particular fanfare. Unlike when her father went anywhere, even a few blocks, they didn't have a motorcycle escort or multiple support cars plus an extra limo, just her car and the follow car with the rest of her detail, but the flashing blue lights on the hoods cleared traffic for them, and ten minutes later they were moving through the west gate onto the White House grounds. The Uniformed Division of the Secret Service was out in force, surrounding the White House in larger numbers than usual, forming an unobtrusive, but obvious to Blair, perimeter preventing the approach of foot and vehicular traffic anywhere near the grounds. She recognized the pattern and what that said about the threat level. Somewhere else she'd been before. Her security would automatically be enhanced, and Cam would be very busy very soon. Hawaii was already a fading fantasy.

Her car came to a halt, and the agent in the right front seat jumped out to open the rear door for them. Cam slid out, waited for Blair, and slipped her hand beneath Blair's elbow as they walked toward the entrance.

"I'm sorry about all of this," Cam murmured, "especially about Adam. From the looks of things, we're not going to make our plane."

"No," Blair murmured. They definitely were not going on vacation. "It's all right. There will be plenty of time for vacations in the future."

She hoped. Service, duty, and responsibility were programmed into Cam's DNA, and Blair had known that when she'd fallen in love with her. But someday, Cam would at least spend more time at a desk than in the field. Until then, their life was what it was.

Cam squeezed her hand as if assuring her she was right, then released it as they entered the West Wing.

Lucinda's assistant met them just inside. "Ms. Powell, Commander, this way please."

Kelly's face was pale, her eyes faintly red rimmed. Shell-shocked, but functioning, exactly as required.

"They're in the conference room," Kelly added as she hurried along.

Not the situation room, at least, where her father met with the top military and security advisors to deal with military emergencies. Here and there staffers passed them, all of them appearing harried but none looking distraught. They didn't know yet. So the meeting she and Cam had been summoned to was for damage control. Everything pointed to something more critical than the already horrifying death of a major member of the president's team.

"Here we are," Kelly said as she opened the heavy mahogany door for them, betraying her distress in that simple unnecessary statement.

"Thank you, Kelly," Blair said gently, and Kelly's eyes filled.

Blair's agents remained outside in the hall as she entered with Cam. They'd be there when she came out. Lucinda stood at the far end of the fifteen-seat conference table, which was nearly full. Blair sat at the opposite end beside Cam and took in the others already gathered there, all of whom she knew. The inner circle.

Lucinda's deputy chief of staff, the White House communications director, the press secretary, the White House chief counsel, the White House medical director, the national security advisor, various deputy directors, and, sitting at the far end across from Lucinda, the campaign press secretary, Esmeralda Alaqua. Esme's hands, folded on the table in front of her, visibly trembled and she stared at Lucinda as if clinging to a life raft, desperate but determined. Blair had always wondered if Esme and Adam were lovers. In that moment, she fervently hoped not. Losing a friend was hard enough, but a partner? Her mind shied away from even imagining the devastation.

The door at the far end of the room opened and everyone rose as her father, flanked by agents Blair recognized, walked in. Oakley Weaver and Evyn Daniels glided into the far corners of the room in their usual unobtrusive fashion. When Tom Turner stepped back, the president motioned him to have a seat at the table. The Secret Service didn't involve themselves in policy. Their role was to protect the presidency, not offer opinions or advice on strategy, but they were key members of the security system that permeated everything around the president like a huge web, invisible but impossible to escape. When decisions impacted their ability to effectively protect the president, or any protectee, it was their duty to speak up. Ultimately, the protectee's decision was final, but most often a workable compromise was possible.

"Please," her father said, indicating the chairs as he sat, and everyone followed suit. He leaned over and murmured something to Esme, and she nodded once.

"Lucinda," her father said.

"I'm sorry to have to inform you," Lucinda said gravely, "that at six thirty-five this morning, Adam Eisley was struck and killed by a hit-and-run driver while jogging."

Blair caught the slightest movement from Oakley Weaver, standing against the wall behind her father's right shoulder. She shuddered for a brief second, her posture stiffening. No other facial expression, other than a visible tightening of her jaw, but she was clearly affected by the news. Just that little bit of reaction was unusual for a seasoned agent, and Oakley had been on the PPD for quite a while now. Blair knew her to say hello to, but she couldn't recall ever actually having a conversation with her. The agents were trained not to engage in conversations beyond polite acknowledgment of a good morning or thank you from the protectee. That she and Paula Stark had become friends was unusual, but then, she'd never followed protocol very well and Stark—well, Paula was Paula. When she was on the job, she was as solid and reliable as Cam. But unlike Cam, whose reserve extended to everyone but Blair beyond the confines of their home, Paula allowed her feelings to show when she wasn't working.

That barest flicker of reaction from Oakley was gone now too. The agent's expression was remote and unreadable.

"What do we know of the circumstances of the event?" Cam asked.

"As of this moment," Lucinda replied, "the driver has not been apprehended. Metropolitan Police are obviously doing everything they can to identify the vehicle. I am still waiting for preliminary reports."

"And our people?" Averill Jensen, the national security advisor, asked.

Lucinda said, "We've asked the Uniformed Division commander to assign a liaison to the Metro force. If we discover there are sensitive security issues, we will assume responsibility for the investigation."

The president said, "We don't know if this was a random act—an accident, and the driver simply fled the scene—or an intentional incident. Until we do, we have to proceed as if this was a targeted assault."

Cam said, "No one has come forth to take credit, I assume?"

"Not as of this time," Lucinda said.

"Do we have any indication of previous threats to Adam?" Cam asked.

All eyes turned to Adam's assistant.

"None that I'm aware of," Esme said, her voice low and flat but steady. "We get our share of crank emails, especially now with the convention coming up, and the usual inflammatory tweets trying to stir things up, but nothing of a violent nature. I think Adam would've told me if there had been."

The communications director interjected, "Forgive me, but what would be gained by targeting Adam? I understand how important his role is to the campaign, but why him? Couldn't it be he was just a convenient target because he was unprotected?"

"That's possible, of course," Lucinda said, "but we can't assume accident or absence of intent. At this juncture, Adam's role in securing the nomination for the president is critical. Despite all the knowledgeable individuals involved in the reelection effort, Adam was the face of our campaign with national recognition. The average citizen knows his name."

The press secretary added, "Some people might believe that removing Adam would cause enough disruption and inflated press coverage to allow Donald Jessup to gain ground."

Philip Brewster, the White House counsel, grimaced. "Is that really likely?"

Lucinda's smile thinned. "That's partly why we're here, Philip. To avert any appearance, real or imagined, of instability in our platform or our position."

"We not only need to be *seen* as carrying on as usual," the president said, "we actually have to do that. We need to keep the campaign organized and on track."

Everyone looked at Esme.

She straightened and her chin lifted. "I don't have the public profile to take Adam's place, and respectfully, I don't want to. I will certainly do whatever is required to assist whoever takes his place."

"You understand," Lucinda said, "such a situation is no reflection on your abilities."

Esme nodded. "Thank you, and I do understand."

"So," Brewster said, "exactly where are we going to get someone at this point with a national profile who will convince the world that Adam's loss is tragic but not debilitating—and someone who can actually do the job? Because we need to do more than hold our ground right now—our margin isn't that large, and public perception can change quickly. We need to continue to gain ground over the next six weeks, because static is not a desirable position."

Blair resisted the urge, just barely, to tell Philip he was a pompous horse's ass. But he was a good attorney, incredibly loyal to her father, and—as cold-hearted as it sounded—he had a point.

"I have a suggestion," Blair said.

Her father glanced down the table and met her eyes for the first time. His gaze almost looked amused. Did he know? "Go ahead, Blair."

"Ari Rostof," Blair said.

A burst of protest sounded simultaneously from multiple voices, Philip's loudest among them.

"Impossible," he intoned. "She'd never accept, and even if she did, she'd never pass the security clearance."

"Talk about a media nightmare," the communications director muttered.

The press secretary leaned back in her seat, a thoughtful expression on her face. "I'm not so sure it's a bad idea. Her security clearance ought to be pretty high already, considering the access she's had working with members of Congress. And she's definitely got the national profile."

"If you like controversial and confrontational," Brewster snapped.

Andrew Powell cleared his throat and the room fell silent.

"Commander Roberts?" the president asked. "Opinion?"

"Let's ask her," Cam said.

Blair kept her eyes on her father, and this time, he smiled back.

Chapter Five

Lucinda Washburn's announcement reverberated in Oakes's bones.

I'm sorry to have to inform you...

Oakes shuddered.

...at six thirty-five this morning...

The words struck over and over with the force of bullets punching into her.

...Adam Eisley was struck and killed...

She set her jaw, force down the shock.

Adam Eisley was struck and killed.

Oakes reeled internally until, after an instant that felt like an eternity, her training kicked in. In those weeks at FLETC and the Beltway, she'd been conditioned to run *toward* the sound of danger when the normal instinct was to flee. Gunfire, explosions, car crashes were all signals for her to act. Fear and pain were relegated to irrelevant background noise. Steely calm spread through her as her mind sharpened, her vision cleared, and though she hadn't moved an inch, every muscle coiled, ready to spring at the first inkling of threat.

The space inside the room contracted until she could sense every detail, while at the same time, her field of view widened, creating a panoramic gestalt of the room at large where every movement was magnified. She automatically cataloged her position. Her back was two inches from the walnut paneled wainscoting behind her. Evyn stood nine and a half feet to her left, at a forty-five-degree angle behind the president's left shoulder, triangulating with her own position on the right. She knew exactly how far she was from the president—an arm's length away. The maximum distance from which she could reach him to cover and evacuate.

Her situational awareness heightened, every image jumped out at her, crisp and razor-edged. The monogrammed pen in Philip Brewster's right hand that he tapped rhythmically, impatiently, against the tabletop. Cameron Roberts's deceptively relaxed posture, hiding the same coiled tension that was second nature to Oakes. Blair Powell, her expression intent, a flicker of impatience in Brewster's direction, but her focus almost unerringly on the president.

Oakes couldn't see his face from where she stood, but his voice was telling. Calm, steady, with just the barest touch of amusement when he addressed his daughter. Oakes had witnessed their unspoken communication many times before, their connection more than familial, a camaraderie between equals.

She was aware of the ache somewhere beneath the readiness, buried deep in her chest, in the core of her brain where emotion lived. Adam, one of her only friends. Two or three mornings a week, she ran with him. She'd begged off running with him that morning to play racquetball with Evyn. If she'd been there—

The pain was swift and lancing. Oakes shut down the doubt, the anger, the rage. She had no time to feel. All that mattered was her job. Maintain situational awareness. Be prepared to protect the president, even here in this apparently unassailable room. No space was impenetrable, no plan infallible, no location completely secure. Her job was to anticipate, to question the obvious, to distrust the appearance of safety. Duty first. There'd be time enough to mourn or rail at the injustice of a pointless death later. Perhaps.

The attorney, Brewster, said, "I suppose Rostof would bring certain assets to the position. Looking beyond the nomination, fund-raising will be a priority. I'm sure she has substantial contacts."

Oakes listened with a portion of her brain. The White House counsel sounded like he was less than impressed with this Rostof woman. Oakes didn't really care. The decisions being made would affect what she would need to do in the short term—in the next few minutes to hours—and, as the lead advance on the convention trip, in the coming weeks as well. Still, her role would remain fundamentally the same. Ari Rostof was a name she recognized only because she'd heard it on television. The woman could be anyone, and Oakes's role would be the same.

"I agree that Rostof is the best choice for a number of reasons," the president said dryly, apparently choosing to ignore Brewster's displeasure. "Our window for action is small, so we need to make immediate arrangements." He turned toward the Chief of Staff. "Lucinda? Anything else?"

"No, Mr. President," Lucinda said briskly. "I'll make the necessary calls."

"Good," the president said. "Thank you all. Tom, Blair, Cam—a moment please."

That was the cue for everyone else to leave, and a minute later the room had cleared. Oakes and Evyn remained as they were, in the background.

Once the doors closed behind the last person, the president looked at his daughter. "All right, how hard do you think it's going to be to convince her?"

Blair waggled her hand. "From what I recall of the two previous campaigns she's run, she's on our side on the majority of issues, so there shouldn't be any insurmountable policy objections. She might not see joining our team as a necessary or desirable career move, though. She going to take heat from the opposition—and maybe some on our side too. Subtly, of course." Blair grimaced. "She doesn't need to put herself in that position—her profile is strong enough as it is."

"Is that all that matters to her?" Lucinda asked. "Her profile on the national stage?"

"I can't really say," Blair replied pensively. "I would guess that career campaign managers at her level are doing it for something other than wide-eyed altruism." She snorted. "That attitude really doesn't last long in the real world."

"Power?" the president asked quietly.

"Possibly. That isn't always a bad thing."

Oakes wondered about Adam. She knew why she'd chosen the Secret Service. What could be more important than protecting the most important man in the Western world? Maybe that was the same thing for Adam—getting that man elected. She'd never thought to ask him—that inborn reticence, reinforced by her training, to breach the personal. To get too close. Now she'd never know.

Cam Roberts said, "Coming in this late will put her at a disadvantage."

"Yes," Lucinda said, "but it also presents a challenge. From what I've seen of her, she likes that sort of thing."

Blair laughed. "I don't think there's anything Ari likes more, except possibly sailing. No matter how high the bar is set, she always wanted it higher. Made it hell for the rest of us."

"I'd forgotten the two of you were at prep school at the same time, weren't you," Lucinda said.

"We were a year apart," Blair said. "For a while there I wanted to be just like her. That was before I mostly wanted to kill her."

The president made a sound somewhere between a laugh and a groan. "For a while there, I was pretty sure you were going to."

Blair smiled, then her face grew serious. "I think if we're going to convince her, it needs to be face-to-face."

"You're saying a call from the President of the United States wouldn't be convincing enough," Lucinda said.

"The Ari I knew—and from what coverage I've caught of her when she ran Jafari's senatorial campaign and recently with Martinez—she hasn't changed. She grew up under the bright lights. Her father... well..." Blair shrugged.

"Yes," Lucinda said with a sigh. "Her father. He might be the wild card in all of this."

Blair shook her head. "Not if you mean that he'll influence Ari, overtly or otherwise. She's spent her whole life proving she was her own person, and that means not only standing up to him but most often taking the exact opposite position."

"Sounds familiar," the president said.

The president's daughter grinned for a fleeting second.

"All the same," Lucinda said, "are we in a position to withstand a witch hunt if the opposition, or even someone in our own party, decides to go digging into the Rostof family businesses?"

"The question is," Roberts said mildly, "is Ari Rostof willing to take that chance?"

The president glanced at Lucinda. "We need to move quickly on this if we're going to contain the media. I believe we've made the right choice, but I'm willing to hear arguments."

No one said anything for a long moment.

Lucinda said, "Next order of business, then, is to get her here and on the job. Ideally, I'd like her in front of the cameras today. Blair, how do you feel about taking the lead in this?"

"I'd want to sit down with her," Blair said. "No video calls. No record at all. We're not exactly best friends, but we've got some history, so I think she'd be open about any concerns."

Cameron Roberts glanced at Blair, one eyebrow imperceptibly lifting. If Oakes hadn't been watching her, she wouldn't have seen it.

"Does anyone know where she is right now?" the president asked.

"I'm sure the senator's office would know how to reach her," Lucinda said. "I'll make some discreet inquiries through confidential channels."

"All right." The president turned to Tom Turner. "The biggest thing on the horizon is the convention, and anyone we get to take Adam's place is going to be one hundred percent buried in that. Can you put someone from your team in on the ground level with Rostof, if she agrees?"

"It might make sense to send someone along with Ms. Powell to be available when Ms. Powell presents the offer. Ms. Rostof's likely to have questions, some of which we may be able to answer."

The president nodded. "Fine, let's do that."

Cam said, "There's another issue we have to consider. The circumstances of Adam's death. If the collision was intentional, if he was targeted because of his position or his *perceived* importance to your reelection, sir, then it is not beyond reason that his successor might be a target also."

"Are you suggesting formal protection?" the president asked. He could request protective services for anyone, and frequently did, although those individuals were most often foreign dignitaries.

"Not until we have more information from Metro and the coroner," Cam said.

"All right then," the president said as he rose. Everyone followed suit. "Let's see that it's done."

He turned and left, and Oakes and Evyn followed him out.

"Oakes," Turner called, "wait a moment."

Oakes fell back while Turner spoke with two of the other members of the detail, who broke away to accompany the president with Evyn.

"Are you good to go?" Turner asked her.

"Yes, sir," Oakes said crisply. Turner must know she and Adam were—*had been*—friends. She didn't need to say anything else. He would trust her to know her own limits.

"Egret's team will advance this trip. I'll advise them to inform you of the details."

"Thank you, sir." Oakes added, "As to briefing Ms. Rostof—"

"Keep it to the obvious—venue details, expected crowd size, that sort of thing—and let her know what you'll need from her. As the president said, she's going to have a steep learning curve and we can't do our jobs if she's not doing hers."

Oakes nodded. From what she'd heard, Ari Rostof sounded like the kind of person who didn't naturally play well with others. That might have to change.

"Good," Turner said. "You're officially reassigned for the length of this mission."

"Yes, sir," Oakes said, fervently hoping the mission would be brief.

After a brisk five-minute walk back to the command center, during which Oakes kept from thinking about Adam by calling up one of her endless mental lists, she pulled her go bag from her locker. On autopilot after having done this hundreds of time before, she checked to make sure everything was there, even though she knew it was. Going through the motions helped keep her focused.

The locker room door opened and Evyn came in.

"Hey," Evyn said, threading her way around the benches to Oakes's side. "I'm really sorry about Adam."

"Yeah." Oakes rearranged her clean shirt and pants for the second time, tucked her bathroom kit into the opposite corner along with a pair of field pants and boots, and zipped up the duffel. "Any other morning, I'd probably have been with him."

"I know," Evyn said.

Oakes appreciated that Evyn didn't tell her that it wouldn't have made a difference if she'd been there, or that she might've been a second victim if she'd been with Adam, or that she couldn't have known what would happen. She already knew all those things. Knowing didn't help.

"So, about this trip—how are you?"

Oakes blew out a breath. "You get the feeling that this Rostof's getting the white glove treatment?"

Evyn snorted. "Just a little bit."

"I don't know what use I'll be." Oakes shook her head.

"Maybe you'll just be along to make everything look good."

Oakes rolled her eyes and Evyn smiled, although the smile didn't reach all the way to her eyes. "I imagine anybody who even thinks about taking over for Adam's going to want to know what the plans are for the biggest event in the president's immediate agenda."

"It's not like I'm going to be able to tell her anything. If we'd gotten an itinerary…" She trailed off. Adam or one of his people would've been responsible for providing the advance team with a skeleton outline of what the president would be doing in the days leading up to and during the convention, but… "So far, nothing."

"Well," Evyn said, "I wouldn't want her job."

"No," Oakes said quietly. "Me neither."

"Give me a holler if you need anything," Evyn said.

"Hey," Oakes said, forcing a smile, "white glove treatment. No problem."

CHAPTER SIX

Newport, Rhode Island
2:10 p.m.

"Ms. Rostof!" Martha—once a stay-at-home mom, she'd grown bored once her children reached their teen years and now came in daily to cook and clean—called down to Ari from the veranda. Somehow she'd managed to be heard over the rumble of the *Castaway*'s engines.

Ari, about to cast off the last line, halted. Shading her face with one hand, she squinted up toward the house. Martha, looking half her age in a plain T-shirt and jeans, made a come-up-here motion with one arm. Ari sighed. Really, was she ever going to escape?

Ari retied the line, climbed up onto the dock, and trotted toward the land end of the pier.

"What is it, Martha?"

"Telephone call for you."

Ari frowned, pulled her cell from the pocket of her cargo shorts, and checked the readout. Missed call. She hadn't heard it above the rumble of the engine.

"I'm about to go out for a sail. Take a message."

Martha shook her head. "You'll want to take this one, Ms. Rostof."

Resigned, Ari called, "Just a minute, then."

She hurried back to the boat, hopped down onto the deck, and shut down the engines. A quick scan to double-check all the lines were secured, and she was on her way back to the house. Someone from the senator's office must want her. If they'd called her cell and then her home number, she wasn't going to be able to avoid addressing whatever was going on. Some piece of negative press or, heaven forbid, some past indiscretion dug up by the opposition come back to haunt the candidate now. Yearbooks should be outlawed, or certainly not kept around to indict someone thirty years after their idiotic college years.

Martha crossed the porch, hurried down the stairs to meet her on the path up from the bay, and held out the portable house phone to Ari. Her expression vacillated between worry and avid curiosity.

"Thank you, Martha," Ari said, waiting for Martha to move out of earshot.

Turning her back to the house, Ari stared out across the harbor. The water had calmed, but the weather report suggested a storm would blow in by later afternoon. Her window for getting in a sail was rapidly shrinking.

"This is Rostof," Ari said absently, mentally calculating how far she'd be able to sail before she'd need to turn around or risk getting caught offshore in a squall.

"Ari, this is Blair Powell."

For a second, Ari struggled with the name. Surely not *that* Blair Powell. But then what other Blair Powell did she know. "Blair?"

"Yes, hello. I'm sorry to catch you without warning, but it's important that I speak with you."

"All right," Ari said, rapidly switching into business mode. "What can I help you with? If it's something to do with an upcoming vote, of course, I'll probably need to confer with the senator or staff. I'm away—well, of course, you know that, don't you. So, some shift in the polls I haven't heard about?"

"Actually, it's not about the senator, at least not directly," Blair said. "It's a bit complicated."

And cryptic, Ari refrained from adding, Blair Powell was one of the most influential figures on the national scene—an effective policy promoter and a wizard at fund-raising. If that wasn't enough, she often represented the president when he was unable to attend some event. For all those reasons, Blair had earned the right to be as cryptic as she liked.

"I have plenty of time," Ari said as the clock face in her mind loomed large, her sailing window fading fast.

"I'd like to speak with you in person," Blair said.

"Oh," Ari said, hoping she didn't sound too relieved as the vision of calm seas and brisk winds returned. She might still get in a sail. "Of course. What's your schedule like? I'm sure I can make mine work with yours, whenever it's convenient. I can be back in DC tomorrow if necessary."

"I'm afraid we're in a bit of a time crunch," Blair said. "How does thirty minutes sound?"

"I'm sorry?" Ari said, confusion descending again. She didn't seem to be tracking very well, and that wasn't like her. This whole conversation seemed to be taking place in a wind tunnel, as if she was hearing sounds that should have made sense but didn't. She could usually predict where a conversation was going after a few moments, either from reading the expressions on the faces of those around her or analyzing the tone of voice, the word choices, the cadence, or the pauses, which were far more important than most people realized. But she was at a loss to quite understand why Blair Powell—the First Daughter—was calling her in the first place. Blair, at least as much as she remembered of her from personal experience, wasn't the sort of person to get involved in backroom politics, and neither, for that matter, was the president. If they wanted something from the senator, they most likely would've simply directed their request to her. If it was something as simple as needing a calendar update, Angelo or one of the other staffers could accommodate.

Usually, the only people who contacted Ari privately were the ones who wanted to influence the senator or, in some far subtler plan, undermine her. She said nothing, waiting for a clue as to what direction the call would go.

"We're at the Newport Naval Base. We could be there in thirty minutes, traffic permitting."

"You're at the naval base," Ari repeated, sounding like a confused parrot even to herself, "here in Newport?"

"Yes," Blair said.

Ari's mind started working again. Blair Powell had no reason to be at the naval base. It certainly wasn't the sort of place where any kind of campaigning would be going on. If she was there, it was because she wanted to meet with Ari. And if that was the case, whatever had brought her here was critical. All of that was moot, anyhow. One did not refuse the First Daughter, not without knowing the circumstances and, very possibly, not even then.

"Of course," Ari said briskly. "I'm at my father's home, but of course you know that. Please come ahead."

"I appreciate you giving up some of your time off," Blair said. "I know how precious it can be."

"Please don't worry about it," Ari said. "Do you need directions?"

"No, our driver is familiar with the area."

That sounded like a military escort. Ari's skin itched with the urge to get inside and turn on the television. What had she missed? But then, if some kind of national emergency had happened, the station would have contacted her father—and he would have informed her already.

"Might I ask how many to expect?"

Blair laughed faintly. "I promise not to inflict the entire entourage on you. I am with Commander Roberts and a number of Secret Service agents. You don't need to make any special arrangements."

"I'll have lunch prepared," Ari said.

"We'll be there shortly. And again, my apologies for the interruption."

"Please don't worry about that," Ari said. "I'll look forward to our discussion."

"Thanks. We'll see you shortly."

The president's daughter disconnected, and Ari tucked her phone back into her pocket. Blair Powell had made a trip for the express purpose of speaking to her. She'd also been pretty confident that Ari would meet with her. She couldn't think of a single reason for this visit, and her father was in the dark too. Something had happened that hadn't yet hit the air.

She pulled her phone back out, hit speed dial, and waited until her assistant in Washington answered.

"Angelo," she said, "it's Ari."

"Hey, boss," Angelo Herrera said with his usual high-octane energy level. "How's the sailing?"

"Just about to go out," Ari said. "How is everything there?"

"The same as always," he said. "The phones are ringing, the volunteers are like eager puppies, and Royster is making his usual sounds about how the senator's liberal policies are going to send the country to hell."

"Is the senator ignoring him?"

"For the time being, but you know how hard it is for her to hold off."

"Just keep her busy and don't let her talk to the press."

Angelo laughed. "So you just calling because you miss me?"

"Is there anything else brewing—anything unusual going on down there?"

A beat of silence, and then Angelo said, "Not that I'm aware of. Have I missed something?"

"I'm not sure, but keep all the lines open. Especially anything coming out of the White House."

"All right, I'll alert our people to sit on any media releases, and I'll shake the rumor tree."

Ari laughed. "Shake gently."

"Always do."

"Good, it's probably nothing. But it has been quiet lately."

"For which I am grateful," he said. "I'll see you in a few days."

"Right, I'll talk to you again soon." Ari disconnected, unable to shake the feeling she'd be seeing him a lot sooner than a few days and that her coveted sailing time had come and gone.

She jogged up to the house, alerted Martha about a possible unexpected luncheon, and continued on down the west wing to her father's study. She rapped on his open door.

"Got a minute?"

He regarded her over his reading glasses, then set them aside. "I thought you were going sailing."

"I was." She crossed the thick Persian carpet and stopped in front of his massive walnut desk. She didn't sit. "Is there anything in the way of breaking news you haven't told me about?"

His gaze sharpened. She'd often been told they had the same eyes, and she wondered if hers ever appeared as lethal as his.

"What's happened?" he said.

"I don't know that anything has, but Blair Powell and Commander Cameron Roberts will be here in"—she checked her watch—"twenty-five minutes."

"Why wasn't I informed?"

His gaze, if possible, grew more remote. Ari knew that look. Her father rarely raised his voice. He didn't need to. He made his displeasure known by actions, not words. Right now he was deciding on a course of action depending on what she said next. She'd learned to volley verbally at a young age, one of the skills that made her so successful.

"Because I just got off the phone with her," Ari said. "I had no notice until five minutes ago."

"A private meeting? And the subject?"

"Blair indicated she wanted to speak to me. I don't have any details."

He picked up his glasses. "I'll be curious to hear about it."

"I'll speak with you later." Making no promises, Ari headed for the door. She estimated it would take him ten seconds to send out inquiries about anything of note on the world scene.

Ari went upstairs to change clothes and await the First Daughter.

While Blair Powell and Cameron Roberts made arrangements to meet with Ari Rostof, Oakes joined the agents on Blair's detail for a walk-around of the vehicles that idled outside the hangar at the Newport Naval Base where they'd landed. She wasn't part of the protective detail, just a tagalong, but she couldn't shake the habit. Once that was done, while the agents waited to escort Blair and the commander to the vehicles, Oakes pulled up her email on the encrypted phone and checked the FYEO report from headquarters.

The dossier was typical of the kind of briefing info she received every day on individuals with whom the president might meet, who might be a potential threat, or whose bodyguards or protective agents she'd have to work with. A passport-type color photo headed the first screen. An attractive Eastern European–appearing, dark-haired, blue-eyed woman with pale skin and sharply etched features.

Subject: Arianna Katarina Rostof
Age: 33
Residence: 3133 Connecticut Ave NW, Washington, DC,
    20008
Phone: (202) 555-0566
Marital Status: Single
Occupation: Political Consultant
Business address: Current campaign manager for Senator
    Alexandria Martinez
Physical Description: WF, 5'9", 135 lbs.
Hair: Black
Eyes: Blue
Distinguishing marks: Appendectomy scar
Education: St. Michael's Country Day School, Newport, RI
    Choate Rosemary Prep, Wallingford, CT
    Georgetown, BA and MA, Political Science and
    International Affairs

Medical Conditions: None
Allergies: Penicillin
Family History: Father, Nikolai, age 55; Mother, Katarina,
    age 54; siblings: none
Security Clearance: Top secret; previous appointment with
    State Department

The dossier was interesting for what it didn't include. Very little family background, and huge red flags surrounded Ari Rostof's father. Oakes knew as much about him as most people in America knew, and most people knew something. Ari Rostof's father owned one of the largest media conglomerates in the world, including cable television channels, newspapers, and magazines, along with several professional sports teams. Oakes had no doubt he also owned interests in many, many other things that weren't as easily accessible to public records. Whereas Ari Rostof's public profile was well-known due to her association with major political candidates, her father's was a mystery below the surface. Nothing in this report shed very much light on it.

Nikolai Rostof was a Russian immigrant who had come to the US as a twenty-year-old. Ari's mother, Katarina, arrived from an Eastern Bloc country several years later. Ari was an American-born citizen and an only child. Oakes wasn't much interested in rumors, although she didn't discount them either. Rumors often were founded in reality. Of course, with a man as successful as Rostof, allusions to the Russian mafia were often the subject of inflammatory journalism. To her knowledge, no evidence had ever surfaced to suggest the rumors were true.

All the same, if Ari Rostof moved into a position where she had daily access to the President of the United States, Oakes had to believe security measures would be adjusted to include the new campaign manager.

"Egret and Hawk are on their way," the agent accompanying the First Daughter and the commander announced over the radio.

Oakes moved into position with the other agents as Blair Powell and Cameron Roberts exited the hangar and strode toward the waiting vehicles. Once the principals along with Paula Stark, the lead agent, were secured in the lead car, Oakes climbed into the follow car with the rest of the detail. Since the president and the First Daughter often traveled together, she knew all Egret's agents with the exception of those pulled from the local office to fill out the ranks for this visit.

Oakes took one side of the facing seats while Felicia Adams and Ozzie Benedict each took window seats. Once the vehicle set out, they kept watch outside.

Oakes had plenty of time to observe the picture-postcard view as they wound through Newport along the harbor, and with no assignment at the moment, she found it hard to ignore the reason for this trip and the ache in her midsection.

Adam had been killed. When reality penetrated, she still reeled with the impact. Like most Secret Service agents on protective details who tended to be young and unattached, she didn't have many close relationships. Any kind of home life was practically impossible. Schedules were more theoretical than real, with constant changes to the itinerary, time off disappearing with a phone call, vacations canceled at the last minute, and weeks or even months away from home. Most agents rotated out of protection after a tour or two, and the ones who stayed long-term, moving up into supervisory positions, often postponed permanent relationships until later in their career.

She was no different than most of her colleagues. She had plenty of opportunities to spend the night with someone during the before and after portions of the innumerable presidential trips, when stress and fatigue and sleep deprivation left everyone's judgment slightly askew. She hadn't been immune to the pressure cooker atmosphere but had never been comfortable with the awkward aftermath of sex with someone she barely knew or, worse, someone she'd considered a friend. She and Evyn had almost gone that way shortly after they'd first met, before Evyn met and fell in love with Wes. Thankfully, they'd made it as far as the hotel room, stared at each other next to the bed, and she'd said, "I don't have many friends."

"Neither do I."

"Let's not do this."

"Good idea."

And that had been the end of it. One of the best decisions she'd ever made in her life. Evyn was still her best friend, but her schedule matched Oakes's for unpredictability. Adam had been the person she spent most of her off hours with, even though they only got together every once in a while. They liked the same movies, they liked the same restaurants, they even liked the same books. The coincidence of their having come from the same hometown astounded her, and even though years had separated them, when they'd been thrown back into the same circle again, that shared history had drawn them together.

And now he was gone.

She squeezed her fists. Now was not the time to think about all that. The vehicles were slowing and she made out arched wrought iron gates, a good ten feet high, set into eight-foot-high stone walls, covered with ivy in places, fifty feet from the main road. A stone gatehouse stood just inside the gate, which swung inward as the lead car pulled slowly forward. A uniformed woman stepped over to the driver's side and leaned down.

Felicia Adams said, "Armed security," relaying a message she'd received from the vehicle preceding them.

After a moment, they moved forward and the gates behind them swung closed. The drive was long and winding, snaking through lawns and gardens filled with massive shrubs and shade trees to a massive sprawling white house on the crest of the hill. The vehicles halted under a portico at the foot of a wide staircase leading to the entrance, and the agents quickly exited, forming a semicircle around the principal's vehicle. Oakes remained in the rear, uncertain of her part in the meeting. The massive mahogany front doors swung open, and a woman walked out. Photos and physical statistics rarely described an individual completely, and in the case of Ari Rostof, far less than usual. For once, Oakes was glad she had the freedom to focus on just one person.

Rostof crossed the wide porch and descended the stairs with a graceful, confident stride as wind blew her thick, shoulder-length dark hair around her face, emphasizing her arched cheekbones and heart-shaped face. Her simple white shirt and slim dark pants somehow managed to create an image of casual elegance and supreme confidence.

"Agent Weaver," Blair Powell said. "Would you join us?"

"Of course." Oakes hid her surprise and fell in just behind the First Daughter as the group moved toward the stairs.

Ari Rostof met them at the bottom, and the two women hugged briefly. Rostof shook Roberts's hand and glanced at Oakes.

"Ari," Blair said, "Special Agent Weaver. She'll be joining us."

Oakes found herself face-to-face with Ari Rostof, who held out her hand and said, "Good to meet you. I'm Ari."

"Oakley Weaver, Ms. Rostof," Oakes said, taking her hand. She looked into blue eyes that perfectly matched the color of the water in the harbor beyond the grand mansion. She couldn't help but think that the woman looking back at her was taking her measure, and she wondered what she saw.

CHAPTER SEVEN

Ari led Blair and her entourage through the wide central hall and into the east wing. The main house—a mid-nineteenth-century three-story mansion—had been expanded with curving wings to either side. From the sea, her home reminded her of a seagull cresting a white-spumed wave. She rarely carried out business at home, but when she did, she preferred the sunroom. Her father's style was to enclose himself and his associates in the dark-paneled, private atmosphere of his office, but Ari had always found that the more casual setting put people at ease. Even adversaries could be unconsciously lulled into revealing more than they wished when immersed in sumptuous comfort, and this room was designed for that. The polished flagstones gleamed with swirls of coral, grays, and greens, reflecting the ocean depths, and the floor-to-ceiling windows, subtly shaded to allow sunlight to bathe the interior without glare, provided views of the harbor and the town nestled along the shore that rivaled any painting for beauty. An arrangement of three floral-print sofas around a large slate-topped coffee table centered on a square natural fiber rug provided seating that enabled conversation while providing everyone with a direct sight line to the others. They might've been sitting around a conference table, which was exactly why the layout had been done that way.

Just as they were all getting seated, Martha appeared with a coffee cart holding a large urn and a tower tray filled with tea sandwiches.

"Coffee? Something to eat?" Ari asked, sitting on the center sofa.

"Just coffee for me," Blair said, taking a seat to Ari's right along with Cameron Roberts.

"Coffee is great," Cam said.

Agent Weaver settled on Ari's left and shook her head. "I'm good, thanks."

The male Secret Service agent who had accompanied Blair and the others from the car had taken up a position just inside the door and were clearly part of the working detail protecting Blair. Interesting that Agent Weaver did not seem to be part of Blair's security detail, and Ari couldn't quite figure out what her role was. She was curious, especially as to the frank appraisal that Weaver made no effort to hide as she studied Ari.

Once Martha had poured, the coffee was distributed, and Martha had pushed the service cart away and silently disappeared, Ari balanced the china saucer on her knee and regarded Blair. "You didn't travel all the way here for the coffee or the view, so how can I help you?"

Blair leaned slightly forward. "We've come on a directive from the president to offer you a job at the White House."

"Ah," Ari said, experienced enough not to show her utter surprise. "I'll need a few details, then."

Cam Roberts laughed. "There are quite a few details you'll probably want, and a lot of answers. Because of the sensitive nature of the problem, we'd like to know you're on board before we divulge a great deal of information."

"Perhaps, then, we should start with the offer?" Ari sipped her coffee and set the cup and saucer down on the coffee table. As she straightened, she caught Agent Weaver's glance. Weaver didn't even try to hide the fact she was watching her and, when she saw Ari looking, smiled an altogether amused smile. There and gone in an instant. At least Ari thought she smiled. Maybe the agent was just enjoying Ari's careful attempts to step around the quicksand of negotiating with two of the most powerful people in Washington, when she had no idea what in heaven's name they were talking about. She wasn't usually distracted during business dealings, but something about the agent's frank regard put her off her stride. Which wouldn't do at all. Not now, not when the stakes were this high and she hadn't a clue as to the game.

Ari shifted subtly and turned her shoulder in Oakley's direction. Whatever odd bit of chemistry might had flared between them, she didn't have the time, inclination, or interest to wonder about it. She never let chaos into her world, and that was the feeling she got every time she saw Agent Weaver studying her. Best to simply close that channel right now.

Oakes noted the move to shut her out. Okay then—Rostof had decided she wasn't a player in this game, and by rights, she wasn't. Not in the immediate hand, perhaps. Except she did have a stake—a very big one. Her duty included not only protecting the president. She was charged with securing his safety, and that of everyone in the kill radius around him, at the biggest public appearance of his political life. And if Rostof planned to take over for Adam, the conductor of that event, they'd be working together daily up until game day. So, yeah, she was in this all the way.

She had to give Ari Rostof credit, though. She was cool under pressure. Anyone would be thrown off-balance by an out-of-the-blue visit from Blair Powell and Cameron Roberts, and they weren't making things easy for Ari by holding back most of the cards. She'd just challenged them to lay down their hand.

"The offer," Blair said, "is this. My father's reelection campaign has had an unexpected shakeup. We need a new campaign manager, and we—*he*—would like that to be you. The question is, do you want the job?"

Ari had more than a few questions, such as had Adam Eisley resigned—or been fired, why was there such a rush that Blair had come in person, and why would the president risk upending his reelection campaign six weeks before the convention? That made absolutely no sense. Something big was being left out of this picture, but she suspected she wasn't going to find out all the information until she committed one way or the other. Blair wouldn't have come in person if the answers were simple, and she must also know Ari wouldn't— couldn't—commit to anything without analyzing all the pros and cons. More than her professional integrity was at stake. Her personal choices had consequences for more than just her.

"You do know," Ari said, "that I already have a commitment with Senator Martinez."

Blair nodded. "Yes, but I think you'll agree, and I'm sure the senator would as well, that the president's reelection is paramount to maintaining the party's stability, which could only benefit the senator as well as every other incumbent up for reelection."

"Well, we're all aware that we can't afford to lose any seats with the margins as close as they are now."

"We're in agreement there," Blair said, accepting the subtle barb with equanimity. She was, after all, a politician's daughter and had been tempered in the fires of politics since she was a preteen.

"What's the status of the campaign," Ari asked. "How sure are you of the votes? How real are the finance numbers we're hearing from the national committee?"

"By all reports, our donors are solid and the polls look good."

"By *whose* report, though? Campaign managers often paint a rosier picture than actually exists." She smiled. "Temporarily at least. If everything is solid, why is Adam leaving?"

Blair glanced at Cam, and some unspoken message passed between them.

Cameron Roberts, the Advisor to the President on Counterterrorism, said, "Ms. Rostof, Adam Eisley was killed this morning in what may have been a hit-and-run accident. The circumstances are as yet unknown. Thus far, the White House has maintained a news blackout, but that can't continue much longer."

"God," Ari said after she caught her breath. "That's horrible." When she glanced at Agent Weaver, a stony mask dropped over her sharply chiseled features, the first real sign of emotion—even if inscrutable— she'd seen from the all-business agent. Something personal with Eisley there. A lover perhaps.

"Why me?" Ari asked quietly.

Blair was silent for long enough to convince Ari that she was searching for an honest answer. Finally Blair said, "Your record speaks for itself—you get your people elected, so we know you can manage all the moving parts. But we need something more than that. We need a figurehead, a national presence, a bannerman to lead the president's forces."

Ari smiled. "I'm not going to ask what you've been reading lately. But I know what you're saying, and I'm a little honored, I guess, that you think that's me."

Cam said, "That's about all we can tell you until we have your answer."

"I understand. You need immediate transition, to maintain the appearance of a solid campaign organization."

"Not just the appearance," Blair said quietly, "but the reality. We are nearly at the eleventh hour. If you've been watching the polls, you know what I'm talking about."

"It's hard to believe Donald Jessup has gained as much ground as he has. Six months ago he was a laughingstock, but now there's this bizarre groundswell of demographics we never would've predicted." Ari shook her head. "I don't think the president is in trouble, but you're right, he can't afford to lose any ground. These things tend to snowball with so little time left."

"Yes," Blair said, "and momentum can swing with just the appearance of weakness."

"How much time do I have to decide?" Ari asked.

Blair looked at her watch. "It's three ten. A transport leaves the naval base to take us back to Andrews at five p.m. We'd like you to be going with us."

Ari laughed and rocked back on the sofa, extending one arm out along the top. Well, that made things simpler. She wouldn't have to wrestle with family responsibility versus personal goals—or ambitions—any longer. "You must know there's absolutely no way that can happen. Even if I were to leave the senator, I need to put a transition team in place, and that would take weeks."

"Unfortunately, we don't have weeks. The convention is six weeks away."

"And you expect me—or any new campaign manager, for that matter—to step in and coordinate a national organization, let alone all the details of the event itself, in that amount of time?"

"We don't have a choice," Blair said. "The convention planning, at least, is already underway."

Ari snorted. "If it is, I would be very surprised. I know what kind of chaos exists up until the last minute." She shook her head. "You're asking the impossible."

"Agent Weaver is the lead advance agent for the president's trip to Philadelphia. Other than Esmeralda Alaqua, the campaign press secretary, she probably knows more about the status of the event than anyone."

Ari swiveled to face the agent, who on the surface now looked as remote as the agent standing by the doorway across the room. Beneath the surface, though, in the depths of her dark gaze, turmoil swirled. Pain perhaps, or anger. "How far along are you with the itinerary?"

Oakes said, "Coordination is underway with local law enforcement, airports, fire-rescue, medical, hotels—all going as planned."

"Of course it is," Ari said dryly. Really, what else could Weaver say? *It's a rat's nest of loose ends surrounding a snarl of chaos*? Did any of them really expect her to buy that? "And the convention organizers? Media and publicity? TV coverage? Ads?"

"That's Adam's…" Oakley flushed. "I don't presently have a status report on those issues."

Ari lifted a brow. Oakley held her gaze. If she was to consider this job—and that was a big *if*—she'd have to work day in and day out with this agent or others like her. She blew out a breath. "That might very well mean Adam's assistant has all those details or, worst case scenario, they were all in Adam's head. What's your take on that, Agent?"

"I can't answer that question, Ms. Rostof, because I don't deal in speculation. But," Oakley said, "my goal is to ensure that every step of the president's convention trip is secured before he ever steps out of the White House. To that end, we'll be on the same team."

Ari appreciated just how carefully Weaver had phrased that reply, as carefully as she had schooled her expression. Weaver had slipped around the obvious difference in their goals. The campaign manager worked for the president to get him reelected. The Secret Service worked for Homeland Security to protect the life of the president. Whoever that might be.

"Give me a moment." Ari rose and walked to the far windows to look at the sea. She'd never undertaken anything of this magnitude before, but the challenge excited her in a way nothing else could. More than just the challenge, the goal. Andrew Powell was a president who stood for many of the things she believed in. She would have to make the decision herself, but she was deciding for more than just herself. If she put herself in the national eye, as would be unavoidable, her father would be in the spotlight with her.

She forced herself to consider what she'd neatly managed to avoid thinking about her whole life. She couldn't be certain, had never been truly certain, that all the speculation she'd heard about her father's business associations wasn't true. Her moving into the sphere of the President of the United States would reawaken all of those old stories, and with them, suspicions of her. The president and his advisors must know what the media would do with that. Blair and Cameron Roberts knew it too, but they were here. They believed in her.

Ari turned around. "I'll need to make a call." She laughed. "Several of them. But I'll be ready to go with you at five p.m."

"Good," Blair said, smiling for the first time. "I'll call ahead. My father will want to meet with you."

"There's quite a few people I'll need to see…yesterday," Ari muttered. "I'll have Martha show you to the study where you can make your calls."

As everyone stood, Ari stopped Weaver with a hand on her arm.

"Ms. Rostof?" Oakes asked.

"Call me Ari," Ari said. "I'll need to see everything you have so far from Adam on the convention."

"Yes, ma'am."

Ari sighed. "Ari."

"All right...Ari. When?"

"Tonight. I'm sorry, I'm afraid it might be late by the time I can get free."

"Not a problem." Oakes hesitated. "And it's Oakes."

Ari smiled. "Thank you." Aware that Blair and the others had moved past them down the hall, and aware too that she still had her fingers curled around Oakes's forearm, Ari reluctantly let go. The night ahead was likely to be the first of many nights spent working, but right at that moment, she didn't mind a bit.

CHAPTER EIGHT

"You won't be disturbed in here," Ari said, opening the paneled mahogany door into a library. The long room faced a flower-bedecked terrace beyond a pair of ornate french doors. The other three walls were covered with floor-to-ceiling shelves filled with books.

"Thanks," Blair said. "We won't be long."

"Just text me," Ari said as she stepped back into the hall. "I'll be ready when you are."

When Ari closed the door behind her, Blair waited a moment before saying, "How secure do you think this is?"

Cam scanned the room and lifted a shoulder. "With those windows alone, someone could probably get a sight line into here with an audio receiver. But…my best guess? It's probably safe. If we are to trust Ari, then we need to trust that she put us in a secure space." Cam shrugged. "And I don't get the sense that this is a location where her father does business. I'm sure wherever *that* is, there are recordings."

Blair dropped into one of a pair of captain's chairs, with broad arms sheathed in supple black leather, arrayed in front of a huge stone fireplace stacked with logs, ready to be fired. She pulled out her phone. "I guess we trust Ari on this."

"When exactly did you decide on her to replace Adam?"

"In the limo on the way to the White House this morning. I didn't have a chance to talk to you about it before we met with my father and the others. Sorry."

Cam sat across from her. "What if I'd disagreed?"

"Do you?"

Cam shook her head. "No. I don't have a history with her, and you do. Besides, I trust your judgment."

Blair laughed. "And I know you well enough that if you'd had an issue, you would've brought it up at the meeting. I wasn't worried about that."

Cam reached across the space between them and Blair took her hand. "About that history."

Blair snorted. "No. And no."

"No, as in...?"

Blair laughed. "No, I wasn't and no, she wasn't."

"Hmm. Maybe her judgment *is* suspect."

"Her judgment is razor sharp," Blair said. "I hope there's enough time. I hope...she's enough."

"All we can do is make the best decisions in the moment," Cam said, "and this is a good one."

"Well," Blair said, punching in the code to the White House, "what's done is done."

"Yes," Cam murmured, her fingers entwined with Blair's.

"This is Blair Powell," Blair said when the operator in the communications center answered the secure line. "I'd like to speak with the president, please."

"Just one moment, Ms. Powell," the operator said in a calm, steady tone.

The faint background static from the electronic scrambler was the only sound for a moment, so subtle that anyone else probably would've missed it, but Blair had been listening to it all her life and knew just what it was.

Then her father said, "Blair. Do we have an answer?"

"Yes. Ari will be accompanying us back to Andrews."

"Excellent."

"Has Adam's family been advised yet?"

"Lucinda called them this morning, explained that there would be no media announcement until later today or possibly tomorrow morning, but"—he sighed—"there's been a leak."

Blair closed her eyes for a second and let out a long breath. "Of course there has. From where?"

"Metro Police."

"Now, that's not surprising. The media has it?"

"The media knows that someone from the White House was involved in the hit-and-run this morning. It's only a matter of time."

"We can't be back until nine tonight at least."

"Hold a moment, I'm going to bring Lucinda and the communications deputy in on this."

Again the very faint static.

"Blair," Lucinda said briskly a few seconds later. "Do we have her?"

"Yes," Blair said.

"Good. We're going to need to get out in front of this leak," Lucinda said.

"I agree," Blair said.

The communications director added, "We need to make some kind of statement within the hour. We'll be lucky if we can keep a cap on it until then."

"We don't have a choice," Blair said. "It's best that we appear to be on top of the situation, even if we can't put Ari on the air."

"I may have a solution for that," Lucinda said.

Blair smiled. "Of course you do."

After Ari left Cam and Blair in the east wing, she asked Martha to show Agent Weaver to a comfortable place to wait and continued on through the house to the west wing. Her father's office door was still closed, and she knocked.

"Come," he said, his voice muffled by the thick, heavy door. She closed it carefully behind her after she entered. Her father still sat behind his desk, but with his chair swiveled toward the windows. From there he could look down on the main entrance, where the vehicles and Secret Service agents from Blair's detail were clearly visible.

"I'll be leaving for Washington in an hour," she said, wondering how he felt about this unexpected intrusion.

He turned back to her and regarded her impassively for a moment. "Does this have something to do with the death of a White House staffer this morning?"

Ari had had years of practice schooling her expression, and she doubted he could see her surprise. She took care not to stiffen or signal her feelings. "I know your networks are remarkably efficient, but you must have mobilized them the moment I left the room."

"You could hardly expect me not to investigate when the First Daughter makes a surprise visit to mine." He smiled, a little wryly. "Some would consider that a meeting of equals, and definitely newsworthy."

Ari scoffed. "If you're trying to boost my ego, I don't need it. And *yours* certainly doesn't."

He smiled, the way he often did when she met him on level ground, answering his challenge with an equally challenging riposte. "I can see you haven't lost your edge, even though you've immersed yourself in a culture where power is not always desirable."

"Power is always desirable," she mused. "It's the cost that's in question."

He raised an eyebrow. "Is there a price you wouldn't pay?"

He probably would think any answer other than no would be a sign of weakness, but Ari wasn't so sure. "I should go—we'll be leaving soon."

"Are you planning to tell me the details?" he asked.

"Are you willing to go off the record?"

He sighed. "If you'll agree to give our reporters in Washington an exclusive when you arrive."

Ari thought it over. Her job was to publicize the president's campaign, and taking over as his new campaign manager was news. Her father's network was one of the largest, and if she could get on the air with her statement before the media had much of a chance to react to the news of Adam's death and her succession, she could get out in front of the uproar she expected her name to generate.

"I can promise you an exclusive interview," Ari said, "but I can't guarantee you'll be the first to break the news. That's entirely up to the White House, and you know there's going to be a press release."

"A generic press release is not nearly as significant as an exclusive. Exactly what will you be doing for the president?"

"I'll be the new campaign manager."

For an instant, his usual impenetrable façade broke and his shock showed through. "Adam Eisley was killed? What happened?"

So his sources in DC hadn't gotten all the information yet. "Off the record, still?"

He grimaced. "Only until the rumor mill identifies him. Once that happens, we will run with the story, quote confirmation from an unnamed source."

She nodded. At that point, none of what transpired would be a secret any longer. "I don't have any details beyond a hit-and-run this morning."

He frowned. "Accident or intentional?"

Ari's heart pounded. That was the question, wasn't it? Could someone actually have targeted Adam? Why? Yes, his role was pivotal in securing the nomination for President Powell, but Adam wasn't a critical power player. He didn't hold a high-level cabinet position or sit on any significant congressional committees. He wasn't a politician in that sense. So why? "I don't know, but I can't figure it's anything other than an accident."

Her father leaned back and folded his hands in his lap. His appraisal carried an air of disbelief. "Can't you?"

Things had always been this way between them. A gauntlet thrown down with a simple question that intimated she had missed some critical point, and she had never been able to avoid being caught up in the verbal jousting. Her mother was the peacekeeper, the one who refused to play the game of power, which was probably why she spent a good part of her time in Italy at the family villa in Tuscany, rather than here where Ari and Nikolai made their home.

"Granted, it's close to the deadline," Ari thought out loud, trying to see what others might have anticipated from Adam's death, "and the public is fickle. Any sign of weakness and, like any other pack, even the staunchest allies will abandon the weak. So I suppose, if Powell's infrastructure weakened—financially or politically—he could lose points in the polls."

"Exactly. And these things tend to escalate. And don't forget, Adam would have been an easy target if the goal was to create chaos. He's not surrounded by Secret Service agents twenty-four hours a day as is the president and those close to him."

A shiver ran down Ari's spine. "Do we really think someone in the opposition would resort to murder? This isn't Nicaragua, you know."

"Why consider it came from the opposition? There could be another group who expects to benefit."

"I suppose you're right," Ari said, not quite ready to embrace a conspiracy theory. "But no matter the circumstances, Powell needs a new campaign manager immediately."

"And you would be a good choice."

Ari laughed shortly. "I certainly hope so."

"You'll need a bodyguard."

"I'm sorry? Why?"

He waved a hand. "Don't be disingenuous. You're an important person and always have been. As a child, you were a target for kidnapping. As an adult, the same is true, and now, in a pivotal public position, where another accident could prove disastrous, you are at risk."

"I don't think…" Ari shook her head. "Really, a bodyguard would be impossible."

"Why? Do you have a lover?"

Ari couldn't prevent heat from rising to her cheeks. "That is beside the point."

"That's the only reason a bodyguard would be inconvenient, and that's not an insurmountable obstacle. Otherwise, you'll have a driver, and you'll have protection."

"Security clearance for a bodyguard is going to be an issue." Ari snorted. "Hell, *my* clearance could be one."

"Those kinds of things can be taken care of with a few phone calls," he said dismissively. "I'll arrange for it."

She knew the tone. There was no changing his mind. She would simply have to make things clear to whoever was assigned to guard her that her private life was private, and she didn't intend to share her living space.

"I'll try it," she said. "I'll leave a message once I know my schedule. It's going to be hectic for a while."

"Very well." As she turned to go, he added, "Be prepared for anything."

"I am," she murmured. At this point it really didn't matter. She'd made her choice.

"If you'll follow me, Agent," Martha said, "you can wait somewhere it's a little more comfortable. If anyone asks, I'll tell them where you are."

"Thank you," Oakes told the housekeeper as she followed her out onto the sweeping veranda at the rear of the house. Before going off to prepare for DC, Ari had taken Blair and Cam somewhere private where Blair could brief the White House on developments. Oakes could have rejoined the rest of Blair's detail outside with the vehicles, but she wasn't really needed out there. On the off chance that Blair— or possibly Ari—might want to speak with her again, she decided to remain available. That was pretty much her assignment, after all.

The housekeeper was right—the view of the sailboats and pleasure craft coursing in the harbor was even more captivating under a clear blue sky dotted with impossibly white powder-puff clouds than it had been from inside. The slanting afternoon sun had just begun to gild the edges of the horizon in swaths of red and gold.

"Would you like something to drink?" Martha asked.

"I'm fine, thank you," Oakes said.

"I just made some lemonade."

Oakes smiled. "Well then, I'll reconsider."

Martha beamed and disappeared inside. Oakes settled into one of the white wicker chairs arranged around a round, glass-topped table beneath a broad, sun-bleached canvas umbrella. A few moments later, the sliding glass doors behind her opened, and footsteps sounded on the flagstones. Oakes turned to thank Martha and rose automatically when she saw Ari approaching with a tray in her hands.

"Ms. Rostof," Oakes said. "Sorry, I…uh…thought you were occupied, or I wouldn't have disappeared."

"Hardly disappeared, Agent," Ari said, setting the tray down and placing a glass in front of Oakes.

"It's Oakes, remember?"

"Yes. Oakes—for Oakley, is it?"

"That's right."

"Unusual—I like it." Ari poured them both lemonade. "Besides, now I have an excuse to linger just a little while longer and pretend I'm still on vacation."

"Can you do that? Forget about the job, I mean?" Oakes asked.

Ari smiled faintly and nodded. "Yes. I'm good at compartmental-izing. Briefly, at least. You're not, I take it?"

"Huh. Not really big on vacations, I guess. I visit family if I'm off over the holidays, but mostly I put in extra time at the gym or the firing range."

"That's sad," Ari said good-naturedly, and Oakes grinned.

"Of course, maybe if I had this view, I might be able to enjoy free time a little more." *Maybe.* For some reason, Oakes didn't want Ari to see her as a work hound and nothing more. Even though she was.

"The view is a factor, I agree. Here…" Ari passed a tray of sandwiches in Oakes's direction. "Go ahead. I'm willing to bet you're starving. I won't tell anyone."

Oakes relented. She wasn't exactly on duty, after all. She took a sandwich along with one of the small sandwich plates adorned with sailboats from the tray. "You'd win that bet."

Ari sat, took half a sandwich, and leaned back in the matching chair beside Oakes's. "So you're not usually part of Blair's detail?"

"No, Presidential Protective Division. I'm just along to..." Oakes hesitated.

"Convince me? Assess my desirability for the job?"

"Not at all. That's up to the president to decide. I'm just an information source today."

"Hmm. All right then." Ari cut another sandwich square in half and divided it between their plates. "I intend to take advantage of that."

Heat coiled between Oakes's shoulder blades. A trickle of anticipation, and warning. She liked the idea and that had to mean something...something she ought to understand and didn't. "Are you packed already?"

Ari gave her a look, as if she'd recognized the deflection. "I don't really need to do much of that. I have an apartment in the city. So I travel light between places." Ari paused. "You must know that, right?"

"Sorry?"

"Where I live. I'm sure you know a great deal more than that about me. That is the Secret Service's job, correct? To *know* about the people who interact with the president?"

"Our job is to do whatever needs to be done to protect the president," Oakes said carefully. "But we're not the FBI or the CIA. The only thing I know about you is vital statistics."

"You mean age, weight, and all the things that some might prefer you not know?" Ari rolled her eyes. "Maybe you shouldn't mention that."

Oakes chuckled. "I can't imagine that's anything you worry about."

Ari's brow lifted. "Oh?"

Oakes flushed. That was stupid. Veering off topic into the personal with Ari Rostof was careless. Thankfully she'd stopped before she'd blurted out the rest of what she'd been thinking. *You're too attractive, too accomplished, too damn together to be worried about something like age or how other people perceive you.* For fuck's sake. Not having an official role had put her entirely off her game. Sitting out here in the sun, sipping lemonade, eating amazing, undoubtedly locally sourced grilled vegetable and pesto sandwiches, had made her soft. The silence went on until Ari laughed.

"If we're going to work together, it would probably be good if we could have a casual conversation. Or," she added with a tiny hint of sarcasm, "are you all business all the time?"

"I thought we were," Oakes said stiffly. She heard the flat tone and so did Ari.

"Technically," Ari went on as if Oakes hadn't just sounded like a socially maladjusted robot, "every appearance the president makes—from big news events like a summit meeting to fund-raisers to a simple trip to the local burger joint—affects his public image and, therefore, his campaign. He's always campaigning—not just running up to election time, but every time a popularity poll is tallied. That's my ballpark, agreed?"

"Yes," Oakes said. How exactly had Ari taken control of this conversation? And where the hell was she going with it?

"And everywhere he goes, his protective detail will be part of it. Which means we'll be working together closely for the foreseeable future."

"That's SOP," Oakes said, more on familiar ground now. "I don't foresee any problem there."

"No, neither do I," Ari said, "but since we are more or less each other's opposite numbers in this scenario, I hope we get to know each other a little bit."

"There's not that much to know," Oakes said. Ari Rostof was direct, and her directness was both fascinating and uncomfortable. They didn't need to have a personal relationship to work together. They certainly didn't need to be friends. She was used to distance in her relationships, even among those she worked with. Evyn and Adam were the exceptions. Now, just Evyn. Her life was too chaotic, too minute to minute, to really care about connections. She liked her colleagues. She depended on them and she trusted them. But their world was circumscribed by their schedules, by the demands of living together sometimes for extended periods, under the most stressful circumstances imaginable. Some used sex and alcohol to deal, and she wasn't above either one of those things on occasion. But no one really talked, not the way Ari seemed to be suggesting. "And I'm not sure why it matters."

"I guess we'll find out, won't we," Ari said quietly, turning her glass on the coaster in front of her. Her fingers were long and slender but, interestingly, did not appear delicate. A scar crossed almost the entire width of the top of her left hand, thin and white. She glanced up and saw Oakes looking at it. "Sailing accident."

And just like that, Oakes wanted to know more—not about the job they'd be doing, about her. "Is that your boat down there in the slip?"

"The *Castaway*—yes, that's mine," Ari said with a note of wistfulness.

"Do you have one in DC?"

Ari shook her head. "No, when I'm there, there's just no time." She laughed a little wryly. "In fact, when I'm *here* there's not much time."

"Why did you do it?" Oakes asked before she could catch herself.

"Take the job?" Ari said, not even bothering to pretend she didn't know what Oakes was asking.

Oakes nodded. She wanted to know, even though the knowledge didn't remotely fall under the umbrella of need-to-know. She wanted to know because she was interested in Ari.

"I'd be a fool to turn it down," Ari said, watching Oakes carefully. "This is a career maker. Sharing the national stage with the president, international media coverage, making contacts it would take me a decade to make otherwise? An opportunity like this only comes along once."

"Purely professional, then," Oakes said.

"Of course," Ari said, still watching her.

"Nope." Oakes shook her head. "I probably would've believed that if I hadn't been in the room when you talked to Blair."

"Oh? And what did you get from that?"

"If your only motivation had been career enhancement, you would've said yes instantly. But you didn't. You hesitated, considering the cost."

Ari straightened, her eyes narrowing. Not defensive. Interested. "The cost?"

Oakes shrugged. "Leaving the senator—which bothers you—breaking that commitment, then putting yourself in the media spotlight in a way that you never have before, and…" She hesitated, wondering whether if she pushed into sensitive areas she'd get shut out. She didn't want that to happen. "There's not just you, is there? Everyone you know, colleagues and…family…will be affected. There's the cost of power to be considered."

"You got all that from the conversation in the sunroom." Ari's pulse jumped in her throat. Had she been that transparent, or was Oakley Weaver far more observant than she'd imagined? She should have realized what lay behind that remote, intensely focused regard. She'd let herself think the scrutiny had been personal because *she* was intrigued, but she might have been wrong. And she couldn't afford to be—not now and certainly not in the days to come.

"Like I said, just guessing."

Very good guess, Ari thought. Irritated by having been so transparent, she said, "Shouldn't these be the sort of observations that you keep to yourself and report to someone?"

"I'm not a spy," Oakes said. "And you are not a threat target."

"Well, that's good to know," Ari said. "But I expect that I'll come under quite a good deal of scrutiny in the next few weeks. From just about everywhere."

"You're right," Oakes said. "But you already knew that."

"Yes," Ari said quietly. "The cost of…something, to be sure."

The doors behind them opened and Blair Powell stepped out onto the veranda.

Ari rose. "I just need a moment to get my things."

"Actually," Blair said, "there's been a change in plans."

Ari hesitated. Perhaps when Blair talked to the White House, they'd rescinded the offer. She could hardly complain and, in fact, would understand if they'd found someone who might be less controversial. "I won't be returning with you?"

"Oh no," Blair said, "you most certainly will. But our timetable has changed slightly. The White House needs to make a press release regarding Adam's death before it breaks in the media."

"There's been a leak," Ari said, wondering if her father had had a hand in that. Almost anyone could be persuaded to reveal what would soon be public anyhow for the right price.

"Yes," Blair said. "The White House must make a statement before the media does."

"What's the timetable?" Ari asked.

"Within the hour."

Ari sighed. "Well, we'll just have to deal with the media response as quickly as we can when we reach DC. We'll be playing catch-up, but we'll handle it."

"Lucinda Washburn has another suggestion that you might find preferable," Blair said.

"Oh?"

"She wants us to hold our press conference here, if you agree."

"Here." Ari laughed. "You do understand my father owns a

television network with a major news channel. If we go ahead here, he's going to want his network to have an exclusive."

"We can't give him that, but we can put his lead network reporter as the main interviewer."

She nodded. "That would work, if we can get all the moving parts assembled. I doubt we can get Dan Yamamoto here at such short notice. The local reporters will have to do."

"Lucinda should be on the line to your father right now to get the go-ahead."

"Does anyone ever say no to Ms. Washburn?" Ari asked, only half seriously.

"Not that I've ever noticed," Blair said with a grin.

"How much time?"

"We're going to coordinate with the White House so we can switch directly from the pressroom to here. Forty minutes."

Ari pushed a hand through her hair. Oakes, who stood just behind her, made a sound that perfectly captured her sense of disbelief. Then she set her misgivings aside. Too late for that. "All right, yes. I'm going to go change now. Hopefully, people from the local station will be here soon to do setup, lights, makeup. That sort of thing."

She paused when her father walked out, strode directly to Blair, and held out his hand. "Ms. Powell, Nikolai Rostof. I'm delighted to meet you."

Blair shook his hand. "Mr. Rostof, I'm sorry I didn't have a chance to speak to you earlier."

"Not at all. I understand you're dealing with some time constraints. I have a helicopter bringing Dan Yamamoto from Providence, where he was on assignment. We are fortunate there—he's only twenty minutes away."

"Excellent," Blair said.

He glanced at Ari. "Nalini Foad is on her way to assist you while the network sets up." He glanced around. "This might be a good location for the interview."

"I think that's a very good idea," Blair said. "Might I suggest, Mr. Rostof, that in order to keep the focus directly on Ari, you not take questions today."

He smiled. "Actually, Ms. Powell, I wasn't planning on attending. I am not all that interested in the spotlight."

"Then," Blair said, "I believe everything is covered at this point. And I appreciate your assistance."

He inclined his head, almost an old-fashioned bow. "My pleasure to assist the daughter of the president." He glanced at Ari. "Arianna."

"Thank you," she murmured as he turned and walked back into the house.

Oakes said quietly, "I've just been drafted by the detail. A press conference changes things a little bit."

Blair sighed. "I know. Sorry."

"Not a problem," Oakes said. "I'm sure Paula Stark will have things covered."

Ari watched Oakes disappear into the house. Their planned briefing would have to wait—possibly indefinitely. The twinge of disappointment was a surprise.

"Is there anything you need?" Blair asked.

"Sorry," Ari said, and quickly added, "oh yes. If you have time, I would appreciate any insights on exactly what direction the White House is taking with this."

Blair nodded. "Of course."

Ari gestured Blair to the table and they sat down side by side.

"This reminds me a bit of the old days in an eleventh-hour study group," Blair said, reaching for a sandwich. "Except you were the one with all the answers then."

Ari snorted. "Hardly."

"Ironic, isn't it," Blair murmured. "We each set out to avoid following in our father's footsteps and here we are." She glanced at Ari. "Or am I being presumptuous?"

Ari laughed quietly and shook her head. "No. You are exactly right."

"I'm devastated over Adam," Blair said, "but I'm glad to have you on our team."

"Thanks," Ari said, hoping none of them came to regret it.

CHAPTER NINE

Philadelphia
3:50 p.m.

"Mustard and chili?" the vendor asked from behind his steam cart on the corner in front of University Hospital as he slapped a street dog into a soft, warm roll.

"Is there any other kind?" Rebecca Frye said. Since she often used the excuse of visiting Catherine at work to indulge in the cart food, he knew her order by heart. Street dogs and cheesesteaks were a staple of police fare.

"There's always the kraut dog," he said seriously as Rebecca passed him the money.

"Only for the faint of heart," she said.

"Not for you, then." He pointedly looked down at the gold badge clipped to her belt. "You want one to go for the doc?"

"That's a good thought. Thanks." She munched on her dog while holding the bag with the extra, one eye on the broad expanse of double doors leading to the main lobby of the Silverstein Pavilion. Dozens of people entered and exited, but she was only interested in one person. She checked the time—3:52—any moment now she would...

Rebecca straightened, popped the last bite into her mouth, and wiped her hands on a paper napkin as she crossed the sidewalk, her gaze on her wife. Today Catherine wore a pale linen jacket and pants with a light green shirt that caught the color of her eyes. Catherine spotted her almost immediately, as if her attention had been drawn through the moving mass of people directly to her. The smile that blossomed on Catherine's face sent a jolt right to her heart. It always did.

Rebecca bounded up the steps and met Catherine halfway down. Catherine put her palm against her chest and kissed her. A few people passing gave them a fleeting glance, but for Rebecca, they might have been standing alone on the steps. Catherine had that effect on her, drawing her away from the tension and frustration that flavored many of her days to a place of quiet contentment.

"Thank you," Catherine murmured, taking the lunch bag Rebecca held out to her. "Hard day?"

"Not really, that's part of the problem." Rebecca turned to walk down the stairs to the sidewalk and slid a hand under Catherine's elbow. Just that light connection settled the indefinable unease that had plagued her all day.

Catherine shot her a look. "You're bored."

Rebecca laughed. "Riding a desk has its own kind of hardships."

"I know, especially for you," Catherine murmured. "And I don't even feel guilty for not feeling sorry for you. I can't help being pleased that you're not *always* out in front of everyone else when there's trouble."

"You don't have to worry about that," Rebecca said.

Catherine didn't comment, because they both knew that wasn't really true.

"Since you've been on that desk a while now, what else is bothering you?" Catherine asked. "Besides not having any bad guys to chase around the streets."

"Knowing that they're out there and not being able to find them."

"Ah. Is it more than that? More than just the generic bad people who will always do bad things? Has something happened?"

"Not exactly. I've got this feeling. Or rather, Sloan has a feeling," Rebecca said. "And you can make book on her feelings."

"I know. You'll be careful, won't you?" Catherine asked. "Whenever what's coming arrives?"

"I always am." Rebecca slid her arm around Catherine's waist, tugging her just a little closer for an instant before releasing her. Being careful and being safe were different things, and they both knew it. Sure, she wasn't a street cop any longer, but her squad was small and they all pulled their time in the field when needed. "Are you done for the day?"

"No, I've got a load of paperwork to do back at the office," Catherine said as they walked west on Spruce to the big old Victorian that had been converted into offices for some of the faculty. "What about you?"

"I'm meeting with the team in a little while to debrief. After that"—she shrugged—"it depends on what they've all got to say."

"You'll call me if you're going to be late?"

That was code for *you'll tell me if you're getting involved in any kind of action.* Rebecca could keep that from her, could save her the worry, but that wasn't part of their deal. Catherine gave Rebecca her heart in exchange for her pledge to share herself, all of herself. Rebecca paused across from the parking lot where she'd left her vehicle and kissed her again. "I will. I love you."

"I love you too." Catherine touched her cheek.

Rebecca slid her hands into her pockets as Catherine turned and walked away. Those first few seconds without her were always a mixture of supreme contentment and a little bit of longing. She watched until Catherine disappeared around the corner, then jogged across the street, climbed into the nondescript gray departmental sedan she preferred when on duty, and headed back downtown. When she pulled up in front of their command center in the converted loft in Old City, Dell arrived on her motorcycle with Sandy riding behind her.

They were both dressed for work—Dell in boots, black jeans, and a short-sleeved T-shirt, Sandy in a nearly crotch-high black leather miniskirt and a sheer red shirt that dipped too low between her breasts for Rebecca to look in that direction for more than an instant. Her dark thick eyeliner, bright red lipstick, long dangling earrings, and messy blond curls reminded Rebecca of how she used to look when they'd first met. Sandy'd been younger then—barely legal age, a tough girl who made her living on the streets with her body. They were colleagues now, but that tough, brave, smart survivor held a special place in Rebecca's heart.

"Either I'm late," Rebecca said, knowing their usual routine was to work the streets all night and sleep most of the day after the morning team meeting, "or you two are very early."

Sandy grinned at Dell. "We've been up for a while."

Dell's sheepish grin made it clear what they'd been doing besides sleeping. Rebecca just shook her head. "Come on, let's head upstairs."

Sloan and Jason were exactly where they'd left them ten hours before, ensconced in front of their monitors, surrounded by coffee cups, take-out containers, and the subtle scent of the hunt. Rebecca knew better than to interrupt them when they were in the zone and headed back to their conference area. She dumped out coffee that looked like it was at least six hours old and set about making a fresh pot. Watts came in while she was watching it drip and grunted a hello. At four thirty, a fresh cup of coffee in hand, she headed back out into the work area.

"You two ready to give us an update?"

Jason said without turning around, "Five minutes."

"Good enough."

Rebecca settled at the conference table with the others, and ten minutes later, which was a little sooner than she'd anticipated, Jason and Sloan wandered in, poured coffee, and joined them.

"Check your devices for a file we just sent," Sloan said immediately. "We made some progress. We've been following breadcrumbs all day long. Most of the associations are loose, but," she said, waiting while everyone downloaded the info via phone or tablet, "we've got some soft links from phone traces between some of our principals."

"Locals?" Rebecca asked.

"Difficult to tell," Sloan said. "We got a lot of undocumented or untraceable addresses. Truthfully, we'll need some luck or a lot more time to pinpoint locations. But we've got names and faces, and we'll have more by morning."

"All right," Rebecca said, scanning the first image, "take us through them."

Sloan reviewed what data they had on each individual as she worked her way down the targets they'd identified so far. In some cases they had name, last known location, associates, group affiliations, criminal records and in others, only aliases. She finished up with surveillance footage they'd pulled from demonstrations, rallies, or local gatherings the targets had been known to attend.

"Wait," Sandy said, straightening. "I know her."

"Which one?" Sloan said.

Sandy turned her tablet to face the others, zoomed the image of a wide-angle crowd shot taken at a student rally at one of the local campuses, and pointed to a twentyish-looking woman with shoulder-length teased blond hair and a sharp-eyed, angry expression. "Her."

The subject stood close to the front of a stage where a man held a microphone and a sign proclaiming the name of a socialist political organization known to be a front for a right-wing supremacy group.

"Did she or the guy onstage pop in your search?" Frye asked Sloan.

"No, but we can run facial recognition through the databases."

"I know where I saw her," Sandy said, an eager edge in her voice. "The Oasis. I've seen her there twice." She lasered in on Rebecca. "I can get close to her."

Studying the keen expression in Sandy's eyes, recognizing the natural cop in her—something no amount of training could instill—Rebecca thought it over. Chasing one possible connection might lead nowhere, but this was the kind of work they did. This was what they'd all been selected for. They worked outside the box, and they worked up close, one thread at a time. She nodded. "Go ahead, but make sure we know where and when you are. Watts—you're her backup."

"Just like old times," he grumbled. "At least the weather's warmer and my balls won't freeze sitting in the car."

Sandy grinned, the spark of the hunter in her eyes. "I'm on it."

"Mitch can go under with her," Dell said. "We can work the inside together."

"Ooh," Sandy crooned, making wide sex eyes at her lover, drawing guffaws and groans, "*that* will be fun."

"Here we go again," Watts muttered. "The guy with the strap-on cock gets all the girls."

"Watts, honey," Sandy purred, "you really need to see Mitch's cock in action."

"No thanks," he said, but he was grinning and so was Dell.

"Okay, enough with the anatomy. Let's run it that way. Hold on—" Rebecca looked down automatically as a network alert announcing a special news briefing from the White House flashed on her screen. Everyone else did the same.

"I think we're going to want to see this," Rebecca said.

Newport Harbor
4:25 p.m.

Oakes walked back to the sunroom where Paula Stark, the lead on Blair Powell's security detail, had scheduled a briefing for the off-the-record news event. Stark stood in front of the sofa where Ari had sat a short while before, along with the agents who were not presently moving the vehicles to more secure locations in one of the Rostof garages. Those agents would remain with the vehicles until Blair was ready to depart, and the rest of the detail, now including Oakes, would be tasked with Blair's personal protection. Ensuring her safety had suddenly become more complicated due to the influx of several dozen reporters, technicians, and TV network personnel who would be descending on the Rostof mansion in just a few moments. None of those individuals would've been prescreened, and all of them would have potential access to Blair.

Stark said, "Mac, Felicia, you'll be screening arrivals—verifying press credentials and IDs. Rostof security will have already checked them at the gate against a list provided by the network. No metal detectors, which leaves us with manual examination of equipment, personal items, and bags."

"What about the press vehicles?" Mac said. "We ought to try to get them a safe distance from the main house."

"There's a large cabana at the far east end of the property—about a quarter mile away—with parking. Their drivers will be instructed to move them there after the passengers have debarked," Stark said. "Mac, you'll accompany the last car down and stay there. Felicia, remain at the front door."

"Got it," Felicia said.

Stark continued, "Weaver, Sato, and I will provide the personal protection."

She took in the gathering, and if she was disturbed by the less than optimal numbers, she didn't show it. "Questions?"

No one had any.

Mac and Felicia left, and Oakes returned to the veranda and took up post to the right of the main doors. Closing in on five p.m., the sun was over her shoulder, an advantage when she'd need to screen the crowd during Ari Rostof's interview. Her vision wouldn't be impaired by the glare. A half dozen men dressed in khaki work clothes appeared, Rostof employees she assumed, and quickly and efficiently moved the tables and chairs out of the way.

Twenty minutes later, a gaggle of press people spilled out onto the veranda. Dan Yamamoto, one of the evening anchors for Rostof Network News, was easily recognizable. In his early forties, he looked like he'd just stepped off the golf course in his dark blue polo and khaki pants. Maybe he had. A makeup technician followed him over to the far edge of the veranda, a portable kit in one hand and a makeup brush in the other.

"Just a minute, Terry," he said, hands on his hips as he surveyed first the shoreline and then the veranda. He made a slow circuit behind the stone balustrade on either side of the stairs leading down to the walkway that eventually ended up at the pier. He pointed to a spot, glanced at the house behind him, then angled slightly. "Let's plan on right about here. We'll want to get a bit of the harbor in view and the corner of the house."

He turned, gazed at Oakes. "You think you could move over about six feet to your right?"

Oakes smiled. "That would depend on where Ms. Powell is standing."

He zeroed in on the lapel pin on her jacket. "Ah, yes. Fine."

He was a veteran, and he understood that the Secret Service did not make concessions for the press. She'd move if she could, but she'd need to be within closing distance of Blair Powell, and since Blair would also be appearing on camera, she was going to be close and probably in camera sight. That was an issue for the cameraman. Not her.

A steady trickle of technicians with equipment, cables, light stands, portable microphones, and all the other paraphernalia necessary for the interview continued to stream out until the broad veranda became a labyrinth of cords, light stands, and people. Blair, Cam, and Ari emerged and met with Dan Yamamoto. Stark and Soto flanked Blair.

Someone called, "Five minutes to airtime."

Ari'd changed into tailored dark slacks and a white open-collared shirt. A gold necklace gleamed in the hollow of her throat, and small diamond-studded gold earrings glinted on each lobe. Her hair was down, and she didn't seem to mind when the wind blew it into disarray. With a practiced flick of one hand, she pushed the thick waves away from her face. What makeup she wore was understated, and she waved away the man with the makeup kit. Oakes smothered a smile at his look of distress. Ari Rostof did not need any help looking camera-ready.

"Ari," Yamamoto said, his voice warm and familiar. "You should be comfortable with this. Anything you need?"

"I'm fine, Dan," she replied.

He smiled. "Never doubted it."

One of Yamamoto's assistants spoke to Blair, pointed, and Blair moved several feet to her left. Oakes shifted to follow her at the regulation distance. Yamamoto frowned, but he said nothing.

Ari looked at her watch, then over her shoulder. Her gaze met Oakes's and she smiled. Oakes nodded. Cam was on Blair's left, Soto to the right rear, and Stark directly behind them, covering the exit. All good. Still, her stomach churned. Too many people moving around.

A woman called out, "Five…four…three…two…on air."

"This is Dan Yamamoto, reporting from the Rostof home on Newport Harbor."

Oakes tuned him out, scanning the faces and bodies arrayed around the perimeter of the veranda, out of the camera line, looking for any untoward movement, any indication of nervousness, anyone intently focused only on Blair.

"…tragic accident…"

"…taking over as the national campaign manager…"

Blair Powell speaking. "…saddened by the loss…friend…"

Roberts answering a question: "…ongoing investigation…"

Standing between Blair and Cam, Ari appeared poised and at ease as she spoke. "…honored by the trust…ready to spearhead the…"

Dan Yamamoto wrapped up the interview and the same woman called out, "Cut. Off air."

The reporters waiting off camera like a pack of jackals all shouted at once.

"Ms. Rostof, Ms.—"

"When will you be returning to Washington?"

"What did the senator say when you told her you were leaving her campaign?"

"Did your father have anything to do with your appointment?"

Questions blurred in a chaotic jumble. Someone handed Ari a microphone.

"I'm sorry, I have no further statement at this time," Ari said.

A male voice rose above all the others. "What can you tell us about the nature of Adam Eisley's death? Is it true he was targeted?"

Ari's expression didn't change. "The investigation into Mr. Eisley's death is ongoing. Thank you all for coming."

Questions continued to pepper the air as Ari turned away. A lean, short-haired brunette walked out onto the veranda and Oakes snapped, "She's armed."

The immaculate cut of her tailored black suit jacket almost but not quite successfully hid the subtle bulge of a holster on her right hip, and if she hadn't held both hands in clear view and obviously well away from her body, she'd already be on the ground in restraints.

"I have her," Stark said, intercepting the stranger. A few words and the quick display of an ID, and Stark nodded her clear.

Ari walked over to the brunette and shook her hand. The brunette, a few inches taller than Ari, leaned close to Ari and murmured something no one else was meant to hear. Ari smiled, touched the brunette's arm briefly, and continued toward the house with Cam and Blair. The brunette fell into step just behind Ari.

Oakes watched the exchange, a prickle of irritation racing down her spine. Whoever the brunette was, she and Ari were clearly acquainted. Maybe it was more than that, and the idea annoyed her. Ari Rostof, however, was none of her concern.

She stood post while the TV people and reporters packed their gear and finally left.

Stark gave the all clear. "Departure in fifteen minutes. Weaver, you ride with Rostof in the follow car. Pick her up in the foyer."

"Copy," Weaver said, and headed that way.

Five minutes before departure time, Ari appeared, carrying a briefcase and an overnight bag. The brunette was with her.

"Agent Weaver," Ari said, "this is Nika Witt. Nika will be traveling with us."

At Oakes's questioning stare, Nika held out her hand. "Rostof Protective Services. I'll be providing Ms. Rostof's security in DC."

Oakes shook her hand. "I see."

"Well," Ari said after a beat of silence, "shall we go?"

"Right." Oakes released Witt's hand. Her grip had been firm—not testing, not challenging—merely confident. If Witt really was going to provide Ari's security, they'd probably be seeing a lot of each other. The idea was far from pleasant on many levels.

CHAPTER TEN

With Blair, Cam, and Stark in the lead car, Oakes, Ari, and Witt in the follow car, and the rest of Blair's detail in the last vehicle, the motorcade pulled down the long, winding drive to the main gate of the Rostof mansion. A police escort of four motorcycle officers and a patrol car waited outside, and with the added assistance of lights and sirens clearing the way, the motorcade made rapid time toward the airstrip at the nearby naval base. Oakes sat across from Ari and Witt in the rear of the vehicle, Witt taking the window seat and Oakes sliding over to the one on the opposite side. They'd positioned themselves automatically to watch both sides of the road, with Ari centered between them. Ari wasn't Oakes's protectee—in fact, now that they were on the road again, no one was—but she couldn't not be situationally aware.

Right now, and for the foreseeable future, Ari Rostof was a high-priority figure. Having a bodyguard was not unreasonable—in fact, considering what had happened to Adam, maybe just one was not enough. Oakes wondered who'd made the call to bring Witt on board—Ari or her father. Oakes's money was on Nikolai Rostof. Ari was already a highly visible public figure and, despite being the heir to an empire, seemed little affected by her notoriety. From her solo meeting with Blair to her rapid decision to accept the White House's offer with no consultation with anyone else, she'd also shown herself confident and capable. A bodyguard just didn't seem her style.

And why Oakes was wondering just why Nika Witt had suddenly made an appearance was another question completely. Neither woman was her concern. Still, she couldn't seem to ignore either of them.

As soon as they'd left the Rostof compound, Ari'd settled back with her phone out, probably scanning emails. Beside her, Witt projected that relaxed kind of wariness that typified security people.

Oakes figured she looked a lot the same herself. A Glock was holstered on Witt's right hip, visible now that she was sitting. If she carried a weapon, presumably she knew how to use it. Otherwise, she was a danger to everyone. Oakes wondered about her training.

Ex-military? Ex-law enforcement? A wannabe cop, like a lot of people in private security? She doubted the last. Witt looked to be in excellent shape, projected a solid air of confidence, and unless she couldn't pass a psych test, would probably be an easy admit to any branch of the military and most of the federal ones. That kind of expertise didn't come from a few weeks of on-the-job security guard training.

Witt must've sensed her scrutiny and met her gaze.

"Ex–Secret Service," Witt said. "Eight years."

Oakes raised a brow. "Get tired of world travel?"

Witt smiled. "Never had much of a chance. Did a tour on protection with an ex-president before four years in New York City."

"Ouch," Oakes said. The New York City posting was a beast, and four years was a long time to stick it out in a pressure cooker office where agents were constantly pulled from investigations to provide protection for dignitaries and others at meetings in the city.

"Then the choice was Atlanta or Kansas City." Witt shrugged. "I don't like hot weather."

Oakes wasn't all that surprised. Quite a few agents choose to leave rather than accept a post in an undesirable city or stick it out at some other posting that proved a hardship for family, even if they stood a chance of advancement. Oakes knew a few who'd gone through training with her who'd opted for transfers to other federal or state law enforcement agencies or, like Witt, private security. She was lucky— she was exactly where she wanted to be.

"I hear you," Oakes said. A least now she knew Ari would have competent security. No one survived FLETC and the Beltway who wasn't skilled, whether they stayed in the service long-term or not.

The motorcade slowed, turned in to the naval base, and the vehicles pulled around beside the small jet that would take them back to Andrews. Two Navy pilots already sat in the dimly lit cockpit. The stairs were down, an officer stood at the bottom, and Blair's detail disembarked from the lead car and immediately climbed aboard. Oakes slid out and held the door for Ari, Witt bringing up the rear. Waiting Navy personnel climbed into the now empty vehicles and drove them off the runway while everyone else boarded.

Blair and Cam sat together toward the front with Stark a few rows behind them. The agents spread out toward the rear of the plane. Ari took an aisle seat in the center, and Witt settled in a row behind her. Oakes was about to walk back and join the rest of the protection detail when Ari looked up and pointed to the empty row across from her.

"If you don't mind me making a few phone calls," Ari said, smiling.

Oakes took the aisle seat across from Ari. "If you don't mind me snoring. Plane rides always put me to sleep."

Ari shook her head, still smiling. "Probably a good idea to grab some sleep when you can."

"You might consider that yourself," Oakes said. "I think you might be in for a long night."

"A lot of them." Ari sighed. "We'd probably better postpone our briefing—by the time we reach DC it will be late, and I'm going to be making a lot of calls."

"I have the late shift tomorrow," Oakes said. "Breakfast meeting?"

"If I possibly can," Ari said.

"No problem," Oakes replied, oddly satisfied. "I'm flexible."

The engines revved and the jet taxied onto the runway. Oakes reclined her seat, leaned back, and closed her eyes. As soon as they were airborne and a voice from the cockpit announced they could now use electronics, including phones, Ari made a call.

"It's me again," Ari said. "I'm on my way back to DC. I guess you saw the briefing." Ari sighed. "I would have warned you if I'd known myself. I didn't. Is the senator there?"

Oakes couldn't help but listen to the conversation, half drifting, half always aware.

"All right," Ari said. "I'll call her at home. Tomorrow, as soon as I know what my schedule will be. You'll do fine." Ari laughed, her laughter tinged with irony. "Yes, it's a whole new game."

For everyone, Oakes thought. Although all that mattered to her was game day—and six weeks was going to go by very quickly.

Philadelphia
9:57 p.m.

Sandy leaned over the bathroom sink finishing her makeup when she heard footsteps behind her. "Give me a sec. I'm almost done."

"Take your time. I have a great view of your ass."

Smiling, she finished putting the final touches on her mascara and turned around. Mitch stood in the doorway, dressed for the street— black jeans, muscle shirt, biker boots, and a wide studded leather belt with a big square buckle that drew attention to the bulge behind his fly. She crooked a finger and said, "Come on over here."

Grinning, he sauntered over and she hooked a finger under his belt and tugged him closer until the faint weight of his cock pressed against her middle. She canted her hips and pressed into him, a surge of satisfaction making her pulse quicken as his eyes widened.

"Come on," he murmured, sliding an arm around her waist while he kissed her behind the ear. "You trying to make me uncomfortable for the rest of the night?"

"Mm-hmm," she said, turning her head to rub her cheek against his. Smoothing her hand down his back, she tugged at his earlobe with her teeth. He hissed and swept his hand down over her ass and under the back of her skirt, his fingertips teasing the curve of her butt. They didn't always work the same schedule, and she wasn't often around when Mitch geared up for a night out under deep cover. Happily, she was often home by the time he returned in the morning and reaped the benefit of him climbing into bed, still strapped, and usually revved from an entire night of tense work. Tonight would be different. They'd be working together, although not as a pair. Not yet, at least.

"Just make sure you don't get too friendly with any of the other girls," Sandy murmured.

"Same goes." With his chest wrapped and his hair slicked back, packing, and carrying a whole lotta attitude in his biker gear, Mitch was the far masculine-of-center of her lover's personae. Lucky for her, she found every variation of Dellon Mitchell's gender expression mind-meltingly sexy.

Sandy lifted one leg and wrapped it around Mitch's thigh, tugging her short skirt up even higher until she could open her legs and tug Mitch between them. She leaned her breasts into him, her heart racing as his breath caught.

"You know," Sandy murmured, "it's going to be a long night. Are you in a big hurry?"

"It *is* important to have a clear head," Mitch whispered, "when working and all."

"Then maybe you should do a little extra prep before we leave."

"Maybe I should." Throat dry and heart thudding like he'd never kissed a girl before, Mitch looped an arm around her thin waist and lifted her off the floor. She, with a practiced movement, braced herself with hands on his shoulders and hiked her hips up around his waist. She settled against him as if their bodies had been carved from one piece, the two parts fitting perfectly as a whole. He swung around, strode out of the bathroom and across the fifteen feet to their bed, and dumped her onto her back. She laughed, and somehow magically, her skirt was lying on the pillow beside her and all that covered her was a flimsy patch of black satin that disappeared between her thighs. Boots still on, Mitch climbed onto the bed and knelt between her thighs. Sandy raised her shoulders, grasped the heavy belt buckle, and yanked it open. Mitch had a hard time catching his breath. She always did this to him, rocketed him from zero to sixty in a couple of heartbeats, all because she wanted him. All of him, right now, however—*whoever*—he was, and all he could think about was giving her everything. Every last bit of him, heart, body, and soul.

Her hand was inside his jeans, slipping out the cock he'd tucked down against the inside of his thigh. Flexible enough to pack but firm enough for working. She tugged him forward and he stretched out above her. With his mouth on hers, he groped around the bedside table, slid open the top drawer, and found a condom.

"In a hurry?" Sandy's voice was husky and her breathing shallow.

"Like you wouldn't believe. But you're in charge, baby," Mitch murmured against her mouth and pressed the condom into her hand. She closed her fist around it, then pushed him upright.

With a few practiced motions, she had it open and rolled onto him and said, "That's your cue, Rookie."

Her eyes were laughing, and as he eased inside her, he watched them widen and grow hazy. Oh yeah, he loved doing that to her. He braced his arms on either side of her slender shoulders and moved with her, following her pace. He'd follow her anywhere, with his last breath.

The push-pull of her hips moving up and down him shoved him even higher, and watching her take her pleasure was enough to jolt him to the edge. The coiled spring in his belly threatened to snap.

"Fuck," he whispered.

"Already?" She laughed, gripped his ass, and pulled him hard inside her. "You're so easy."

Mitch closed his eyes and gritted his teeth to hold back the explosion, but he couldn't stop. She did that to him. Every time. He shuddered, heard himself groan and her laughing. And right on top of that, the quick catch of her breath, the strangled cry, and she was bucking beneath him, joining him.

His arms gave out, but he caught himself before he could crush her. He wasn't really much bigger, but more muscular, heavier where she was lithe and willowy. Breathing hard, he buried his face in her neck. "I love you."

She stroked his hair, slid a hand under the back of his jeans, and squeezed his ass.

"You are so hot," she whispered.

He chuckled a little raggedly. She wore him out. His legs felt like jelly.

"I'm going to need a minute."

"Uh-huh." She gripped his hip bones and pushed him back, eased him out of her.

"You okay?" Mitch whispered. "Need more?"

Sandy massaged his shoulders, loving the way his body, loose and vulnerable, felt atop her. "I could go again. A couple of times."

He raised his head. A hint of panic in his dark eyes. "Now?"

She laughed and kissed him. "In the morning. Make sure you save a little something for me."

He grinned and settled back with his head on her shoulder. "Always do."

She stroked his face, kissed the top of his head. "I know you do."

"You'll be careful, right? If we make contact and this girl leads us to some kind of organized cell—"

"I know, I know. I'll be fine." If she didn't know how much Mitch loved her, she might be annoyed. She was a cop after all, even if he had seniority. Even if when they'd met, she'd still been just a CI. But it wasn't the cop worrying over her, it was her lover. So she let it go.

All the same, she bounced a fist lightly on his shoulder. "You too, you know."

"Always, baby."

"Then get your sweet ass up and get yourself back together. I have to check my makeup."

His strength finally returning, he propped himself up on his arms and regarded her with a tilt of his head. "Looks good to me." He kissed her. "Oops. Smeared your lipstick."

Laughing, he avoided the playful slap and climbed off the bed. After rearranging himself and zipping up his pants, he waited by the door while she double-checked her makeup and got her weapon out of the drawer. He watched her slide her backup piece into a tiny holster that fit inside her even tinier skirt at the base of her spine. He didn't know how she hid that there. His was in a leg holster just above the top of his boot. Not a quick draw but inconspicuous.

She turned, gave him the once-over, and nodded. "Give me a few minutes' head start."

"Okay, babe." Mitch squeezed her hand as she passed him. "Take good care of my girl."

"I'll see you back here in the morning, Rookie," Sandy said. "Love you."

"Yeah," Mitch whispered, watching her stroll down the hall with a sexy sway that would draw the attention of anyone with a pulse. "Love you."

CHAPTER ELEVEN

"We're beginning the descent to Andrews. We'll be on the ground in twenty-five minutes," the pilot announced.

Ari checked the time. A bit after nine. She'd been too revved to sleep, too busy mentally reviewing the events of the day and her recent phone calls to relax. Antonio had taken the news of her departure from the senator's campaign about the way she'd expected. Partly resigned, a little bit angry and trying hard not to be, and a little bit envious and pretending he wasn't. She couldn't blame him. She had just made a colossal career leap forward, and she hadn't looked back. But that was the business they were in, and none of it was personal. Business was never personal. The only thing personal to her was the end result. Winning, for her client and therefore herself, was everything.

The senator, whom she'd decided to try at home, had answered instantly, her first words, "I saw the news briefing. I doubt they gave you much time—or much choice."

Her rough ex-smoker's voice had sounded faintly amused.

"It was rushed," Ari had admitted, "but the choice was mine. I'm sorry to be leaving."

"But you'd be an idiot not to," Senator Martinez said.

"Yes."

"Well, now the president owes me a bit of consideration in the future, since he stole my political consultant at a critical point in my reelection campaign." She laughed. "Good thing I'm winning."

"I don't believe that's in doubt," Ari said, wisely avoiding any comment about the president. "And Antonio will steer the course well."

"Just see that you get Powell through November ahead of the jackals, ours *and* theirs," Martinez said sharply. "Or else we're all screwed."

"That's my plan," Ari said.

"Good luck," Martinez said as she ended the call.

Ari hoped she wouldn't need it. She'd depended on her wits and her drive her whole life. Of course, with the unexpected appearance of Blair Powell on her doorstep, her life had suddenly taken a sharp right-angle turn, maybe more of a hairpin turn—she was still headed for the summit, but she'd taken a detour. An unexpected one, and from a very unexpected source. Had Blair just been the messenger because they had some history, ancient though it was? She knew who Blair was *now*, of course, but they'd both been different in prep school. She remembered Blair as being young, privileged, and so very angry. Ari'd seen a lot of herself in Blair. From the outside, they both seemed to have everything anyone could ever want. Both had arrived at school with bodyguards in the background, Blair because her father was a governor. Hers had been necessary because her father was…well, because he was Nikolai Rostof.

Ari still didn't know all that meant, and she didn't lie to herself and pretend that she wanted to know. Of course with his last name and his history, and his incredible ascendancy to power and wealth, there were clichéd rumors. But rumors abounded in her world, and all that mattered was proof. And about the only proof that really mattered was evidence that couldn't be fabricated. Not much was incontrovertible—except digital records. Fakes were easy to spot and the real thing was impossible to deny. She was very careful about where she discussed business, and she'd installed software on her personal phone to scramble calls. She was doubly careful of where she was seen in public and with whom, especially if an outing was personal. The constant media attention and the inevitable rumor mill were good reasons not to foster significant personal connections.

Cloak-and-dagger, perhaps, but she'd grown up under an umbrella of paranoia and caution. In her own way, Blair had too. Blair'd had state police escorts and plainclothes state agents protecting her, but nothing like the Secret Service detail she had now. Ari had thought she'd left most of that behind, but now she had a bodyguard too. She still had to sort out how she was going to conduct her life with someone as close to her as Witt was going to be.

She knew Nika Witt only slightly. Witt had been with Rostof Protective Services for about six months, and Ari had met her at one of her father's functions. She would have noticed her in any case. She was good looking, in a dark intense kind of way. Ari smiled to herself.

A lot like Oakes Weaver. The two rather resembled bookends, although Witt was more lithe where Weaver was lean and, Ari suspected, tightly muscled underneath that surprisingly nice fitting charcoal suit. That was not an off-the-rack suit. Unusual for the security types, and she liked that little quirk about Weaver. Found it interesting. So often the security types, ex-military or federal, had all the personality trained out of them, or maybe they never had any to begin with.

Oakes Weaver struck her as being a lot more complicated than she wanted to let on. Ari turned her head and watched Oakes sleeping. Or perhaps pretending to sleep. She looked relaxed, but as Ari had come to appreciate about so many things, that might just be a façade.

"Are you really sleeping?" she asked, low enough that she doubted anyone could hear over the low purr of the engines.

"What gave me away?" Oakes opened her eyes and glanced across the aisle at Ari, a light dancing in her eyes that Ari hadn't seen before. Could that possibly be humor?

"Nothing, really. I just had a feeling you were really good at pretending."

Oakes's brows drew down and she cocked her head as if surprised. "I think I might have been insulted."

"Oh, I doubt that," Ari said. "Doesn't that sort of go along with your line of work? Maybe not pretending, but hiding?"

"Okay, now I've definitely been insulted."

"Why?" Ari could tell from the subtle playful tone in her voice that she wasn't really. "You're not supposed to be noticed. In the background, no opinions, no reactions, no investment. All about the job, right?"

"And is that a lot different than what you do?"

"Totally," Ari said, keeping it light. "I spend a lot of my time in front of a camera, or getting my clients in front of one. I'm visible."

"Right, and the camera never lies."

Ari smiled. "You know, sometimes it does."

"So what are you hiding? Or is it hiding *from*?"

Ari caught her breath. "That's rather personal."

"You started it."

"All right," Ari said carefully, sensing danger and, for some reason, walking closer to the edge of the cliff. Her entire life had been about caution. Being careful not to reveal too much to anyone about who she was, who her family was. Sometimes, not even to herself. And here was a stranger tempting her to drop her cloak. Taunting her.

Challenging her. And she liked the challenge. If this was a game, she was intrigued enough to play.

"None of what I do is about me," Ari said. "It's all about the client. So if I'm on camera, all I'm doing is trying to get people to think about my client. I should be invisible."

Oakes chuckled. "I think you're deluding yourself. You are almost as important as the person you represent. People associate certain things with you, like success. Besides that, you'd be hard to overlook no matter what you were doing."

Ari felt heat rise to her cheeks, and she was very glad for the relatively dim lighting inside the jet. Revealing what she wanted to reveal was one thing, but letting Oakes know that the compliment pleased her was something else entirely. Being susceptible to anyone, particularly an attractive woman, was enough to make the edge of the cliff crumble under her feet. Still, she didn't step back. "All right, I won't pretend I don't know what you're talking about in terms of professional reputation. Of course I want people to associate success with me. My success is my client's success."

"And it works the other way too," Oakes said. "When the senator is reelected, and she will be, people are going to remember *you*. Not whoever takes your place for the last stretch." And now Oakes shrugged. "And now, well, you'll be standing there with the president."

Ari sighed. "Yes," she said almost to herself, "the president."

"Are you nervous?"

The question was so personal, should have been too personal to answer. She answered without thinking. "No. I'm excited."

Oakes gave her a long look. "Then it sounds like you're just the person for the job."

"Tell me that in a week."

"Chances are we'll know in a day or two."

The cabin lights dimmed further for landing, and Ari could barely see Oakes's outline in the dark. "We still need to get together. Hopefully before that."

"I'm available," Oakes said in the dark.

Watts pulled down a narrow cobblestone street running along the waterfront in Fishtown, a section of the city that had once been a working-class neighborhood with some decent factory jobs in the big brick buildings along the Delaware River. Now the factories were broken-windowed shells, and parts of Fishtown were still a cesspool of gangs and drugs. He parked midway down the block where he had a good view in both directions approaching the Oasis, a half-assed name for a dingy, one-story roadside joint that hadn't looked like much twenty years ago when it was built. Now it looked like the pit it was—a single grimy window with a neon palm-tree shaped sign in glowing puke green to the left of a plain black wooden door, a flat-topped roof, and peeling red-painted sides. He still had half an hour before one of his team showed up, so he slid his seat back and got comfortable while he cooled his heels.

Not much happening on the street yet. Too early still for most of the scumbags who spent the best part of the night at the club to show up. Most of them probably didn't roll outta their flops or their gangbanger clubhouses until ten or eleven at night anyhow. The night crawlers didn't emerge until the sun was way down and the righteous citizens were all home in front of their televisions. Prime time for crime and cops.

Watts rearranged his ass on the uncomfortable fake-leather seat of the beater car he'd sweet-talked the guys in the impound lot into letting him use. No way was he sitting out on the street in a car that screamed cop so he could get his ass capped by some skinny gangbanger wannabe who needed to make his bones. His much skinnier ass. Having a heart attack and nearly croaking had scared him, although he wouldn't admit it to anyone. Scared him enough that he cut down on the chips and the beer after dinner at night. And, okay, maybe in secret he was walking a couple miles every morning. But now his bony ass got sore without all the padding.

To say nothing of being bored with nothing to do but watch the door and listen in on Mitch and Sandy's conversations to make sure they kept *their* skinny asses out of trouble. But that was okay. Somebody had to look out for them. The two of them, fearless crazy-ass kids. Not really kids, but new kinda cops. They never would've made it through the academy in his day. Sandy, an ex-hooker. Mitch—Dell—what the hell—he'd stopped trying to figure that out. He just took them for who they were. The only thing he knew for sure was they were his, and he'd sit in this trash can of a street or anywhere else to make sure they got their skinny asses home safe and sound.

At a little before eleven, a cab pulled around the corner, stopped, and Sandy got out. She waved at the cabbie as he pulled away, going slow enough that Watts figured he was cruising her ass as she sashayed down the street. Couldn't blame him. She had a nice ass, and it was practically hanging out of that little miniskirt she wore. If it was up to him, he'd tell her to cover up some so he wouldn't have to worry about every pervert in a ten-mile radius sniffing after her—but then, it wasn't up to him how many risks she took to get the job done. It was up to the Loo. And he had to admit, Frye looked after the squad the way no one else could. She kept them all safe, she kept the brass from squeezing their nuts, and she got results.

So here he sat.

Sandy didn't look in his direction. Of course, she wouldn't. She'd know he was there. She trusted him to be there. Maybe that was the real reason he dragged himself out of bed at the crack of dawn to go traipsing around the track at the football field a mile from his apartment every morning. So he could be there when he was needed.

Sandy sauntered up to the Oasis, hitched her skirt down an inch—like that did much good—fluffed her hair, and strolled inside. Twenty minutes later, a motorcycle came around the other end of the block, roared down the street, and angled into the curb along the line of other bikes. The scrawny guy all in black—of course—swung a leg over, stood and hooked his helmet to the bike, adjusted his…well, whatever he had in his jeans, and slouched over to the door, looking neither right or left, and shoved his way inside. So all the players were onstage.

Watts thumbed his phone to wake the screen, checked he had plenty of battery, and watched until it lit up.

"You read me," Sandy said on the conference channel.

"Yeah. You're good," Watts replied.

"Loud and clear, babe." Mitch's voice came through.

Good, they were all hooked in together now. Watts set the phone down beside him, leaving it on so he could hear them. "You kids have fun."

CHAPTER TWELVE

Sandy slipped her phone into the pocket of her skirt, flushed, and checked her makeup one more time. Damn, Mitch really had smeared her lipstick. She smoothed the little bit of a smudge away with her fingertips and smiled at the memory. Good sex always got her in the mood for an op. Her skin tingled, and her heart raced, and she couldn't wait to see what happened. Being a cop was the most fun she'd ever had, except of course when she was in bed with Dellon Mitchell.

She headed back out, ordered a gin and tonic—extra lime and not much ice—and put her back to the bar to watch the room. Not too crowded yet—just the usual mix of drug dealers, bikers, a couple of working girls, and here and there a few guys in too-clean tees and brand name jeans who didn't quite fit the place. Not tourists or college boys looking to score drugs or girls, but not lowlifes either. Those were the ones who interested her. What were they doing here?

She didn't see who she was looking for, but she tended to be lucky and patient. Hell, she was inside, warm and dry, and not working on her back. She could wait forever at this rate. So she nursed her drink and made sure anyone looking in her direction saw a street girl who wasn't quite ready to start earning her nightly wage. In the meantime, she found a little eye candy to take the edge off the waiting.

At the far end of the bar, Mitch was talking up a young black woman in a silver-spangled halter top that barely covered her nipples, and jeans cut so low her ass crack showed. The girl was leaning over so far Mitch probably could've stuck his tongue down between her tits. Sandy thought that was hot. The girl liked the looks of Mitch too. She had her hand on his arm and he was laughing. Yup. Definitely hot. Sandy angled a bit more so she could keep an eye on the door and watch them out of the corner of her eye.

Ten minutes later the blonde from the photo came through the door. Quickly, Sandy turned her back to the room, leaned on the bar, and showed a little cleavage of her own. The bartender, a muscle-bound white dude without much hair, who made up for it with such a large bulge in his pants she wondered if it was real, strolled over, leaned his elbow on the bar, and looked down her shirt.

"I know you, don't I?" he said. How original.

"Not the way you're thinking." Sandy smiled at him and watched the blonde do a quick circuit of the room and come over to the bar to get a drink.

"How do you know what I'm thinking?" he said, in what he probably thought was a low sexy voice.

"Well, I can sorta tell from the way you're looking at my tits."

He laughed. "Baby, if you're not doing anything later—"

"Have to check my list." She laughed and he good-naturedly winked and moved down the bar to take the blonde's order.

Sandy turned casually, cocked her head, and said, "Hey, do you remember me?"

The blonde didn't answer for a second, as if she wasn't sure Sandy was talking to her. Finally she looked over at her, a disinterested smirk on her face, and said, "I think you got the wrong girl, honey."

"No—I don't think so." Sandy put as much eager into her voice as she could. A little bit of airheadedness too. "Let me think…it was March, maybe." She flashed a proud smile. "Yeah, that's it! March. March up at University. You know, when the guy from…Intensity America…was there talking."

"You mean Identity America," the blonde said, a bit more interested now but still suspicious. "You were there? I don't remember you."

"Oh yeah. I was standing, like, right near you."

The blonde's brows came down. "Jeez, there were an awful lot of people there and everybody was yelling and shouting." She laughed. "That was something, wasn't it?"

"*Amazing.*" Sandy smiled like she was used to being overlooked, while mentally bringing up the crowd shot Sloan had shown with the blonde standing by the stage. "Yeah, I guess that's why you don't remember me. I was with some other people. Tall skinny guy wearing a cowboy hat?"

The blonde snapped her fingers. "I remember him. Oh yeah, you too. That was a cool demonstration, huh?"

"Totally. Do you go there…to school, I mean."

The blonde snorted. "Not hardly. A friend...my boyfriend," she added, lowering her voice like she was exposing a big secret, "he knew the speaker...you know, the guy on the stage. That's why we were there."

Sandy leaned closer, as if sharing the secret. "No kidding. Wow. So you're, like, part of their...what do you call it..."

"Organization," the blonde said.

Sandy smiled widely. "Yeah, that."

"Well"—the blonde straightened up a little bit, almost preening—"yeah, I guess you could say that."

Sandy moved down the bar carrying her drink. Now they were shoulder to shoulder. The bartender had passed the blonde a beer and moved off. "That is *so* cool. Is there, like, you know, someplace I can join. I'd love to, you know, do something to help out. They're so"—she looked around and lowered her voice—"*right*, you know. Their what do you call it...message or whatever. About the people who really matter, and the ones who don't."

Sandy figured she'd laid it on enough and backed off a little bit, waiting for the blonde to pick up the tune.

"I know, huh," the blonde said, looking around the room. "You know, my boyfriend, he's really tight with the important people."

"No shit," Sandy whispered. "I bet that's like...hot."

The blonde rolled her eyes. "Yeah, you'd think so, huh. But it's all I can do to talk him into getting it up. He's always so busy making *plans*."

"Guys." Sandy laughed. "And they say we're the ones that are always holding out."

"Hey," the blonde said, holding out her hand, "I'm Trish."

Sandy took the bony hand bedecked with a couple of cheap silver rings with turquoise stones and shook it, keeping her fingers limp and lose. A girly handshake. "I'm Elle—you know, like the letter."

Trish brightened. "Yeah? Cool name. Say, you want to get a table?"

Sandy said, "Yeah, that would be awesome."

Washington, DC
11:05 p.m.

A motorcade of four vehicles, visible by their taillights all in a line, waited for them at Andrews in front of one of the outlying hangars.

Ari wasn't exactly sure what she should do after they landed. She still needed to get to DC. Fortunately, she wouldn't be dragging luggage around. Call a cab? An Uber? Probably the better choice at that hour. Apparently reading her mind, the agent in the right front seat turned and looked into the back.

"We'll be happy to escort you home, Ms. Rostof." He looked over at Oakes, sitting across from Ari. "You're on your own, sport."

Oakes grinned. "I'll just ride back with you to the motor pool. I can find my way home from there."

"You'd be closer if we dropped you off with Ms. Rostof," the agent said.

Ari had a feeling she was missing something in this back-and-forth.

Oakes narrowed her eyes, wondering if she'd heard a bit of a taunt in O'Cleary's voice. Sometimes her fellow agents could be such assholes.

"I'll manage," Oakes said.

Abruptly, Ari said, "I'm actually too wired to sleep. I know it's late, but if you're not working tonight and have an hour or two, we could get that briefing out of the way. There's a great all-night diner…" She hesitated. "Of course, if that's not convenient or…"

"It's fine," Oakes said. She was pretty certain she heard a snort from the front seat. Across from her, Nika Witt tensed. Huh. She didn't seem to like Ari's suggestion very much. Of course, she might have had plans of her own that didn't include shadowing Rostof in the middle of the night. Or maybe it was something more personal, although Oakes kinda doubted that Witt would compromise her position with Rostof Protective Services by making a move on Rostof's daughter, but you never knew. After all, Cameron Roberts was sitting in the first car with her wife, the First Daughter of the United States, and way back when, Roberts had been the chief of Blair Powell's detail. Sometimes, life just happened and you had to roll with it. At the moment, she kinda felt like rolling with it.

"The question is," Oakes added, "does this place have decent coffee?"

"It's not an espresso boutique, but they've got good french roast and," Ari said with a playful smile Oakes hadn't seen before, "they've got killer cinnamon buns that they'll grill for you."

"Butter and raisins?"

"And walnuts."

"Sold," Oakes said.

Witt's facial expression hadn't changed an iota, so either she didn't mind extra work or she was very, very good at keeping her thoughts to herself. Likely both.

As if just realizing that she had an extension to her life now, Ari turned on the seat and faced Nika. "The diner's a couple blocks from my apartment. I'm not sure what living arrangements you're going to make, but I won't need you for the rest of the night." She frowned. "As a matter of fact, do you even have a suitcase? Or a hotel reservation somewhere?"

Witt finally cracked a smile, and Oakes had to admit, she was good-looking. For some reason, that bothered her. Okay, so Witt was gonna spend a lot of time up close and personal with Ari Rostof. So what? That made Oakes's life easier. Because after what happened to Adam, accident or not, somebody was going to need to worry about Rostof. She was pretty sure Tom Turner had already thought about that, and he wouldn't be above suggesting to the president that Ari needed security. She wasn't the usual protectee, but that wouldn't be the first time Secret Service agents were detailed to civilians. At the president's pleasure, Secret Service agents could be assigned to anyone for protection— visiting dignitaries were the most common, but government hopefuls, cabinet members, and anyone else the president deemed at risk. Why not someone in a key position like Rostof's? Maybe with Witt in place, that wouldn't be necessary. The idea should have pleased her, but it didn't, actually. She didn't know Witt, and just because Witt was a former Secret Service agent didn't necessarily mean she'd been good at it. Oakes made it a priority to find out.

Witt said quietly, "I have an apartment in the Kennedy-Warren. All of my things should have been delivered earlier, according to your father."

"An apartment in the Kennedy-Warren," Ari said slowly and decidedly coolly. "And where exactly would that be?"

Witt hesitated for just a moment too long. That was a big mistake.

Ari's shoulders stiffened. "Ten floor? North wing?"

Witt bit the bullet. "1014."

"Across the hall from my apartment."

"Yes, ma'am, that is correct."

Ari blew out a breath. "Of course you knew that when we left Newport. And forget the *ma'am*."

"Yes, I'd been briefed," Witt said.

"But it wasn't your place to mention it. I understand."

Oakes could put the picture together as well as Ari. No way did that apartment just come available. Nikolai Rostof had been keeping an eye on her, or at least had planned to by having an apartment available if needed.

"Did someone need to move out so you could move in?" Ari asked.

What she was really asking was if someone had been watching her all this time without her knowing it.

"That information is not available to me," Witt said.

Ari's jaw was set, and Oakes was pretty sure she could hear her molars grinding. Couldn't blame her. Finding out your father was spying on you had to suck.

"Well, then," Ari said, "you won't have far to go when they drop us off. I will not be needing your…services for the rest of this night."

Witt wisely said nothing and neither did Oakes. Her training came in handy when she needed to appear as if she hadn't heard a word of a conversation.

The motorcade reached DC and made pretty good time through the late-night traffic, pulling to a stop in front of Blair and Cam's building around midnight. The First Daughter's detail piled out along with Blair and Cam, and as soon as they entered the building, the lead car pulled away to return to the motor pool garage. The remaining cars followed suit, and fifteen minutes later the vehicle carrying Ari, Oakes, and Witt broke off to head up Connecticut Avenue.

The silence that filled the vehicle was thick enough to walk on. Oakes smiled to herself. Rostof was pissed. She was certain she never wanted Ari pissed at her. Her fury was a cold thing, like a steel blade sliding silently from a sheath. No hot, raging inferno for her. Oakes wondered if she ever raged. She wondered if anything ever set her on fire.

She glanced at Witt, who seemed preternaturally comfortable, a posture Oakes recognized. The relaxed coil of tension, deep inside. The appearance of calm when every nerve ending was set to spark. Yeah, she could see the agent in Witt coming through, and a weird competitive urge flashed through her. What the hell?

"Here we are," O'Cleary said from the front seat with a suspicious degree of jocularity in his voice. Yeah, he was enjoying this whole scene. Oakes wondered why. She was certain she hadn't given anything away.

Not that there was anything to reveal.

As soon as the vehicle pulled around the circular drive and stopped in front of the main lobby of the apartment complex, Ari slid across the seat and reached for the door.

"Thank you," she said, grasping for the handle.

Oakes got there first, and for an instant, their hands joined. Ari's skin was anything but cool. Heat rushed up Oakes's arm and her heart thudded.

"That's my job," Oakes said, gently evading Ari's touch and gripping the handle.

Witt somehow managed to get in front of her as the door swung open. She said as she passed Oakes, "Actually, it's mine."

CHAPTER THIRTEEN

"Good night," Blair said to Sato, as she stepped into the elevators. He'd spend the rest of the night standing post in the lobby. The doors closed behind them, and she glanced at Cam. "Some start to the vacation."

Cam grinned wryly. "Not exactly what I had planned."

Blair raised an eyebrow. "I seem to remember that you had an agenda. Only partially fulfilled."

Chuckling, Cam hooked an arm around her waist, and Blair rested her head against Cam's shoulder. Cam kissed the top of her head. "Tired?"

"Beyond tired." The elevator doors opened and they walked down the hall to their apartment. Cam greeted the agent there and keyed them inside. "There's always tomorrow."

Blair took her hand. "Isn't that how we started the day?"

"Never gets old."

Blair kissed her. "No, it never does. You are the only sane thing in my life."

Cam framed her face. "Same goes."

"What do you think about Ari Rostof?" Blair asked as she dropped onto the sofa with a sigh.

"About like I expected, since you recommended her." Cam settled beside her and cupped her nape. Massaging the tight muscles there, she sifted Blair's hair through her fingers. "Decisive. Savvy. Handled the press well."

"That sounds like a positive endorsement."

"Granted. She reminds me a little bit of you."

"Oh?" Blair said, casting Cam a sideways glance. "How so?"

"Confident, capable, independent. Did you notice she didn't consult with anyone before she made her decision?"

"I know. I'm not surprised, given her situation. Nikolai Rostof could smother anyone who wasn't strong enough to make their own way."

"Maybe that's why she reminds me of you," Cam said. "You've both had to struggle to shape your own lives in the face of some pretty restrictive family dynamics."

"Maybe. Our fathers are very different, though. Mine was controlling, but because he had to be. Hers, I think, because that's his basic nature."

"A fine distinction," Cam mused, drawing her closer, "but I imagine it felt the same when you were young."

Blair closed her eyes and rested her head against Cam's shoulder. "Yes, it did, and that's why I love you. Because you understand that." She searched Cam's face. "You're caught up in all that now too. Just look at what happened to our vacation."

"That would have happened anyway, even if I wasn't madly in love with the president's daughter." Blair laughed and Cam kissed her. "My job, after all."

"Between the two of us, our life isn't really our own," Blair said.

Happily, the note of sadness that had once accompanied that truth was gone from her voice. Cam nodded. "Yep. We've still got a long ways to go, with your father looking at another term as president."

"I know. Does it feel like a sacrifice to you?"

"No. Does it to you?" Cam said.

"Not as long as I have you." Blair took a deep breath. "You know, bed sounds really good right now."

Cam read the weariness in her eyes, stood, and tugged her down the hall to the bedroom.

"Sit," she said, guiding Blair gently down onto the side of the bed.

Intrigued, Blair did as she was told. Cam knelt before her and slipped off her shoes. The act was so intimate that Blair's heart tumbled in her chest. When she reached out to stroke Cam's cheek, her fingers trembled. "How can you do this to me after all this time."

Cam looked up, and her gray eyes were as calm as a vast ocean that promised of storms to come, still far out to sea but moving slowly closer. "I adore you."

"I believe you."

"Good." Carefully, with infinite precision, Cam unbuttoned Blair's shirt. Then the top of her pants. Sliding both hands around Blair's hips, she eased her up to her feet and drew her clothing off one piece at a time. When Blair was naked except for her bra and panties, Cam rose and pulled her against her body. "You are the most beautiful, amazing, sexy woman I've ever seen."

"Fancy stuff. I hope you intend to make good on that," Blair murmured against Cam's throat. Touched to her soul, she kissed her, lightly tasted her with the tip of her tongue. "I want you to touch me."

Cam stepped back, shed her suit one garment at a time, as Blair watched her slowly reveal herself. She wasn't sure what moved her more—Cam's beautiful body or the way she shed her pristine control, one piece of armor at a time, just for Blair. The weapon harness, into the top drawer. The commission book and badge to the dresser top. The watch, set down carefully next to the badge, until she was naked and adorned only by the glittering ring on her left hand.

Blair's throat was dry, her pulse was pounding, and urgency pulsed deep inside. She gestured to her bra and panties with a flick of a finger against satin. "You forgot something."

"No, I didn't. I just like to see you in your lacy bits."

Blair laughed. "I didn't even wear my most sexy ones."

"I don't care. It always works for me."

"Are you done looking?"

"For a minute." Cam reached behind Blair's back, unhooked her bra, and with the other hand, skimmed inside her panties and pushed them down. Blair stepped free of everything, pulled the sheets down, and stretched out. Cam slid in beside her and wrapped her in her arms.

Blair nestled her cheek on Cam's shoulder. "I'm not sure I can move."

"You don't have to," Cam murmured, stroking her back, the hollow at the base of her spine, the curve of her ass.

Blair closed her eyes and gave in to the indulgence of simply being loved. When Cam traced a finger over the curve of her hip, down the hollow inside, and ever so lightly between her thighs, she arched, so ready, so easy.

"I feel positively selfish here," Blair whispered.

"Oh, I don't think so." Cam turned her gently onto her back and, easing down her body, kissed her between her thighs. "I've got exactly what I want."

"Lucky me." Blair closed her eyes, already soaring, and surrendered to the wonder that was Cam. The orgasm stripping her to the core was a gift, given and received.

"Come here," Blair whispered an eternity later.

When Cam folded her in her arms, Blair slid one leg between Cam's thighs. Satin heat welcomed her. "I love it when you feel like that."

Cam's breath hitched, igniting a surge of satisfaction in Blair's depths. She rocked into her, steadily building the pace and pressure to take Cam where she needed to go. Faster, harder, her own heart racing, her breath caught in her throat. Cam's fingers tensed on her shoulders.

"That's it," Blair murmured, head spinning with aching wonder as Cam went rigid and groaned.

When Cam slid limply onto her back, a long sigh escaping her, Blair curled up beside her and rested her cheek on her chest. She lightly stroked Cam's abdomen. "I think that checks all the boxes on today's agenda."

"Mm, I think you're right." Cam kissed her.

"Get some sleep," Blair murmured on the cusp of drifting off. "Tomorrow is going to be another big day."

"I know," Cam whispered. Tomorrow was the start of a whole new game.

The Oasis
Philadelphia
Midnight

Mitch palmed the hand that was slowly sliding up the inside of his left thigh and gently moved it around to the top of his leg.

Mavis, as she had introduced herself, frowned. "Now why'd you do that, baby. I just know we'd be good together."

She leaned even farther forward, as if he hadn't already had an outstanding view of her outstanding assets. He smiled. "I can't imagine anything with you could be less than amazing."

She probably heard that about a million times from other guys or girls wanting to score, but he meant it, and she must have known it, because something in her eyes softened and she moved her hand.

"You know," she said quietly, the street accent dropping away, "my real name is Mary, but I read this book, you know, where one of the really cool chicks was named Mavis, and I really liked it, so I figured, why not. Who's to know, right?"

Mitch nodded. "I think you ought to be called whatever you want. They're both nice names."

She smiled. "So, really, what's a decent guy like you doing in a pit like this?"

"What makes you think I'm so decent?"

She looked down where his hand still gently held hers. "I know what I got to offer, and most guys wouldn't say no." She raised a brow. "Unless you got a girl?"

He shook his head. He did, but not on the job. All the same, he didn't take advantage. He didn't need to go that far, and he didn't want to.

"So," Mavis said quizzically, "just not your type, then?"

"Another night, absolutely."

She laughed and moved her hand all the way off his leg. "So? Who is she? The one who caught your eye? Cause if you don't have someone at home, and you're in here looking, she's got to be here."

He couldn't really blush on command, but he was practiced enough to pretend he'd been caught out. He shrugged.

"Uh-huh, though so." She poked him in the chest. "It's a good thing I'm not supersensitive or I'd be crushed."

"Oh, come on," Mitch said, "you gotta know how hot you are."

"I do, and you are avoiding the question. So who'd you see that tripped your trigger?" She ran a fingertip down his neck and chuckled when he shivered. He was human, after all, and his body had a will of its own. Lucky for him, he had a lot of practice steering the ship out of the shallows when temptation beckoned.

Mitch turned his head a fraction and glanced across the room to where Sandy sat at a table with the blonde from the surveillance photo.

"Okay, which blonde are you fantasizing about naked?" Mavis asked archly.

"The one with the red top. And it's not what you think."

"Oh, right." She laughed like she really meant it, tilted her head, and narrowed her eyes a little bit. Her lashes were long and dark, and real. "She *is* awfully cute. I bet she'd be hot in bed. Can't say as I'd mind a taste of that."

Mitch's stomach curled just a little because, boy, was Mavis right. "Not touching that one."

"Oh, like you don't want to." Mavis asked, "So what is it about her? Is it the blond thing? Because it usually is the freaking hair—it's a dick magnet. That's why I don't like blondes."

Mavis's black hair gleamed with some kind of glittery stuff in a dozen gorgeous shoulder-length braids.

"Not the hair—and yours is great, by the way. To tell you the truth, it's her ass. So, do you know her?"

Mavis laughed. "No, I don't. The other one comes in quite a bit, usually with one of those earnest white boys who take themselves too seriously. And you really are a dick."

Mitch's gut tightened. Maybe they were on the right trail. "You mad?"

"No, not really. You know why?"

He shook his head, because he really didn't. Turning down a girl, and then talking about another one, usually was not a great idea.

"Because you're honest. You didn't take what you could have had, when you didn't really want it."

"Well, to my way of thinking," he said, "you should have what you deserve."

"Thank you." She gave him a little shove. "And since you're ruining my game, you should take off now."

Mitch signaled the bartender to send her another drink, left money on the counter, and said, "You be careful now, Mavis."

She leaned over and kissed him. "I always am. You too, baby."

He picked up his drink and wended his way through the tables to where Sandy was sitting with the target. They both looked up at him questioningly.

"I was wondering if you two would like some company." Lame, but sure to get a response.

Sandy barked a laugh. "You think we're together?"

"I—"

"Because if we were," Sandy said, "do you really think we'd want you around?"

"Okay, sorry, my mistake," he said as he backed away.

Rolling her eyes, Sandy glanced over at the blonde. "What do you think—you want to do him?"

The blonde looked a little nonplussed for an instant, then seemed to get into it. She pursed her lips. "Well, my boyfriend might want in on it too."

Sandy raised the shoulder. "Yeah, okay. I can do that."

Mitch held up a hand, gesturing with the beer bottle in the other. "Okay, my mistake. Really, I'll just leave you two ladies to your evening."

Sandy snaked a hand out and grabbed his wrist. "Oh, relax, snowflake. You're safe with us. Have a seat." Sandy looked over at the blonde. "Okay with you?"

"Sure, but I'm not gonna fuck him."

Sandy grinned. "Neither am I. At least not until he buys me a drink."

Washington, DC
Midnight

The detail vehicles pulled away, leaving the three of them in front of the sprawling Kennedy-Warren complex that spanned a block and a half adjacent to the zoo. The night was just cool enough to require a jacket, and Oakes wondered if Ari was cold in only the silk shirt and pants she'd worn for the TV interview.

Nika Witt said, "If you have need of me, Ms. Rostof, you should have my number."

"Yes, that was provided to me. I should be fine, thank you," Ari said.

Oakes waited silently while Witt turned, walked inside the foyer, and spoke to the security guard outfitted as a bellman who buzzed her through into the main lobby. She didn't stop at the desk but went straight for the elevators.

"No check-in," Oakes said.

"That's because she's been here before." Ari spun on her heel and walked down the curving sidewalk toward Connecticut Avenue. Oakes fell in beside her.

"That would be my guess too." Oakes hesitated a second, then added, "Probably why she doesn't have a suitcase, either."

"No, she's all moved in. Probably has been for a while."

"She'd be hard to miss," Oakes said, keeping her tone conversational. Ari was both angry and upset, and Oakes didn't have any reason or desire to make either one of those emotions any worse. Interesting, because she was used to sparring with the closest people in her life all the time. Living and working with a bunch of Secret Service agents was a lot like living in a frat house, or sorority house, or mixed house, to be totally accurate. Everyone always subtly jostling for position, playing a friendly game of one-upmanship, looking for the weaknesses to poke.

Because, after all, that's what friendly competitors—or competitive friends, maybe—did with one another.

Ari didn't fit into either of those categories, and not just because she wasn't one of Oakes's colleagues. She was different because, well, because she was such a fascinating woman, and Oakes didn't see any of her fellow agents—male or female—in quite that way.

"That doesn't necessarily mean that she's been watching you," Oakes added. "I suspect if she was living there, you would've run into her in the hall or the elevator or the lobby."

Ari shot her a sideways glance. "Really. And if you had been assigned to *watch* me," she said, putting a particularly acid twist to the word *watch* that made it sound a lot like *spy*, "I would've noticed you?"

"Well," Oakes said, caught between pride, honesty, and a desire to smooth over the rough waters she'd just stirred up, "possibly not."

Ari snorted. "Tell me that you are being humble."

Oakes laughed, glad for the little bit of levity that had snuck into Ari's voice. Her being upset was upsetting. Another thing she wasn't quite used to. "Okay, I was being humble."

"You don't really do it all that well, by the way."

"Hey, I think that's the third time tonight you've insulted me."

"Uh-huh. And I can see how much of an effect it had."

"So you *were* trying to insult me."

"Hardly." Ari cast her a sideways smile. "Just testing."

"Did I pass?" Oakes wasn't sure what the test was, but she most definitely did not want to disappoint.

"I'll let you know."

Oakes laughed. This was a different kind of sparring than Oakes was used to. Exciting, in a different way than the usual aggressive endorphin kind of rush knocking heads with another agent produced. Arousing, actually. What it was, Oakes realized on a wave of slowly building electricity skittering over her skin, was flirting.

Not the best of ideas, and she could think of a number of reasons without even trying very hard. She didn't know a damn thing about Ari Rostof, other than what she had read in her bio, and what had been in her bio had raised a few flags. Her father's questionable business associations aside, Ari was about to take over one of the most important jobs in the president's administration, at least until the next election, and that meant she was going to be on the opposite side of the playing field from Oakes.

Her job was to secure the president's safety, and that was pretty much going to be a twenty-four-hour-a-day job right up until the election. Her experience with Adam, as much as she'd liked him, was that he wanted to get as much face time for the president as possible, while Oakes and every other Secret Service agent in the Presidential Protective Division wanted to keep him in a bulletproof bubble as far away from the public as possible. Yeah, she and Ari were definitely on opposite sides of this court.

"The diner's right here," Ari said, leading her around the corner to an old-fashioned subway car diner squeezed between a building with an art house movie theater on the first level and a Thai restaurant on the other side. A row of square windows ran down the middle of the aluminum-sided structure, and quite a few booths were full.

"I hope they haven't run out of cinnamon buns," Oakes said.

Ari laughed and reached for the door. Oakes grabbed it automatically.

"You know, I am quite capable of opening my own doors," Ari murmured as she stepped inside.

Oakes followed her down the aisle to a red vinyl booth and slid in across from her. "I have no doubt you're supremely competent at any number of things. It's habit."

"I didn't actually say I didn't like it." Ari picked up a menu.

"Good." Oakes grabbed a menu herself.

A waitress in a black skirt, a red and white striped apron, and a short-sleeved white shirt with frilly caps appeared beside them.

"Grilled cinnamon bun?" she said, looking at Ari. "Coffee?"

"Yes to both," Ari said.

"You can double that, and an order of eggs and ham," Oakes said.

"Gotcha." The waitress moved away without writing anything down.

"You really *do* like the cinnamon buns," Oakes said.

"When I like something, I don't change my mind," Ari said.

"Good to know." Oakes's belly was buzzing again for no good reason. They were talking about pastry, for cripes' sake.

Two cups of coffee appeared in front of them, and Ari added cream to hers, picked it up, and leaned back in the booth. "So, let's start with the areas we probably agree on."

Oakes laughed and tried her own coffee. Strong but rich. Nice. "Let's hope there are some."

Ari smiled thinly. Oakes apparently had the same reservations she did. She hadn't had any difficulty working with the senator's private security detail, since they pretty much did whatever the senator wanted them to do, and the senator did whatever Ari wanted *her* to do, which included all kinds of interactions with the public—town meetings, fund-raisers, walkabouts in farm country, television appearances, commencement speeches. Anything and everything to get her face in front of the public and, more importantly, her hand shaking those of her potential constituents. Security was important, but not a major concern. Yes, the security guards needed to keep overzealous constituents from crowding the senator, and after what happened to Congresswoman Gabby Giffords, crowd control and weapon surveillance were heightened. But the senator was far from being a public symbol like the President of the United States. The issue of the public's access to him was going to be a major stumbling block, and one she would rather leave until she'd garnered some goodwill with the Secret Service detail. Oakes seemed like a reasonable place to start.

"The convention agenda…" Ari said, choosing a neutral topic. "Do you have an itinerary yet?"

"Adam assured me that he had one, but I haven't seen it," Oakes said, a note of annoyance trickling into her usually inscrutable tone.

"All right, that'll be one of the first things on my list. Hotel?"

"Still being vetted."

"I don't need to know about the hospitals, but I'd like the plans for the motorcade route as soon as possible."

"Why is that?" Oakes asked casually. Ari seemed to know a little bit more about how things worked than she'd expected. But then, why wouldn't she. She worked on the Hill, the senator had been at plenty of functions where the president was also present, and the bones of what happened when he traveled were obvious. The details were never shared with anyone, and she didn't intend to share them now.

"In case a stop along the way would be advantageous," Ari said.

Oakes shook her head. "There won't be any stops along the way."

Ari smiled. "Well, you never know."

The back of Oakes's neck started to itch. So much for flirting. It looked like the game was on. Ari didn't seem to notice Oakes's reticence as she typed notes into her phone.

"Who's interfacing with media from your team, anyone yet?"

"That would be Evyn Daniels," Oakes said.

"I'll need to speak with him."

"Her."

"Her," Ari said with another smile.

She was beautiful when she smiled. The observation irritated Oakes at the moment. "I'll let her know."

"I'll talk to the heads of the major networks covering the event— who they plan to have doing personal interviews, where they're going to be held."

"I imagine Rostof Network News will be involved," Oakes said.

Ari's brows flickered for just an instant before her facial expression smoothed out again. "Of course. But that won't be the only network there."

"I'll arrange a meeting between you, Evyn, and myself as soon as possible."

"I'll also need the layout for the Convention Center," Ari said.

"Why?"

"I want to see where the president is positioned when he accepts the nomination to check camera angles, sight lines to the broadcast booths, where he'll be staging before the appearance, the walk-on position—everything that has to do with his personal presentation."

"You really plan to manage him," Oakes said.

"That's my job, managing people." Ari looked up from her phone, a gleam in her eyes that reminded Oakes of a professional athlete before a major tournament. Rostof was in this to win, all right, and it looked like things were going to be very different with her calling the plays.

CHAPTER FOURTEEN

The Oasis
1:20 a.m.

A tall skinny guy with hair cut so short it barely left a shadow on his skull and features so nondescript the average person wouldn't be able to describe him a few hours later appeared beside their table. The guy wore dark cargo pants and a plain T-shirt, no pockets and no logos. His whole appearance suggested he was trying to pass as unremarkable. That might have worked if it wasn't for the black lightning bolt tattoo on the left side of his neck. Mitch laughed to himself. That was an identifying mark if he'd ever seen one.

"Who are you?" the guy said after a moment, looking at Mitch. He dropped his hand on the back of Trish's neck, a gesture that was more controlling than possessive.

"Hey, baby," Trish said with a tone that belied her almost dismissive sneer when she looked up at him, although Mitch supposed her expression could be construed as a smile. Maybe if you weren't looking too closely, and this guy wasn't. He probably never really looked at her—she was just there, background noise—and she probably knew it.

"Hey," Mitch said, holding out a hand. "I'm Mitch."

"Uh-huh," the guy said, taking his hand and squeezing just a little harder than a handshake required. Mitch didn't take the bait and slouched back in his chair after extracting his hand.

"Elle," Sandy said, not offering her hand.

The guy didn't offer his either.

"I'm…Mark," the guy said.

The hesitation gave him away. Not Mark, then. Chances were it was an *M*-name. People often subconsciously chose aliases with their own initials.

Mark pulled out a chair and sat down next to Trish.

"First time here?" Mark said, as if he owned the place and was taking a customer survey.

"Not me," Sandy said. "The music sucks, but the drinks are pretty good." She laughed. "And the bartender's hot."

Trish laughed with her. Mitch didn't and neither did Mark.

"So, what about you, Mitch. What'd you come here for?"

"I heard this was a good place for guys to meet chicks." Mitch draped his arm around the back of Sandy's chair but didn't touch her. "I'm working on that."

"Make sure you work on the right girl." Mark let a beat pass while he looked Sandy over. He tugged Trish an inch closer. "'Cause this one's mine."

Mitch could see his fingers tighten on Trish's neck, and he worked to keep his face blank as he raised his hands. "Absolutely. Never poach another guy's girl."

"So, you a student?" Mark signaled to one of the harried waitresses hustling by with a full tray. "Another round here, if you please."

She shot him a look as if his polite request hadn't fooled her at all. His superior tone still came through loud and clear. "When I get to it."

"I went to City College for a while," Mitch said, "but it wasn't for me. Too many bleeding-heart liberals." He snorted. "Teachers *and* students."

Mark's eyes glinted as if he'd just noticed Mitch for the first time. "Well, yeah, you see that a lot on campuses these days. But you know, there's a lot of us there too."

"Us regular guys, you mean." Mitch backed off and waited. Mark struck him as being cautious and experienced enough to pick up on being pumped for information.

"I was thinking along the lines of all-American guys, you know?"

"I hear that."

Mark tilted his head, as if studying Mitch for some sign he was serious. Mitch stayed relaxed and let him look. Mark seemed to come to some kind of decision, because he relaxed for the first time, settling against the back of his chair. "So what do you do now?"

"Whatever I can to make a few bucks," Mitch said.

"You dealing?" Mark asked.

"Hell, no," Mitch said, going by instinct. "I'm clean and so's my record. Never been busted and never plan to be."

"Good," Mark said, "that's real good."

Washington, DC
1:30 a.m.

"I think that about covers the immediate issues," Ari said, pushing her coffee cup aside. "Thanks for sacrificing a few hours' sleep."

"No problem," Oakes said. "I don't need a lot of sleep, and I'm an expert at grabbing what I need when I can."

"There's going to be a lot of that going around the next few weeks," Ari said.

"True. Besides, you're right about the cinnamon buns. They're great—the rest of the food too."

"Just got lucky," Ari said, placing bills on the table. "I found the right incentive to keep you up half the night."

"You did," Oakes said, placing her hand over Ari's.

Ari caught her breath, her heart jumping. She hadn't been anticipating anything personal, or at least she hadn't let her mind go there even though Oakes was damnably attractive with just the right blend of confidence tempered by professionalism and tinged with arrogance. And here she was making a move when Ari was positive she hadn't sent any signals to encourage her. How could she have—she wasn't interested. Okay, maybe not that exactly, but she didn't have the time, space, or emotional fortitude to take on a complicated woman right now, and Oakes would be anything but simple.

"Why don't you let me get the check," Oakes said. "I'm not carrying any cash, so I can't chip in otherwise."

Something that felt a lot like a blush crept up Ari's throat, and she prayed Oakes didn't notice. Read *that* one all wrong. She must be a little more tired than she'd thought. Not a good start to a new job that was going to require her to spend a lot of time with Agent Weaver.

"No, that's fine." Ari carefully but not too quickly extracted her hand from beneath Oakes's warm palm and sat back a little so she could pull her hand safely into her lap without looking like she was running away. Which she definitely was. "I almost never use cash either, except for here. I just like the waitresses to get their tips that way."

"Nice of you. They don't have an easy job. Did you ever wait tables?"

Ari shook her head. "No, I'm afraid my summer jobs were interning at my father's firms, when I wasn't crewing on one of his racing sailboats."

Oakes laughed. "Okay, then. Tough work."

"Hey," Ari said with mock archness, "you've never worked for my father."

"True enough. But I imagine it's a lot like working for the president. Your time is never your own, everything you schedule gets changed, and no matter what you see or hear, you're not supposed to have any opinions."

"You're absolutely right." Ari laughed. "So I guess I'm well prepared. Well, except for the last thing. I didn't score highly on the no-opinion part."

"Yeah, I imagine that's true."

"Hm. What exactly are you saying there, Agent?"

Oakes grinned. "You strike me as a woman who speaks her mind."

"You're only partially right," Ari said. "Professionally I keep a lot to myself—I'm managing someone else's image, remember."

"And personally? No secrets there?" Oakes asked quietly.

"I didn't say that," Ari answered just as quietly. No, she wouldn't pretend she didn't hold back parts of herself. Why should she? She *did* need to turn this conversation onto safer paths, though. Somehow a casual conversation with Oakes had a way of getting way too close very quickly. "What about you? What did you do before the Secret Service got a hold of you?"

"Work, you mean?" When Ari nodded, Oakes said, "I did wait tables for a while—not in a diner like this, but in my grandparents' restaurant. They owned a resort in the Blue Ridge Mountains, with a little café that went with it. Just open during the summer. It's been in the family for a hundred years. I worked there summers at the counter."

"Really. That sounds awesome," Ari said.

"I don't know how awesome you'd find it, with not much to do except hike, bike, and read. They didn't even have decent internet until the last few years."

Ari laughed. "Okay, I'd find it a little difficult without the internet, being a compulsive news junkie, but the biking and hiking part sounds okay. Of course, my experience doing either is at a resort in the Berkshires. Something about what you describe sounds like a whole lot more fun."

"Looking back, it was," Oakes said.

"Do they still own the place?"

"Retired and moved to year-round warmer climes. My parents didn't want to take it over, but one of my cousins did. She seems to be making a go of it, even though places like that aren't as popular as they used to be. Everybody wants amenities."

"Sometimes, getting away from the amenities is exactly what we need." Ari's plan for a few hours on the sea seemed like a long time ago now, but the time for regrets was past. She'd made her choice.

"I don't know," Oakes mused. "I can't remember the last time I actually had a vacation."

"You do get them, right?" Ari sounded genuinely curious.

"Yeah, we do. But like as not, they get changed at the last minute."

"I guess in your line of work, your time is never really your own."

"I'm not complaining," Oakes said. "They don't keep anything secret about the job when you sign up." She laughed. "Well, that's not literally true. Obviously."

Ari sighed and rose. "Well, I guess if we're going to be ready for tomorrow, we'd better get some sleep."

Oakes followed Ari outside, and when Ari turned right toward the Kennedy-Warren, Oakes said, "I'll walk you back."

"It's really not far, and not necessary."

"Yeah, it is."

Shaking her head, Ari said, "You're chivalrous."

Oaks laughed. "Well, now there is something I've never been accused of before."

"It's really not an accusation, you know."

"Well, then," Oakes said quietly, "thank you."

"What about you?" Ari said. "You're going to end up walking home alone now. Are you sure you don't need *my* protection?"

"I'm only twenty minutes away on Nineteenth. Makes it an easy commute." She lowered her voice. "And besides, I'm armed."

"True. In that case, I won't worry about you."

"Well, then," Oaks said, surprised by her reluctance to leave. "Good night."

"Good night, Oakes."

Oakes waited until Ari was through the main doors and into the lobby before turning and heading home. She wondered if Nika Witt was awake in the apartment across the hall from Ari or if indeed Ari's father had kept tabs on her. She supposed he might have just been looking out for her safety, and she couldn't fault him for that. Ari might not have been a prime target before today, but she would be now. Still, Oakes couldn't prevent a ripple of irritation when she envisioned Nika by Ari's side.

She picked up her pace. The sooner she got back to doing what she did best, the better, and Ari Rostof could be someone else's problem.

The hallway leading to Ari's apartment was deserted, no sounds coming from beneath the doors of the adjoining units. Superior soundproofing notwithstanding, the Kennedy-Warren in general was quiet, occupied primarily by professionals who were out during the day and rarely home in the evening, much like herself. She paused before inserting her key in the lock, conscious of the closed door at her back. 1014, Nika Witt's apartment. Or rather, the apartment her father kept in her building, ostensibly for just this reason. For when he wanted someone to keep watch over her. To him that meant keeping her safe. To her, it meant intruding on her life. Worse, it meant a lack of trust in her own ability to take care of herself. She shouldn't have been surprised, really, and Witt was already installed in her life. That battle was lost and not worth wasting energy on.

With a sigh, she unlocked the door and stepped into her apartment. She engaged the deadbolt, slid the security chain into place, and, moving by memory, found the table lamp by the sofa and clicked it on. She hadn't left any lights on when she'd left the previous week, since she hadn't planned on coming back right away. She'd have to notify management in the morning that she had returned early, so they didn't come in to water plants or check the apartment as they routinely did if tenants were away for a while. She had a two-bedroom apartment, one of the few larger units in a building constructed during an era when people did not need quite as much room. In addition to being spacious, the ceilings were high, the windows plentiful, and the kitchen just big enough for a table for two. She loved the place despite not spending all that much time there.

Not until she'd stepped inside and shut the door on the rest of the world did she realize just how tired she was. Her shoulders ached, her back ached, and her head was muzzy as a result of a day filled with incredible emotional challenges, both good and bad. She was beyond excited to have the President of the United States as her new client, concerned about all that needed to be done, and surprisingly, intrigued that none of her thoughts really lingered on the job confronting her as they ordinarily would. Instead, as she went about getting ready for bed, she thought of Oakes Weaver. At once charming and humorous, intelligent and challenging, and at other times, barricaded behind a professional façade that was more than just window dressing. Oakes was one of those people for whom duty was a tangible thing. Something she could feel, that she lived and breathed. Ari had met a few people like that in her life, but the quality was rare. In her experience, those individuals could be remarkable and admirable, and also incredibly stubborn and royal pains in the behind. She suspected Oakes would be a little bit of both. She needed to work with her, and that was likely to require all her talent. She couldn't afford distractions, no matter how charming the package.

In panties and a loose T-shirt, she got into bed and immediately kicked the sheets aside in the unseasonably warm room. She cracked a window, and the night breeze drifted in along with traffic sounds. City lullabies. Morning would come all too soon, and she willed her racing mind to still. A minute later she checked her watch. She'd been home seventeen minutes. Oakes should be arriving at her destination just about now. Ari glanced at her phone on her bedside table, and for one insane moment, contemplated texting Oakes to ask if she made it home uneventfully. Laughing at her own insanity, she ignored the thought, turned over, and closed her eyes.

The Oasis
Philadelphia
1:45 a.m.

When the bartender announced last call, Sandy stood and finished off her drink, only the second she'd had the entire evening since she'd managed to look like she was drinking a lot more by passing her half-full glass back to the waitress every time someone bought another round.

"Well, I'm done. It's been fun." She glanced at Trish. "Maybe I'll see you again, huh?"

"Yeah, sure," Trish said, not sounding all that into it, but she'd handed Sandy her phone at one point while everyone was talking and said, "Put your number in."

Contact had been made. Maybe it would go somewhere, and maybe not. But that's how the job was done. Just a few more scenes to play now.

Sandy leaned down and kissed Mitch on the cheek. "Thanks for the drinks."

Right on cue, Mitch jumped up. "Uh, I could give you a ride home, if you're into motorcycles. If you need one, I mean."

Sandy cocked her head, aware that Mark, or whatever his real name was, and Trish were watching.

She shrugged. "Beats walking. But remember what I said. I'm not going to fuck you."

"Yeah, I got that message." Mitch grinned. "The offer for a ride is still open, though. And who knows, maybe next time I see you here, I'll get lucky."

Sandy laughed and rolled her eyes.

Mark finally said, "So maybe I'll see you again, huh, Mitch? You know, like-minded guys, they don't come around that often."

"Totally," Mitch said, keeping his attention on Sandy. Now was not the time to look too eager. He set his hand in the small of her back. "You ready?"

"'Night all," Sandy called, and walked away.

Once outside, Mitch unhooked the second helmet from behind his seat and handed it to her. "That skirt is not made for riding on the bike."

"That's not why I'm wearing it." Sandy hiked it up to climb on behind him. After he kick-started the bike and pulled away, she wrapped her arms around his waist like they'd done a hundred times before. She didn't look in Watts's direction, but she knew he was there. Probably bored out of his skull, listening to their inane conversation most of the night. Of course, he could've been scanning sports scores on his phone. If there'd been trouble, he would've been there. That was all she needed to know.

As they climbed the stairs to their second-floor apartment, she said, "If there's anything there at all, it's him, don't you think?"

"I think so." Mitch unlocked the door and held it so she could go in before him. "He's got the rhetoric down. Trish…" He shrugged. "I don't know why she's in it. He's an asshole."

"He is, but plenty of girls hook up with assholes if there's no other choice." Sandy shed her skirt and shirt, aware that Mitch was watching her. "You tired?"

"You offering?"

She unhooked her bra, pushed down her panties, and climbed into bed. "Could be convinced."

Laughing, Dell kicked off the boots, then peeled off the T-shirt and the wrap binding her chest. Last came the pants and Mitch's gear. Naked, she approached the bed. "I like watching you watch me do that."

Sandy leaned on an elbow. "That's cause you know watching you strip makes me hot."

"Does it?"

"Come see for yourself."

Dell stretched out between her thighs, smiling as she kissed her belly and then her clit. Sandy let out a little hiss as Dell's mouth moved over her.

"I like that too," she murmured, her throat getting tighter with every second.

Dell murmured agreement against her sex, and Sandy gritted her teeth to stay in the moment. Not for long, though. She couldn't stop her body from rolling against Dell's mouth. Just too damn good. Dell kept it up, and she came hard and fast, somewhere in the midst of the orgasm losing her grip and falling bonelessly back to the bed. The next thing she knew Dell was beside her, wrapping her up in her arms.

"Hey," she said sleepily, kissing her. "You are unbelievably hot."

"Yeah," Dell whispered. "I am."

Laughing, Sandy cupped her sex, found her hot and wet, and started to stroke.

Dell moaned, closed her eyes, and didn't even try to hold back.

"That's what I call good teamwork," Sandy murmured when Dell rested her cheek on her shoulder, breathing hard. When Dell's quiet breathing was the only answer, she held her tighter and closed her eyes.

CHAPTER FIFTEEN

Ari slept better than she'd expected, waking at just before six surprisingly clearheaded. The room had chilled with the window open overnight, but the breeze felt great, and she gave herself a minute to just lie there while her brain clicked in and she organized everything she needed to do. As it had the night before, snippets of her conversations with Oakes, random glimpses of her, recollections of the timbre of her voice and the expressive turn of her smile, kept intruding on her thoughts. Rather than being annoyed by the interferences, she enjoyed each one for a brief few seconds before setting the memory aside and focusing again on what had to be her priority.

After a quick shower, she dressed in a navy suit and blue and white striped shirt, checked her messages, and saw a text from Esmeralda Alaqua, introducing herself and letting Ari know she would be available after seven. She smiled to herself. She liked that. Her new associate, Adam's second in command and, if she proved as efficient and amenable as her texts suggested, soon to be Ari's right hand, had made her presence known without waiting to be contacted. Ari needed forward-thinking people who took the reins and did what needed to be done. She'd need a lot of them if *she* was going to do what needed to be done in the infinitesimally short period of time she'd been given.

The trick was not to let everyone know exactly how far underwater she was starting out. But that's what she was good at. Keeping misgivings and insecurities to herself. Projecting the aura of having everything under control, always. Of being absolutely certain of her decisions. That's what being in charge was all about. Oh, she'd listen to good advice and reasonable consultation, but in the end, the decisions she made were her own, and doubt was not permissible.

She grabbed her slim bifold case with her tablet inside, slipped her key card into the inside pocket of her suit jacket, and left the apartment. The door across from hers instantly opened, and Nika Witt stepped out, dressed in perfectly fitted black pants, a gray open-collared shirt, and fashionable boots that nevertheless looked like she could move quickly in them.

"Good morning, Ms. Rostof," Nika said.

Ari paused. "All right, how did you know I was leaving? Please tell me there aren't cameras in my apartment."

"To my knowledge, there are not," Nika said, not breaking a smile. Humor was not high on her list of personality traits. "And if there were any, you have my word that I would not be using them."

"Did you by any chance sweep the apartment for listening devices or some such thing?"

Nika held her gaze as she said, "Before you returned last night. I detected nothing of the sort. Nor did I interfere with any of your possessions while scanning the rooms."

Ari managed not to gape. She'd been kidding. "How did you get access?"

"I have a key, to be used only if I feel that you are endangered."

A chill ran down Ari's spine. "Were you ever going to tell me that?"

"Not unless you asked."

"And since I don't know what else I need to know, you're not going to tell me."

"My job is to safeguard you. By whatever means necessary."

"I'm not in any danger, and I can assure you that following me around will bore you to tears while greatly inconveniencing me." Incensed by the intrusion and annoyed at the unnecessary disruption to her already overcrowded schedule, Ari turned and strode toward the elevators. Nika fell in silently at her side.

"You don't know what threats might be directed at you," Nika said. "And I would be more than happy to have absolutely nothing to do other than stay by your side for the duration of the assignment."

Ari stabbed the elevator button, admitting her entire reaction was childish, as she'd already accepted Nika's presence. Taking it out on someone who was only doing their job was beneath her. "I appreciate that you have a job to do, and I'm sure you understand why it's problematic for me. So let's agree to make it as pleasant as possible. What do you need from me?"

"An itinerary if you have one, and advance notice as soon as you know of any changes. Public appearances are always the most difficult to secure, so it would be helpful for me to know the agenda in advance."

"I have absolutely no idea what my schedule is going to be," Ari said as they rode down to the lobby. Crossing to the doors to the street, she added, "But if and when I do, I'll be sure that you're advised." She paused on the sidewalk in front of the main entrance. "I actually don't even know where I'm going other than the White House, since that's where Adam's office is. My office."

"Very well. The car is waiting," Nika said, gesturing to a black SUV idling a few feet away.

"What car is that?"

"Yours."

"I don't have a car. I don't use one in the city. I Uber."

Nika smiled, walked over, and opened the rear door. "Not anymore."

With a sigh, Ari climbed in, and after closing the door, Nika went around to the driver's side. So now she had a chauffeur as well as a bodyguard. She didn't even have a pass to get into the White House, and she hoped her ID would be enough. That someone actually knew she was coming. Wouldn't that be just perfect—all dressed up and nowhere to go. On impulse, she texted Oakes Weaver.

Morning. Hope I didn't wake you. Am I going to be able to get in to work this morning?

She wasn't sure what to expect. Oakes could be doing anything right now—sleeping, working, running. Didn't she mention she ran when they were at the diner? Ten seconds later the three little dots appeared in her message window telling her that a text was coming. Ridiculously, her heart raced.

I'll meet you at the west gate and walk you through
Thanks. Sorry to bother
No bother

And that was that. Professional, to the point. And her damn heart still raced.

OEOB, White House Complex
6:35 a.m.

"I'm going down to meet the new campaign manager and escort her to her office," Oakes said, rising from the desk where she'd been watching the closed-circuit television cameras along with the rest of the security shift in the control room.

"You're not on until this afternoon, are you?" Evyn said, walking over with coffee and pastries. "Missed us?"

"No, but with everything going on, I thought I'd come in for the morning push."

"Showing initiative. Going above and beyond." Evyn shook her head. "That's a bad habit to establish. It makes the rest of us look bad."

"Unusual circumstances."

"Uh-huh. So you say."

What it meant was that she didn't have much of a life. True, a hell of a lot had happened between the racquetball game and now. Adam had been killed. She still couldn't wrap her mind around that, and every time she tried, a knot of sadness and anger formed in her chest. She'd have to deal with it somehow, if it didn't just go away on its own. That probably wouldn't happen, but finding out exactly what *had* happened would help. Still waiting on that. Then the rushed flight to Newport, one of the prettiest places she'd ever seen. And Ari Rostof burst on the scene. More beautiful, really, than she'd appeared in media photos. And a whole lot more than that. More—of everything.

"Oakes?" Evyn stood two feet away with the bakery bag in her outstretched hand.

Oakes jolted. "What? Sorry."

"If I didn't know better, I'd say you were daydreaming. But you never do that." Evyn tilted her head, narrowed her eyes. "Do you want a Danish?"

"Oh, no, sorry. I better get down to the gate."

Evyn put her coffee and the Danish down on the counter and walked along beside her. "So, what's she like?"

"Who?"

Evyn huffed. "For crying out loud. Rostof?"

"You must've seen the news briefing yesterday."

"I did. Cool, capable, great television presence."

"Yup."

"And that's not what I'm asking. What's she really like?"

Oakes gave her a look. "That's what she's like."

Heat prickled the back of her neck. Ari was a lot more than that. Thinking about sitting in the diner subtly sorting out their positions, the two of them circling a little bit at first, trying to stake out their territory without actually showing any claws. Nobody peed on the border of their territory. And then, once they'd more or less agreed to where the line was gonna be drawn between who had control of what, for now, relaxing, and just…talking. About things she never talked about with anyone, not even Evyn. Certainly not with the others on her team.

How the hell did she end up talking about the little diner in the mountains? Like who could possibly care about that? But Ari had seemed interested. Maybe even a little envious. That was weird. Especially when thinking about Ari, whose idea of a vacation was some fancy-ass resort in the Berkshires where the hiking trails were probably groomed and the food catered. Okay, that was an exaggeration, and not fair. Maybe she was a bit envious herself. But the facts were indisputable—they couldn't be more different. Her, the child of average middle-class parents, whose family had lived in the foothills of the Blue Ridge Mountains for a hundred and fifty years. And Ari, the daughter of a Russian immigrant who had risen to become one of the most powerful figures in the country. Ari, whose privilege had come at a cost. Somehow Ari'd pried those bars of her gilded cage apart and made her own way. That couldn't have been easy.

"So do you like her, or what?" Evyn said.

"Hmm? Ari? I suppose." Like was an inadequate word for what she felt about her—curious, fascinated, impressed. Definitely impressed.

"Ari is it," Evyn said softly. "You *like* her."

Damn it, she could feel herself blushing. "Cut it out."

"Wow." Evyn's eyes gleamed. "You really do. Is she…you know, available?"

Frowning, Oakes nodded to the security officer standing post at the elevators. "I don't know. How the hell would I know that. And it doesn't matter."

"Okay," Evyn said lightly, as if she meant something totally different. She gave a little wave. "See you at the push."

"Right," Oakes said, stepping into the elevator. Evyn's grin was damned annoying. Probably too much to hope Ari was single. Hell, a woman like her—brains, looks, amazing personality. Just—hell. She had to get her head out of the vapor she'd somehow stumbled into and back in the game. The damn big game she was in.

She glanced at her phone, checking the time, as the elevator settled and the doors swished open. Considering traffic, she ought to make it to the guard post at the west entrance before Ari. She didn't want her to have any trouble there and, just to be sure, picked up her pace.

She'd only been waiting a few minutes when a black SUV pulled up to the gate with Nika Witt at the wheel. That was a surprise but really shouldn't have been. Witt couldn't exactly guard her if she wasn't *with* her. Oakes wondered if Ari enjoyed the personal attention. The idea curdled in her stomach. Nika said something to the uniformed Secret Service agent on duty as Oakes walked over.

"Morning, Sergeant Kovacs," Oakes said.

The guard nodded. "Agent Weaver. Morning."

"Do you have Ms. Rostof on your admit list?" Oakes asked.

"Just checking it now," the officer said, swiping through a tablet.

The rear window rolled down, and Ari looked out. "Hi."

Oakes's stomach did a weird turn, the sour feeling giving way to excitement. "Morning. How did you sleep?"

As soon as she said it, she wanted to take it back. That was stupid and way too personal.

Ari didn't seem to think so, though. She smiled. "A lot better than I expected. You?"

"Uh, good. Fine." She wasn't about to say she'd tossed and turned for a couple of hours, trying to unwind and failing, before she'd finally gotten out of bed, done twenty push-ups, until some of the jitters settled down. Then she'd slept a hard and dreamless sleep. She still wasn't sure what had spiked the restlessness. Not like her at all. Yep. Not mentioning that. "Fine."

"You're clear to enter, Ms. Rostof," the officer said. "But your driver isn't, and you can't bring the car in here anyhow. No parking authorization."

Oakes added, "Leave your personal devices locked in here too. You'll be issued secured electronics via your office."

"Oh, right. Thank you." Ari got out and passed her devices to Nika through the open window. "I'll be inside all morning. You should…go do something touristy or something."

Witt said, "Please text me as needed."

The faint crease between Witt's thick dark brows deepened. Not happy to be excluded. Oakes smiled. "She'll be fine with us."

Nika gave her a long look, eased the windows up, and drove away.

As they walked toward the West Wing entrance, Oakes said, "She's not happy."

"I really wouldn't want to be her." Ari sighed.

"That's charitable of you," Oakes said.

Ari laughed. "Not really. If she were less of a professional, she could spend her days doing something enjoyable, but I know damn well she's going to be within a block of here all day waiting to hear from me. Probably at some Starbucks. That has got to be the most boring thing in the world."

"Any protection service is a lot like that," Oakes said. "A whole lot of standing around, a few minutes of moving from one place to the next, and then more of the same. If you're lucky, that's it. Nobody wants excitement in this line of work because it always means something bad."

"And that's okay?"

Oakes shrugged. "It's the job. Don't worry about her. She'll be fine."

"She was in my apartment last night," Ari said quietly. She wasn't even sure why she volunteered that information, but it bothered her, and…Oakes was a good listener.

Oakes let out a long whistle. "You mean when you weren't there."

Ari gave her a look. "Yes, of course. While we were having coffee."

"So she was checking the place out."

"That's weird, isn't it?"

"Not really. It's her job."

"She wasn't going to tell me."

"I don't have any defense for her," Oakes said slowly. "You're not used to that sort of thing, and it must have seemed like an incredible invasion of privacy."

"It was and it did. But?"

"At the risk of sounding lame, she was doing her job—the one your father hired her to do."

Ari sighed as they went through yet another security checkpoint before entering the West Wing. "You're right. I'll get over it."

"I'm not saying you should like it—or even get used to it. You didn't ask for it, after all."

"Maybe if I thought it was the least bit necessary, I wouldn't mind so much."

Oakes's chest tightened. She didn't even want to consider Ari might need protecting. "Give things a little time to settle down, and maybe you can convince your father you don't need her."

Ari squeezed Oakes's arm. "Thanks. You're right."

Oakes sucked in a breath. Ari had already moved her hand, but every spot her fingers touched tingled. She swallowed around the dust in her throat. "You know where you're going?"

Ari laughed. "No. But I bet someone can point me to the right place."

"I'll take you up."

"You don't have to. I know you've got your own job to do."

She did, and she would do it. Just not right this minute. "I've got time."

Ari smiled. "Then thank you. I owe you for this."

"All right," Oakes said, grinning at Ari's surprised look. "Dinner?"

Laughing, Ari shook her head. "Why not. Can't promise when, but I'll call you, Agent Weaver."

Oakes took that as a win. "Like I said. Anytime. I'm flexible."

Way too soon, they reached the junction between the main hall and a suite of offices.

"This is it."

"Thanks again," Ari said.

"My pleasure." Oakes smiled. "Besides, I scored a…" She almost said *date* and caught herself. Whoa. Talk about a close call. "Dinner."

"You did," Ari said with a warm glow in her eyes that could melt the polar ice cap. "I'll find time—I just can't promise when. You pick the place, my treat."

Oakes wanted to say she'd be happy to wait as long as needed, but that wasn't exactly true. She wanted it to happen yesterday. She took a breath. "That works. Good luck today."

"Thanks," Ari murmured as Oakes turned to head back. "Let's hope luck is the last thing I need."

CHAPTER SIXTEEN

Control Room, OEOB
Washington, DC

Oakes slid into an open seat at the conference table next to Evyn at a minute before seven. Evyn shot her a sidelong glance.

"Package delivered?"

"All set," Oakes said, trying to sound casual. Funny, she didn't feel casual or relaxed. She also didn't feel the way she did before the morning push on a day when she didn't have much to look forward to other than constructing every possible scenario where the president might be at risk and planning a counteroffensive. War games on an uncertain battleground against indistinguishable and unidentifiable adversaries. Tasks guaranteed to give her a headache and night sweats, the closer they got to game day. But right at this moment, none of those sensations registered.

Oddly, her head buzzed and her stomach churned the way it often did when setting out on a tense trip with the principal. No reason for that now. No one was in danger, no one needed her protection, and no threat lurked just beyond her field of vision. None in physical form, at least. Something had her fight-or-flight hormones revving—or someone, she should say. And *who* was no damn mystery. Something about Ari Rostof triggered all her warning bells. Just being around Ari put her on guard, put her on edge, and stirred up the same deep-seated excitement that accompanied the possibility of danger. Ari ignited her sense of uncertainty in a way that felt primitively good. She felt the taunting challenge in the animal part of her brain—come out and play, and catch me if you can. The feeling was exhilarating and dumbfounding.

What the hell was becoming her go-to refrain to self.

"You with us, Weaver?" Tom Turner said.

Oakes jumped. A surreptitious glance at her phone lying on the tabletop showed 7:06. Where had she gone for five minutes? What had she missed?

"Present, sir." Oakes hoped she sounded awake and alert.

"You get any sleep last night?"

Okay, maybe not. She felt heat rise to her cheeks. Every other agent in the room was looking at her curiously. As if sleep was something none of them needed except her.

"Plenty, thank you."

"Then why don't you bring us up to speed on what happened in Newport." He didn't sound disturbed—he sounded exactly as he always did. Calm, in control, and undeniably in charge. "The news briefing was more flash than substance, although impressive considering how quickly they got it together. I'm a lot more interested in what they didn't show us on television, though."

Oakes's throat was dry. What was she supposed to say? That the news briefing went off so well because Ari Rostof was impressive? That she was hard to get out of her head once she came into focus? That she was beautiful and accomplished? Oakes didn't think so. What was it he was actually looking for? Knowing the answer seemed critical, as if a misstep here would send her down a road she definitely did not want to tread. "From what I observed, the First Daughter presented the offer to take over for Adam, without going into detail why the position was open, and with no other explanation at all. After a brief deliberation and a few questions we'd anticipated regarding the upcoming convention, Rostof accepted. Likewise, straightforward and without any probative questions."

"Took it all on face value?" Evyn asked, sounding a bit incredulous.

Oakes almost said *more like on faith*, but held it back. Ari trusted Blair Powell, that much had been clear, and where that trust had come from was something she'd like to know a lot more about. Not because anyone in this room needed to know—she couldn't see how it was need-to-know information—but because *she* wanted to know more about Ari. "My impression was that Ari...Ms. Rostof...concluded that a visit from the president's daughter to extend the offer personally was all the convincing she needed to say yes."

"Patriotism?" Turner asked without a hint of sarcasm.

Oakes hesitated. "I couldn't say, sir. Professionalism, for certain."

Turner nodded. "What about Nikolai Rostof? What was his response?"

Pulse skittering, aware of the footing beneath starting to give way, Oakes replied, "I don't know that there was one, at least, none that I witnessed. And none that impacted Ms. Rostov's decision. She agreed without any consultation with him."

"Interesting," Turner said. "Well, then, for the time being, that avenue is closed."

Oakes didn't needed clarification. Nikolai Rostof was a highly recognizable figure on the political scene and a power broker whose source of power was closely guarded.

Across from her, an agent cleared his throat. "Shouldn't we keep an eye out for, ah, intrusion from that direction? Rostof—the daughter—is going to be exposed to a lot of key intelligence just by virtue of her access and proximity to POTUS. Considering her father's connections, that could be compromising."

Turner regarded him with the same cool expression he always wore. "We are not an investigative division, number one. Number two, Nikolai Rostof is an American citizen who is not under suspicion for anything, and if he was, again, we are not an investigative division. So, McMichael, the answer to your question is no."

"Right, sorry," McMichael said, obviously chagrined.

The slowly tightening rope of tension that had twisted around Oakes's spine relaxed, and she eased back in her chair. If she'd been asked to spy on Ari, she wouldn't have been able to do it. The idea sent her world spinning. She'd never encountered a situation where her duty was at odds with her personal interest. The very idea curdled her stomach.

What the hell? How had the personal even entered into this equation? She should have known Tom wouldn't ask her to do that anyhow, but hearing him say it out loud helped settle the unrest in her midsection.

"Daniels, do you have anything on the follow-up to those reports out of Philadelphia about some kind of pattern they're chasing that suggests a local cell?"

"Not yet," Evyn said. "I contacted this investigator, JT Sloan, who basically said, in not so many words, they were tracking a hunch."

Someone at the end of the table snorted. "Are they using psychics too?"

Evyn smiled, but she didn't laugh. "This team of theirs has an impressive record, and a lot of it is propagated by Sloan's cyberinvestigations. Apparently, she's some kind of genius."

"Yeah," the same agent said, "but a hunch is still a hunch. Probably a waste of time."

"Possibly," Turner said, "but let's keep an eye on those threads they're pulling on." He looked at Oakes. "And that brings us to the question of the day. Where do we stand on the advance?"

"Uh, I..." Oakes had meant to review the reports when she'd gotten in that morning and hadn't had a chance to do that since she'd volunteered to escort Ari to her destination.

Evyn cut in before Oakes could offer a lame excuse. "Since Weaver was out of pocket all day yesterday and not due in until split shift, I pulled all the reports we currently have."

Okay, Oakes thought, *I owe her one* as Evyn summarized where they stood in their planning.

"So," Turner said, "we're pretty much in the same place we were yesterday, with media and the itinerary still in the wind. And now we've got someone brand new in charge of that."

"I did have a chance to review some of the basics with Ms. Rostov last night," Oakes said. "I got the impression she hit the ground running this morning, so we should be getting some info soon."

"Good, because we can't afford any gaps or surprises down the road." Turner rose. "All right, then, we've got the president in Atlanta in a week. Warren, Santos, are we ready?"

"Absolutely," Warren, a petite redhead who made no secret she wanted to step into Turner's shoes when he eventually retired or moved up, said briskly.

They'd all be on their way to Atlanta where the president was stumping for the party's incumbent senator in a tight race. Oakes hated Atlanta. It was hot, buggy, and filled with right-wing nutcases. But what she liked or didn't like didn't matter. She'd be going.

As everyone rose and filed out, Evyn sidled up to Oakes. "Are you okay? You were sweating in there."

"I'm fine."

"There's no problem, is there? With Rostof?"

"What?" Oakes took a second to cool the hot burst of defensive temper. This was Evyn, her friend and, technically, her superior. "No. None."

"Good. So...when exactly did you have time to fill in Ari... oh, excuse me, *Ms. Rostov*...on some of the basics?" Her grin was infuriating.

"It was a long trip back."

"Hey, didn't you fly military to Andrews?"

"Yes."

"So you spent the flight debriefing?"

Oakes gave up. "No, I slept."

"And then..."

"We spent an hour or so in a diner around the corner from Ari's place. Just talking about...work."

"And when were you going to tell me that part?"

"There isn't any *part* to it."

"You're protesting a lot."

"You're bugging me more."

Evyn laughed. "Okay. Whatever you say. Going home for a while?"

"Yeah, probably," Oakes said, although she had some catching up to do on reports first. And she wasn't tired. Wired was more like it. "Let me know what you hear from that Sloan person, huh?"

Suddenly serious, Evyn nodded. "I'm going to do a little bit more digging. I'll let you know if there's anything."

"Thanks," Oakes said. "The last thing we want is to be out of the loop."

As Evyn nodded and walked away, Oakes considered the same was true with media. She needed to know what Ari was planning, and she could only hope nothing conflicted with the best interests of protecting the president.

Ari followed the corridor to a constellation of offices clustered around a central mini-lobby with a scattering of chairs and a few side tables. The carpet was a pleasing blue gray but otherwise industrial wall-to-wall. Must be where visitors, interns, and other staff waited to meet with the campaign staffers. The press secretary, who was responsible for getting out the message Ari and the president agreed on and coordinating meetings and interviews with the press, would have an office somewhere close. For Ari to keep the campaign on track, she'd need a press secretary who could finish her sentences. How in hell was that going to happen under these circumstances, in this amount of time? A question she couldn't answer. She hesitated before the door with Adam Eisley's name on it. It was closed.

"Ms. Rostof." A slender woman in her late thirties, wearing a black skirt with an iron-gray silk shirt and short black heels, came out of a nearby office. She was probably quite beautiful, given her deep brown eyes, sculpted cheekbones, and full expressive mouth, when she wasn't struggling with grief and exhaustion.

"Yes." Ari held out her hand. "Ms. Alaqua?"

"Esmeralda, please." She smiled a little sadly. "I would say welcome aboard, but it somehow just doesn't seem appropriate given... Adam. But I am glad that you're here."

"I understand completely. I'm also glad to be here, but happy isn't quite the word I would use either. Where should I set up camp?"

Esmeralda let out a relieved sigh. "If it's all right with you, I cleared one of the temporary spaces down the hall. Adam didn't have very many personal items in his office, and I'll pack those up as soon as I get a break today. Then, of course, it will be yours."

"There's no rush." Ari hadn't known Adam personally, but the senselessness of his death still moved her. "Is there going to be a service?"

"Not here. His parents are elderly, and he's going to go home when he's released by the coroner."

"I understand that." Ari wanted to ask if there was any further information on the nature of his death, but this woman, steeped in sorrow, was not the one to ask. Maybe Blair, if she got the chance to connect with her. The White House suddenly seemed like a continent all to itself, one vast new world she needed to learn to navigate, and quickly. Oakes would know too, wouldn't she? She could text her to ask. Ari took a breath. What she could do was get on with her job and put Oakes Weaver from her mind. More easily said than done, but she'd managed harder things. "If there's anything that I can help with, please let me know."

"I will."

"Well, then," Ari said briskly. "What's first?"

Again, Esmeralda looked relieved. "I've printed out what would've been Adam's agenda for the next few days. Some meetings with key people are ones that you should take."

"All right. Can you give me notes on who they are, what projects are outstanding with them, and anything that you feel I should know."

"Of course."

"Then I need to speak with the finance director."

"That's Zach Bigelow. He's already called this morning. I'll give you his number."

"Good. Where are we with an official statement from campaign headquarters on Adam's death and my appointment?" She held Esmeralda's gaze as she asked. She didn't have the luxury to ease into her new position, as difficult as it was going to be for everyone.

"I can have something for you within the hour to review and make the morning news."

"Good. Do that. Then you and I need to sit down and review the campaign plan. We can look over what Adam had in mind, but you should probably anticipate changes."

"I understand. Adam was terrific, but he kept an awful lot in his head, and I expect there're going to be gaps."

"Well, we'll make filling them a priority. But I'll have my own game plan."

Esmeralda never hesitated. "Absolutely."

"Do I have an official email address yet?"

"Yes. I'll text it to you. Your electronics have already been loaded with the necessary contacts."

"Perfect."

Ari followed Esmeralda to the temporary office, set up the laptop, and started going through her correspondence. This could not be an easy transition for someone who had known and worked with Adam for so long. She appreciated Esmeralda's professionalism and her openness. One hurdle, and a big one, was over.

An hour later Esmeralda texted her.

The president wishes to see you at 1 pm

Ari read the message several times. She'd expected something like this eventually, but still, it was a jolt. A little bit of a thrill, a little bit of anticipatory nerves in the pit of her stomach, and a lot of pressure. Good thing she thrived on all three.

What do I need to know?

No agenda cited.

As she started to text a reply, a call came through. Her father's number.

Ari stared at the readout and let it go to voice mail.
A minute later another text, this time from him.
Call me We need to talk
And so it began.

Chapter Seventeen

The Oval Office
12:45 p.m.

Blair nodded to the Secret Service agent posted outside in the foyer adjoining the Oval Office and headed for the presidential secretary's desk. Sybil Gretzsky, midforties, trim, stylish, and an absolute commanding general when it came to keeping the president's schedule and protecting his free time, smiled as Blair approached.

"Is he free?" Blair asked.

"Until the one o'clock meeting. I think he's having a sandwich."

"Can I bug him?"

Sybil smiled. "I don't think he would consider you dropping in at any time to be bugging. Go on in."

Her father looked up as she entered, pushed aside a crumpled sandwich wrapper, and wiped his hands on a paper napkin stenciled with a red rooster.

"Are you eating one of those chicken doughnut things again?" Blair asked. Her father managed a fairly regular exercise program of weights and elliptical workouts, and he'd kept in good physical condition, considering the demands of his office, so she was mostly teasing. She had a thing for those evil fried chicken and doughnut sandwiches herself.

He laughed, and when he did, some of the weariness of almost four years in office dropped away. For an instant, she glimpsed the man she'd grown up with. He'd always carried the burden of responsibility for thousands on his shoulders, as he'd been governing in one form or another as long as she could remember. As a child, she'd thought everyone's father had an office in a big, ornate building with spacious, high-ceilinged lobbies, lots of security guards, and people rushing to and fro who looked at her as if she was different than any other child they'd ever seen. An oddity, someone not quite approachable. She *had* been different, and it had taken her forever to figure out why. Eventually she'd understood that people treated her differently not because of anything she'd done or hadn't done, but just because she was her father's daughter. She resented that for a very long time. Maybe until she'd learned to embrace the very uniqueness of being who she was. Cam had never looked away from who she was and had never allowed her to forget it. She'd resented her at first too.

She smiled, thinking how much had changed and how, truly, all that had changed was her.

"What?" Andrew said.

Blair shook her head, stepped around behind the big Lincoln desk that he used, and kissed his cheek. "Nothing. Just remembering."

"Good memories?"

"Yes."

He leaned back in the high-backed leather chair and folded his hands on his stomach, looking as if he had all the time in the world instead of all the world to be concerned with. "So, what did you want to tell me in private?"

Blair laughed and sat down in front of his desk in one of the floral patterned, upholstered chairs. "I'm that obvious, am I?"

"No, but we go back a long ways, and I'm familiar with your habits."

Blair laughed again. "You're in a really good mood today. Any particular reason?" His expression grew solemn for a moment, and her chest tightened. "Is there something wrong?"

"Not exactly. Not at all, really." He sat forward and fidgeted with a pen.

Her father never fidgeted.

"Are you going to tell me, or are you going to make me guess?" She'd seen him in just about every crisis possible—from the death of her mother to a terrorist attack—and she'd never seen him look the least bit unsure of himself. "Dad?"

"It's a secret."

Mentally, Blair rolled her eyes. "You mean, like ninety-nine percent of what goes on in here?"

"More than that."

"Okay. My lips are forever sealed."

"I asked Lucinda to marry me this morning—well, more accurately, last night."

Blair caught her breath, carefully blotting out any mental images of what last night might have entailed between her father and the woman who had been at the center of his professional and personal life for almost two decades. For the first time in a very long while, she couldn't think of a single thing to say.

"You approve?" He sounded anxious.

The air rushed out on something that was very close to a girlish squeal. She jumped up, raced back around the desk, and hugged him. "I so totally approve. It's about fucking time."

"She didn't say so, but I think Lucinda was thinking something along the same lines." The light jumped back into his eyes, and Blair's heart swelled.

"When?" she asked, settling back in her chair.

"After the election. Win or lose."

"Wow." Still a little shocked, Blair blurted, "And what about, you know, her job?"

Andrew winced. "We haven't quite figured that out, but four years as Chief of Staff is practically as wearing as four years of the presidency. She'll likely be ready for a change, and most presidents go through their chiefs of staff a lot faster than I have. So the job description would change, depending on her interests and where I need her most."

"Well, she'd already have a job, after all. First Lady."

"About that…" Andrew said.

"Uh-oh." The picture Blair was forming rapidly morphed into something very different. "That's not really Lucinda, is it?"

"No," Andrew said with a wry smile. "We're thinking that we might not make the marriage public for a while."

"Define a while," Blair said.

"Undetermined at this time. I know it puts a lot of pressure on you, filling in for me so frequently when an official presence is needed."

"It does, true, but I'll do whatever you need me to do. That includes whatever you and Lucinda need."

"Some people will be unhappy when word finally gets out that she isn't filling the prescribed role."

Blair waved a hand. "Let them complain. You won't be breaking any laws. Lucinda has years of political experience and ought to continue to work where she's most effective. You've given up enough for this job, Dad. The public doesn't have the right to know every single thing about your life, and Congress doesn't have the right to dictate your personal life."

"Well, all of this is on a tentative timetable, because if I'm not reelected, most of the issues become moot."

"You're going to be reelected. Number one, because you deserve to be. Number two, because you've got a kick-ass campaign manager who will pretty much take no prisoners when we get to the bloody part."

"It probably will get bloody," Andrew said. "I'll be challenged at the national convention, and if I'm nominated, the election will probably be even more brutal."

Blair shrugged. "You'll have the best team in your corner."

"And what did you want to tell me about Ari Rostof, since I've shared my news."

"What makes you think I'm here about Ari?"

"Educated guess."

"Okay, fair enough. Good guess." Blair paused. "We didn't get a chance to review what went on up in Newport when I got back. I thought you might have questions."

"If there'd been a problem, you would have told me. So…what do I need to know before the meeting today?"

"I think there're going to be quite a few people who aren't happy about her appointment, and some of them are going to be in your ear about it."

"There are always people unhappy about one appointment or another, but her position is not only key, but high-profile. So I expect you're right. Anything I need to be concerned with?"

"No," Blair said immediately. "I don't think any of the issues people might bring up have anything to do with Ari. Her father is the one everyone is really worried about, and whatever he may or may *not* have done, whoever he is beneath the billionaire façade, she's not part of it."

"How can you be sure?"

"Because I've known her since I was fifteen. Ari was sixteen when we met. I saw her struggle back then to stretch the ties between them, to make room for her own ambitions, and I've seen how she's constructed her life since then. If he had been what a lot of people think, I believe she would've broken the ties."

"That's not an easy thing to do for family," he observed neutrally.

"I know, but I trust her integrity. And her judgment. If I didn't, I never would've suggested her. So all I want is for you to trust me, give her a chance, and let her guide you."

"Well, that's easy," Andrew said. "I've always trusted you. You and Lucinda are the two smartest people I know. Well, three now, considering your wife. Who's just downright scary."

Cam. Scary? Oh yes, scary amazing. Blair smiled at her father. "Isn't she just."

Cameron Roberts walked into the control room and every eye turned in her direction.

"Afternoon," she said to the agents working shift. "Tom around?"

"In the conference room," Warren said.

"Thanks."

She went down the hall and knocked on the open door. Tom, Oakes Weaver, and Evyn Daniels were leaning over the conference table, looking at an old-fashioned paper map spread out on the tabletop. "Got a minute?"

Tom looked over. "Morning, Commander. Need to see me?"

"You can all stay," Cam said, walking in and surveying the map. "I didn't even think they made those things anymore."

"This is the first time I've ever seen one," Oakes said. "It's like something from the prehistoric age."

Tom snorted. "Bullshit. The digital feed in here is down, and I wanted to look at motorcade routes. Besides, what's wrong with looking at an honest to God map instead of a projection?"

"You know you can do that on your iPads," Cam said.

"Not the same thing. You can't run your finger over it like you can with this." Tom tapped the map.

Cam studied the four alternative routes from Philadelphia International Airport into the city, marked in black. Running out from each one were crisscrosses of red lines, connecting the motorcade path to hotels, hospitals, safe houses, and emergency exit routes from the city.

"You settle on the main yet?" Cam asked.

Tom tapped one black line that traveled more or less directly from the airport into Center City Philadelphia. "This would be the anticipated route, so we're going to use this one"—he moved his finger—"which is a little bit longer but is actually the one preferred by Philadelphia police. Doesn't snarl the traffic quite as badly." He shook his head. "Center City Philadelphia is a nightmare of streets no bigger than alleys—hell, some of those streets are barely wide enough for a horse and buggy."

"That's because they were built over two hundred years ago for horses and buggies, remember," Cam said.

"I don't know, I'm from Dallas where the streets are actually wide enough to accommodate modern cars."

"You're not gonna get the Beast through some of these streets," Cam said. "I guess you'll find that out when you run the routes during the advance."

Oakes said, "We've done that. We've identified the chokepoints around the Convention Center and mapped out ways around. Once the perimeter is set and barricaded, we'll sail right in."

Cam smiled. "You're going to get some scratches on it."

"The motor pool can complain about that when we get back." Oakes grinned.

Tom straightened. "What can we do for you, Commander?"

"I just got off the phone with Metro. They pulled some videos from witnesses—a whole bunch of tourists happened to be watching and taking pics of what they mistakenly thought was the president's motorcade going by. Several caught the accident on their phones."

Tom's expression flattened. "And?"

"They're still analyzing what they've got, comparing different angles of view, running time stamps, estimating vehicular speeds—the usual forensic accident stuff. None of the videos are great quality, but the techs are confident in what they have so far." Cam paused. These people had known Adam. His death was personal and the news would be too. "The vehicle that struck Adam accelerated rather than braked as it got closer to him. From the direction it was traveling, no attempt was made to avoid him."

"Son of a bitch," Oakes muttered. She looked around quickly. "Sorry, sir."

"My feelings exactly, Weaver," Tom said. "Conclusive? Not just some distracted driver gawking at the rotunda or something?"

"No indication from the vehicle travel pattern that the driver was impaired. The reading is intentional."

"Anything from the license plate?" Evyn asked.

"They've got a nice clear shot in one video, but the plates belong to a Lexus that was left in the parking lot at Reagan National. They traced the owner of that vehicle, who's currently in Barbados."

"And of course, they're not a suspect."

Cam shook her head. "The FBI is running them, but they're a retired couple—both schoolteachers, longtime Georgetown residents. No political connections."

"Well that makes it pretty sure this was no accident. But why?" Tom said. "Adam Eisley. Why him?"

"A few possible reasons," Cam said. "He was a relatively easy target—his habits were fairly regular, the route he ran was one of only two. He's close to the president and important—no, critical at this juncture—to his reelection efforts. Maybe someone thought taking him out of the picture would be enough to disrupt the campaign, destabilize the forward momentum. There's the outside possibility Adam was into something we don't even know about. Something that would make him a target."

"No," Oakes said quickly. "Not Adam. I know him. He is—was—exactly as he seemed to be. He wouldn't be into anything illegal or disloyal."

"I agree with you," Cam said, "but the FBI will be looking into it regardless."

"So currently we have no suspects," Tom said.

"No, and it's possible—probable—that the driver and those behind the attack will remain undetected."

Oakes's gut clenched. Adam might have been nothing more than a pawn—and his killers would likely go free. Crimes like that happened every day and often were only solved by luck. As a federal agent, she understood that. As his friend, she raged.

After a few seconds, Oakes set aside the personal feelings that had no place here, as Cam continued, "But what we *do* have appears to be a well-organized and successfully executed attack on someone who is often in the immediate vicinity of the president. Adam was an insider. I wanted you to know right away."

"You think there's a chance of a repeat on someone else close to the president?" Oakes asked.

"Impossible to tell." Cam didn't need to voice the unspoken. Every person in the room was aware that her wife was often in the kill zone, the area right around the president where any assassination attempt was likely to incur casualties. These agents were paid to stand in that zone. Blair did it out of love and duty. The only way to keep all of them safe was to see that any threat to the president, no matter how remote or impossible-seeming, was neutralized. She trusted the agents on this detail with far more than the security of an office. She trusted them with the most important person in her life.

Chapter Eighteen

Philadelphia
Game Day minus 35 days
9:17 p.m.

Five minutes into the second half of an evening of Vivaldi presented by the Philadelphia Orchestra, Rebecca's phone vibrated in her pants pocket. Trying to be as unobtrusive as possible, she slid it out and shielded the screen with her hand. Beside her, Catherine was raptly immersed in the visiting conductor's interpretation of "Summer" from *The Four Seasons*, her favorite concerto by one of her favorite composers. Rebecca's tastes ran more to rhythm and blues, but any evening spent with Catherine was a pleasure. And Catherine's pleasure was always hers. Too often, the evening ended the way she was concerned this one might.

Hey whatcha doin

Sandy's code for *call me*. When Sandy or Dell was working the streets, they always carried burner phones that could not be traced and never used any official lines of communication. Or uncoded messages.

Rebecca leaned close and whispered, "I have to take this call."

Still watching the first violinist, Catherine slid her hand onto Rebecca's thigh and squeezed. "I know. Text me if you're leaving."

"I will. I love you."

Catherine smile, as always, lit her world. "I know. Go."

Muttering apologies to half a dozen patrons—why were they always in the middle seats anyhow—Rebecca made it into the aisle and out to the lobby. She hit the call icon above Sandy's message and waited.

"Hey," Sandy said, her voice a whisper. "Trish invited me back to her place. Not sure exactly what the plans are or location, but we're leaving any minute."

"Do you have any backup?"

"No. I wasn't planning on hitting the Oasis tonight, didn't want to push too hard and make them suspicious, but Trish texted me to meet her. It all went down fast."

"What about Dell?"

"Uh. She's got a meet with the Diablos tonight. Something about that gun deal."

"Can you stall until I can get Watts or McCurdy over there?"

"I don't think so. I'm in the bathroom and Trish is waiting. I don't want to lose this. There's something not right about these two, but I can't figure it."

"Leave your phone open," Rebecca said. "I'm ten minutes from you. I'm on my way."

"Thanks, Loo."

Leaving the call open, Rebecca switched screens to text Catherine.

Have to go love you

She didn't expect an answer. Catherine would stay, enjoy the concert, and take an Uber home. They'd done this before. Too many times, but she'd stopped apologizing. The first year they were together, she'd apologized every time she'd canceled a dinner date, run out halfway through a movie, or never showed at all for an evening with friends. For a long while, she'd wondered—and worried—just how long Catherine would tolerate being shunted aside. Catherine, being Catherine, called her on it before six months had passed.

"Every time you say you're sorry," Catherine said as Rebecca headed for the door one night, "you insult me."

"What?" Rebecca stopped short. "How?"

Catherine put her arms around Rebecca's neck and looked into her eyes. "I fell in love with a cop, eyes wide open. Every time you have to *be* a cop at a less than convenient time and then apologize, you're saying I was either naïve or self-deluding."

"What?" Rebecca repeated, even more astounded. "I'm just sorry I have to disappoint you!"

"I *am* a little disappointed our plans were disrupted, but I imagine you are too."

"Well, yeah."

"Then there's no need to apologize." Catherine had kissed her and shoved her gently toward the door. "Go be a cop, Rebecca. I love you."

Rebecca had laughed at the time, but she hadn't forgotten it. She still said she was sorry from time to time, but she'd learned the better words were *I love you*.

Bounding down the wide marble stairs to the street, she signaled the valet with her badge in one hand, handed him her tag, and said, "Police business. Make it fast."

"Yes, ma'am," he snapped. Spinning around, he trotted away.

The valet parking lot was just around the corner, and three minutes later, she jumped into Catherine's Audi, slapped the emergency light she kept on the floor in the back onto the dash, and headed downtown. Her phone was open on the seat beside her, the speaker icon glowing.

"So, you want to finish your drink?" Sandy said. "I could use another."

"No, I'm done with it. He waters them anyways."

Sandy snorted. "They all do that."

"We got stuff at the apartment. You got a ride?"

"No," Sandy said. "I was with some friends when you tagged me. I left them and my ride behind. Cabbed over here. You?"

"Yeah, we're across the river, so I got to drive."

"Cool. In Camden, you mean?"

"Yeah. Crappy neighborhood, but the view's not bad." She laughed, and it didn't sound like she found it all that funny. "If you like looking at boats and the ass end of Philadelphia."

"So what's the deal?" Sandy's voice was muffled by the white noise inside the bar for a few seconds, but then the background sounds dropped away. "Man, this weather sucks. I'm gonna freeze my tits off out here. Where's your car?"

They'd left the Oasis.

"Just around the corner on Arch." Trish laughed. "I think your tits will survive the walk."

Rebecca cut around a backup on Nineteenth that wasn't going to unlock whether she had lights flashing or not. No place on the narrow street for people to move over. She was still a few minutes away from the Oasis.

"So, about this thing at your place," Sandy said. "Are we looking at sex? Because, you know, I'm into you, but—"

"Not Ma—Mark. I have to practically strip naked and start doing myself before he even notices."

Sandy laughed. "So maybe we should find Mitch, have him go along. Might be more Mark's thing."

Trish snorted. "You know, Mitch's hot. You think he'd fuck Mark?"

"Hey, his deal's his deal. You'd have to ask him."

"Kinda like to see that." A car alarm beeped, and a door opened and closed. "I don't think Mark would be into it, though."

"Too bad," Sandy said. "So, is there a party?"

"No, there's a meeting."

"Okay, that's weird." Sandy laughed.

"Some friends of Matt's." Trish huffed. "Stupid name thing—like it matters. Anyhow, you'll like these dudes. There's a couple hot chicks, 'cause you kinda swing that way mostly, don't you?"

"Well, if I had my choice, I'd rather you than him."

"Yeah, I wish that did it for me. But anyhow, they're people Matt knows from the rally."

"Oh," Sandy said. "That's cool, then. I really dug that speaker. And like I said—makes so much sense, you know?"

"Yeah," Trish said, not sounding all that enthusiastic.

"So, this is a nice ride," Sandy said. "I dig muscle cars, especially red ones like this."

"It's got flash. It's probably the only thing about him that's flashy."

"Well, every Corvette is flashy."

Rebecca smiled to herself as Sandy ID'd the car for her. Only a couple of bridges crossed the Delaware River into Camden, and from the Oasis, the Ben Franklin was the closest. Hoping to pick them up before they crossed, Rebecca changed course away from the Oasis on Arch, swung down Vine, and took a chance that she'd hit the intersection to the bridge before they did. She was almost to the approach lane when a red Corvette shot up onto the bridge. She fell into line three cars behind with a buzzing in her stomach. Her animal instincts had kicked in, the sharp focus of the predator that had spied its prey. She had the target in sight, and a surge of adrenaline laced with hunger and anticipation shot through her. She only wished she wasn't using one of her people as the bait.

❖

Atlanta, Georgia
12:59 a.m.

Oakes slid onto a stool next to Ari in the Marriott bar. A throng of Braves fans crowded around the opposite end, boisterous and already in their pregame lubricated state.

"Evening," she said to Ari. "Mind company?"

"Hi. Not at all." Ari smiled and tilted her head toward the group at the far end of the bar. "As long as you promise not to talk about baseball stats."

"I don't think we'll be able to avoid that. Big doubleheader tomorrow." When the bartender approached, Oakes added, "Scotch on the rocks. Glenlivet if you've got it."

He rolled his eyes. "Full-service here, Mac."

"Feels like a big doubleheader to me too," Ari said.

"You mean the president's first big trip with you running the show?"

"I'm not exactly sure I'm running the show, not even close," Ari said, swirling the surprisingly good white burgundy in her glass. She wasn't naïve enough to think she could control anything on the president's schedule. Her job was to analyze polls, take the temperature of the electorate, read where the media was headed in term of the next big story, and *suggest* a path through all that for the president that would put him and his message in front of as many people as possible in the best light possible. "I recommend, the president decides."

"Yep, that's the way it goes." Oakes sipped the scotch. Smoky and smooth. Nice. "I thought you'd be riding down on Air Force One this weekend. That'd be your first trip, right?"

"I wanted to meet with a couple of the producers down here before he arrived. I'm still playing catch-up."

"Well, considering it's only been a week, I'm not surprised. How's it going?" Oakes had seen Ari passing in the halls in the West Wing during the past week, when she'd been standing post and unable to have a conversation. Ari had looked busy, but not frazzled. But then, she suspected Ari never looked frazzled. She had earned a smile and a nod from Ari each time, and oddly, that had felt like a reward.

"I did tell you to ask me in ten days. Time is not up yet," Ari said with a bit of a tease.

Oakes laughed. "I always have been one to get in ahead of a deadline if I could."

"Hmm. Impatient?" Ari swiveled on her stool to face Oakes, her eyes alight with amusement. She'd been working nonstop, eighteen hours a day, for a week and this was the first moment she'd had to relax. Her earlier vision of a drink and a long warm shower before curling up with a book vanished the instant Oakes appeared. She was remarkably awake all of a sudden. "Or just competitive? First one in with your homework, first in line for a lab bench in chem lab?"

Oakes shook her head. "Never took chemistry. I was a history major."

Ari murmured, "Okay, you surprised me again."

"Me? I can't imagine very much about me that's surprising," Oakes said.

"Oh, you'd be surprised. But don't change the subject. How did you go from history to law enforcement?"

Oakes was glad for the low lighting in the bar. She was blushing. She'd opened the door to talking about herself, hadn't she. That happened every time she and Ari talked. The weird thing was, she didn't mind. Too much. "Okay. Well, I guess it started when I heard Obama speak at a town meeting. I was a junior in college. I suddenly realized that I didn't want to study the things that had already happened—I wanted to be part of what was happening."

"And you made a right-angle turn into law enforcement."

"Well, not exactly," Oakes said. "More into history, living history."

Ari was silent for a long moment, and Oakes started to feel foolish. She'd just said that, right? Jeez, if she'd made that comment to any of her team, they'd laugh their asses off. Maybe that's why she kept a lot of things to herself.

"Are you trying to tell me that you're a Secret Service agent because you wanted to be close to the person most likely to be making history?"

"You make it sound kind of creepy," Oakes muttered.

"I'm sorry. I didn't mean it that way at all." Ari put her hand on Oakes's arm where it rested on the top of the bar.

"No worries," Oakes said, distracted by Ari's hand. It was damn hot in Atlanta and she was off duty, wearing a polo shirt, one of her go-to shirts when she was dressing down, and her arm was bare. Ari's fingers were cool on her very hot skin.

"It's fascinating, that's all," Ari went on, seemingly oblivious to the fire kindling beneath her fingertips. "That you didn't become a Secret Service agent because you wanted to be a supercop or something."

Oakes laughed. "Well, don't ever say that out loud around anyone on the detail. We're not cops. We're big bad federal agents. There's no one like us."

"Of course. Forgive me. How foolish of me. Okay, I'm still trying to figure out why the Secret Service?"

"When I started, all I knew is what I *didn't* want to be."

"Mm-hmm. And?" Ari said, leaning closer.

The noise level from the sports crowd had picked up. That had to be the reason Ari leaned closer. So close their shoulders touched. The scent of Ari's perfume—dark blossoms and spice—made Oakes's head swim for a second. She took a deep breath and tugged at the open collar of her polo. Damn, it was hot in Atlanta. "Didn't want to be behind a desk. I hate computers pretty much, and I like to travel. FBI is mostly in country, CIA is too cloak-and-dagger for me, and the Foreign Service is mostly diplomatic postings. Not my style. So that left joining the military or the Secret Service."

"I can't quite see you in the military, although in uniform—" Ari broke off abruptly.

"Are you one of those women that goes for people in uniform?"

"I can't say I wouldn't give a *woman* in uniform a second look," Ari said.

The tension in Oakes's belly that had been coiling tighter and tighter as they'd talked ratcheted up a notch. That answered one really important question. And Ari's hand was still on her arm. Oakes finished her scotch in one big gulp. "What are you drinking?"

"Wine. I've still got some left," Ari said. "And a big meeting tomorrow at eight, so I think I'll stick to one. But by all means, go ahead."

"Two's my limit," Oakes said. She'd never been much of a drinker, and despite the propensity for her and her colleagues to unwind after a big event with a lot of steam being let off around a bar, she managed to keep it to that almost all the time. When the bartender looked her way, she tipped her glass in his direction and said, "A short one."

"So you're saying logic brought you around to the Secret Service?" Ari said after the bartender topped off Oakes's glass.

"Never looked at it quite that way, but I suppose so. I thought about the things that I was good at. I like physical things, I like order, I'm pretty good on a team—I was pretty much into sports in high school and college—and I wanted to do something meaningful with my life."

"Not an overwhelming sense of duty and patriotism?"

Oakes flushed. Ari sounded serious, so she answered that way. "Maybe a little bit of that too."

"Can I ask you something personal?" Ari asked.

Oakes snorted. "Ah, isn't that what you've been doing?"

"I guess," Ari said contemplatively, "but this one seems more so."

"Okay, you ask, and I'll tell you if you're treading somewhere off-limits."

"When you considered your job, did you consider that it might cost your life?"

"That's not a rare question," Oakes said. "And the answer is, we don't think about it. It's part of the job. We're trained to react to danger in a certain way, to respond with action, to run toward the burning building, and not away. You don't think about all the rest of it."

"Okay," Ari said. "It takes a certain kind of person who's willing to do that."

"That's why not everyone does it."

"Yes, I get the part where special comes in."

The slow, deep warmth in Ari's voice hit hard in the pit of Oakes's stomach. She wasn't just hot any longer, she was freaking blazing. She wasn't even close to drunk, but her head reeled and she wanted to forget about being smart. She wanted to cross those last few inches and kiss Ari Rostof more than she'd ever wanted anything or anyone in her life. Fucking Atlanta always made her nuts.

"What about you," Oakes said before she lost the last little bit of her mind. "How did you end up doing what you're doing?"

"A little bit the same way you did. I discovered that I'm good at organization. And political consultation is nothing if it's not about organizing—organizing people to do certain work, gathering data and sorting through opinions and then organizing a message. It's about getting other people to do what you want."

"Somehow, I bet you'd be good at that." Oakes was pretty sure Ari could get people to do anything, just by looking at them the way she looked at Oakes right now. As if Oakes was the only person in the room.

"In high school, and then in college, I found myself heading lots of different committees, and it occurred to me that that happened because I was able to synthesize the opinions of others and come up with a message that people would agree to. Or buy in to."

"Yeah, that sounds like politics."

"Mm. True." Ari smiled as if she was laughing at herself. "I also discovered that I liked it. It's satisfying. I guess it's my way of imposing order on chaos."

"You could've done that in the network newsroom. I imagine a job was waiting for you."

For an instant, Ari's face shuttered closed. "There was a lot waiting for me, but none of it was what I chose."

"Sorry, if I stepped over the line there," Oakes said, sipping at the scotch she wasn't actually interested in finishing. The last thing she wanted was to cloud her head any more than it already was. Ari was much too interesting to miss anything.

"That's all right, you didn't. It's natural to ask." Ari finished her wine and pushed the empty glass across the bar. "While it was made very clear to me what my father's aspirations for me were, he never strong-armed me in that direction. He's resilient. That's why he's so successful. When I changed course, so did he. At least, in his expectations."

"It sounds like he raised a daughter in his own image, at least in terms of being independent and determined," Oakes said.

"Thank you." Ari shook her head. "I'm not sure he would've been all that happy had he known that was happening."

"Well, it's clear he doesn't give up easily. I see that Witt is still with you." Oakes had seen her as soon as she'd walked in, sitting alone at a two-top with a view of the entrance as well as the bar. Typical positioning for someone doing what she was doing, which was watching Ari.

"Yes, she has the remarkably boring job of watching me talk on the telephone a great part of the day, waiting around while I have meetings with TV producers and reporters, hold staff meetings, and have a nightcap at a hotel bar. A horrible job, really."

"You eat dinner together?" The idea of the two of them spending their off time together made the hair on the back of Oakes's neck stand up.

"What? With Nika? No." Ari's brow quirked. "Most of the time I eat all my meals at my desk. Nika and I are cordial but not friendly. We're not *friends*. I have no idea how she doesn't absolutely lose her mind doing this work."

"You get really good at talking to yourself," Oakes said.

"You must," Ari said. "Speaking of your work. What are you doing until Saturday? Or am I not allowed to ask?"

Oakes grinned. "I'll be standing post on the hotel floor where the president is staying until he arrives. And anything else the advance team leader needs me to do."

"Okay, that sounds boring."

"Well, considering the floor has been completely cleared so there are no guests, I won't be seeing much of anything, hopefully. If I did, then I'd have some work to do."

Ari's face suddenly grew solemn. "I didn't mean to make light of what you do. I'm sorry."

"Hey," Oakes said quickly. "I wasn't bothered. And you're right. It's going to be boring."

"Perhaps I can buy you dinner tomorrow night. That is, if you're not working then."

Oakes's pulse did a little jitter, which did nothing to the lightness in her head or the want churning in her depths. "I've got the day shift tomorrow. I'll be done at four."

"Shall we say seven?" Ari asked.

"Sounds perfect," Oakes said.

CHAPTER NINETEEN

Washington, DC
Game Day minus 35 days
11:05 p.m.

The only light in the bedroom came from the digital clock on the bedside table, a faintly eerie red glow. The only sound was…the silence of wakefulness. Cam slid her arm around Blair's shoulders and tugged her close. "You're not sleeping."

Blair sighed and nestled her cheek on Cam's shoulder. "Sorry. I'm keeping you awake."

"No, you aren't. I was sleeping, but I could hear you thinking in my dreams."

Blair laughed and ran her hand down the center of Cam's body, letting it rest on her abdomen. "That's a very scary thought, you know. I don't think I should be invading your innermost private places."

"Oh, I don't know. I live in hope."

Blair nipped at her throat. "Careful what you wish for."

"Only you, baby."

Smiling, Blair closed her eyes. She wasn't having much success shutting off her brain, and she obviously hadn't managed not to disturb Cam either. Since they were both awake now, no point struggling in silence. "I keep thinking about my father and Lucinda."

"Not in graphic detail, I hope."

"God," Blair said, "absolutely not."

Cam kissed the top of Blair's head and massaged the tight muscles in Blair's shoulders. After a few moments, the kinks slowly began to relax, but Blair's body still radiated tension. Something important had to be going on to keep Blair awake. Blair was not a worrier. She lived very much in the present and dealt with whatever came along *as* it came along. The only event she worried about in advance was the danger of Cam's job, and they'd both learned to live with that. "What's bothering you?"

"Not bothered so much, just worried a little."

"About?"

"All my life, the father I've known has belonged more to the public, to the people, than to any one person. Maybe even to himself. I think I might be jealous that's changing."

"You mean that Lucinda has a special place in his life?"

"Mostly that he's willing to change his life for her."

And not for me went unspoken, but Cam heard it all the same.

"I can see how that would bother you," Cam said.

Blair sighed. "Selfish, isn't it."

"No, it's natural. He's your father, and that makes him one of the most important people in your life."

"Yes, but I shouldn't be jealous that he has fallen in love, that he's happy. Really, I'm not twelve anymore."

"No," Cam said gently, "but when you were twelve, everything changed, and you didn't have anything to say about it. You lost one of the most important people in your life, and that left a hole that at twelve was enormous and never gets completely filled, no matter how old you are."

"I am such an idiot," Blair murmured.

Cam frowned. "Okay, that's a non sequitur."

Blair raised up on her elbow, her face a flickering canvas of light and dark in the dim illumination. So beautiful, Cam's heart stopped for a second.

"When you were twelve," Blair said, "you lost someone special too. Horribly, with no chance to prepare. And what did you do about it? You turned what could have been a life of anger and bitterness into one of meaning. You became this incredibly brave, strong, determined person who is willing to sacrifice for other people."

"I love that you see me that way," Cam said, "but that's not why I do what I do." She had secret places, places she feared might tarnish Blair's image of her, but for Blair, she would always choose truth. "I don't think I consciously chose to be brave or admirable. I wasn't brave that day, and some part of me is always trying to make up for that failure. Maybe even punish myself for it."

"And risking your life for others is part of the punishment?" Blair said.

"I don't think of it that way, but it does help me balance the scales somehow."

"You can call it whatever you like," Blair said, "but I know who you are. And I love you for it."

"I know, and that is what I count on every day." Cam tightened her hold. "And I think you should give yourself a chance to adjust to Andrew's news. By the time they're married, chances are you'll feel a lot differently."

"You're right. We have to get through the next six months first." Blair let out a long breath. "I don't ever remember the other campaigns being this crazy. It's like a sharkfest, with loyalties changing every day."

"The climate in the country has changed," Cam said. "Even the parties have fractured, so allegiances are constantly shifting."

"And we're looking at nonstop campaigning from now until the convention," Blair grumbled. "I just *love* living out of my suitcase in one hotel after another."

"I don't suppose you'd consider cutting back on some of—"

"You know I can't. And I don't want to. One thing I'm absolutely sure of—my father is the best person for the job."

"Then we'll just pack a really big suitcase," Cam said.

"Well, there is one good thing about being on the campaign trail," Blair said.

"What's that?"

Blair kissed her. "I really like hotel sex."

"Do we have to wait for Atlanta?"

Laughing, Blair slid on top of her. "Well, since I'm awake…"

Camden

After trailing the Corvette off the bridge into Camden, Rebecca dropped back on the nearly empty streets until Trish turned onto Front Street, a narrow street running parallel to the waterfront. The area had once been a working-class neighborhood of families living in identical row houses with stoops lined up along the sidewalks like gapped teeth, and tiny backyards barely big enough for the clotheslines strung between the porches and telephone poles. Now the factories that had sustained those families were closed, and the port activity had shifted across the river to Philadelphia. The neighborhoods deteriorated, drugs and crime—the byproducts of poverty—rose, and urban decay spread through the streets like a blight.

Rebecca eased around the corner and saw the Corvette pull into a parking place half a block away. Keeping a steady pace, she drove by as Trish and Sandy got out, and mentally marked the building they entered as she watched in her rearview mirror. On her second pass around the block, she noted the number, fortunately illuminated by a nearby streetlight, and proceeded to park where she'd have a view of the front entrance.

With her phone still open to Sandy's call, she texted Sloan.

Need a rundown occupants 332 Front St Camden. Alert Watts and McCurdy. May need backup that address

Sloan would be up. She almost always was. Sure enough, ten seconds later her screen lit up.

Copy that

Undercover work took a wild love of risk and an uncanny instinct for reading danger signs. Sandy had both. Rebecca settled back behind the wheel to watch and listen.

"Hey," Sandy said, slipping into a narrow space on the sofa, already crowded with two guys and a girl. The girl was next to her, twentysomething, long straight flyaway red hair, faded jeans with holes in the knees, scoop-neck white T-shirt with a black swirly design, and strappy sandals too cool for the weather.

"Hey," the girl said, shooting a quick look in her direction. "I'm Ireland."

"Elle," Sandy said, scanning the rest of the living room where Trish had guided her. From what she could make out on the quick trip from the bland gray metal security door and the dank hall outside the second-floor flat, the place had one bedroom, a galley kitchen, and a bathroom in addition to this ten by fifteen room with a pair of windows facing the river. The space was crowded with more guys than girls, seven not counting Trish and the guy who called himself Mark but whose name was obviously Matt. A few people had beers, and a screw-top gallon bottle of cheap white wine sat in the middle of a fake walnut coffee table. Definitely not a party.

"So, Ireland," Sandy murmured, sliding her phone out and slipping it into her lap so the lieutenant would hear their whispers, "what's going on?"

"First time?" asked the girl who almost certainly hadn't been christened Ireland.

"Yeah, pretty much. I hooked up with Trish and…Matt from the rally, you know." Sandy took a chance, hoping she was headed in the right direction, and embellished a little. Maybe more than a little, considering she had zero idea what all these people were about. She was really just following her intuition, and if she was way off base, what's the worst that could happen? No way was anybody going to do anything other than toss her out with this many witnesses. The trick to creating a background in this situation was to connect the dots for everyone else before they realized there were gaps in the outline. "I have been into things for a while. I just couldn't find the right place, the right people. You know what I mean?"

"That's because most people talk the talk, but that's as far as it goes."

Sandy got the buzz then, that instinctive thrill telling her she was on the right trail. "That's *totally* it. I tagged into a couple groups online, you know, but that's all you ever get. Just a lot of words."

Ireland shifted until her eyes met Sandy's and she looked at her for a long, silent moment. Sandy had been scrutinized by a lot tougher people than this girl, who looked like she'd never gone hungry a day in her life, and let her look. People only saw what she wanted them to see. And right now, Ireland would see someone a little bit naïve, a lot eager, and tough enough to play in the big leagues. That was all good, because Sandy had one of those feelings that this might be a bigger game than anyone suspected, and she intended to have a front row seat.

"This is my floor," Ari said, as the elevator door opened on three. Oakes had pushed five. Hurrying before the doors began their inevitable cycle to close, she said, "I've got coffee, seltzer, and an unopened bottle of red in my room…if you're not quite ready for bed."

Oakes reached above Ari's head and held the door open with her arm. The hall beyond, like the elevator they'd rode up in, was empty except for them. Ari's back was against the open door, and Oakes was very close. So close she could count her eyelashes, if she hadn't been so absorbed in her mouth. Her very sexy, full, kissable mouth. Ari blinked.

"I appreciate the offer," Oakes said. "But—"

"Right," Ari said quickly. "I forgot you have the early shift tomorrow." She laughed. "And I've got an eight o'clock meeting."

"That's not what I was about to say."

No parts of their bodies touched, but every cell in Ari's vibrated. The inch of space between them tingled with charged electricity, like the heavy ozone-laden air right before a storm broke free and lashed the earth with spears of lightning. "Sorry, didn't mean to interrupt."

"The problem is," Oakes murmured, "I *am* ready for bed."

Ari started to smile. Oakes's mouth got in the way. The kiss was one hundred percent Oakes. Confident, skillful, and challenging. Oakes's mouth slanted to cover hers completely, the tip of her tongue teasing at the seam of Ari's mouth until she opened for her. And then, when she'd expected—*wanted*—Oakes to explore, she'd disappeared with just a flicker of sensation over the surface of her lower lip. Teasing her, *toying* with her. Oh no—not so fast.

Ari grabbed a handful of Oakes's cotton polo shirt, twisted it in her grip, and pushed her way deeper into Oakes's mouth. If Oakes wouldn't give when she'd obviously offered, she'd take. God, she tasted good.

Oakes grunted, sounding surprised and every bit as ready as Ari. She slid an arm around Ari's waist and kissed her back, probing and demanding. Heat flared and tension coiled just below Ari's rib cage, forcing the breath from her body.

As abruptly as she had begun, Oakes drew back. "Cameras."

"Of course," Ari said, working to catch her breath. "Your people?"

Oakes shook her head. "Not on this floor. Just routine security and probably no one's actually monitoring, but"—she drew her finger along the edge of Ari's jaw, brushed her thumb over Ari's lower lip—"this is personal. Private."

"Yes, it is." Especially given she'd been about to reach under Oakes's shirt.

"Not out of line, then?" Oakes murmured.

Ari shook her head, releasing the grip she had on Oakes's polo shirt and smoothing out the wrinkles with her fingertips. "Most definitely not. After all, I made the first move."

Oakes grinned. "You did."

"So," Ari said, trying for cool but aware her voice was shaking, "dinner, then? Tomorrow."

"Seven. I'll be there. Wait—where?"

"I'll text you."

Oakes nodded and backed into the elevator.

Ari stepped out and watched Oakes as the doors slowly slid closed. She'd known what she was offering when she'd invited Oakes back to her room. That wasn't at all her typical style, but then nothing about the way Oakley Weaver made her feel was usual.

Oakes exited on the fifth floor, her heart still pounding. She hadn't meant to do that, but she was damn glad she did. She been wanting to kiss Ari Rostof since the first time she'd seen her. Before she'd even known her. Just being in the same space with her, buffeted by her energy, bombarded by the intensity that radiated from her with every word and every movement, that was a storm that had put her on edge. Now that edge was honed to blade sharpness.

Blood still humming, she let herself into the room she was sharing with Evyn and tiptoed in the dark toward the bed.

"Didn't expect to see you tonight," Evyn said from the darkness.

"Why?"

"You didn't notice me downstairs in the bar. You were too busy with Ari Rostof."

"Just having a drink and a friendly conversation." Oakes shed her clothes in a pile on the floor and flopped down on the other double bed.

"Uh-huh. I'll bet. Did you kiss her?"

"Shut up, Daniels."

Evyn laughed and Oakes could imagine the know-it-all grin. "Yup, you kissed her."

Oakes smiled to herself. Yes, she'd kissed her. And she couldn't wait for the next time.

The message light was flashing on the bedside phone when Ari got into her room. She called down for the message and got transferred to voice mail.

"You're avoiding my texts," her father said. "I'll expect you for breakfast, say, seven in the hotel dining room? You should have plenty of time to make it to your eight o'clock meeting."

The message ended there, and Ari put the phone down. She didn't have to think too hard to put the pieces together. Witt knew her schedule, and if Witt did, her father did too. Hell, he probably knew she'd been having a drink with Oakes not an hour earlier. Since Witt had the good sense not to follow them up in the elevator, he didn't know about the kiss. She couldn't imagine why that would matter, but a fierce protectiveness welled up in her when she considered that Oakes might come under any kind of pressure from or because of her father.

She'd deal with that problem in the morning. For the moment, she planned on indulging herself in the memory of a very hot kiss. Smiling as she stripped and stepped into the shower, she pictured Oakes Weaver with one arm braced against the door, effectively caging her in. Not what she'd been looking for. Not what she'd expected, or expected to like.

But oh, she had.

CHAPTER TWENTY

After an agitated night fractured by the lingering unease from her father's message and the distinctly different restlessness brought on by Oakes's kiss, Ari rose, dressed, and went down to the hotel lobby in search of coffee well before her father's appointed time to meet. Annoyed though she might be at the unexpected request—or more accurately, his *demand*—refusing was out of the question. He was there in the hotel, and he would be waiting at a table, probably having already ordered breakfast for both of them, at seven. Whatever he needed to say to her was important enough for him to make the trip in person, and despite her aggravation and resentment at having her movements not so subtly reported by her bodyguard, he was her father and she had no reason to avoid him. Pique was something she simply didn't have time for.

"Double espresso, please," she said to the barista at the coffee kiosk at 6:02. Within moments, she knew, the kiosk would be crowded, and all she wanted was a few moments of quiet, alone in the corner, to read her email, enjoy her first caffeine jolt of the day, and mentally prepare for whatever the meeting with her father would bring.

"Morning," Oakes said from behind her.

All thoughts of quietly reading her email flew from her mind as she reached for her coffee. She half turned, totally unprepared for the better-than-caffeine buzz the sight of Oakes provoked. She wore a crisp white shirt, tailored charcoal pants with a thin black belt, and black loafers. Nothing out of the ordinary, just typical business attire, but somehow she looked dashing, and Ari's mind instantly envisioned the two of them having dinner together and afterward... Dragging her imagination well away from any images of *after*, Ari said, "Morning. Can I buy you a cup of coffee?"

"As long as you promise to drink it with me."

"I have a bit of time," Ari said, pleased her voice sounded casually friendly. "What's your pleasure?"

Oakes shrugged, her gaze traveling over Ari's face before delving into her eyes. "As long as it's strong and fresh, I'm there."

For no reason Ari could fathom, a ripple of anticipation coursed down her spine. Ari turned away, afraid she'd give away her flustered state if Oakes kept looking at her that way—all dark-eyed and intense and so annoyingly sure of herself. Women never looked at her that way, and she'd never stopped to wonder why not. Nor had she ever cared. How was she to know she'd like it so damn much?

"Something else?" the barista asked.

"Oh! Sorry, yes. Another of the same, please."

The barista nodded silently and Ari concentrated on making normal friendly conversation. She turned, determined not to fall into the trap of looking into Oakes's eyes. A woman could get lost in there. "Are you on your way to work?"

"Technically," Oakes said, "I'm not due for another forty-five minutes or so. I usually wander over before the push." At Ari's questioning look, she added, "When the shift changes and everyone debriefs. Just to see what's going on."

Ari signed the receipt and handed Oakes her coffee. Just as well—she didn't need the distraction this morning. Email was much safer when she needed a clear head. Being around Oakes tended to make her lose track of…everything. Time, caution, good intentions. "Well, I won't keep you."

"Oh, I really wish you would." Oakes's grin was maddeningly disarming, and just as pleasantly appealing. "And you did promise."

"Sorry?"

"To drink your coffee with me if I let you treat."

"I did, didn't I." Ari surrendered. Damn it, she wanted a little more of the heady excitement spending time with Oakes inspired. "Well, I suppose I can spare you a few minutes."

Oakes's grin widened. "Then it's my lucky day."

Ari led the way to a small two-top in the corner as the line behind them grew. As she set her coffee down and pulled out the chair, her attention snagged on a woman in BDUs, laced-up black boots, and an ID hanging around her neck on a lanyard who entered the area with one of the most gorgeous dogs Ari had ever seen. She watched her as the woman stepped into line and the dog calmly settled by her left side.

"Forget it," Oakes said. "She's taken."

Ari jerked her gaze to Oakes. "You might have mentioned that before now."

"No," Oakes said with a laugh, "not by *me*. One of the reporters in the press crew. You probably met her—brunette, thirtyish. Vivian Elliot."

"Yes, I remember her." The relief flooding through her was a bit of an embarrassment. Why she'd never considered that Oakes might be attached was completely unlike her. She couldn't afford any kind of mental lapse these days, and she seemed off her game when it came to Oakes.

Of course, Oakes might just as likely have no interest in attachment with her or anyone else. But then, neither did she.

Did she?

Of course not. *Definitely* not in her short-term or even long-term game plan. Who could think that far ahead, when she was constantly on the move following one politician after another on the campaign trail, state after state, month after month? She hadn't even been able to eke out four days to herself to go sailing. A relationship? Out of the question.

Oakes tilted her head. "There's a lot going on in your head right now, but I'll be damned if I know what it is. Did you think Dusty Nash was my type? She's one of us, by the way. K9 division."

Ari laughed. "You have a type?"

"Don't you?"

"I suppose, but you can't tell just by looking."

Oakes draped her arm over the back of her chair and leaned back, supremely at ease and annoyingly attractive. "Really?"

"You know," Ari said, pointing a finger, "I never noticed before, but you are supremely arrogant."

"Just now you figured that out."

"Mm. Not so much when it comes to talking about your work, but your love life—"

The smugness left Oakes's face and her fathomless blue gaze grew even deeper. "Is that what we're talking about?"

Damn it. Ari felt her cheeks redden. What was she doing? Love life? *Really.* "No, of course not."

"Okay," Oakes said slowly, "since we're not talking about romantic relationships, we must be talking about sex."

Ari straightened. "No, we most certainly are not."

"Are you sure?"

Ari never played games. Well, actually, totally not true, at least professionally. She was a great games maven when it came to politics, when it came to wrapping the truth in a message that worked for her purposes. She never fabricated, never lied, never made promises she didn't intend to keep, but the truth came in a variety of colors, shades, and hues. She took advantage of a full palette to paint a picture with the intended effect on her audience. In her personal life, she was black and white. Or at least until this moment, she'd always considered herself to be. "Okay, enough."

Oakes surprised her, resting her hand on her wrist. "If I've offended you, I'm sorry."

"No, you haven't at all. What you've done is...confuse me."

"Not my intention."

"I know. It's me. I don't totally understand what happens every time I talk to you." Ari frowned. "See—right there."

"What happened?"

"I blurt out things I have no intention of saying. That never happens to me. I don't have feelings that are foreign to me, only...I do when I'm with you."

"Maybe," Oakes said quietly, intently, the relentless focus in her eyes pinning Ari to the spot, "you just never noticed before."

"Maybe, but here are the facts," Ari said, taking a breath and committing to what might very well be the craziest thing she'd ever done. "I find you incredibly attractive. I invited you back to my room last night because I wanted to have sex with you. And I'd really like to kiss you again."

"Before or after we have sex?"

The line was delivered without the slightest smile, but Ari felt the laughter behind it. "Before, after, and during. Oh, and I fully expect dinner first. One date at least."

"Anything else that I should be aware of?" Oakes said. "Because I'm making a list."

"I want to hear more about that little café in the mountains."

Oakes blinked. There, she'd caught her off guard. Ari smiled inwardly. At least she wasn't the only one not totally on top of her game here.

"Really?" Oakes's brow furrowed. "You don't want to hear about what the president has for breakfast every day, or what he's really like when he's not on camera, or whether or not he has women coming into the White House through some secret tunnel instead?"

"God, no. Do people actually ask you that?"

"You'd be surprised how many dates I've been on where that's the topic of conversation."

"No, I don't want to know those things. I'm happy to hear whatever you want to tell me about what you do. If it's important to you, then it would be important to me. But I'm not a voyeur at a distance."

"Okay. Anything else?"

"No," Ari said, laughing. She'd never enjoyed a negotiation so much. Come to think of it, she'd never negotiated a date before.

"My turn," Oakes said quietly.

Ari's heart jumped around in her chest the way her sailboat rocked at its mooring during a gale. She thought for a second to reach out, grab the towline, strap it down, keep it from drifting into dangerous waters, but she didn't. The little element of danger that fluttered through her was exciting. "All right. Do I need to take notes?"

Oakes shook her head. "Just for the record, I've been wanting to kiss you since that first afternoon in Newport. When I got back to my room last night, I thought about it, imagined it. So I just wanted you to know tonight feels like a long, *long* way off."

Imagining Oakes thinking about them together brought heat to her throat. Ari swallowed around the desire following close behind. "Unfortunately, I have a full schedule."

"Yeah, me too." Oakes stroked Ari's bare arm. "But we have a date for tonight."

"Yes, we do," Ari said thickly. God, she was going to need to take a walk to get this woman out of her head before she met with her father. Ari extricated her arm from beneath Oakes's warm fingers. "I'm afraid I have an appointment in a few minutes."

"And I do too."

Oakes leaned closer, so close for a wild moment Ari thought she was about to kiss her. And she didn't pull away. Couldn't.

"Just so you know," Oakes murmured, "I'll be thinking about kissing you all day while I'm standing in one spot doing pretty much nothing else."

"I'm delighted to provide a little amusement." Ari forced herself to stand, gathered her shredded control, and walked away.

Oakes's laughter trailed behind her like a warm caress.

❖

Philadelphia
6:40 a.m.

"I'm not so sure I like you getting in with these people on your own," Dell said, sitting on the side of the bed and pulling on her socks.

Sandy finished with her mascara, closed the tube, and set it down along with her other makeup on the bathroom counter. She looked like she'd been up half the night, which she had, but that was not the point. That would never do. She added concealer under her eyes, decided she no longer looked half dead, and walked into the bedroom. "It's fine. These are not drug dealers, who—I might mention—*you* deal with every night."

Frowning, Dell flipped the lock of dark hair off her forehead with a quick jerk of her head. "Yeah, but—"

Sandy leaned down, gripped the hair at the back of Dell's head, and pulled until Dell was looking up at her. She kissed her, smearing her damn lipstick, and not caring. "Don't even say it. I'm a cop just like you. And just because you think you're tougher doesn't make it true."

"What I was going to say," Dell said, her pupils wide and her voice husky, "was I'd feel better if you had backup closer than down the street in the car."

"Yeah, like you do when you're out there alone on your bike. Double standard, Dell."

Dell slid her arms around Sandy's waist. "I just love you."

Sandy smiled. "I know. And that's why I'm here, despite the attitude, Rookie."

"Okay, point taken."

Dell let her go and Sandy strapped on her thigh holster beneath her short denim skirt.

"What do you think about them," Dell said, sliding her weapon holster onto her belt loop.

Sandy though back on the night. The vibes were weird—like everyone knew each other but no one was really friends. No small talk, no flirting or usual party chatter. Matt, who she'd been careful not to call by name, moved from small group to small group and spoke in low tones about casual stuff that could pass as ordinary conversation, but she'd had the feeling he was asking for updates on something.

What, she couldn't tell. "I'm not sure. They're not your usual bunch of privileged college kids, going on about the system and how it all needs to change, and never having a plan for anything."

"Actual activists, you mean," Dell said.

"Different." Sandy chewed her lip, wishing she could pinpoint what bothered her so much about the general atmosphere. "They're all a little paranoid. Like no one really wanted to talk to anyone else and they wouldn't have been there except for Matt—that's definitely his real name. He's a relay point of some kind."

Dell narrowed her eyes. "Are they violent?"

Sandy shrugged. "Hard to tell. For all I know they could be a bunch of computer hackers, planning to take on Google or Amazon or the damn Pentagon. No details that I could get, not yet anyways. But there's *something*."

"And you're in?"

"Hard to tell. I connected with a few people. A girl and a couple of guys. Trish likes me, but I think that's just because she doesn't have a girlfriend to complain to about what a dickhead Matt is."

"Well," Dell said, holding the door open for her, "now at least Sloan has an address, a license plate number, and part of a name. We'll be able to get some background on them."

"Yep. And I'm pretty sure Trish will be contacting me again." Sandy kissed her. "We can't push too hard, but it would be good if you don't worry."

Dell rolled her eyes. "Yeah, that's gonna happen in the next century or so."

Sandy laughed and grabbed her hand. "Come on, Rookie. Let's go for a ride."

Atlanta Marriott
6:55 a.m.

Totally buzzed, not from the caffeine but the conversation, Oakes grabbed a couple of mochas, a latte, and a bag full of assorted pastries, and headed up to the tenth floor to their control center. The president would be staying on the ninth floor, and the eighth and seventh had already been cleared. Until he arrived, agents from the PPD as well as the Atlanta field office would rotate shifts to ensure no one accessed the off-limits areas. The advance agents had vetted any hotel employees who might deliver bedding or amenities prior to his arrival. Agents from the protective detail would oversee the president's own food staff preparing any meals in the hotel kitchen for the president and his party.

Balancing the drink tray and pastry bag, Oakes shouldered through the door into the rooms that had been connected for their use, and greeted the overnight and oncoming day shift agents gathered there.

Evyn lounged on a sofa looking half asleep. She perked up when she saw Oakes. "Coffee. Doughnuts?"

"Muffins, croissants, and..." Oakes dangled the bag in her direction. "Bavarian cream."

"I love you," Evyn said. "Give."

One of the guys whistled. "Hey, what's going on in that room you two are sharing?"

Evyn smiled sweetly. "Let your imagination run wild, and it won't even be close."

Several other agents hooted, and Oakes dropped onto the sofa next to Evyn. She fished out a cherry Danish and took a bite.

"How'd you sleep?" Evyn said coyly. "Have nice dreams?"

Oakes took her time swallowing and sipped her coffee. "Like a baby. Dreamless sleep."

"I'll just bet."

"Wes give you a wake-up call like usual?" Oakes asked, hoping to divert Evyn's curiosity.

"Of course. That's as much as I'll probably hear from her until they all arrive," Evyn said, referring to her wife, the White House physician. Wes always traveled with the president and remained within the kill zone whenever he was in public. She had to be that close to render lifesaving aid if he was ever injured. If Evyn was bothered by the danger, she didn't show it.

"Maybe you can sneak her into the room for a midnight visit one of these nights."

"Wanna watch?"

"Uh, no," Oakes said, laughing.

Tom Turner walked in and the aimless conversation throughout the room instantly disappeared.

"Morning, everyone," he said. He picked up one of the available coffees. "Latte?"

"With almond milk," Oakes informed him.

"Excellent." He leaned against one of the long tables they'd transported and set up. "Anything from the night shift?"

The team leader shook her head. "All quiet, chief."

"Surveillance?"

"Nothing out of the ordinary," Warren said, then added with a totally fake air of uncertainty, "although, maybe something worth noting."

Tom's eyebrows rose. "Such as?"

"A new arrival, came in last night. We picked him up at the registration desk around midnight." Again the slight hitch, as if trying to ratchet up the suspense. "Nikolai Rostof. Kind of a coincidence, huh?"

Every muscle in Oakes's body tensed. Had Ari known? How could she not? She hadn't said anything, but then why should she?"

Beside her, Evyn muttered, "Uh-oh. Warren's got the scent."

"It's a free country," Turner said.

"Yes, sir." Warren, ever the Rottweiler, wouldn't let go of the bone. "But his being here at the same time as the president, who's stumping for the liberal candidate, does kind of feel a little connected, don't you think?"

"What I think," Tom said, "is that it's our business to know what's going on in any environment in which the president will be making a personal appearance. Nikolai Rostof is not a person of interest, but I didn't say we weren't interested."

Warren's eyes glinted.

"So we'll do our jobs and pay attention to who he sees," Tom said. "But remember, he is, after all, the owner of the largest media network in the civilized world. And the president is news. It's most likely he's just here doing his job like the rest of us."

"And it's just coincidence that his daughter is the president's campaign manager and one of the closest people to him?" Warren said.

Oakes ground her teeth. This had to come up sooner or later, and as much as she wanted to yank on Warren's leash and tell her to back off, she couldn't refute any of the concerns being put forward. Ari had to know her father's activities would be scrutinized, and as a consequence, hers would be too. This was a battle Ari would have to fight on her own.

What really had her stomach in a knot was wondering why Ari hadn't mentioned anything when they'd had coffee less than an hour before.

CHAPTER TWENTY-ONE

Atlanta Marriott
5:05 p.m.

Just as Ari turned on the shower, a knock sounded on her hotel room door. She frowned. Couldn't be room service, since she had dinner plans. Must be the maid. Smiling to herself, she wrapped a towel around her torso and padded into the lounge area of her suite.

"I'm fine," she called. "I won't be needing any service tonight. Thank you."

"Ari, it's Oakes."

"Oakes?" Ari took a step toward the door and stopped. She was wearing a towel. And they'd agreed to meet at a steakhouse a short walk from the hotel in two hours. So what was Oakes doing there now? "I'm not ready."

"Can we talk?"

"Yes, of course. Wait just a minute." She hurried into the bathroom, turned off the shower, shed her towel, and pulled on the complimentary hotel robe hanging behind the door. It covered her from neck to knees, and rather than keep Oakes waiting, she belted it securely around her waist. Good enough for a minute or two's conversation. Oakes must need to change their plans—cancel? Disappointment rolled through her and she pushed it aside. This would happen—they were both busy. As to why Oakes hadn't just texted—well, at least this was more personal.

"Just a sec!" Ari released the security chain and opened the door partway, realizing as she did she'd never told Oakes her room number. But of course, anything a Secret Service agent wanted to know, they could find out. The thought was fleetingly disquieting.

Oakes stood at the threshold, looking uncomfortable, even a little flustered. She still wore the clothes she'd had on that morning. She must've just gotten off shift.

A knot of tension formed in Ari's chest. This picture was not the one she'd been expecting.

"Something's wrong." She stepped back, giving Oakes room so she could pass her without their bodies touching. A minute or two was not going to be long enough for whatever had brought Oakes unannounced to her door. "Come in. I think I'd better get dressed. Just give me a moment."

"I'm sorry about this, I just..." Oakes slid her hands into her pockets and looked over Ari's shoulder, avoiding eye contact.

Yes, something was definitely wrong.

"It's fine," Ari said briskly, pulling on her professional armor. Whatever *this* was, it was more than personal. Unfortunately, mixing the professional with the personal was a bad idea, and she knew that. She'd let her attraction to Oakes, her fascination with her, interfere with her better judgment. In fact, she hadn't been using any judgment at all. That would need to stop.

She pulled a clean shirt and a pair of casual khaki pants from her closet and retreated to the bathroom. When she emerged, feeling a little less vulnerable, despite the fact that she was still barefoot and without underwear, Oakes hadn't budged from the middle of the room.

Ari indicated the sofa. "Why don't you sit down."

She took the chair facing the sofa.

"This is awkward," Oakes said.

"It doesn't have to be," Ari said. "Whatever's on your mind, just say it. I assure you, whatever the problem, there will be a solution. Is there an issue with the president's itinerary?"

"This isn't about the president," Oakes said, "not directly at least."

"Then this is a personal visit?" That didn't make any sense to her. What kind of problem could have arisen in less than twelve hours, something serious enough to bring Oakes to her door looking upset? They had a relationship, although without any kind of shape or form at this point. They hadn't set any ground rules. They hadn't even had a first date, although somehow that night in the diner had felt like one. She'd revealed more about herself than she had to anyone in a very, very long time. Perhaps that was the problem. Did Oakes want to back off, slow down?

They'd only kissed, for goodness' sake. Although she *had* mentioned wanting to go to bed with her. She might have made assumptions that were inaccurate—not like her, but then nothing about her feelings for Oakes Weaver were typical. Still, there *was* something between them. Something powerful and innate, instinctive. Undeniable.

"It's both. Hell, maybe it's nothing." Oakes ran a hand through her hair. "Damn it, I'm usually never at a loss for words."

"Is there something about our…seeing each other that's causing a problem? I wasn't aware that there was any rule against it. Our responsibilities bring us together, but neither of us answers to the other." She laughed shortly. "I can't imagine anyone thinks there's any undue influence in either direction."

"No, and I'm not here…" Oakes blew out a breath. "It's about your father."

Ari stiffened. That was not what she'd been expecting, but why hadn't she? One thing her father was not, was invisible. Wherever he went, people noticed. "I see. What about him?"

"He's here, for one thing."

"Yes, he is. In room 2509 on the penthouse floor, but you probably already know that."

Oakes winced. "You didn't mention your meeting with him when we had coffee this morning."

"No, I didn't. I didn't think it was germane. I still fail to see why it is of concern to you." Ari crossed her legs and studied Oakes. "Is he under investigation? Is that what this is about?"

"If he is, I don't have any knowledge of it."

"Am I?"

Oakes shook her head. "Again, same answer."

"Would you tell me the truth?"

Oakes flushed. "Yes, I would. I wouldn't have come here if it compromised an ongoing investigation. I wouldn't have planned to have dinner with you tonight if that was an issue."

"Then why are you here?"

Oakes paced across the room, stood with her back to Ari, and looked out the window. "Because I couldn't have dinner with you tonight and go to bed with you tonight without, I don't know, making sure that our personal and professional lives won't be at odds."

"And this is because I had breakfast with my father." Ari had had a lifetime of being Nikolai Rostof's daughter. She'd lost friends because of it—she'd cut people out of her life because they'd only wanted to be close to her to get close to him—and she'd reaped the benefits as well. She'd always been safe. And she'd known, to him, she was special. She hadn't expected to lose a lover—one she hadn't even been to bed with yet.

"With Nikolai Rostof—a powerful man with ties so deep around the world I'm willing to bet you aren't even aware of them all."

"You're saying," Ari said from behind Oakes, her tone so cold Oakes's blood froze, "that you don't trust me. That you think I'm, what, a spy?"

Oakes spun around, took in the set of Ari's stiff shoulders. She was making a mess of this.

"I'm trying to say I never want you to feel I'm with you for any other reason than our personal feelings. Damn it, Ari. I never expected to want someone as much as I want you."

Ari stood and faced her. "You can walk away, Oakes."

"Is that what you want me to do?" Oakes winced. The words hit like a gut punch.

"No," Ari said swiftly. "It isn't. But I don't want to put you in a compromising position. I don't want anything about us being involved to interfere with your duty or put you under any kind of suspicion."

"That's for me to worry about and for me to deal with," Oakes said.

"I don't want you to doubt whatever we may have." Ari shook her head. "The president trusts me, or he wouldn't have put me in this position. You know as well as I do that every investigative agency in this country has looked at my father and me for years. Assuming they are all competent, we couldn't possibly have been vetted more thoroughly before I even took this job."

"There are still some people who wonder about your father," Oakes said.

"Are you one of them?"

"No."

"My father made a personal visit this morning," Ari said, "because I have been intentionally avoiding him since I took this new position. For exactly the reason that brought you over here tonight. He's my father and I won't deny him, but I'm trying to keep the personal at a distance from the professional." She laughed ruefully. "I haven't done a very good job of that, have I."

"You can't do any more than you've done." Oakes went to her, took her hand. Relief eased some of the knots in her insides when Ari didn't jerk away. She wouldn't have blamed her if she had. "I came here to say this one thing—I need you to know that when I'm with you, I'm not reporting to anyone about anything. And I won't."

"I'm not asking you for that promise," Ari said. "I would never ask you to compromise your ethics, and I certainly would never expect you to skirt a direct order in any way." Ari put both hands flat against Oakes's chest. "I believe you. Now believe this. I have never had any knowledge, or even suspicions, that my father has broken a law or engaged in criminal activity."

"I believe you." Oakes met Ari's gaze, let her look into her own eyes for the truth. "You or your father may come under some additional scrutiny while he's here, possibly longer. You had to know that."

"Yes, I know that." Ari took a breath. "What will you do if you're ordered to investigate him? Or to use your association with me to do that?"

"I'll refuse." Oakes had never been more certain in her life.

"We could stop this right now," Ari said softly. "Everything would be simpler."

"No, it wouldn't. Not for me." Oakes gripped the nape of her neck and kissed her. Nothing would be simpler, not now, not after she'd touched her, not after she'd already kissed her. "You're under my skin, Ari Rostof. Deeper than that. I'm not walking away from you."

"I'm so glad." Ari gripped her shirt, pressed against her, and closed her eyes. After a long moment, she whispered, "I heard they have excellent room service here." Her voice was throaty, her breasts soft against Oakes's chest. "I vote for canceling dinner reservations and having room service. A little bit later."

Oakes picked her up, provoking a startled half laugh from Ari, and turned toward the king-size bed in the adjoining room. "I like that idea."

Ari threaded her arms around Oakes's neck. "I can't believe you're carrying me."

"One of the benefits of our training."

Oakes walked through to the bedroom and settled Ari on the bed. She leaned over her to unbutton Ari's shirt, her fingers fumbling the buttons as the soft cotton parted. Ari wasn't wearing anything under it, and the vision of Ari's breasts suddenly eclipsed her awareness of every sensation other than the frantic beating of her heart. Oakes swallowed hard. "I really liked the robe, but this is pretty nice too."

"I was in a hurry," Ari said, reaching up to tug Oakes's shirt out of her trousers.

"Your breasts are beautiful," Oakes muttered, scooping her hand beneath Ari's shirt to cradle one.

Ari gasped. "Your hands feel so good on my skin."

Oakes bent her head and traced a slow circle around the deep rose nipple with her tongue. "May I?"

"God, yes." Ari pressed Oakes's head closer to her breast, her shoulders arching, rubbing her nipple over Oakes's lips. "Please, yes."

Groaning, Oakes drew her in, closing her lips in a gentle vise, teasing her with the tip of her tongue. Ari's sharp cry of pleasure made her clit pound. *Fuck.* Heat flared in her center and she desperately wanted to entice Ari to cry out again. She worked another button free and cupped Ari's other breast, rubbing her nipple with the pad of her thumb.

Ari hissed and covered Oakes's hand, squeezing Oakes's fingers around her breast. "You could make me come like that."

"Give me a second, then," Oakes muttered, pushing Ari's shirt aside and kissing her opposite breast.

Ari shoved her back so unexpectedly, Oakes cursed. "Hey!"

"Not yet." Ari laughed. "Get naked. Please."

Oakes toed off her shoes and shed her clothes, watching Ari watch her as she did. She took her time, enjoying the way Ari's eyes moved over her body as she stripped off her shirt, pushed down her pants. When Ari ran a finger down the center of her abdomen, she shuddered. Right at that moment, she would have done any damn thing Ari told her to do—as long as she kept looking at her and touching her the way she was.

"Take your time," Ari said slowly. "I only get to see you for the first time once. I want plenty of opportunity to take it all in."

"This isn't exactly how I pictured it," Oakes said.

"No?" Ari's smile was slow and sensuous. "Let me guess. You pictured being totally in control, didn't you?"

"That's one way of putting it."

Leaning forward, Ari eased her fingers under the waistband of Oakes's briefs, the backs of her fingers setting fire to Oakes's skin. "I like disrupting your pictures."

"You have a knack for it."

"Do I? Mm. I like that too." Ari swung around until she was sitting on the side of the bed, her shirt parting down the center, her breasts exposed. She kissed Oakes's middle and rubbed her cheek against her.

Oakes's skin ignited. Sweat trickled down the back of her neck.

She wasn't shy, but she'd never actually been the object of a woman's scrutiny before, at least, none that she'd been so aware of. Everywhere that Ari's gaze slid over her body, her skin tingled. She quickened, nerves and flesh ready to explode. Her thighs trembled so much she was sure Ari could see.

"I'm pretty much at your command," she said, her voice sounding as thick and slow and hot as her blood.

Ari placed her palms on either side of Oakes's navel and scratched lightly with her nails. The sensation was exquisite and Oakes closed her eyes. Another second and she'd be panting. God, she might even be begging. What the fuck was happening here? Oakes buried her fingers in Ari's hair. "I could get off just looking down and watching you touch me."

Ari tilted her head, smiled again. "In a hurry?"

"I am now." Oakes lifted Ari to her feet and pushed her shirt down her arms and off. Pulling her close, she kissed her again, her breasts against Ari's, her skin hot and tight. Ari's hand skimmed down her back, under her briefs, and pushed them down. Oakes reached between them and unbuttoned Ari's pants. "You're making me a little crazy here."

"Something you need?" Ari said, kissing Oakes's throat.

"More of you."

Ari stepped away and shed the last of her clothing. "You should be careful what you ask for, because I can think of a lot of things I want to do to you."

"You're not gonna get a chance if you keep that up."

Laughing, Ari wrapped an arm around Oakes's waist and tugged her down onto the bed. Off-balance, Oakes nearly tumbled full-length on top of her and just managed to catch herself on her outstretched arms. Her hips settled between Ari's as naturally as if they'd done this a thousand times before. But they hadn't, and her flesh knew it. She caught her breath, vision tunneling, and teetered on the edge.

"Don't move for a second," Oakes gasped. "Just...don't."

Ari's eyes had gone wide, her pupils dark inviting pools, daring Oakes to drown.

"I can't." Ari shivered. "If I do, I won't last another second."

"I don't know what you're doing to me, but I like it. And it scares the hell out of me."

As if to taunt her, Ari raised her thigh, pressed it hard against her center. "You'd better like it, because this is just the beginning."

Oakes panted, struggling to tamp down the tornado swirling in the pit of her being. "Ari, I'm not kidding. You gotta ease up on me."

"Oh, not a chance."

Ari circled an arm around Oakes's neck and kissed her. Oakes lost herself in the sultry taste of Ari's kiss, surrendering to the knife edge of pleasure striking deep within her.

Ari broke the kiss with a gasp. "Oakes...Oakes, I can't..."

"Yes," Oakes urged. "Now. Now?"

"Yes, *now*." Ari's fingers dug into Oakes's shoulders, her body a taut arch lifting beneath her. A strangled cry tore from Ari's throat.

Carried away on the tide of Ari's passion, Oakes relinquished the last threads of her control. Oakes kissed her throat, her heart beating wildly as her body convulsed. Holding as still as she could while her body shattered, she rode the excruciating whirlwind to the edge and finally tumbled.

"You never asked me the details of my meeting with my father this morning," Ari said softly, tracing the curve of Oakes's breast. She lay stretched out half on top of her, her cheek nestled in the curve of Oakes's shoulder.

Oakes traced lazy circles on Ari's back, her limbs loose and languorous. She wanted her again, but she couldn't move. Didn't want to move and dispel the wonder of Ari in her arms. Her body was sated. She was happy. Content. "I figured that was between you and your father."

"And you're satisfied to leave it that way?" Ari said.

"Yes."

"Thank you," Ari said. "If I totally understood exactly what he was trying to tell me, I might've told you sooner. My father is generally not circumspect, but he was today."

"How so?"

"I've been replaying the conversation all day. I think he was trying to send me a message about the election, that I should pay attention to who is supporting President Powell's opponents in both parties."

"Okay, that sounds like advice you don't need."

"That's what I thought too. That's my job, after all, to understand voting blocs, financial supporters, donors, and benefactors. So why would he go to all the trouble to point that out? Why come all this way— why not just be clear about who or what he saw as a complication?"

"Or a threat," Oakes mused.

"What do you mean?"

"Your father has a lot of contacts throughout the world, right?"

"Of course. His business interests are incredibly diverse."

"Maybe he was trying to get a message to someone else, through you," Oakes said.

"That seems awfully hit or miss. Why wouldn't he just send the message himself?"

"Maybe he can't."

"You mean, he might jeopardize his association with someone if he did."

"Possible. Or maybe there's some other risk involved." Oakes didn't mention the possibility of physical danger—raising concerns about Rostof's safety would only frighten Ari and leave them no closer to an answer. "Did he mention anyone in particular he thought you should be aware of? Or speak to, for that matter?"

"No, but I got the sense he meant in President Powell's own party. Someone may be changing sides or withdrawing support, I suppose."

"He does have competition for the nomination from within," Oakes said. "Is any of it serious?"

Ari blew out a breath. "Right at this moment—moderately. But we still have a ways to go, and the tide of public opinion can turn quickly."

"Did you get the sense he wanted to send a warning?" Oakes asked carefully.

"A warning? Like someone was a physical threat to the president?" Ari sat up, her back against the mound of pillows. "No, and if he had known something like that, I'm sure he would have said. But..." Ari contemplated the conversation she had with her father that morning. "He might have been trying to say someone was being influenced or sharing information in some questionable dealings. Collusion?"

"Possibly," Oakes said.

"Do you think I'm supposed to pass this message on?"

"Your father knows how smart you are, doesn't he?"

Ari laughed softly. "I like to think so."

"My guess is he can't directly contact any of the agencies, but he knows you could. *And* he trusts you to figure it out."

Ari leaned back to look at her face. "I need to talk to Cam Roberts."

Oakes grinned. Ari was reading her mind. She liked that. "I think you're right. If your father wants to send a message to someone with the power to investigate anyone or anything, Cameron Roberts is the person. You have direct access to her, and you're outside every other federal agency."

"I'll call her tonight," Ari said. "I also intend to extract a price from my father. No more Witt."

Oakes grinned. "I won't complain. Room service first?"

"You order," Ari said, "I'll call, and"—she straddled Oakes's midsection, her hair draping down around Oakes's face as she leaned forward to kiss her—"then I'll come up with something to fill the time until we eat."

Oakes murmured, "Sounds like a perfect plan."

CHAPTER TWENTY-TWO

The Trump Taj Mahal Casino
Atlantic City, New Jersey
Game Day minus 14 days
1:10 a.m.

Matthew fed dollar tokens into the slot machine and pulled the arm, disinterestedly watching the symbols rotate on the three cylinders. Cherries, lemons, and a freaking banana. Only an idiot played these stupid machines. Everyone knew the odds favored the house. He fed in another coin. Three cherries lined up and tokens vomited out the bottom. A few tumbled free of the tray and bounced on his loafers, spinning off onto the grimy gray carpeted floor. He scooped the coins out of the tray into the plastic bucket he'd picked up when he'd traded real American money for the fake tokens at the little window with the bars. An Arab girl sat behind the bars taking money and passing back useless colored chips and silver tokens. That at least looked right. Her behind bars. Probably a jihadist.

All around him foreigners brandished wealth they'd gotten by taking advantage of American generosity. American stupidity. Foreign aid. What a joke. The foreigners were doing just fine, while American working men couldn't find jobs and lived in run-down shacks while offshore workers stole their paychecks, and the people in power looked the other way.

Not for much longer.

"Hey buddy, hey man! You're losing your money," exclaimed a bearded white guy with a beer gut in a faded blue work shirt and baggy black pants, pointing to the litter of coins.

Matthew almost told him to take it, but he wasn't supposed to be standing out.

Play the slots, keep a low profile. You'll be contacted.

Giving the money away would probably make him memorable.

"Yeah. Thanks, man. I missed that." Hurriedly, he raked up the loose fake coins and dumped them in his plastic bucket with the stupid palm tree on the side.

He fed another coin into the slot and yanked the arm.

"Excuse me," a redhead in a silver spangled top and skintight black capri pants murmured, moving in close. "I think you dropped your room key by the elevator."

She held out a keycard. "1609, right?"

"Yes, thanks," Matthew said, taking the card printed with an image of the sparkling shoreline and boardwalk. Another fake. The shoreline was a garbage dump.

"No problem." She turned away and a second later disappeared into the throng.

Matthew slid off the stool, swinging his little plastic bucket, and headed for the elevators. He hadn't booked a room.

1609 was empty when he let himself in except for a small blue and green nylon cold bag, the kind you got from L.L.Bean to pack lunch in or beer for an afternoon pickup game, sitting in the center of a round fake-wood table by the windows. His breath hitched, and he stared at it for a long moment. He was pretty sure he knew what was in it, but he'd never quite believed he'd be looking at it. All this waiting—years, it seemed, though it had been less than eight months since he'd first been contacted by a like-minded guy who'd seen his YouTube posts on what would really make America great again, asking him if he wanted to connect with others like himself who were going to do something, not just talk.

He unzipped the bag.

The canisters looked harmless enough. Silver tubes an inch or so in diameter, eight inches long, with a valve at one flattened end. Ordinary tear gas canisters, used by riot police the world over. Only the gas inside these would do a lot more than irritate the eyes and burn the lungs. It would paralyze the nervous system, cause seizures and cardiac arrhythmias, and kill you. In minutes. Sometimes less.

Matthew zipped up the bag and tucked it under his arm, took the elevator back down to the lobby, dropped his room key in the slot reserved for express checkouts, and went to pick up his Corvette from the self-park lot down the street.

He left his plastic bucket of fake coins on an empty stool in the casino.

The Hilton Hotel
Bethlehem, Pennsylvania
4:03 a.m.

Ari's Apple Watch chimed at the same time Oakes's phone beeped. She lifted a wrist, peered at the too-bright glowing face through a half-open eye, and hit stop as Oakes, groaning, rolled over, fumbled on the bedside table, and knocked her phone onto the floor.

"Damn it," Oakes grumbled, leaning out of the bed to search on the floor for her phone.

When she found it and flopped back with another groan, Ari leaned over and kissed her. "It's not my fault you have to be there hours ahead of everyone else."

"Where are we again?" Oakes mumbled.

"The president is touring the Bethlehem Steel Mill this morning." Ari laughed. "I realize we've been in four cities in the last fourteen days, but I can't believe you've lost track of the itinerary."

"It must be because my brain is leaking out of my ears."

"We can always cut down on the sex," Ari said lightly.

Oakes's eyes snapped open, clear and sharp in the sparse light seeping in through the half-open bathroom door.

"You're wide-awake just like that," Ari said accusingly. "That's unfair. I at least need coffee."

"Waking up with you tends to wake me up…all over."

Ari kissed her again. "I know. I have the same feeling. I've spent a lot of time in hotels while campaigning, but I've never enjoyed it quite so much. Even room service tastes better."

"You know, there's no way this is a secret."

"Do you want it to be?" Ari had already dealt with the reality of their relationship. They spent days on end with the same group of people: the Secret Service agents on the president's detail, the White House medical staff, her own campaign staff, the press corps, the White House press secretary, the First Daughter and her wife. Pretending she wasn't involved with Oakes Weaver would be impossible, foolish, and to her way of thinking, insulting to them both. They were adults, they weren't doing anything wrong, and nothing about their relationship impinged on their professional obligations or duties. Oakes hadn't answered, and Ari's heart climbed into her throat. Had she misjudged? She was in trouble if she had—she'd thought they were building something here. She'd gone all in, even if she hadn't said so out loud. Oakes owned a part of her now—a part of her no one had ever touched. A part of her she hadn't even known she'd wanted to give to someone until she already had. "Oakes? Do you want this to be a secret?"

"What? No! Sorry, I just like watching you think."

Ari laughed despite wanting to strangle her. "And how do you know that's what I was doing?"

"You get this little line between your eyebrows and—"

Ari slapped her on the shoulder. "I do *not* get lines or…frowny faces."

Oakes grinned and tugged Ari on top of her. "Frowny face. That's what it is. You get a frowny face."

Ari narrowed her eyes and said threateningly, "Oakes, you're on thin ice here."

"Nah. You're always beautiful." Watching Ari's eyes soften, Oakes swept a hand down Ari's back and into the dip at the base of her spine. She loved that landscape, the womanly grace and strength of her. She loved it even more when Ari caught her breath and arched above her, pressing their lower bodies closer together. "Really awake now."

"We don't have time," Ari said.

"I can be fast *and* good," Oakes said.

Ari nipped at Oakes's lower lip. "You can be very, very good, but fast is not really one of my preferences. So if you don't mind, we'll wait until you can tend to me properly."

"Oh yeah, I like that idea."

"Good, hold on to it." Ari rolled away, and Oakes reluctantly rose. "I probably won't see much of you today. After he does this meeting with the steelworkers and we finish up in Lehigh with the donor luncheon, I have a meeting scheduled in Newark with the producer airing the debate."

"I know," Oakes said. "You think that will run late?"

Ari gathered the clothes she'd strewn around the room in her haste to get naked the night before. "The debate's the last big televised event before the national convention. I need to be sure the coverage is aimed in the right direction and they're prepared for this to be a free-for-all."

"Don't worry, he's a natural."

"Oh, I'm not worried about his performance," Ari said, "but if the moderators are as unprepared as the last two, the atmosphere could turn on us quickly."

"I'm sure you'll get them prepped properly." Still naked, Oakes cupped Ari's nape and kissed her, long and thoroughly, making sure Ari didn't forget what they had planned for later.

Ari cupped Oakes's cheek. "You don't really think I could forget."

"How do you do that, know what I'm thinking?"

Ari speared her fingers through Oakes's disheveled hair, making it even more tousled and loving the rough and roguish way she looked, as if she'd been making love half the night. Which, of course, she had. "It's the way you kiss me. I can hear a thousand words in every touch."

Oakes wondered if Ari could hear the three words she hadn't said. The three that kept playing in her mind every time she looked at her, every time she touched her, every time she was away from her, and every time she saw her again after they'd been apart. The three words she thought every time her heart leapt in her chest and her soul sparked into life.

The three words that, once said, would change her world forever.

"I'd better get into the shower," Oakes said.

"Hey." Ari threaded her arms around Oakes's neck and kissed her. "Room for two?"

"Can you behave?"

"I wouldn't swear to it."

"Good." Oakes took her hand. "Then you can join me."

Philadelphia
6:58 a.m.

Sandy met Rebecca in the cavernous first floor of Sloan's building just as the big grates on the industrial elevator slid soundlessly open.

"Morning, Loo," Sandy said.

"Morning, Detective," Rebecca said.

Dell dove in as the doors neared closing and they reversed course.

Watts lumbered on. "Good move, kid."

Ignoring him, Dell said, "Did I just hear that right?" She shot Sandy a glance, her eyes gleaming. "Detective?"

"Promotions posted this morning," Rebecca said. "Ceremony's next week." She held out her hand. "Congratulations, Detective."

Sandy took her hand. Hers was shaking. She was *not* going to cry in front of everyone. "Thank you."

There, she sounded just fine. Her vision was a little blurry but no one needed to know that.

"Wahoo," Dell burst out, grabbing Sandy and lifting her off her feet. She swung her in a half circle, squeezing what little air she'd managed to suck in right out again.

"Yo, watch the flying feet before you nail me in the nuts," Watts exclaimed.

"I'm so proud of you," Dell said, planting a big one right on her mouth.

"Okay, that makes up for it," Watts said.

Laughing, Sandy punched Dell in the arm. "Put me down."

"I love you," Dell said as she released her.

Sandy tugged her shirt into shape and tried to look cool. Hopping up and down and squealing would just have to wait. But oh my God, *detective*!

The elevator opened on the third floor, and she trooped out with the others. Sloan was already seated at the table in the conference area with a cup of coffee. That was weird. She was routinely a few minutes late.

Rebecca paused on her way to the coffee area. "You get something for us?"

"The breadcrumbs are starting to settle," Sloan said. "A few more pieces, we might actually have an entire slice."

"I was rather hoping for a loaf," Rebecca said, pouring herself coffee.

Jason was the last to come in, his hair tousled and circles under his eyes, but his step was brisk and his eyes bright. He plopped into a chair next to Sloan, giving her a brief grin.

Oh yeah, those two had something. Sandy's heart kicked up, and her shiny new rank moved to the back seat.

"All right," Rebecca said as everyone settled around the table. "Let's hear what you two supersleuths have come up with."

"As you know," Sloan said, "we didn't get a whole lot out of the Corvette ID other than Ford's name."

Sandy'd been psyched when Rebecca had run the plates on the Corvette and come up with the name *Matthew Ford*. He hadn't bothered to change the registration on his vehicle. Sounded like Basic Criminal Skills 101, but sometimes even the most experienced criminals made careless mistakes. Zealots like Ford and his crowd were often naïve and inexperienced, thinking themselves far more invisible than they actually were.

Disappointingly, ID'ing Matthew Ford had been a dead end. He was like a couple million other twentysomething white men: college-educated at a third-tier conservative Christian school in Georgia, no criminal record, and no history of subversive activity or associations beyond the alt-right rally he'd attended. At least, none they'd been able to dig up.

Sandy tapped her foot impatiently, waiting for Sloan to give her a thread to pull, a weak spot to poke at—something, *anything*—until she could shake something loose. Because she just knew there was something there, boiling under the surface, but she hadn't seen a hint of the usual operations—no drugs, no large amounts of cash changing hands, no underage girls—or boys of dubious origin—suddenly making an appearance.

Sloan must have sensed her nerves fraying, because she sent her a big grin. "But last night we finally found Ford's real story on YouTube."

"YouTube?" Sandy blurted. "He's got a YouTube channel? I can't believe that. He's too paranoid."

"You're right, he is," Sloan said, "but what he isn't is internet savvy. He's using an alias, but if you feed in enough keywords and cross-references, hit all the major platforms, and crawl through about a billion bytes of archived videos with a really vigorous search function, you can find him. He's using the name *Matthew Frank*."

"Original," Watts muttered.

"Matthew Frank," Sloan went on, "is into some serious white supremacist ideology. Hard-core. We've been able to track his viewing history back over eighteen months when the escalation of his posts and the extremism of what he was viewing really started to pick up."

"Associations?" Frye asked.

"Plenty of them," Jason put in, "and here's what gets interesting. Sandy's right about him being paranoid. In the last six months, he's abandoned at least ten forums where he was previously a major player. He's entirely eliminated his YouTube presence in the last three months. When he surfaced in New Jersey."

"Going undercover?" Rebecca asked.

"That's what it looks like," Sloan said. "The pattern resembles what we see in geographic analysis when members of disparate cells converge. How organized or what their agenda might be, still unknown."

"Include everything we have and send it off to the national center," Rebecca said to Sloan.

"Already done."

"Of course." Rebecca turned to Sandy. "Nothing?"

"No," Sandy said, frustration making her voice hard-edged. "I think the only way I'm gonna get anything is through Trish. I'm gonna have to push her harder."

"Cautiously," Rebecca said pointedly. "You're our only avenue in."

"Absolutely, always." Sandy's stomach tightened. Frye hadn't pointed out they couldn't give her close backup either. She didn't have to. That didn't matter anyhow. Her job was to find out if Matthew Ford and the people slowly assembling around him were dangerous, or if, like so many angry pseudomilitants, they burned hot with rhetoric and eventually flamed out. Most of the individuals and groups on the myriad domestic and international terrorism watch lists ended up that way, but they all had to be treated with serious respect because, as the Oklahoma City bombing, the torching of Southern Black churches, and the assaults on mosques and temples proved all too frequently, sometimes the rhetoric transformed into violent action.

She'd be careful, as long as caution didn't prevent her from getting the job done.

CHAPTER TWENTY-THREE

"Morning." Blair slipped into the seat between her father and Lucinda at a table for six in the corner of the private dining room and kissed her father's cheek. The adjacent tables were empty in a ring four tables deep around them, a subtle barrier providing as much privacy as they ever managed in public. Which was not much, but at least their conversation would be private. Like the president's quarters on the tenth floor and any other area he was likely to visit, the room was sequestered from any kind of civilian traffic before, during, and immediately after his stay. The Secret Service agents stationed at each door checked the room at frequent intervals throughout the day and night, whether the room was in use or not, for listening devices, cameras, and explosives.

A few tables at the far end of the room were occupied by members of the White House press corps, the elite group who actually traveled with the president to all his major appearances. These were the senior network and news agency reporters, most of whom had worked the White House beat for decades. They'd seen presidents come and go, witnessed parties in power change practically overnight, and been privy to all the internal power struggles, squabbles, and coups that were the lifeblood of politics. They stayed close to the president in the event of some breaking developments, but otherwise gave him and his family a respectful berth.

Andrew was dressed in his meet-the-people garb of navy polo and khakis. With him, it wasn't a publicity thing—he just liked to dress that way. Lucinda looked effortlessly stylish as usual in a mint green silk shirt, tailored taupe pants, and low heels a shade darker than the pants. Blair fell somewhere in between the two on the style spectrum in low-rise slim black pants, a red silk shirt, and—since she'd be accompanying her father most of the day, which meant half running to keep pace with him—black flats.

"Hi, honey," Andrew said. "Cam coming?"

"No—she left at daybreak, I think. It might have been midnight. She texted me to say she was held up at a meeting."

Lucinda laughed. "I wish I could sleep the way you do."

"I need to conserve my strength," Blair said, only half kidding.

"How are you holding up?" Lucinda smiled and passed the coffee carafe to Blair.

"Considering how close we are to the end of this particular road trip," Blair said, "not bad at all. But I am more than ready to sleep in my own bed and *not* talk to a reporter as soon as we get this nomination sewn up."

"If we win," her father said, "you'll only have a little more than four more years of this."

Blair gave him a look. "I'm on board as long as you want, although once you two—you know—make it official, that could change."

Lucinda did something Blair had never seen her do before. She blushed. That was a side of her Blair rarely saw when they were in private, and that was a rare occurrence these days.

"If...*when*...that happens," Lucinda said, "I may have moved on from politics. Carnegie Mellon has offered me a place in their policy development department."

"That's code for think tank, isn't it?" Blair glanced at her father, who seemed happy with the possibility of Lucinda no longer serving as his most important advisor. "Wow, that would be great. And weird."

"Yes," Lucinda said, "it would."

"We've got a lot of votes to count before we need to worry about any of that," Andrew said. He tilted his chin toward the far door. "Looks like Cam made it after all."

"Oh?" Blair looked over her shoulder, pleased but surprised. Maybe Cam just wanted to grab breakfast, but Blair didn't think so. Cam was not a spontaneous person. None of them were, really. Their days were too regimented, too scheduled, and the only disruptions to the schedules unfortunately consisted of earth-shattering emergencies, for real.

Cam never revealed anything in her facial expression, and she didn't now. Blair could usually read her body language, but all she sensed was intensity and purpose. And that was just Cam.

"I'm sorry to interrupt breakfast, Mr. President"—Cam pulled out a chair at the table and sat down—"but I wanted to brief you personally, and I know you're heading straight from here to tour the mill."

"You haven't interrupted anything yet," Andrew said. "They're just about to serve. You can let them know what you want."

"Thanks, I'm good."

Blair reached over and squeezed Cam's hand. "I didn't hear you get up this morning."

"You were sleeping...soundly." Cam briefly entwined their fingers before turning to the president. "I got a call from a contact at the CIA a little after six this morning. He wanted to brief me personally on some emerging intelligence."

"An early-morning call from the CIA is never good news," Lucinda said, pouring herself a little more coffee.

While she didn't appear perturbed, Blair detected the ice in her tone. Lucinda did not like being out of the loop.

"At this point," Cam said, "he didn't have enough to put in an official report, and I don't think he wanted to. He has his own sources to protect."

Lucinda grimaced. "The Agency always does. But he obviously thought he had something, or he wouldn't have reached out to you."

Blair read that as Lucinda's way of saying she wouldn't hunt out the source of Cam's intel, at least not so anyone would notice. Lucinda would be an asset to any think tank in the nation, but she'd be better off just waiting to run for president when Andrew's second term was up. The idea was exhilarating, and a tad terrifying.

Cam fell silent as the White House servers brought in breakfast on a rolling cart, served the plates, and inquired of Cam if she wanted anything.

"No, thanks," Cam said, and the servers withdrew, leaving them in their circle of silence again.

"All right," Andrew said, calmly slicing into his avocado and eggs on toast, "let's hear it."

"You'll remember we received some soft intelligence several weeks ago, nothing very specific, that suggested one of your political rivals might be receiving assistance from outside sources."

"Foreign sources," Lucinda said with a bite of distaste.

Cam nodded.

No one said anything else. No one had to. Cam had briefed them after Ari's father had met with Cam and told her his sources, unnamed, had uncovered a trail leading from Eastern Europe into the inner circles of one of her father's challengers. The trail was murky at best, but Cam had carefully tapped the lines of her own covert contacts. One had obviously borne fruit.

"Does the name Farris Palmer ring any bells?" Cam said.

"Yes, wait a minute," Lucinda said, getting the distant look in her eyes she often got as she called up information from her voluminous encyclopedic memory. "He's a journalist, of sorts, writes op-ed columns for the *Post*, conservative, not a friend of Andrew's."

Blair added, "He's gotten very popular in the last year or so. I don't remember hearing much from him before that."

"That's because Palmer is an alias," Cam said.

"Well, a lot of writers write under pseudonyms," Blair pointed out. "Although I've never read anything about his original identity."

"His real name is Frank Plummer. He used to work on Anthony Russo's campaign and was a big supporter of Graves's freedom patriot party."

A crease formed between Lucinda's brows. "He's been on a watch list for years because of his white nationalist ties. How has he established this new profile?"

Blair said, "You're kidding. How could we not know this?"

Cam shrugged. "Two different managing editors said almost the same thing—they took his bio at face value since the facts were verifiable. He'd been building the alias for some time—talk shows, articles, even a book."

"And now there's evidence he's attempting to influence the election with help from outside the country?"

"That's what Rostof suspected, and my contact agrees."

Andrew carefully folded his napkin and set it aside. "We already knew our friends in Moscow have an interest in our elections, and plenty of avenues to apply influence. That's not the reason the CIA contacted you at six in the morning."

"No," Cam said. "The real worry is Plummer's previous connection to violent alt-right groups suspected of being behind hate crimes and other terrorist incidents."

"So what does that mean for us?" Blair asked. "Is there a potential threat?"

"We don't know. This could be a coincidence, or it could be part of a larger, more organized initiative. On my way down here, I got another report from a group in Philadelphia. They've been investigating some soft findings suggestive of an active alt-right group in the Philadelphia area."

"That's pretty common in most major cities," Lucinda said, "and unfortunately, more and more, campuses everywhere."

"Absolutely, but this one appears to be active and escalating. They only picked it up because they've got a couple of extremely sharp cyberinvestigators with some algorithmic programs that I would very much like to get a look at."

Blair laughed. "You mean unregistered programs?"

"Something of their own development, yes," Cam said.

"What's the bottom line here?" Andrew said.

"There are too many threads, all leading to the same place," Cam said, "and that's Philadelphia. I'm heading up there ahead of your arrival to get a look at this operation and assess the information they have, but Tom needs to be alerted to an enhanced threat level. We have to expect some kind of action that may affect your agenda."

"What about your contact?" Lucinda said. "Are they going to move on Plummer? If he's culpable of facilitating foreign interests in our electoral process, he's vulnerable."

"Yes," Cam said. "It's a multijurisdictional nightmare, but I've suggested they move quickly. He may have information vital to the security of the president." Cam rose. "Sorry. I need to go. I set up a briefing with Tom and his people and Ari Rostof to discuss potential changes to your itinerary."

"Oh, boy," Blair said as she watched Cam thread her way between the tables, nod to the agent on the door, and disappear. "That's a meeting I'm happy to miss."

"We can't make substantial changes now," Ari said. "The president is scheduled for major television network appearances as well as public appearances at fund-raisers and donor receptions. We have to be seen going in strong and coming out even stronger when he has the nomination."

Oakes glanced at Commander Roberts, who had just confirmed the increased threat level they'd be facing in Philadelphia. Ari wasn't happy, and she was right from her point of view, considering her priorities. But her priorities were not essential or really even relevant. The president's candidacy would be moot if they couldn't protect him. As lead on the

Philadelphia advance, the final call on all security matters, including where and when the president would ultimately engage with the public, would be hers. The president could override her, but no one else.

Roberts and Tom Turner had tossed the ball into her court, and she'd just have to hit it back.

"Your concerns are noted," Oakes said, "and it's possible we won't have to adjust any of the president's itinerary. However, the enhanced threat level means we'll be reevaluating the agenda item by item and reconfiguring as needed."

"Reconfiguring," Ari repeated. "That would be code for canceling?"

The sarcasm was subtle, but Oakes was intimately familiar with Ari's tone. Oh yeah. Not happy at all. She said, "In some instances that might be necessary, but we always try to work with the staffers."

Ari sighed. "Can I expect any immediate changes? We've finalized the network schedules already, and those will be the hardest to alter."

"Those would be the least likely to be affected."

"Donor receptions?"

Oakes sent what she hoped was a sympathetic grimace. "All instances in which he will be exposed to large groups of people will be assessed on a case-by-case basis."

"All right," Ari said. "I'll review our agenda with my staff and the president with that in mind. I'd rather reschedule some of those things now than cancel at the last moment." She regarded Oakes steadily. "Any disruption at this point can shake the confidence of the voters—and the donors. I hope you'll keep that in mind."

Oakes nodded. She couldn't agree to something she might not be able to do, and Ari would know that.

Commander Roberts stood. "Let's keep ahead of this situation."

Tom and the others followed Roberts out of the conference room, until only Oakes and Ari remained.

"And that," Ari said dryly, "is what you and I had hoped wouldn't happen."

Oakes shook her head. "Nah. I knew it would happen—it always does, sometimes in a big way, sometimes not so much."

"You could have warned me," Ari said grumpily.

Having the good sense not to laugh, Oakes just shook her head. "I don't see how, since I'm just hearing the details now."

Ari sighed. "That makes it hard for me to be angry. I need a bad guy to focus my frustration on."

"I'd rather you be mad at me," Oakes said, "because if there's a real bad guy in this picture, we've got more than just a potential threat."

"I know you're right." Ari took Oakes's hand. "And I don't want you in any kind of danger. But damn—I don't want you messing with my campaign plans."

Oakes lifted Ari's hand and rubbed her cheek against it. "I'll do what I can. Trust me."

Ari linked their fingers. "I do."

CHAPTER TWENTY-FOUR

The Oasis
Philadelphia
Game Day minus 33 hours
11:10 p.m.

"Hey," Sandy said, plopping into the chair next to Trish at their usual table in the corner. Funny how that had gotten to be their place. She'd been meeting her there several times a week, sometimes ending up at the apartment where Matt and the weird group of people would be gathered, talking among themselves in twos and threes, with Matt passing between them, saying a few words, and then everyone would disperse. No one gave Sandy much of a look after the first few times. A friend of Trish's seemed to be enough of a credential.

"Hey," Trish said, slurring a bit already. She'd worn a scoop-neck cami top, and one thin strap hung down her arm like a fragile noose. Her hair and makeup looked a bit worn out too.

"I didn't think I was going to be able to get here," Sandy said. "All the roads coming into this area are blocked. What a pain. I had to walk like six blocks, and it's freakin' hot tonight."

"Yeah, the big deal convention," Trish scoffed. "It's all about that, all the time now. Like all the rest of us don't really matter, so it's cool to fuck up our lives."

"Yeah. 'Course it's not like we're really on anybody's radar, right?" Sandy said.

"Well, maybe that's about to change." Trish took a big gulp of her mixed drink. "Maybe they'll get the message this time."

Sandy's pulse sped up. "That would be good, you know, to get the message out. To, I dunno, make people pay attention."

"That's the thing, you know? Messages. No one ever really listens. Not about being fucked over by everything and everybody." Trish pointed her swizzle stick at Sandy. "But they'll pay attention if it's more than talk, right?"

"All true." Sandy approached the subject as if she was holding out her hand to a wild animal, one that would run at the first sign of a threat. "Matt knows how to make people listen, though. Right?"

"Matt." Trish shook her head as if she'd changed her mind about what she wanted to say and drained her drink. "I need another drink."

"Hey, I'll get it."

Sandy took her time getting to the bar, hoping a little break would distract Trish from her obvious goal of getting blind drunk. She needed her to be talking, not passed out.

"Go easy on the gin," she said the bartender. "My friend might be driving later."

He frowned. Even in a place like this, the bartenders were careful not to let drunk customers out on the street who might get into accidents that would come back on them. Their motives weren't altruistic—they were just personally motivated. "Don't let her do that, hear?"

"Yeah, I've got her covered. But she'll notice if there's nothing in it."

Her handed her a watered-down version of Trish's usual, and Sandy carried it back to the table. As she sat down, she said, "So, is Matt coming? I haven't seen him for a while, except, you know, last week at your place. But he didn't have much to say."

"Not to you and me," Trish said. "*We're* not the important ones."

Sandy laughed. "I kinda noticed no one really talks to anybody except their own little groups. That's weird for a bunch of friends."

"That's because they're not friends. They probably never even met each other until a few weeks ago. That's the whole point, you know? So that nobody really knows anything, so nobody could involve anyone."

"Um, uh-huh," Sandy said, feigning confusion. "I get it, I guess. They're all there because of Matt—he's the...what do you call it, the organizer."

"Not exactly. He's up there, but he doesn't make the plans." Trish narrowed her eyes. "He doesn't even tell me very much. Like I haven't been around for the last six months, listening to his freaking super-private phone calls with the burn phones you can't use more than once." She fished a phone out of her pocket. "Like I would really throw these things away. That's just stupid."

"Shit. You stole his phone?" Sandy nodded approvingly. "That's savage."

"Well, he replaces them every couple of days, and there's about a million minutes left on them. Besides, I think he only ever talks to one person, so what's the big deal?"

"I guess he's just private," Sandy said.

"Paranoid is more like it." Trish leaned forward, her expression halfway between intense and unfocused. "Matt's thing is, he doesn't just want to send a message, he wants to be famous. He wants his face on television."

"Well, if he's so secretive, I don't get that." Sandy held off probing as much as she dared, feeling the thrill of a nibble on the end of her line but afraid her quarry would slip the hook if she tried to set it too quickly.

"He needs to keep everything quiet until the very last minute. Because, you know, the wrong people might hear about it."

"Whoa." Sandy feigned excitement. "You mean, police or something?"

"I guess. They're planning more than just carrying signs and stuff. That's what he's been doing, telling them where and when."

"Oh," Sandy said, the tug of the hook digging in making her blood race. "It's gonna be at the Convention Center…gotta be. That's where all the TV people will be."

Trish shrugged and reached for her glass. She fumbled it and almost knocked it over, but Sandy caught it upright. "Who knows? He doesn't tell me the details."

"You're not going?"

She shook her head. "No. I'm not part of that in crowd."

"That blows."

And that's where Matt had made his mistake. He'd made Trish feel like an outsider. He'd kept her in the dark, as if he didn't trust her, and by doing so, he'd *made* her untrustworthy.

"Just tell him he's being a dick in front of everyone else, and he'll have to take you along. They all know you—he'll cave."

"Not happening." Trish drained her drink. "That's not the way it's going to go down. It's not a group thing, and he's not going with them anyhow. He's got something else planned."

An icy shiver ran down Sandy's spine. "He does?"

Trish sagged back in her chair, the alcohol making her features slack, almost as if she was melting. "I told you, he wants his face on television. You gotta do something big to get that."

Trish was too out of it to provide any more details, so Sandy got her outside and into a cab. Trish might remember what she'd told her, but she was pretty confident that no matter how much Trish remembered, she wouldn't tell Matt anything about it.

As soon as Sandy saw the cab disappear around the corner, she punched in Rebecca's number.

"Sorry to wake you, Loo," Sandy said, "but I didn't think this ought to wait until morning."

"You all right?"

"Fine. I'm at the Oasis and Trish just left. I think they're planning some kind of action at the Convention Center, maybe in several places at once."

"Details?"

Sandy waved at a cab, and miraculously, it pulled over. "I don't have much, but I figured the brain trust could fit some pieces together." She patted the faint weight in her teensy, mostly useless back pocket. The phone Trish had lifted from Matt nestled against her butt, safe and sound. "And I've got a little something for them to play with."

"I'll call the team in."

"Right. See you." Sandy slid into the cab and gave him Sloan's address. The excitement of closing in on her quarry made her pulse race, but the nagging feeling that the stakes were a lot higher than any of them realized seethed in the pit of her stomach. Not close enough yet—and not much time left.

University Hospital
Philadelphia
Game Day minus 27 hours

"Morning, Dr. Torveau," Oakes said to Ali Torveau, the Chief of Emergency Services at University Hospital. Some might carelessly call the brunette with short tousled hair, matching dark eyes, and delicately etched features pretty, but her high-bridged nose and dark, dramatic brows emboldened her profile and pushed her into the striking category.

Even more important to Oakes, Torveau's emergency medical team had a rep for being the best in the Northeast, which was why Oakes was there at five a.m.

Ali shook her hand with an easy smile. "Agent Weaver. Good to see you again."

"Thanks for making time in your schedule, Doctor," Oakes said as they walked through the emergency room towards the trauma admitting area. "You're number one for medevac."

Torveau never broke stride, as if she was on call to treat the President of the United States in a life-threatening situation every day. "We've planned for that since we knew we were on the list, and run emergency scenarios with that in mind. We're ready."

"If you don't mind walking me through it," Oakes said, "I can get out of your way and let you get back to work."

They stopped at the trauma admitting entrance. "For the duration of the president's stay," Ali said, "we've cleared a direct cordon from the street to this entrance. Other emergency vehicles will be circling around to the main ER entrance on the north side of the lot."

"You have three designated bays down here, correct? All capable of full surgical procedures if needed?"

"That's correct. We plan to hold two open and reroute everything we can for the duration of his time in the city."

"Wheels down to wheels up," Oakes said, "will be five days."

Torveau nodded. "We're also holding two rooms open in the main OR as well. The chiefs of trauma and surgery, as well as the neuro, ortho, and cardiothoracic chiefs, will all be in-house seven to seven and within fifteen minutes' arrival time during their off times. Senior staff members will be on-site around the clock."

"No additions or changes to the list of personnel we were provided previously?" Oakes asked.

"No, all the same. I plan to stay on-site twenty-four seven."

"Appreciate that, Doctor. I think that covers it."

Ali stopped in the trauma triage area and held out her hand. "I'm confident my staff can handle anything, but I hope not to see you again after this morning."

Oakes shook her hand. "That's exactly my thought. You'll be advised when POTUS is on the ground."

"You have my direct number."

Oakes left through the main trauma admitting doors and jogged the route their vehicles would take from the street in the event the president needed medical assistance. She noted sight lines to other buildings in the hospital complex, locations that needed to be cleared of vehicles that might impede their progress, and a dumpster that had not yet been removed per protocol. Agents would be posted to all those areas before the morning was out. All that remained now was for the president to arrive at eight the next day.

These last few hours before kickoff were always the worst. The shifts were all set for the next twenty-four, and as shift leader, she was at loose ends—left to checking and rechecking and generally trying not to get in the way of everyone doing their jobs. What she needed was a diversion.

As she reached Thirty-Third Street and signaled to her ride, she reconsidered. What she *needed* was to see Ari. She'd been on-site in Philadelphia for a week, and the few days before that had been so hectic, they'd barely had a moment together. She missed Ari in a way she hadn't expected, in a way she'd never experienced before. The longer they were apart, the more she was plagued with the feeling of something needing to be done, of something needing to be completed, until she finally realized it was *her*. She felt incomplete, like a hollow place inside her had been filled with heat and life and joy, and without Ari, that place echoed with the absence.

Evyn pulled the Suburban to the curb and Oakes jumped into the front passenger seat.

"All clear?"

"Yes," Oakes said, watching the crowds of pedestrians, mostly hospital workers from the way they were dressed, stream across the intersection. She glanced at Evyn. "Do you miss Wes?"

Evyn shot her a curious look. "Sure. I try not to think about it, because I can't do anything to change things. You'll get used to it."

"Uh…"

Evyn snorted. "Come on, I know you and Ari are a thing." She paused. "A serious thing?"

"Yeah, pretty serious."

"Good. I like her. She knows what she's about. She's no pushover. A pain in the ass, sometimes, but she's doing her job."

"Yeah," Oakes said with a laugh. "I noticed that."

"But you're working that out?"

"I think we understand each other. Our goals aren't exactly the same, but we respect the jobs we have to do."

"You know Warren has still got a spur in her butt about Nikolai

Rostof," Evyn said. "Once you and Ari go public—officially—she's going to be all over you."

"She can poke all she wants to." Oakes stretched her legs out as much as she could under the dash. "If there'd been anything there to find, someone would have by now. But no matter what her father's interests or involvements might be, Ari is not part of it."

"So when do you plan to make your move?"

Oakes frowned. "What do you mean?"

Evyn sighed and turned in to the entrance to the Hyatt parking garage. They had cleared the entire lower level for their vehicles. "Have you told her yet?"

"Oh. No."

"Is it because you're not sure?" Evyn shut off the engine and turned in the seat to face her.

"I'm sure," Oakes said. "I guess I've been holding back because that's just a big first step, right? And then there will be a lot of changes."

"That's what it's all about, isn't it?" Evyn said softly. "Life is change."

"I know, but look at how lousy most of us are at relationships."

"You can break pattern."

"That's the plan. Hold on—" Oakes's phone vibrated, and she checked the readout.

just landed Philadelphia airport can I see you?

Oakes's breath rushed out. "I guess I'm about to get my chance. Ari's here."

Laughing, Evyn clapped her on the shoulder. "At least you'll have something to do for the rest of the day besides bug the rest of us."

CHAPTER TWENTY-FIVE

Gramercy Park
New York City
6:20 a.m.

Cam tapped lightly on the open door to Blair's studio. "Can I interest you in coffee?"

Blair turned, a slightly befuddled look on her face. "Hi. Um, what time is it?"

"Time for some fuel. You've been in here since one o'clock in the morning."

"Oh. I woke up, and I just had this image…" Blair raised her hands, the paintbrush in her right hand flaming with deep red paint.

"Can I see?" Cam asked. Sometimes Blair was ready for a work in progress to be viewed. Other times she kept a canvas sequestered until she was happy with it.

"Sure." Blair reached out for the coffee cup. "You had a really good idea, us sneaking back here for a few days before Philadelphia. I didn't realize how much I missed being able to work."

"I did." Cam kissed her. "You get fidgety."

"Do I?" Laughing, Blair reached for Cam and abruptly pulled back. "You're dressed for work. Why is that?"

"Let me see what you're working on first," Cam said.

Blair sipped her coffee, leaving a smudge of crimson on the side of the white porcelain. "Are you going back to DC early?"

"No, Philadelphia." Cam edged around her and studied the brilliant washes of color slashing across the canvas. She recognized the general location of the abstract landscape. Central Park, at dawn.

A wash of morning sunlight, flush with the promise of a new day, rode above the myriad greens of lawn and trees.

"I like it," Cam said. "I feel...energized...just looking at it."

Blair's expression softened. "You always have gotten it. You and Diane are among the few who see what I see. Thank you."

"I'm glad, but I think you have to thank my mother for that," Cam said. "I grew up watching her paint, trying to make sense of things in a logical way until she told me to stop thinking and just feel."

"Your mother is a very wise woman."

"She is. I was lucky she raised me, and I'm lucky to have you to fill my life with beauty like this."

Blair kissed her. "If you plan on staying in those very dapper clothes much longer, you should stop with the compliments."

Cam cupped her chin to look into her eyes. "Will you promise to get some sleep today?"

"I have to be back in DC this evening so I can get up tomorrow and fly to Philadelphia with my father. I've got a few hours left here, and then I'll head back. I promise I'll get a good night's sleep."

"Thanks."

"Why are you changing plans and heading up there today?" Blair asked. "Problems?"

Cam raised a shoulder. "I'm not sure. I got a call from Rebecca Frye a bit ago, and her team is putting together a picture that's a little worrisome. I want to look at things myself."

"The advance detail is there, right?" Blair said. "You won't be on your own."

"I'll have plenty of backup, but I'm just reviewing their investigation, not apprehending anyone. I don't expect any problems."

She meant every word, but Blair knew as well as she did investigations had a way of morphing into something different.

"All right. Call me?" Blair said.

"I will. I'll see you in the morning." Cam pulled her close and kissed her, ignoring Blair's muffled protest. A smear of paint here or there was a small price to pay for the sensation of Blair's body fitting to hers. She ended the kiss and stroked a finger down the edge of Blair's jaw. "Take care of yourself until I see you again."

"And you do the same, Commander," Blair murmured, squeezing her ass as Cam backed away.

Cam smiled and flicked at the fleck of red on the sleeve of her charcoal suit. Totally worth it.

❖

Oakes paced in front of the revolving doors in the Hyatt lobby, realized she was pacing, and forced herself to stop. Considering she spent literally days of her life standing in one spot, her behavior was distinctly unusual. So was the agitation that roiled her insides like a swarm of bees. She rubbed her stomach, but it didn't quiet things down in there. She was as jittery as if she'd had two double espressos back to back.

She tensed as another black Uber pulled up in front of the hotel, and the bees suddenly took flight as Ari stepped out. Oakes shouldered through the revolving door and commandeered Ari's luggage as soon as the driver opened the trunk.

"I got it," she said and pulled it out of the back of the vehicle. When she turned, Ari was watching her with a quirky smile.

"Carrying luggage, Agent," she murmured too low for the driver to hear.

"Making an exception," Oakes said. She'd told Ari about the time the spoiled teen son of a visiting diplomat had cavalierly instructed the agents on the protection detail to get his bag before he swept grandly into the hotel. He'd been very surprised to look outside a few minutes later to see his bags piled on the sidewalk where they'd been deposited by the limo driver. Secret Service agents never carried bags, not when they needed hands free to secure a protectee.

"Well, thank you very much. I feel special." Ari's smile chased away the last of Oakes's nerves, and a different kind of restlessness settled in the pit of her stomach.

"Did you have breakfast?" Oakes asked, fervently hoping the answer was yes. No way could she eat. She wasn't sure how long she could wait to touch her.

Ari shouldered her briefcase and gave Oakes a long look. "How much time do you have?"

"Hard to say. If something comes up, and something always does, I'll have to take care of it. Right now I've got time."

"Then right now, I'd like to go to my room if we can."

"Oh yeah, we can." Oakes waved off the bellman and pushed Ari's wheeled suitcase toward the entrance. Ari went ahead to register.

"I didn't expect to see you today," Oakes said when Ari rejoined her and they crossed the lobby toward the bank of elevators the detail had sequestered for the duration. She used the key card that only the Secret Service agents had been issued to call the elevator.

As they stepped inside, Ari said, "I have several meetings scheduled, but they're later today."

"That was lucky."

Ari grinned. "Actually, it was an excuse to come up earlier."

Oakes swallowed around the sudden surge of raw lust that mushroomed in her chest. "Was it now."

"Mm-hmm. I missed you," Ari said.

"I missed you too," Oakes said. "A lot."

Ari smiled as if Oakes had said something particularly eloquent or special. She wished she could think of something like that to say, but her mind was a little fuzzy, so she just confessed the one thing that had been on her mind for days. "I missed touching you."

Ari's bemused expression changed in a heartbeat, her lips curving into a satisfied smile and her eyes sweeping down Oakes's body like a brush of fire. "You'll have to show me just how much."

"I plan to."

The doors opened and Oakes pushed Ari's suitcase out. "The staffers have rooms here too, but you're the first to arrive."

"Sounds perfect," Ari said and keyed them into her room.

As soon as she crossed the threshold, Oakes shoved Ari's suitcase to one side and tugged Ari in for a kiss. Ari's arms came around her neck, and that empty place within her immediately filled with light and heat.

The urgency she'd felt just moments ago transformed into the desperate need to get as close as she could, for as long as she could, to speak the truth of her desire with her hands and her mouth and her lips on Ari's flesh. "Come to bed with me?"

"Oh yes." Ari leaned away, one hand trailing down Oakes's throat to curl against her chest. "I've missed your hands on me. I've missed feeling you everywhere."

Ari grasped Oakes's hand and led her to the bed. While Oakes yanked down the covers, Ari turned her back. "Unzip me?"

Hands shaking, Oakes slowly drew the zipper down the back of Ari's navy blue dress and brushed the garment off her shoulders. She lifted Ari's hair and kissed the back of her neck. As Ari drew the sleeves down her arms and pushed it lower, Oakes circled her middle with one arm and pulled her close. She kissed just below her ear, and Ari shuddered against her with a soft moan.

"Ari," Oakes said quietly.

Ari tilted her head back against Oakes's shoulder, turning so their eyes met.

"I love you," Oakes said.

Ari's breath quickened, and she turned in Oakes's arms. Her dress fell to the floor, leaving her in just her bra and panties. She cupped Oakes's face and kissed her. "Show me."

Oakes's heart nearly hammered out of her chest. She released the clasp on Ari's bra, drew the straps down her arms, and let it fall as Ari stepped free of her dress. Oakes kissed her and cupped her breast, molding it in her hand. Ari's purr of satisfaction ignited fireworks in her depths, sweet and sharp. She'd be content to stroke and caress her just to hear that sound again and again.

Ari wasn't waiting. She unbuttoned Oakes's shirt, pulled it from her pants, and pushed Oakes away. "Shed it."

Grinning, Oakes pulled off her shirt and the bra underneath while Ari unbuckled her belt and opened her pants. Naked, Oakes gripped Ari's hips, guided her down onto the bed, and gently drew Ari's panties off. Ari made a grumbling noise and a hurry-up gesture with a tilt of her hips, but Oakes held back. So sweet and sharp. She settled one thigh between Ari's, leaned over her on bent elbows, and kissed her. Her gaze fixed on Ari's, drinking her in, she swept down Ari's body and stroked between her thighs.

Ari caught her lower lip between her teeth and lifted her hips to meet her. "You feel so good."

"I want to go slow," Oakes said, "so I can tell you all the things I feel. Things I've never felt for anyone else before. Things I never knew I *could* feel."

Ari raked her nails down Oakes's forearm and covered the hand that caressed between her legs. "Come inside me and tell me. Tell me everything."

Oakes's vision swam, desire slammed through her blood, and she eased inside her.

"I don't want slow," Ari whispered. "I need you now. I need to feel you love me."

Guided by the rise and fall of Ari's hips, Oakes delved into the heat, stroked faster, deeper, as Ari clutched her shoulders. Ari's need, her unbridled desire, stoked Oakes's arousal and she rocked against Ari's thigh. She took Ari higher and higher, harder and faster and deeper. With every stroke, the urgency in the pit of Oakes's stomach tightened, coiling until she threatened to break.

Panting, Oakes braced herself on her outstretched arm and held Ari's gaze. "Feel me? I love you."

"Yes, everywhere. Make me come," Ari gasped in a desperate, wild plea.

Oakes's breath stopped in her chest. All she needed, all she would ever need, was that single image of Ari's pleasure—over and over unending. When Ari came with a sharp, keening cry of pleasure and release, Oakes snapped, her orgasm boiling through her like flame.

Ari's strength rekindled quickly, and she edged Oakes over onto her back. "I want mine—I want you."

"I'm all yours, always," Oakes said, drawing Ari down for a kiss. The insistent buzzing of her phone penetrated her foggy brain and she groaned. "Damn it."

Ari laughed and dropped her head on Oakes's shoulder. "Could have been worse."

"Not much," Oakes muttered and checked the message. "And I have to go. I'm sorry."

"No, I understand—I wasn't sure I'd see you at all," Ari said. "So I'll see you whenever you're free next."

Oakes said, "That may not be for a few days."

"I know." Ari tangled Oakes's hair in her fingers and pulled her back for a last kiss. "That's fine. It won't always be this way. We'll probably have a few hours now and then to ourselves."

"Are you okay with that?"

"It's our life." Ari sat up, naked, with the sheets around her hips as Oakes pulled on her clothes. The look in her eyes was enough to make Oakes crazy.

"I love you," Ari said. "All the rest is just part of it, who you are, and who we are. I'm sure I'll complain sometimes, but we'll figure it out."

Oakes clipped her weapon to her belt and kissed her. "We will. I can't wait."

CHAPTER TWENTY-SIX

Oakes called Evyn and handed off the detail to her before leaving the Hyatt and driving ten blocks into Old City to the address Commander Roberts had texted. She parked on a narrow street in a section of downtown Philadelphia that still bore the hallmarks of the city's history. The waterfront a few blocks away, once fronted by three-story residential row houses, now bristled with high-rise condos, but this area was a maze of narrow streets no wider than most alleys, some of them still cobblestoned, and rows of attached brick and stone buildings, many with the first floors converted into retail shops with the upper floors divided into apartments.

Her destination was an exception to the cramped and crowded commercial buildings—a brick structure four stories high that encompassed most of the block, with granite crenulations adorning the eaves. The only entrances at street level were a double-wide solid metal roll-down door to what must be a garage and, a distance away, a plain windowless entrance up a set of four granite steps. The place was a fortress.

Oakes strode up the four stone steps and looked for a bell. A security camera set into a grated recess in the upper right corner of the shallow alcove swiveled and focused on her.

A distinctly human voice that held the barest hint of AI inquired, "ID?"

Intrigued with the sophisticated tech that she'd rarely seen outside of Quantico, Oakes faced the camera and held up her commission card and badge. "Special Agent Oakes Weaver, Unites States Secret Service."

"Please enter and take the elevator to the third floor, Special Agent Weaver."

"Thanks," Oakes said dryly.

"You're welcome."

A faint click announced the entry was unlocked, and Oakes walked into a spacious, pristine garage housing several SUVs, a very flashy black Porsche, and a motorcycle. On the far wall, a large freight elevator converted for passenger use with a sliding brass grate and modern mechanics stood waiting. She stepped in, pushed 3, and looked for the other security cameras while the silent hydraulics rapidly activated her ascent. Inner doors slid open on another cavernous workspace, this one lit with recessed LED lights in the loft's high ceilings. A warren of workspaces filled with equipment that rivaled the control center in DC divided up the floor space.

"Oakes," Commander Roberts called as she emerged from an aisle in the depths of the room. "Thanks for getting here so quickly."

"Morning, Commander. I was close," Oakes said as a formality, since she'd hardly had a choice. Roberts hadn't been scheduled to arrive until the next day, but now she was here and calling for an emergency briefing. Oakes's trouble meter pinged the red zone and promised to stay there until whatever going on was handled. Tom Turner was coming up on Air Force One the next morning, and until he arrived, she was acting SAIC. Her ball, her call.

A tall blonde with the glacially cool, precision-carved features of an ice sculpture emerged from a doorway and strode toward them. Her bespoke navy blue suit hardly screamed cop but everything else about her did—the confident carriage, the assessing blue eyes, the smile that could turn lethal in a heartbeat.

"Commander Roberts, Special Agent Weaver," the blonde said, holding out her hand, "Detective Lieutenant Rebecca Frye. Thank you for coming in. We've turned up some new intelligence I thought you'd want sooner rather than not."

Cam shook her hand, as did Oakes.

"I appreciate you reading us in on this, Lieutenant," Cam said, offering the standard promise of interagency cooperation they all knew could change if the situation became one that involved the security of the president.

"Our cyberinvestigators can tell you what they've put together," Frye said as they walked. "We've also had a detective undercover with the same group, and we've made some connections there. The associations are tenuous, but they're getting tighter all the time."

The conference room held a big table in the center with a dozen chairs around it, plenty to accommodate everyone who filed in. Oakes took an open seat and studied the other people at the table. A heavyset guy in his middle years, sharp eyed, in a rumpled suit and a disinterested gaze that belied the sharp appraisal directed her way. Cop. A preppy-looking young guy in a plaid shirt and unwrinkled khakis, thin, with an intriguing face—masculine and, somehow, seductively female at the same time. The effect was unexpectedly attractive, since guys had never been her thing. Next to him, a dark-haired, remote-looking woman, broad shouldered and fit, maybe a cop, but maybe something else there too. Frye, clearly the leader, and two other women Oakes couldn't really peg. One, a rangy and dark-haired woman about her age, in a tight black T-shirt and a tattoo on her right forearm that looked like Army, and an even younger blonde in a skimpy top, dangling earrings, makeup, and ice blue fingernails. Oakes wouldn't have pegged her for cop if she hadn't looked into her eyes and found them fixed on her with laser intensity. Cop, all right.

"Sandy," Frye said to the young blonde, "why don't you give Commander Roberts and Special Agent Weaver a rundown while Sloan brings up the idents."

An image appeared on a screen that lowered at one end of the room. White male, late twenties to early thirties, in a dark T-shirt and jeans, in a crowd of similarly aged people in front of a stage at some kind of gathering.

"This is Matthew Ford," Sandy said, her voice a little husky and confident, "who we now believe is the leader of an alt-right cell we've been watching for the last few months. He is currently located across the river in Camden."

A second image came up and slid into place next to Matthew's. Another blonde, who on first glance somewhat resembled Sandy, but Oakes instantly saw the difference. This woman's features were softer, almost smudged, and her eyes lacked the eagle-like focus of the cop across from her. Instead of appearing like a coiled spring ready to burst into action, she seemed deflated. Superficial similarities, and a world of difference.

"Trish Edwards. Ford's girlfriend," Sandy said.

A group shot came up with half a dozen heads circled.

"These are some of the individuals in direct contact with Ford recently who were also present at an Identity America rally in Manhattan late last year and again"—another photo, with several more heads circled—"at a local university four months ago. We now believe all of them to be members of different cells, and they've all converged here recently." She glanced at Sloan. "You two want to do your geek thing and explain that?"

Sloan grinned, and the distant cast of her bold features flashed with lethal brilliance.

"You have the initial report from when we first tripped over the pattern," Sloan said, "and we've been tracking movements of known associates since that time. As Sandy noted, there's been a convergence in this area, and we can trace ninety percent of the individuals back to this one group. What we haven't been able to determine is the next level of the cell. Until last night."

Frye interjected, "Sandy was able to get us a phone that Ford had used to communicate with someone else in the organization, probably one of several upper-level individuals controlling the cells. Sloan and Jason pulled us up a name."

As another image of a dark-haired, middle-aged Caucasian male with broad, heavy features in a severe black suit and open-collared white shirt exiting a black SUV appeared on-screen, Sloan said, "Vladimir Kharkov."

Roberts said, "You're running him?"

Sloan said, "We supplied it to all the counterterrorism units as soon as we got it, but"—she glanced at Frye, who subtly nodded—"we decided to do a run ourselves."

Oakes glanced at Cam, who regarded Sloan with a faint smile. This unit, whoever they were and whatever their stated mission, was a lot more than appeared on the surface. Just look at their physical setup. Frye and the others worked outside the usual constraints of an urban police department and clearly had clearance to chase whatever they found worth chasing. She envied them the freedom as much as she appreciated their intel.

"I'd really like to see that program," Roberts said evenly.

Sloan smiled back, and Oakes was reminded of a documentary she'd once seen of two alpha wolves staring each other down. Opposite her at the table, Rebecca Frye looked like she was enjoying herself. She'd seen this little bit of theater before, that was clear.

"It's in the development stage," Sloan said with a shrug, "still a little rough."

"I understand," Roberts said. "Maybe when it's a little more refined, you'll share."

"Maybe we can trade," Sloan said. "You know—a show me yours kind of thing."

Roberts laughed. "Maybe we can. So...what do you know?"

Sloan's features settled back into the sharp planes and angles of a stone warrior statue. "If you dig a little bit into Kharkov's background, it gets very fuzzy a decade or so back. Whoever he is, he wasn't born with that name and probably wasn't born where his ID and traceable history suggests. He's here in the US as part of an international consortium that ostensibly works on enhanced computer memory hardware. A place called CompuDyne located, conveniently, in Maryland. No overt connections to any of the alt-right activist groups. *But* he has friends in high places."

A new image flashed, revealing Kharkov with a younger slim hipster type with neatly cropped brown hair, smooth WASPish features, and a precisely tailored suit.

"Frank Plummer," Roberts said, "aka Farris Palmer."

"Exactly," Sloan said, flicking an appreciative nod in Roberts's direction. "And he has ties to Identity America that go back a long way."

"Which he has very successfully buried beneath his alias," Roberts added.

Oakes's stomach tightened. Palmer didn't just have ties to Identity America—he was somehow connected to Nikolai Rostof. The Commander had gotten his name from Ari's father, but what Nikolai knew about him or *how* he knew was still a mystery. At least to Oakes. Cam Roberts almost certainly knew.

"You have a pretty good program somewhere yourself, Commander," Sloan said dryly.

Cam's small smile echoed Sloan's. "We had one piece, and you have the rest. The picture looks pretty clear. This can't be a coincidence that this is happening now, when the president will be in town tomorrow."

"We've got one more piece," Frye said. "Sandy."

"They're planning an action, possibly several, and"—Sandy's brows knit in obvious frustration—"I can't pin down what, where, and when. I'm close, but I think I'm running out of time."

"Violent?" Roberts asked.

"That's my read," Sandy said.

Oakes found her assessment credible. The detective might've

looked young, but if she was part of this group, she was exceptional. With any potential threat to the president, the Secret Service would have to take point. And that meant her.

Oakes said, "Have you seen any sign of weapons?"

Sandy shook her head. "No. Not one word. Nothing to suggest they've got a stockpile of firearms, and I've been in Ford's apartment. There's nothing there. And…none of them look like shooters."

"What's your read on them, then," Oakes asked.

"They're not fanatics in the usual sense," Sandy said, "but a couple of them I could see being willing to take extreme action."

"Suicide bombers? Chemical agents? Bioweapons?"

Sandy was quiet a long moment. "The secrecy, the extreme loyalty to the group, the general sense of fatalism about anything other than violent action being effective—yeah, I can see a couple of them would fit the profile of suicide bombers. I don't think the others are aware of that, though."

"That's often the case," Oakes said. "But given the choices for an effective strike here, we have to consider it a high-probability threat."

Sandy straightened, the glint in her eyes distinctly predatory. "And that would fit if one person in each group self-terminated, taking others with them. What a mess that would be—that kind of action often results in enhanced recruitment." She shook her head. "Go figure."

"The Secret Service will take point in this," Oakes said to Frye.

Frye said, "We'll keep working our end. The PPD will need to be put on alert."

"Select teams only," Commander Roberts said. "We don't want this leaking. We need to round up all of these individuals. If we shatter the cells, they'll need time to rebuild."

"Understood," Frye said. "My unit will spearhead the SWAT teams."

Oakes rose. "We need these images for our details," Oakes said. "We have to find them before they get into the streets."

"We can hit the ones we've identified tonight," Frye said. "That should throw the cells into enough chaos to disrupt what they have planned for tomorrow."

"And what about Ford?" Oakes asked. "What's his game?"

Sandy grimaced. "Whatever he's planning, it's his own story. And he wants it to be unforgettable."

CHAPTER TWENTY-SEVEN

Game Day minus 22 hours

"If you'll excuse me just a moment," Ari said to Wayne Lorenzo, the regional network producer for Rostof media, "but I need to take this."

"Of course, Ms. Rostof," he said, hiding the annoyance he probably felt at the interruption. His aura of self-importance had been barely restrained since she'd arrived for the pre-production meeting.

She stepped out of his corner office with its two walls of windows overlooking downtown Philadelphia and the waterfront into the private waiting area that was almost as spacious. The receptionist manned a semicircular desk that rivaled the command deck on the *Enterprise* in the center of the rich maroon-carpeted expanse opposite the bank of elevators.

"Hello," Ari said as she walked to the far end of the room and stood in front of the windows. Barges and oil tankers plowed up and down the river, leaving muddy gray troughs in their wake.

"It's me," Oakes said. "I'm sorry to interrupt you, but I need to see you as soon as you can."

"Of course. I'm just finishing up here. Where are you?"

"I'm on my way back to the hotel. I need to brief Evyn and then I'll be free. Half an hour?"

"Where?" Ari asked.

"Your room."

"All right. I'll see you then."

Ari slid the phone into her jacket pocket and returned to finish her meeting. She'd really only needed to finish up reviewing the week's broadcast schedule, and undoubtedly Lorenzo's barely disguised irritation stemmed from his opinion that sort of thing was beneath him. However, Ari didn't agree. She'd wanted to confirm the timing of on-air coverage, vet the reporters who would be doing the in-person interviews with the president, establish when and where the interviews would take place, and check the blocks reserved for prime-time ad placement. A snafu at this late date would result in canceled interviews and the loss of millions of dollars of advertising and on-air exposure.

"Thank you, Wayne," Ari said as she walked back into the office. "I think we've about covered the essentials. Please be sure any change in plans, no matter how small, is relayed to me or Ms. Alaqua immediately. Thank you for your time."

Lorenzo stood and extended his hand over the desk.

"We're very glad to see you in your new position, Ms. Rostof," he said, with all but a wink.

She returned his handshake. "I'm meeting with cable and broadcast networks later today. President Powell's campaign is of international importance, and we of course want to be sure that the coverage is as extensive."

His smile faltered just a little, and he nodded. "Of course. Of course. Anything you need—anything at all—please call my direct number."

"Thank you." She left his luxurious office, took the silent, speedy elevator down to the first floor, and exited out to the street. She rather missed Witt as she texted for an Uber. The convenience of having a driver waiting, however, did not override the knowledge that her every movement was being noted, if not reported. Witt was probably equally happy to be somewhere else.

She arrived back at the hotel twenty minutes later and found she couldn't really work while waiting for Oakes. Usually, her concentration was total, and even five minutes was enough time for her to be productive. When the knock sounded on her hotel room door, she hurried to open it.

Oakes entered, and when she didn't kiss her, Ari steeled herself. Whatever the problem, it wasn't simple.

"Hi," Ari said. "I didn't order coffee or anything. I wasn't sure how much time you had."

"I'm fine." Oakes strode past her into the lounge area of the large suite and Ari followed.

"What's going on?" Ari asked.

"Two things," Oakes said abruptly. "The president's schedule throughout the day tomorrow—possibly longer—is likely to change on short notice."

Ari stiffened. Worse than she'd expected, then. "I see. Can you be more specific?"

"I'm afraid not yet. I may have more details for you later."

"I can't do any kind of damage control until you tell me exactly how the itinerary will be disrupted, but I don't need to tell you how critical it is at this late date that we not alter the appearances we already have scheduled. Aside from the cost, the public perception—"

"This isn't open to discussion," Oakes said.

"I see," Ari repeated. "Is this you pulling rank?"

"When matters of security are concerned, the Secret Service has the final word."

"Except for the president's."

A muscle on the left side of Oakes's jaw tensed. "Yes, that's correct." She ran a hand through her hair. "Don't fight me on this, Ari. I'm not trying to make your life difficult."

Ari huffed. "As if fighting it were even possible. Is this matter above my pay grade, then, that you can't give me any explanation?"

"It's a matter of national security, at this point."

Ari reined back her irritation. Oakes was doing her job, and right now, their jobs were at odds. "A credible threat—that's what you're saying."

Oakes held her gaze silently.

"All right." Ari blew out a breath. "Since I have no choice, I'll need all the time you can give me."

"That's why I'm here now. And one other reason." Oakes grimaced. She wasn't handling this very well, but the president wasn't the only one at risk. Anyone in the kill zone could be a target, and that included Ari. After her immediate reaction to what the HPCU's intel meant for the president's security, her next thought had been of Ari. That Ari could be in mortal danger. The image shorted out her brain. Her professional control went out the window whenever she thought about that. "If it's at all possible, I'd like you to limit your exposure. Curtail your personal appearances with him until further notice."

Ari laughed incredulously. "Now? At the biggest event of the year? We have donor dinners scheduled, meetings with high-ranking congressional supporters, lobbyists. You can't be serious."

"I am. I don't—" Oakes squeezed the bridge of her nose. "You realize if there's a threat to him and you're anywhere nearby—"

Ari cupped her jaw. "Oakes, stop. I know what you're trying to say, and I feel the same way whenever I think about what *you* do for a living. It scares the hell out of me. But you'll do what you have to do, and so will I. And I don't want you thinking about me when you're trying to do your job."

Oakes grasped her shoulders and pulled her close. Pressing her cheek to Ari's hair, she closed her eyes and just breathed her in. Slowly, she shoved the fear back into the recesses of her mind where it belonged. "It's hard for me not to think of you. It's pretty much all I do."

"That part is all good," Ari whispered as her mouth moved over Oakes's neck. "You just have to get used to me being in your life, and quickly. Because I'm here, and I'm staying here. You need to do what you do best with no worries, no second thoughts, and no distractions."

"No distractions?" Oaks laughed. Being in the same space with Ari made her head spin. Being away from her made her a little bit crazy. Touching her set her on fire. "You're the best distraction that's ever happened to me."

Ari's arms circled her neck as she leaned back, giving Oakes a satisfied smile. "Couldn't be happier, then." She pressed her fingers to Oakes's mouth. "I heard everything you said. I understand. I'm not at all happy about any of it, especially the possibility of you needing to put yourself in harm's way, but…" Her voice wavered. "We are who we are, the two of us together. Tell me what you can, as soon as you can."

Oakes kissed her with all the heat and longing and tenderness she could convey. "I love you."

Ari tightened her grip and closed her eyes. She'd never known that love could make her so strong, and so incredibly vulnerable at the same time. "I love you back."

Cam and Oakes logged in to the video conference from the Secret Service control center at the Hyatt on a secure line.

Tom Turner came on first. "Cam, Oakes. Hold for the president."

The others appeared on her monitor one after the other: Blair, the president, Lucinda.

"We've got a situation up here," Cam said. "All evidence points to a violent alt-right group planning an action which we believe may target the president."

"How credible?" Andrew asked.

"High threat level." Cam ran down the details of her briefing with the High Profile Crimes Unit. "They're good, and their evidence is solid. We're mobilizing here with the FBI and local law enforcement."

"Nothing specific," Lucinda asked, "in terms of time, place, or target?"

"Unfortunately, no," Cam said.

The president said, "I can't see that we'll be able to do anything other than we typically would in terms of security. Tom?"

"We can bring in more agents to widen our perimeters on the ground. I also recommend changing the motorcade route just in case we've had any kind of breach in security thus far. Oakes?"

"Not a problem," Oakes said. "No details will be provided to the police escort on the route until Air Force One is in the air. I recommend alternate route B."

Tom nodded. "We won't scramble the escort or file the flight plans until just before takeoff."

"Sir," Oakes added, "I recommend we proceed directly to the hotel from the airport. We can approach on a parallel street and enter via the secondary rear garage entrance."

"That would mean canceling the televised arrival," Lucinda said.

Andrew shook his head. "No, I don't think that's going to be possible, Agent Weaver. I understand your recommendations, but we need to be seen arriving with the expectation that I will be the party's nominee, and that means publicly visible and confident."

"We can arrive at the main entrance but cancel the rope line," Tom said.

"Not for my first public exposure," the president said. "First impressions, as you all know," he added with a wry expression, "are critical."

"I'd strongly advise you to reconsider, Mr. President," Cam said.

Andrew glanced at Lucinda, who nodded, her expression completely unreadable. But apparently, the president could read behind her veiled eyes.

"The rope line stays," he said.

After the video call was ended, Oakes left to confer with the rest of the detail. Alone for a few moments at least, Cam dialed Blair's number.

"How serious is this?" Blair said.

"Just short of confirmed red. We've identified half a dozen active cells, possibly all staging an attack at the same time. Best-case scenario is we apprehend the majority before tomorrow."

"And if you don't? What exactly are you expecting?"

Cam wished she could bridge the infuriating distance separating them and touch her. "Suicide attacks."

"God," Blair murmured.

"Blair, if there's any way you can alter your travel plans, come up earlier, or delay until—"

"You know I can't do that. Besides, I couldn't be any safer than next to my father when I have you and the entire Secret Service, the FBI, and countless others protecting us."

"I knew you'd say that," Cam said.

"Of course you did. And you'll have expected this too—promise me, Commander, since I know you won't be sitting back, leading from some safe zone—don't let anything happen to you."

"I won't," Cam said, promising as she always did the one thing she couldn't really promise, and they both knew it.

"You're going to call the feebs in, aren't you," Watts said.

"Have to," Frye said. "Domestic terrorism. Their game, their ball."

A chorus of groans emanated from around the table.

"But," Frye added, "I won't let them shut us out. If they want our intelligence, they have to let us in on the takedowns."

"Lieutenant," Sandy said.

"Sandy?" Frye said.

"I think the only way I'm going to get any more useful intelligence is to turn Trish."

Beside her, Dell jolted upright. "If that goes bad, your cover will be blown. And these people won't hesitate to take you out."

Sandy bit back a retort. Dell always did this—one of the things she loved about Dell was how protective she was, even when she was being a jerk and treating her like her girlfriend instead of another cop. It was knee-jerk, and she knew absolutely that Dell respected her abilities and was proud of her. Dell was just scared. And Sandy knew how to handle scared. "Thank you very much, Detective Mitchell. I *never* thought of that."

Dell flushed. "Sorry."

"Detective Mitchell has a point," Frye said coolly, having refereed the same situation in different combinations within the group many times before. The strength of their unit was their loyalty to and, contrary to popular teaching, their dependence on one another. Any one of them would die for any other. "What makes you think she'll turn?"

"She's been excluded, and she's angry about that. She's also not ideologically committed like the others. She is Matthew Ford's girlfriend first and foremost, and that's her main connection to all of this. He's pulled away from her lately. His attention's directed elsewhere. She's angry, and I think a little bit frightened. If she knew she could get pulled down by what the same people who've pulled Matthew away from her were planning, I think there's a good chance she'd want out."

"I think the kid's got a point," Watts said. "I've been sitting out in that car enough nights to get a good sense of this Trish girl. She's no revolutionary, or whatever they call themselves. She's just one of those girls that hangs on to a guy because that's what she thinks she should do, who believes that's all she can do, and she got sucked into this thing."

"Thanks, Watts." Sandy smiled at him. He was so much more than he wanted people to know, and he always seemed a little embarrassed when it showed.

"I didn't say it'd be easy, and you're going to need backup. But"—he looked at Frye—"considering what's at stake here, it's worth a shot. They might not get close to the president—they'll have agents six feet deep around him—but what about all the civilians at risk? Those are our responsibility."

"Make contact," Frye said, "but at the first sign she's in deeper than we think, you pull out for good. I want you to disappear before they can retaliate."

"Got it," Sandy said, wondering how she was going to do that if Matthew was anywhere around.

CHAPTER TWENTY-EIGHT

The Oasis
Game Day minus 8 hours

Eleven p.m. came and passed, then midnight, as Sandy watched the door waiting for Trish to show up. A few minutes later, Sandy ordered her third beer, took a couple of swallows as she had with the first two glasses, and left it on an empty table. At 12:35, she slipped into the rear of the bar and headed down the narrow hallway toward the bathrooms, grateful for the dim lighting that saved her from seeing the grunge on the floor and God knows what else on the walls, and pulled out her phone.

"There's nothing—no call, no reply to my texts," she said. "I'm going to Camden."

"I'll be behind you," Watts said.

Sandy left the bar, walked to the closest cross street that wasn't barricaded for the president's arrival the following morning, and miraculously only waited six minutes for a cab. She slid in and texted Watts. *ETA, 10 minutes.*

On your tail, sweet thing.

She smiled and slid her phone away. She and Watts were the only ones not attached to the joint antiterrorist task force operation set to commence at 0400. Dell, Frye, Oakes and another Secret Service agent, and the PPD SWAT were embedded with the FBI strike teams planning to hit the cell members the HPCU and federal counterterrorism units had identified from vehicle IDs, photographs, phone records, and known associate networks in simultaneous strikes on six different locations within a twenty-five-mile radius of Center City. The FBI, of course, had taken over the operation as soon as they'd been notified, and none of the HPCU were happy about it. Their case, should be their arrests too. At least the team was still involved. Jason and Sloan, who were technically civilian consultants, were handling all the communication and electronic surveillance from HPCU headquarters.

Sandy didn't see Matthew's Corvette where he usually parked it near the corner. That didn't necessarily mean he wasn't home. They needed to find him and take him in before the strikes. If he got word, he'd disappear.

She texted Trish again, still no response. The apartment windows on the street side were dark. Something in her gut insisted this was all wrong, but if Matthew was home and she tipped them off before the raid, she might jeopardize the entire operation. She hesitated, knowing Watts was parked somewhere nearby, waiting for her to make the call.

She did the only thing she could do, the only thing she truly trusted. She went with her gut, rang the buzzer, and waited. Nothing. She tried the door and, like with so many of the run-down buildings in the area, security wasn't a big priority. The deadbolt wasn't operational, and the lock itself took a little jiggling before it gave. The foyer, with a row of dented brass mailboxes with jimmied locks left over from an earlier era and a scattering of trampled flyers on the cracked tile floor, opened directly into a dingy hallway with dust balls, food litter, and cat pee making the whole place smell like a latrine.

No light showed from beneath the single door at the far end of the hall. The two apartments on the second floor were all quiet as she passed by their doors as well. She climbed to the third floor and knocked on Matthew Ford's door. She was working on her story for appearing unannounced when it opened. Trish was backlit by the light from the galley kitchen down the hall. Her hair was disheveled, her makeup smeared, and her face puffy.

"Trish," Sandy said. "I've been calling you. Didn't you get my texts?"

"The fucker took my phone. Too bad he didn't take the rest of the trash."

"What?" Sandy peered around Trish's shoulder. Empty take-out containers, beer bottles, and plastic cups, some still holding wine dregs, littered the coffee table and floor.

"He took his duffel and every fucking phone he could find. Gone." She snapped her fingers, managing only a muted thud. "Just like that."

"Gone where?" Trish shrugged helplessly, and Sandy eased inside and closed the door. Trish seemed too upset to question why Sandy had just shown up. She might be on her way to being high too. "Let me take a look around. Maybe he left a note or something."

Trish snorted and wiped her eyes. "He didn't. I looked, but"—she waved an arm—"feel free."

Sandy did a quick scan of the room, confirmed it was empty, and checked the kitchen. The refrigerator held half-open cans and bottles and a few take-out containers. "At least he left the food."

"Yeah, decent of him, the prick."

"Did he say anything?" Sandy called as she headed toward the single bedroom. "That he was leaving or something. Or if something happened?"

"I told you I haven't seen much of him the last week, the last two weeks, really. He'd come and go at all hours, wouldn't say much to me. Wouldn't tell me what he was doing or what was happening. He didn't even say good-bye." Trish slumped on a cracked fake-leather stool in the corner of the kitchen. "I knew as soon as the others showed up this would happen."

Sandy hurriedly searched the bedroom closet, found it was empty. A few of Matthew's shirts hung on hangers, but no duffel. He left most of his clothes, so he had something else in the duffel. Weapons? Nothing under the bed, and the single chest of drawers revealed nothing but a few T-shirts, underwear, and Trish's clothes. He was gone and he hadn't taken much with him. Maybe he planned to come back, but then, why not tell Trish he was leaving?

"Trish," Sandy said as she came back into the kitchen. "Where would he go? Was he meeting one of the others?"

"How would I know? I'm not important enough to tell."

Trish was angry, and definitely more than a little drunk. Sandy grabbed her hands, gave them a little shake to get her attention.

"This is really important, Trish. Matthew could be in trouble. Maybe they all are. If you know where he is, have any idea at all, it's important you tell me."

Trish frowned. "What do you mean, trouble?"

"If they're planning something violent, they could all be in danger. Did he tell you anything? Where or what they were going to do?"

"What does it matter now? He's gone. They're all doing their special thing. Because they're all so smart and important."

"It matters, Trish. They could get hurt. Other people could get hurt. Matthew could stop it."

"I don't know where he went," Trish said. "I don't know what they're planning. It all felt like some kind of big game, you know? All the secret talks and the phone calls and the meetings. But I don't think they're really going to do anything." She gave Sandy a confused look. "That would be crazy, right?"

Sandy believed her. Trish wasn't part of Ford's plan, and now she'd lost him.

Philadelphia
3:45 a.m.

Rebecca's phone rang as the armored vehicle slipped silently through the streets of Fishtown.

"Frye," she said.

"Ford's in the wind," Sloan said. "Sandy couldn't get anything from Trish, but he's gone."

"We'll get something when we hit the other cells," Frye said. "Someone will talk."

She didn't add, *if any of them know anything beyond their own small act in the larger play.* To date, Ford had been smart enough to go unnoticed by a dozen counterterrorism agencies. He might have been smart enough to keep critical details from the others too. But they could get lucky. Sometimes being lucky beat being good.

"Good luck," Sloan said, echoing Frye's thoughts.

"Everyone on schedule to hit their targets?"

"So far. We've got them all on closed-circuit here." Sloan laughed. "The FBI has joined us. It's a real fun party."

Frye half smiled. Yet another government agency envious of Sloan's toys.

"Keep me informed."

"Keep your head down, Frye," Sloan said.

"Plan on it."

Alpha team—go!
Bravo team—go!
Charlie Delta Echo—go go!
Strike teams all over the city simultaneously took down doors in

houses and apartments, SWAT and CAT—the Secret Service counter-assault unit—swarming inside, apprehending anyone they found. FBI and Secret Service canine teams followed, the bomb dogs and their handlers scouring the buildings and grounds. Rebecca counted a dozen detonators, C-4 explosives, and vests wired and ready to be armed in the back room of the apartment her team raided.

Within fifteen minutes, all targets had been swept and cleared. Forensic teams stayed behind at each site to log evidence, bag and tag all electronics, and photograph the scene.

Fourteen people were sequestered at the Edward N. Cahn Federal Building for interrogation. Rebecca and an FBI interrogator, along with a half dozen other teams of two, began the questioning after the detainees were printed and photographed.

The interrogation room resembled a hundred others she'd seen over the years, although this one smelled a little better than most. Four straight-backed metal chairs, two on each side, flanked the long metal table in the center of the room. A pale redhead in a shapeless V-neck jersey tee and institutional orange canvas pants was handcuffed to a ring on the far side of the table. She'd obviously been sleeping in the tee and little else and someone had issued her the pants, which were going to be part of her standard wardrobe for a long time.

"Ms. Rothman," FBI Special Agent Renée Savard said, "what time were you instructed to initiate your action this morning?"

"Lawyer," the redhead said instantly.

Special Agent Renée Savard shook her head. "You've been detained under suspicion of domestic terrorism, supported by the presence of explosives with the clear intent to harm. According to the Patriot Act, this action falls under the jurisdiction of military law, and as such, we are not required to bring charges prior to questioning, and thus"—Savard smiled as if everything she said was the best news of the day—"you are not entitled to an attorney at this time."

Rebecca slid out a chair and sat across from the prisoner. "The more you cooperate, the more you help yourself."

She didn't mind playing good cop if she could get a lead on Matthew Ford.

In a dozen other interrogation rooms the same conversations were taking place. And in every one, the question of the hour was where was Matthew Ford.

❖

A knock on her door roused Ari from a light, restless sleep a little before six. Her alarm was due to go off any moment, and she massaged her gritty eyelids with her fingertips. She hadn't expected to sleep at all, but the fear and tension of waiting while Oakes took part in the takedowns eventually wore her out.

When she let Oakes in, her heart pounded with relief. "Is it over?"

"Not yet. Ford is still whereabouts unknown." Oakes rubbed her face. Dark circles ringed her eyes, and she looked pale and thinner than the last time Ari had seen her.

Ari's stomach tightened. *Not over yet.* "You need coffee and some food. Do you have time?"

"Just a little."

Ari kissed her and gave her a little push in the direction of the sofa in the seating area. "Go sit down. I'll get something up here right away."

Everyone on the president's staff got the fastest service possible, and ten minutes later, a pot of coffee, several baskets of bread and pastries, and breakfast food arrived.

"What about everyone else?" Ari asked after Oakes had her first cup of coffee. "Are they giving you more information about their organization—who's in charge?"

"It's early yet, but some people are talking." Oakes snorted. "Most people are talking. Now that everything is coming apart, only a few of them are hard-core. Those are the ones we suspect would have worn the vests."

The horror of that image tightened Ari's throat, and she wrapped her arms around her midsection to quiet the turmoil that roiled there. "How can anyone believe suicide could achieve anything?"

"When fear and helplessness are the goals, it's a pretty good weapon." Oakes sighed and poured a second cup of coffee. "As near as we can tell, four individual cells were mobilized, and we have eighty percent of their members in custody." She grimaced. "But not Ford."

"What does that mean for the president's arrival?" Ari asked.

Oakes gave her a long look. "Will the president change his mind about appearing in public, walking the rope line?"

"I doubt it."

"My thoughts too. So we'll have to find Ford in a crowd of tens of thousands before he gets close enough to harm anyone."

CHAPTER TWENTY-NINE

Game Day
Philadelphia
National Convention, Day 1

Ari pulled on the cobalt blue blazer that nearly matched the color of her eyes, smoothed out the white textured silk shirt, and checked that her makeup was camera ready.

Oakes knocked at seven a.m. exactly.

"Hi," Ari said when she opened the door.

Oakes, in a charcoal suit, her lapel pin signifying Secret Service on the left side, and a dark, intense expression on her face, stepped inside. "We've got about thirty seconds."

"I know." Ari kissed her and pressed both hands to her shoulders. "Be careful today."

"Stay close to the agents today," Oakes said, and kissed her again. "I love you."

Ari ran her fingers through Oakes's hair, leaving it ever so slightly disheveled, leaving her mark even if only she could see it. Oakes wouldn't be riding in the motorcade to meet the president. She'd be staying behind with the hundreds of law enforcement agents securing the area and hunting for Matthew Ford. "I love you too."

They didn't speak on the way down to the basement level where a line of black SUVs idled at the top of the entrance ramp, the lead cars bearing US flags and presidential symbols. The mobile hazmat, bomb control, and medical vans followed later in the line. As they approached, Cam Roberts climbed into the back seat of the lead car. An agent opened the rear door of the third car in the line.

"Ms. Rostof," she said.

"Thank you," Ari said, pausing to catch Oakes's gaze. "I'll see you after the press conference."

There was nothing left for her to say. Agents were posted on floors above and below the one the president would occupy, in the garage, at the hotel entrances and surveillance points inside, and at strategic locations on the inner perimeter surrounding the hotel. Secret Service agents, local police, and FBI swarmed the outer perimeter in plain clothes, hunting for Ford.

Everything was in place. Everyone had seen the image of his face.

Now all they could do was follow protocol. Oakes and the others would do their jobs and she would do hers.

Oakes stepped back as Ari stepped into the car, and almost as soon as she'd snapped her seat belt into place, the vehicles moved out. Out her smoked glass window, the city streets along the motorcade route appeared eerily deserted. No traffic, no irritated cabbies blaring horns, and no pedestrians. At the inner perimeter line, she caught her first glimpse of crowds milling about behind police barricades. Scores of uniformed police erected more metal barriers to allow civilians to line the route for a fleeting glimpse of the president's car passing.

A dozen motorcycle police fell into line in front of the lead car to escort them over the bridge to the airport. With no traffic on the bridge, they arrived at the airfield in less than fifteen minutes. The vehicles pulled into line along the runway. People crowded six deep along the length of a chain-link fence bordering a grassy expanse on the far side of the runway. Uniformed police on foot and in patrol cars with light bars flashing stood ready to stop any eager onlookers who decided to climb the fence for a better view of the president's arrival. The press congregated behind temporary barricades set out along the runway behind the wall of Secret Service vehicles.

At eight a.m., Air Force One set down and taxied alongside the waiting cars. Ari got out and stood beside the SUV along with the agents and watched the majestic 747 taxi to a stop. As the engines wound down, the staircase slowly descended and the military escorts exited and took their position at the foot of the stairs. The president and Blair stepped out together, followed by Lucinda, the first doctor, the protective detail, White House staffers, and the press. Secret Service agents hurriedly crossed the tarmac to flank the president on his way to the vehicles.

Blair motioned Ari up to the second car in line. "Ride with me."

Ari slid into the back seat with Blair and Commander Roberts.

Within moments, they were on their way back to the city.

"How are we doing?" Blair said.

"The polls are positive," Ari said. "The president has maintained a healthy lead, the delegates are all solid in their plans to vote as expected, and the economy has been helping us out. Everything looks good."

Blair nodded. "His handling of health care and the minimum wage questions at the debates really solidified his support."

"It helps that he knows what he's talking about, and it shows."

"That's why he is going to win," Blair said.

"He wouldn't have had any competition at all except the democratic socialist candidate just won't give up the spotlight." Ari shrugged. "In four days, none of that will matter. We'll be moving on to the campaign trail in a whole new game."

They were over the bridge and entering Center City within moments. The closer they got to the hotel, the more Ari's heart pounded. She curled her fingers to hide the tremor. Oakes expected something to happen, although she hadn't said so in so many words. Across from her, Cameron Roberts emanated fierce tension with the unswerving focus of a jungle cat poised to take down prey. Silent, powerful, deadly.

The motorcade turned onto Market Street, the main avenue bisecting the city from north to south. Only a few blocks now. The streets were lined with people and police.

Cam said, "Upon disembarking, you and Blair will join the president and proceed directly to the entrance."

"Lars Anderson from RBN news will do a thirty-second on-air interview at the entrance to the hotel," Ari said.

"Of course," Cam said. "Agents will be waiting to accompany you."

What she meant was that Secret Service agents, Oakes among them, would be waiting to stand between them and any threat from the public, who waited just feet away beyond the rope line to catch a glimpse of President Andrew Powell. Today, Matthew Ford would almost certainly be among them.

Eagle's ETA three minutes

Evyn, driving the lead car, alerted the agents on the ground the president was about to arrive at the hotel.

Oakes, waiting at the entrance to the semicircular drive fronting the Hyatt, scanned the crowds surrounding her. Agents to her left and right, interspersed with the crowd, were doing the same. Hundreds of faces, young and old, of every race and nationality, jostling, pressing forward, jockeying for a place against the metal barricades bordering the deep blue carpet extending from the point where the president's limo would stop to the hotel entrance.

Ford could be among them, possibly close enough to fire a shot or toss a grenade, or even launch himself in a suicide vest into the president's path. She and every law enforcement agent for a hundred miles had his picture, but he could've disguised his appearance or donned a uniform that at first glance would be bypassed, or any number of a dozen things. Oakes was trained to look for the odd detail or a traditional terrorist tool—the backpack containing explosives, the out-of-place coat on a hot summer day covering a suicide vest, the one person moving against the crowd in an unwavering path toward the principal or displaying some sign of agitation or excitement.

Ford was out there, Oakes knew it. They all knew it. None of the cell members they'd apprehended claimed to know of Ford's plan. They were probably telling the truth. According to Commander Roberts, the CIA was interrogating Ford's Russian contact—his presumed handler with the ties to a congressman—but he was a professional and would be a lot harder to break than the untrained fanatics they'd arrested the night before. She had no hard intelligence. All she had to go on was instinct. And her instinct said he was out there.

ETA one minute, Evyn announced.

And she was out of time.

Sandy worked her way through the crowd, moving from one end of the street in front of the Hyatt to the other, back and forth, searching for him. He wouldn't wait. He *couldn't* wait, not now that whatever he'd planned had failed. He must know they were looking for him, and unless he abandoned the plan entirely, it would have to be now. Somewhere in those thirty feet between the time the president stepped out of the armored vehicle and when he entered the hotel lobby, when he was most exposed, Ford would have to act.

Suicide vest like he'd planned with the others? The June morning was on their side, clear and bright and already close to seventy degrees. Hardly anyone wore a jacket.

Something else, then. A handgun was most likely. Small, easy to conceal under a T-shirt or inside a waistband until the last second. All it took was one well-placed shot or even a wild spray of automatic fire. But she didn't think so—not showy enough somehow, too simple. Too *ordinary*.

Matthew Ford wanted to be remembered—that's what Trish had said. He wanted his face to be known. Something bigger, something unforgettable. The sound of the motorcycle escort, sirens blaring, announced the president's imminent arrival. Sandy pushed closer toward the entrance. He would need to be close. He was close. She could feel it.

He'd known since five a.m. he would be alone in this. None of his contacts had checked in with him. There would be no diversions along the outer perimeters to draw police and FBI and Secret Service agents away at the last moment. He still held an advantage. They wouldn't know where he was. They wouldn't know what he looked like now. He'd been in position for hours, sitting in a Starbucks among a crowd of people waiting to see the motorcade. He'd watched the bursts of color across the sky at sunrise. His last sunrise.

When the emergency vehicles and news vans had arrived at six, and scores of people filled the cordoned-off area reserved for them, he'd left the Starbucks where he'd been waiting and tossed the light nylon windbreaker he'd used to cover the navy blue shirt with the paramedic emblem on the sleeve into a trash can. Mingling with the dozens of first responders wasn't difficult. Paramedics, EMTs, firefighters all too busy with their own preparations to notice someone from a different rig.

Secret Service agents and police were heavy on the ground, but so far his shaved head, camouflaged like his face with tanner, had been enough of an alteration to let him go unnoticed. He worked his way behind the press of reporters closest to the rope line. When he slipped the long, slim canister from his equipment belt and held it aloft, he wanted them to focus on him. He'd have just enough time to be captured on film for the world to see his face before he depressed the plunger on the aerosol canister and, along with the president and anyone standing within a hundred feet of him, died.

❖

The motorcade pulled up in front of the hotel and Oakes took one last look through the crowd. Sandy Sullivan, fifteen feet away, did the same, and their eyes met for an instant.

Oakes's call now. She took a breath and radioed the agents inside the cars.

"All clear."

The lead car stopped, Evyn came around the front and stood opposite the agent who opened the rear door for President Powell and Lucinda Washburn. Ari stepped out of the second vehicle with Blair and Cam Roberts. Cameras flashed. The two groups converged and started up the blue carpet. Secret Service agents kept pace at points around them.

Evyn's job was to protect them now. Oakes forced her gaze away from Ari and tracked back to Sandy.

The detective, blond hair a beacon in the sea of shifting humanity, suddenly surged forward against the crowd. A man forged a line directly toward the entrance, leaving people stumbling in his wake, his hand aloft, glinting silver.

Sandy, closing in on the man, shouted, "Matthew! Is that you?"

Oakes surged into the breach.

CHAPTER THIRTY

National Convention, Day 4

"You look great, babe," Dell said as Sandy pulled off her top and grabbed another one out of the closet.

"That color's not quite right," she said distractedly.

Dell leaned back on the bed on her elbows and crossed her legs, enjoying the show. She'd been dressed for half an hour. Pulling on a pair of good pants, a pressed white shirt, belt, and loafers didn't take a lot of time. Making sure her hair was lying right, which it was, took longer than that. Sandy, on the other hand, had been through four outfits and counting.

"You're always the best-looking woman in the room," Dell commented.

Sandy looked over her shoulder with an eye roll. "You already got yours today. So enough with the compliments." She set her hands on her hips, pulled the last shirt from the closet, and slipped it on. "Besides, it isn't every day you get to meet the president, you know."

"It isn't every day a crazy-ass cop saves the president's life."

"It wasn't me who jumped on him," Sandy said. The image of Oakes sailing through the air, clamping a hand around Matthew's wrist, and taking him down with that silver canister clutched between them still woke her at night. If that had been an explosive, Oakes would be dead. If Ford had managed to depress the release valve on the aerosol container, hundreds might have died. All she did was distract him for that extra second it took for Oakes to make contact. She shivered.

Dell was at her side in an instant, cupping her face. "Hey. It's over, you got him."

"We all got him," Sandy said.

"If you hadn't picked him up cutting through the crowd, if you hadn't drawn Oakes's attention, if you hadn't called his name..." Dell shook her head.

None of the agents or police could have discharged a weapon in that crowd. The only choice had been to physically intercept him or block his weapon with their bodies. If they hadn't had that one second of hesitation, long enough for Oakes and then half a dozen other Secret Service agents to pile onto him, the body count would have been inestimable. The president could have been killed. Sandy could be gone.

Dell rested her forehead against Sandy's and closed her eyes. "You're a hero, babe. And the best cop I know."

"Everything I know about being a cop, you and the rest of the team taught me." Sandy threaded her arms around Dell's waist and kissed her. "And you're the best teachers I know. Just remember that when you start worrying."

"I love you." Dell kissed her. "Just don't try to be a hero too often."

"Oh, I'm so done with that." Sandy laughed and took Dell's hand. "Come on, Rookie, let's go see the president."

"You know," Cam said, slipping her arms around Blair's waist as she stood before the mirror putting in her earrings, "even when Lucinda is First Lady, it will always be you the public will remember at his side. You're a big reason he's where he is today."

Blair turned and circled Cam's shoulders. She smiled a bit ruefully. "As hard as it's been—and as much as I fought it sometimes—I don't regret any of it...except for the reason it's been me and not my mom."

Cam kissed her. "You've made both your parents proud."

Blair's eyes filled. "I love you for that. I love you for being here with me."

"Wouldn't want to be anywhere else. Ever."

"Well, then," Blair said, "it's time to jump back on the merry-go-round."

Cam shrugged into her suit jacket and smiled as Blair straightened her collar. "Should be a fun ride."

Blair snorted. "I would rather a nice, long, quiet *stroll* for the next four years."

"Somehow, I don't think that's likely to happen. But"—Cam slid her hand inside her jacket and pulled out two airline tickets—"in three days, we'll be on a plane, and I'm not telling anyone where we're going." She kissed her. "Even you."

Blair's eyes lit up. "Oh my God. Yes, please."

Laughing, Cam kissed her again. "Anytime you say."

"Every day, for all time."

"I'll be there." Cam took her hand, and together they walked out to join her father for his acceptance speech.

Oakes walked over to the staging area in the huge convention hall where Ari stood directing her staffers. The doors would open in less than five minutes, and thousands of delegates would pour in for the last day of political jostling, dealmaking, speech making, and celebration.

"We're going to need to move the podium to the other side of the stage," Oakes said.

Ari looked up from her tablet where she'd been checking off last-minute details. "We can't do that. The cameramen are all set up in the broadcast booth—"

"Have to do it," Oakes said. "It's in direct line with the exit path to the backstage exit."

"We're just now figuring that out?" Ari never got frazzled, but she sounded close. No, actually, she sounded very, very annoyed.

Oakes shrugged. "Water main broke on Eleventh. We had to remap our emergency extraction routes." Ari blew out a breath and a lock of hair floated up from her forehead. Oakes smoothed it down with a finger. "The media people will adjust. They always get the shot."

Ari caught her breath. Dozens of cameras had caught Oakes for the world to watch over and over in endless loops, her body in flight as she intercepted Matthew Ford the instant before he released sarin into the crowd, fifty feet from the president. She'd seen the image hundreds of times, until she should have been numb, but she wasn't. In some deep place inside her, she was still terrified. And incredibly proud.

When Oakes and a handful of agents tackled Ford, the Secret Service agents surrounding her and the others with the president closed in on them and herded them inside the lobby, everyone moving like a wave spreading outward from the seismic center of a tsunami. Oakes and the other law enforcement agents had done their jobs without thought to themselves, and the thousands of onlookers out of sight of the brief disturbance barely sensed the ripple. What could have been mass panic with hundreds of injuries dissolved into little more than transitory confusion.

Ari poked Oakes in the chest. "I love you, but you're going to drive me crazy with these last-minutes changes for the next four years, aren't you?"

Oaks laughed and, not caring that two dozen cameras were focused in their direction, kissed her. "I plan on making you crazy in a lot of ways, a hell of a lot longer than that. That's the price you pay for falling for a Secret Service agent."

Ari kissed her back. "Believe me when I say the cost is worth it."

About the Author

Radclyffe has written over sixty romance and romantic intrigue novels as well as a paranormal romance series, The Midnight Hunters, as L.L. Raand.

She is a three-time Lambda Literary Award winner in romance and erotica and received the Dr. James Duggins Outstanding Mid-Career Novelist Award by the Lambda Literary Foundation. A member of the Saints and Sinners Literary Hall of Fame, she is also an RWA/FF&P Prism Award winner for *Secrets in the Stone*, an RWA FTHRW Lories and RWA HODRW winner for *Firestorm*, an RWA Bean Pot winner for *Crossroads*, an RWA Laurel Wreath winner for *Blood Hunt*, and a Book Buyers Best award winner for *Price of Honor* and *Secret Hearts*. She is also a featured author in the 2015 documentary film *Love Between the Covers*, from Blueberry Hill Productions. In 2019 she was recognized as a "Trailblazer of Romance" by the Romance Writers of America.

In 2004 she founded Bold Strokes Books, one of the world's largest independent LGBTQ publishing companies, and is the current president and publisher.

Find her at facebook.com/Radclyffe.BSB, follow her on Twitter @RadclyffeBSB, and visit her website at Radfic.com.

Books Available From Bold Strokes Books

A Moment in Time by Lisa Moreau. A longstanding family feud separates two women who unexpectedly fall in love at an antique clock shop in a small Louisiana town. (978-1-63555-419-9)

Aspen in Moonlight by Kelly Wacker. When art historian Melissa Warren meets Sula Johansen, director of a local bear conservancy, she discovers that love can come in unexpected and unusual forms. (978-1-63555-470-0)

Back to September by Melissa Brayden. Small bookshop owner Hannah Shepard and famous romance novelist Parker Bristow maneuver the landscape of their two very different worlds to find out if love can win out in the end. (978-1-63555-576-9)

Changing Course by Brey Willows. When the woman of her dreams falls from the sky, intergalactic space captain Jessa Arbelle had better be ready to catch her. (978-1-63555-335-2)

Cost of Honor by Radclyffe. First Daughter Blair Powell and Homeland Security Director Cameron Roberts face adversity when their enemies stop at nothing to prevent President Andrew Powell's reelection. Book 11 in the Honor series. (978-1-63555-582-0)

Fearless by Tina Michele. Determined to overcome her debilitating fear through exposure therapy, Laura Carter all but fails before she's even begun until dolphin trainer Jillian Marshall dedicates herself to helping Laura defeat the nightmares of her past. (978-1-63555-495-3)

Not Dead Enough by J.M. Redmann. In the tenth book of the Mickey Knight mystery series, a woman who may or may not be dead drags Micky into a messy con game. (978-1-63555-543-1)

Not Since You by Fiona Riley. When Charlotte boards her honeymoon cruise single and comes face-to-face with Lexi, the high school love she left behind, she questions every decision she has ever made. (978-1-63555-474-8)

Not Your Average Love Spell by Barbara Ann Wright. In this romantic fantasy, four women struggle with who to love and who to hate while fighting to rid a kingdom of an evil invading force. (978-1-63555-327-7)

Tennessee Whiskey by Donna K. Ford. After losing her job, Dane Foster starts spiraling out of control. She wants to put her life on pause and ask for a redo, a chance for something that matters. Emma Reynolds is that chance. (978-1-63555-556-1)

30 Dates in 30 Days by Elle Spencer. In this sophisticated contemporary romance, Veronica Welch is a busy lawyer who tries to find love the fast way—thirty dates in thirty days. (978-1-63555-498-4)

Finding Sky by Cass Sellars. Skylar Addison's search for a career intersects with her new boss's search for butterflies, but Skylar can't forgive Jess's intrusion into her life. Romance is the last thing they expect. (978-1-63555-521-9)

Hammers, Strings, and Beautiful Things by Morgan Lee Miller. While on tour with the biggest pop star in the world, rising musician Blair Bennett falls in love for the first time while coping with loss and depression. (978-1-63555-538-7)

Heart of a Killer by Yolanda Wallace. Contract killer Santana Masters's only interest is her next assignment—until a chance meeting with a beautiful stranger tempts her to change her ways. (978-1-63555-547-9)

Leading the Witness by Carsen Taite. When defense attorney Catherine Landauer reluctantly becomes the key witness in prosecutor Starr Rio's latest criminal trial, their hearts, careers, and lives may be at risk. (978-1-63555-512-7)

No Experience Required by Kimberly Cooper Griffin. Izzy Treadway has resigned herself to a life without romance because of her bipolar illness but wonders what she's gotten herself into when she agrees to write a book about love. (978-1-63555-561-5)

One Walk in Winter by Georgia Beers. Olivia Santini and Hayley Boyd Markham might be rivals at work, but they discover that lonely hearts often find company in the most unexpected of places. (978-1-63555-541-7)

The Inn at Netherfield Green by Aurora Rey. Advertising executive Lauren Montgomery and gin distiller Camden Crawley don't agree on anything except saving the Rose & Crown, the old English pub that's brought them together. (978-1-63555-445-8)

Top of Her Game by M. Ullrich. When it comes to life on the field and matters of the heart, losing isn't an option for pro athletes Kenzie Shaw and Sutton Flores. (978-1-63555-500-4)

Vanished by Eden Darry. First came the storm, and then the blinding white light that made everyone in town disappear. Another storm is coming, and Ellery and Loveday must find the chosen one or they won't survive. (978-1-63555-437-3)

All She Wants by Larkin Rose. Marci Jones and Tessa Dalton get more than they bargained for when their plans for a one-night stand turn into an opportunity for love. (978-1-63555-476-2)

Beautiful Accidents by Erin Zak. Stevie Adams doesn't believe in fate, not after losing her parents in a car crash. But she's about to discover that sometimes the best things in life happen purely by accident. (978-1-63555-497-7)

Before Now by Joy Argento. The instant Delaney Peyton and Jade Taylor meet, they sense a connection neither can explain. Can they overcome a betrayal that spans the centuries to reignite a love that can't be broken? (978-1-63555-525-7)

Breathe by Cari Hunter. Paramedic Jemima Pardon's chronic bad luck seems to be improving when she meets police officer Rosie Jones. But they face a battle to survive before they can find love. (978-1-63555-523-3)

Double-Crossed by Ali Vali. Hired thief and killer Reed Gable finds something in her scope that will change her life forever when she gets a contract to end casino accountant Brinley Myers's life. (978-1-63555-302-4)

False Horizons by CJ Birch. Jordan and Ash struggle with different views on the alien agenda and must find their way back to each other before they're swallowed up by a centuries-old war. Third in the New Horizons series. (978-1-63555-519-6)

Legacy by Charlotte Greene. In this paranormal mystery, five women hike to a remote cabin deep inside a national park—and unsettling events suggest that they should have stayed home. (978-1-63555-490-8)

Somewhere Along the Way by Kathleen Knowles. When Maxine Cooper moves to San Francisco during the summer of 1981, she learns that wherever you run, you cannot escape yourself. (978-1-63555-383-3)

Blood of the Pack by Jenny Frame. When Alpha of the Scottish pack Kenrick Wulver visits the Wolfgangs, she falls for Zaria Lupa, a wolf on the run. (978-1-63555-431-1)

Cause of Death by Sheri Lewis Wohl. Medical student Vi Akiak and K9 Search and Rescue officer Kate Renard must work together to find a killer before they end up the next targets. In the race for survival, they discover that love may be the biggest risk of all. (978-1-63555-441-0)

Chasing Sunset by Missouri Vaun. Hijinks and mishaps ensue as Iris and Finn set off on a road trip adventure, chasing the sunset, and falling in love along the way. (978-1-63555-454-0)

Double Down by MB Austin. When an unlikely friendship with Spanish pop star Erlea turns deeper, Celeste, in-house physician for the hotel hosting Erlea's show, has a choice to make—run or double down on love. (978-1-63555-423-6)

Party of Three by Sandy Lowe. Three friends are in for a wild night at billionaire heiress Eleanor McGregor's twenty-fifth birthday party. Love, lust, and doing the right thing, even when it hurts, turn the evening into one that will change their lives forever. (978-1-63555-246-1)

Sit. Stay. Love. by Karis Walsh. City girl Alana Brendt and country vet Tegan Evans both know they don't belong together. Only problem is, they're falling in love. (978-1-63555-439-7)

Where the Lies Hide by Renee Roman. As P.I. Camdyn Stark gets closer to solving the case, will her dark secrets and the lies she's buried jeopardize her future with the quietly beautiful Sarah Peters? (978-1-63555-371-0)

Beautiful Dreamer by Melissa Brayden. With love on the line, can Devyn Winters find it in her heart to stay in the small town of Dreamer's Bay, the one place she swore she'd never remain? (978-1-63555-305-5)

Create a Life to Love by Erin Zak. When sixteen-year-old Beth shows up at her birth mother's door, three lives will change forever. (978-1-63555-425-0)

Deadeye by Meredith Doench. Stranded while hunting the serial predator Deadeye, Special Agent Luce Hansen fights for survival while her lover, forensic pathologist Harper Bennett, hunts for clues to Hansen's disappearance along the killer's trail. (978-1-63555-253-9)

Endangered by Michelle Larkin. Shapeshifters Officer Aspen Wolfe and Dr. Tora Madigan fight their growing attraction as they work together to destroy a secret government agency that exterminates their kind. (978-1-63555-377-2)

Incognito by VK Powell. The only thing Evan Spears is focused on is capturing a fleeing murder suspect until wild card Frankie Strong is added to her team and causes chaos on and off the job. (978-1-63555-389-5)

Insult to Injury by Gun Brooke. After losing everything, Gail Owen withdraws to her old farmhouse and finds a destitute young woman, Romi Shepherd, living in a secret room. (978-1-63555-323-9)

Just One Moment by Dena Blake. If you were given the chance to have the love of your life back, could you ignore everything that went wrong and start over again? (978-1-63555-387-1)

Scene of the Crime by MJ Williamz. Cullen Matthews finds herself caught between the woman she thinks she loves but can no longer trust and a beautiful detective she can't stop thinking about who will stop at nothing to find the truth. (978-1-63555-405-2)

Fear of Falling by Georgia Beers. Singer Sophie James is ready to shake up her career, but her new manager, the gorgeous Dana Landon, has other ideas. (978-1-63555-443-4)

Daughter of No One by Sam Ledel. When their worlds are threatened, a princess and a village outcast must overcome their differences and embrace a budding attraction if they want to survive. (978-1-63555-427-4)

Playing with Fire by Lesley Davis. When Takira Lathan and Dante Groves meet at Takira's restaurant, love may find its way onto the menu. (978-1-63555-433-5)

Practice Makes Perfect by Carsen Taite. Meet law school friends Campbell, Abby, and Grace, law partners at Austin's premier boutique legal firm for young, hip entrepreneurs. Legal Affairs: one law firm, three best friends, three chances to fall in love. (978-1-63555-357-4)

The Last Seduction by Ronica Black. When you allow true love to elude you once and you desperately regret it, are you brave enough to grab it when it comes around again? (978-1-63555-211-9)

Wavering Convictions by Erin Dutton. After a traumatic event, Maggie has vowed to regain her strength and independence. So how can Ally be both the woman who makes her feel safe and a constant reminder of the person who took her security away? (978-1-63555-403-8)